REBEL'S CAGE

KATE JACOBY

Copyright © Tracey Oliphant 2001
All rights reserved

The right of Tracey Oliphant to be identified as the author
of this work has been asserted by her in accordance
with the Copyright, Designs and Patents Act 1988.

This edition published in Great Britain in 2002 by

Gollancz
An imprint of the Orion Publishing Group
Orion House, 5 Upper St Martin's Lane,
London WC2H 9EA

A CIP catalogue record for this book
is available from the British Library

ISBN 0 57507 295 4

Typeset at The Spartan Press Ltd,
Lymington, Hants

Printed in Great Britain by
Clays Ltd, St Ives plc

Acknowledgements

As always, a huge thank you to my family, and to my friends for all their support and understanding. Thank you again to Jo and to Karen – your efforts are always appreciated.

Much has been said about Robert Douglas, the man at the centre of this history; about his character, his honour and about the sometimes secret forces behind his actions. Many stories have been told, of his brave deeds, his strength and his determination to deliver his people from tyranny.

But Robert Douglas was a man both more and less than what legend made of him. The people saw in him the hero they needed; those close to him saw the soul tortured by a prophecy handed to him at the age of nine – an event which would shape not only the rest of his life, but also that of his beloved country.

When Robert Douglas returned from his self-imposed exile, he found Lusara struggling under the rule of the conqueror Selar, the Church floundering for leadership and the powerful Guilde growing stronger under Proctor Vaughn. While Selar had once been a close friend, Vaughn had been Robert's sworn enemy, for the Proctor had discovered the secret of Robert's sorcery and was determined to destroy him.

The secret Enclave, hidden high in the Goleth Mountains, was home to sorcerers who no longer dared to live in the country, fearing for their lives, from both Guilde and sorcerer Malachi. The Enclave was protected by the powerful talisman known as the Key, which was also used as a guide and a source of information by the leader, the Jaibir. It was the Key which had given Robert the Prophecy.

While the people needed a release from tyranny, those within the Enclave, the Salti, begged Robert to help them – but Robert was a man of honour, and could not reconcile the responsibilities placed upon him with his oath of allegiance to Selar, nor with the terrible fate promised by the Prophecy: that Robert would, in the act of salvation, destroy that which

1

he loved most. This conflict raged within him, shaped his character and informed too many of his choices. Over thirty and more years it grew, becoming something he both despised and feared, a dark stain inside himself he could neither control nor destroy. In his own mind, he called it the demon.

But there was one person who understood both Robert and his demon. Jennifer Ross was abducted as a child by Nash and set to live in Shan Moss forest. Fourteen years later Robert rescued her, discovering she was not only a sorcerer, with vastly different magical powers, but the daughter of the Earl of Elita. Robert returned her to her father, but even as he realised his feelings for her were changing, he discovered that she was part of the Prophecy, the Ally – and if he allowed it to come true, *she* would be the one he would destroy.

King Selar had a new friend, Samdon Nash. A sorcerer of incredible power and evil, Nash was known as Carlan to his people, the Malachi. He would stop at nothing to possess the Key – and Jenn, the Ally.

Then an accident caught Robert and his brother Finnlay, and the secret sorcerers were no longer secret. Word flew across the land.

As Nash secured his position at court, he used a hideous perversion of the ancient Bonding to tie Selar to him, so the King would lose all free will and become Nash's puppet. Robert helped the Queen flee to safety with her two children, but Jenn's impending marriage finally broke him. Despite all his promises to himself, Robert spent the night with her, giving into the Bonding foretold by the prophecy, then he left, sending himself into exile once again – this time determined to stay there and do no more harm.

Though heartbroken, Jenn went through with the marriage to Duke Tiege Eachern, Selar's brutish cousin. When she found she was carrying Robert's child, she kept the secret, allowing her husband to believe it his.

This time Robert exiled himself in a remote abbey, hiding even his identity from the brothers. There he met Bishop Aiden McCauly, recently imprisoned by Selar, then rescued, and now living in hiding. The seeds of a deep and powerful friendship were born between the two, who were drawn from their sanctuary by threats to Robert's brother and an attack on Jenn at Elita.

They raced across the country and arrived at the castle in time to discover those holding siege were evil Malachi sorcerers under control of the third figure in the prophecy, the Angel of Darkness. Even as Jenn went into labour, even as her father was killed and her son born, the enemy was closing in on them, threatening to overrun the castle. Exhausting all his defences, the demon within Robert finally cracked and broke, flooding through him with a fury that could not be denied. From the highest battlements, he let loose the terrifying Word of Destruction, obliterating the Malachi and severely wounding the Angel of Darkness.

Five years later, Robert returned again to Lusara, having researched the prophecy as much as he could. But this time he came with a more urgent mission. Selar was determined to invade neighbouring Mayenne, ruled by his brother. Robert knew that Lusara was not strong enough for such a fight, that the only outcome would be defeat, and another tyrant on the throne of Lusara. He sent out word to lords still loyal, asking them to gather their armies and meet him at Bleakstone Castle, in friendly Flan'har.

With her husband's death, Jenn took her son, Andrew, to live with her sister while she joined the rebels, where she volunteered to help research the Prophecy by making a trip to Bu, in the southern continent. Horrified that she should go alone, Robert went with her. While they found nothing of immediate use to the Prophecy, the trip did heal the rift between them, and Robert vowed to marry her, despite the Prophecy – even as he was forced to accept he might not have a way out of it.

When they returned to Bleakstone, loyal lords insisted that Robert marry Selar's daughter, Galiena, and upon victory, that he take the crown. Stricken, Robert went to Jenn, but she insisted that he agree, saying that their country was more important than their love. After the wedding, word arrived that

Selar was heading for the border. The rebel forces were mobilised.

Jenn headed to the Enclave and was chosen by the Key to replace the dead Jaibir. Trying to stop her, Robert arrived too late – but the Key possessed him, changing both their bodies so they would not age, but last as long as this battle against evil would require them. With Jenn now joined to the Key for life, Robert could no longer trust her, and left to rejoin his army.

Marching with Selar's army, Nash made an ally of Prince Kenrick. Jenn joined Robert's army; one night their camp was attacked by Malachi, and a young woman was captured. She gave up no information; Robert was not to know that she was Sairead, the girl Micah, his closest friend, had fallen in love with. Micah had left her to fight alongside Robert.

Kenrick stole into the rebel camp and poisoned his sister, Robert's young wife. Devastated by her death, Robert prepared his army the following morning, knowing where to lay the blame.

At dawn, the armies faced each other and the fight was engaged. Robert sought out Selar and faced him, struggling to control the demon. But he killed Selar, and night fell, and still the battle was not won.

That night, as Robert slept fitfully, ignoring the pain of his wounds, Malachi once more crept into the camp, freed Sairead, and abducted Micah. The following morning, as the armies lined up for battle, Robert rode into the heart of Shan Moss forest to save his friend.

Robert found Micah in a clearing, bound and gagged, and fought off Malachi attacks before Nash appeared. Robert was stabbed in the back by Sairead – and discovered that she was the girl Micah had fallen in love with. Feeling betrayed, he sent Micah back to camp to warn the rebels, then began his assault on Nash, chasing him through the forest.

They emerged onto the battlefield between the two terrified armies. Nash was severely wounded, his power virtually gone. Robert too was hurt, but determined to last as long as it took. The two sorcerers fired bolts at each other, then Jenn felt the build-up of power and knew Robert was preparing to use the

Word of Destruction to kill both himself and Nash: he would defy the Prophecy that had ruled his life with his *own* death.

Jenn rushed between them, using her own awesome powers to split them apart. Nash was spent, but alive, and Kenrick's men rescued him from the field. Robert remained standing long enough to see Kenrick's army racing away in terror and to hear the cheers of his own men. Then he collapsed into Finnlay's arms.

The war was over and Kenrick, now King, was fleeing back to Marsay, the wounded Nash and dispirited Malachi with him. Micah, desolate to be banished from Robert's side, left to play bodyguard to his friend's son, Andrew. Robert's army buried its dead that night, but Robert himself lay dying, his wounds severe, the demon inside him making them worse.

Finnlay fetched Jenn, hoping she would tell Robert that she loved him and that Andrew was his son, so Robert might have something to fight for. Jenn was shocked by Robert's injuries. Mindspeaking him, she discovered the demon had all but overtaken him and would kill him before the night was over. She saw that telling him the truth would not make things better. She needed to give the demon something else to focus on – so she told him that she had never loved him, that their one night together had been just the Bonding and nothing else and that surely it was time they put their brief moments together into the past.

The demon struck out at her, but with Robert so weak, it could do no damage. She opened her eyes to find the demon working to heal him – but she saw only hatred in his eyes. Jenn left for the Enclave, knowing that she had lost his love, but that he was now finally free of her, free to fulfil the destiny his country cried out for.

For eight years, Jenn lived and worked at the Enclave, teaching and learning, growing closer to the Key, strengthening their bond. She saw her son regularly, but never enough. Rarely would a day pass that she would not wonder about the Prophecy and how it would finally unfold.

Of Nash, there was little word as the years flew by. It was

assumed he was recovering, rebuilding himself, using his evil powers to take the blood of other sorcerers. Few were fooled into believing his silence meant that he was finished. They all knew that this was a period of watchfulness, of preparation.

Kenrick grew into his role as King in his father's place, more than surpassing his sire's tyranny. Piece by piece, Lusara fell apart around him, and nobody seemed able to stop it.

During those eight years, when it seemed darkness would engulf Lusara and swallow it whole, the country prayed for deliverance. This was the time of the Silent Rebellion. And Robert Douglas, Duke of Haddon, rebel and outlaw, waited for something many people should have foreseen.

For Robert, the time of waiting came to an end one frosty winter evening, not long after Caslemas in 1370.

Excerpt from *The Secret History of Lusara* – Ruel

Where are you who would but stand by me,
When sodden ground beneath my feet doth
Trample all the rosy rotten leaves
And winter's light in ribbon streams right
Through my cold forgotten heart?

Where would you stand then, my love,
When I am needy, grey and pale,
And washed upon this desert shore
Blind with memories of your face
And the touch of ice upon my soul?

Lady Anna Douglas

Prologue

1363

Alone, he crashed through the forest, his horse stumbling in the deep snow, losing purchase, almost falling, but gaining balance again, sweating, panicking at the chase, the noise, the scent of blood in the air, the cry of the soldiers pursuing him, and his horse stumbling again, grunting, tiring. It was too much to ask. Far too much.

The night was absolute, a yawning cavern of inkiness into which he plunged headlong, escaping fate, escaping punishment and due retribution. Icy air stole his breath away, pine-scented and raw, drawing him further and further in, where safety was nothing more than a promise, but where peace was assured for a time.

The horse went down and he tumbled over its shoulder, slipping and rolling down the slope, his path unchecked, gathering snow, sliding, suffocating, disappearing.

He came to a halt, buried in darkness too deep to touch.

Silence surrounded him: thick, cloying silence sinking into his bones like treacle, holding him in place like a stake through the heart. No bones broken. No fatal cuts. Nothing that would not heal, given enough time. Only the older wounds still plagued him, those that refused to stay closed.

He listened to the silence, wanting to believe it. The snap and rustle of snow flakes around him sank into the background as he searched for harsher, more immediate noises. The soldiers were gone now, chasing some other figure in the night, losing him in the snow. He tried to reach out with his Senses, but again his injuries cut him short, blinding him to everything he had once taken for granted, making him mercilessly, terrifyingly normal again.

9

He sighed, patted the snow around his face to pack clear a breathing hole, then settled down, comfortable in his hiding place, resting in the darkness, his natural home.

The cold winter night gave him a cold winter dream. His body floated, insubstantial, torn from his control, lost in the maze. He was surrounded. Hurting. Lifted from the elements to feel shapes around him not part of this world. He knew what this was; knew the place, the time, the weapons. Knew what he had to do. He'd already been here a hundred times before.

He ran, plunging through a forest now bare of snow, shifting seasons and years as though time passed in the blink of a lazy eye. He chased the dream Nash, dodging blasts, inflicting his own, wishing he knew Shan Moss better, praying his wounds would not strike him down before he could destroy his enemy, this creature of unspeakable evil. But Nash stayed just ahead of him, too close to ignore, too far away to kill. Even when they emerged onto the battlefield, armies either side of them terrified, shifting back, but not leaving, not deserting him. He didn't deserve such loyalty. But it wasn't *his* loyalty – it belonged to Lusara, to the country he would defend if fate would let him. So the armies could only stand by and watch this battle rage between him and Nash as they threw blasts of heavy power at one another, as Robert danced and feinted, deflected and returned, as his blood seeped out of a dozen deep wounds, as Nash's powers drained too slowly. Until the moment finally came.

He gathered together all the demon had bred in him, all the anger and fury, frustration, hatred, fear and self-loathing. He pulled it all together inside him, knowing what it would do – and knowing made it worthwhile. Stirring within the depths he felt the Word of Destruction grow inside, pushing up to be spoken aloud, where he could destroy Nash – and himself as well, defying his terrible destiny, even as he fulfilled it. The Word rose in him, perched upon his lips, a heartbeat away from being spoken—

And the ground beneath his feet split open, shuddering and rattling the balance from him, throwing him down, opening a cavern between him and his enemy. Cut loose, the demon soared through him, unfettered and unchallenged, denying every breath of sense and hope. He staggered to his feet. He turned and faced *her*, knowing what she'd done, knowing she'd betrayed him, knowing he should have known it would happen.

His fist rose to strike, to let the demon loose upon her, letting the pain free to destroy the love that he still felt for her—

He froze. The air of this dreamworld rippled around him, making even the ground under his feet insubstantial. She stood before him, her face expressionless, nothing of meaning in her deep blue eyes.

He would have destroyed her. Just as the Prophecy had said. He would have destroyed her. Even though he loved her.

The voice that came to him was not his own. Nor hers. This was a man he'd left behind too many years ago.

'You are strong, Robert Douglas. Very strong. Your will is unbroken. But you are also weak. You hesitate. You will never win unless you can learn to be ruthless.'

Before him stood David Maclean, old, white-haired, looking too much like his son, Micah – the man Robert had once considered his closest friend. The father now shook his head, disparaging as always, determined to prove that Robert had always been a traitor to his people.

'You are weak, Douglas. See, even now you hesitate. The power sits within you. Strike her down now and rid this country of her evil. He has said you must give her up to beat him. Fulfil your destiny as it is written in your heart and destroy her now.'

He felt a trickle of something warm flow over his eye, then saw the red blood as it trailed from a wound on his forehead. He could barely see her now, even as she stood close to him, her hand upon his arm, concern in her gaze.

'I never loved you, Robert. How could you think otherwise? How could I love a man with such darkness inside him?'

'Strike her down now, Douglas, while you can!'

And voices rose along with this chant, loud, surrounding

11

him, coming from the armies in the field, their swords raised and glinting in the cold grey sky. The heavens wept, as he wished he could.

The chant became deafening as his knees gave way beneath him, his sword falling from fingers already dying. He'd wanted this to end, and now it was ending. Only the chanting didn't stop. Instead, it changed pitch, quieted, became a plea. A cry. A call for—

'*Help! Help me!*'

Robert wrenched himself from sleep, scrambling out of his snow shelter, eyes blinking back the bright morning light. For a moment, he recognised nothing, then the cry came again and he stumbled forward, the old wound in his side screaming protest. He staggered and slipped down the hill, reaching out for any hand-hold, keeping track of the faint voice, tiny, desperate and young.

He tripped and rolled, coming to a stop on flat ground. A horse, choked and panting, eyed him warily, reins dangling against cracked ice. Before him, stretched out into the distance, was a lake bound in winter, an ice-hole black on its surface out of which thrashed limbs even now losing their last strength.

Robert moved, so swiftly, the horse had no time to react. He wrapped the reins around his ankle, then knelt on the ice, stretching out on his stomach to reach the ice hole. He called out, urging, reassuring, calming. He could hear the ice creak and groan beneath him, feel it shifting, cracking further. If he didn't get the child to safety soon, they'd both be dead.

He pushed further, until his hands reached water, grasping hold of an arm mid-flail. The cold sent shock waves through him and the arms slipped from his grip. He came forward another inch and the ice cracked open beneath his chest. But it was enough to get hold of the boy with both hands, grab his clothing and pull. Chunks of ice splashed up into his face, the water blinded him and the stabbing pain in his side sucked the breath from his body, but he didn't let go. He dragged the boy clear of the water, soaking himself in the process, using his legs to inch them back towards the bank, calling out to the horse to back up, to help pull them both to safety.

12

The boy was still and silent now as Robert hurried the last few feet off the ice. Even as he dragged the frozen body towards the trees, he was already rubbing limbs, stripping off sodden clothing, pulling his own cloak free to wrap around the boy. He set him down carefully, then immediately set to work, kicking snow aside to find damp scrappy wood he could use for a fire. He didn't care what it looked like, it just needed to be warm. He used his powers to set it alight, turning it into a blaze that would burn quickly, warming air frozen from months of winter. Only when he was sure the boy was no longer in danger of freezing to death did he turn and eye the horse.

It watched him warily, as though able to read his thoughts. He chose to ignore it, clearing more snow from the ground to give the animal somewhere to forage. Give it time to calm down, that was the thing. Give them both time.

He gathered more wood, stoked up the fire, making sure he kept himself warm, since he'd lost his cloak. The pain in his side sank to a dull heavy throb. Two years and still the wound hadn't healed. He doubted it ever would now, though the doctors insisted it was just a matter of time. But he didn't have time. None of them did.

The boy hadn't moved, he just lay wrapped in Robert's cloak, white face, blue lips, dark hair. Small and slight, a pale shadow about seven or eight years old. Out here alone. On a horse bearing a fine-quality saddle which . . .

Robert fell to his knees beside the boy, tugging the cloth back from his face to reveal young features that were far too familiar for him to ignore.

'Andrew?' Robert whispered. 'But what in the name of the gods are you doing . . .' He stopped, looked up across the lake, putting together last night, and the night before, the directions, the raid, the chase, the route to escape. In the dark, it had been impossible to tell how far he'd gone, exactly where his horse had finally thrown him.

'Serin's blood! I have to get you home before . . .' No, he didn't think how this boy's mother was the woman he'd once loved, the woman who'd betrayed him. He had learned long before that such thoughts were anathema. Instead, he kept

13

everything centred on warming the still body, on gaining the horse's trust, on putting the fire out and getting Andrew up onto the saddle in front of him. Then, before it could start snowing again, he urged the horse to move and followed the trail back. He could only hope it would take them towards Maitland.

Mist rose between the trees as the sun hit last night's snow. Their passage was hidden by grey, lit by golden rays too weak to warm. But the movement did that, and the horse beneath them. Robert held onto Andrew, keeping as much of his body covered as possible, feeling, eventually, some twitches, and then shivers begin to rattle through the slight frame.

How in Mineah's name had he got so far out here alone? Why hadn't anybody missed him yet? Had he been running from some trouble?

Was his mother nearby?

Such a question almost froze him on his journey, but Andrew began to cough and Robert kicked the horse into greater movement. Soon he no longer needed to follow the tracks, he recognised the landscape.

He paused while still under cover and some small distance from the cottage to Seek for possible trouble, to find out if there was more than one person behind those walls.

All was well, as quiet as it appeared. Carefully, Robert brought the horse to the edge of the trees, where a clearing opened out to face the house. To one side was a tiny stable, large enough perhaps for two horses and a bale of hay. Keeping hold of Andrew, Robert slid from his horse to the ground and made his way around the building to duck into the stable unseen from the house. There he laid Andrew down where he would be safe. The child was shivering violently. Soon his muscles would start to ache and the pain would be enough to wake him up. Robert would have to be gone before then.

He had a moment, no longer, a moment in which to feel a thread of excitement run through him. He had an idea, no more, probably foolish, probably doomed to failure.

He reached out, brushed the hair from Andrew's pale forehead and pressed two fingers there. 'Know me,' he

14

whispered, exerting the power needed to enforce the command. 'Always know my aura. I will not forget yours. Listen and learn.'

He could hear movement from within the house. He had to go or he would be discovered. 'Know me, Andrew. I *will* come back.'

Seconds later, he was back within the darkness of the trees, hiding again, the reins between his fingers, waiting, watching the door, hope rising in him again.

The door opened and a man stepped outside, a frown on his face, a face Robert knew better than his own. Dark red curls shook as Micah turned this way and that, as though he'd heard something and had come out into the cold to investigate. Some other instinct sent his gaze to the ground, to where Robert's footprints gathered before the stable door. In a flash Micah was inside. A moment later, he emerged, the boy in his arms and words of fear and concern echoed across the clearing before Micah took Andrew to safety inside.

Safety and warmth. Maitland Manor was a ten minute ride away, where Andrew's aunt and uncle lived, where Andrew lived. The boy was well-loved, cherished and kept close.

But still that thread of excitement ran through Robert, touching something inside him he'd never encountered before. So he was still standing there, in the shadows, when Micah opened the door once more. But he didn't go far. He simply stood there, staring hard into the trees before nodding once.

'Thank you.'

Robert said nothing, gave no sign that he was there. He waited for Micah to go back inside, then mounted the boy's horse and rode into the morning with a fine sense of purpose.

He had a lot of work to do.

1

1370

The field shimmered in a golden haze of autumn sun and sumptuous cloth. Huge pavilions stretched out to the north and west, rippling in the afternoon breeze: a statement of outrageous wealth and prosperity, and not a little audacity. Pennants of every colour ringed the field, their flapping drowned out by the constant movement of people in the background, cooks roasting whole sides of beef, bakers working a stone-built oven and, behind them, row after row of spit-fires over which fish and fowl were grilled on pikes. To the east, within the shadows of a tidy wood, minstrels and tumblers practised, making ready.

Osbert's head ached. His feet hurt and his back tingled with the strain of standing for so long. He should never have made the long ride from Marsay in one day without giving himself some time to recover for this event. Better still, he should have had the courage to stay away altogether.

But courage had never been his greatest strength.

At least he was not alone in his suffering. Most of the court was there along with him: the King's Council, magnates, lords, ladies, priests and his highest ranking Guildesmen. They stood there, in the cleared space between pavilions his Guilde engineers had spent six months creating, circling the long table at which the King sat, all bedecked in their best finery, glittering and glowing with the opulence the King wished to display to the visiting envoy from Mayenne.

But there was something so wretchedly transparent about the whole thing that made Osbert's head ache more, gave his stomach a queasy sinking feeling; he knew he wouldn't eat a mouthful of the feast even now being prepared.

'Would you like some wine, my lord?'

Osbert refused to look at the priest who stood beside him, whispering to avoid drawing attention to himself. Kenrick sat no more than twenty feet away from them, engrossed in his conversation with the ambassador from Mayenne, almost his entire court watching the exchange. It would not do well to interrupt such a tense moment.

'No,' Osbert murmured, barely moving. 'I would not like some wine. I would like to go to my bed, fall asleep and find this was all some sort of sick joke.'

'I would imagine the King would find such an action mildly amusing,' Godfrey replied. 'He is indeed well known for his sense of humour.'

'As is your good self,' Osbert added dryly. Judging his moment, he glanced aside at the tall Archdeacon, recognising the familiar ironic expression on a face he'd grown to know almost too well over the years.

As Proctor of the Guilde, Osbert's place at such events as this was unarguable. Godfrey, however, had won his by sheer determination. With Bishop Brome in frequent ill health, Godfrey was more and more often requested to stand in his place. Without doubt, Godfrey lent any occasion far more dignity than his superior ever could.

Lean and strong, Godfrey's long face was framed with dark hair which showed little of the passing years, his tonsure still proudly shaved. He, unlike everyone else here, wore only the simplest of habits, black robes lightened by the silver stole draped around his neck, urged upon him by the Bishop himself.

On his better days, Osbert allowed that he and Godfrey had become friends through trials shared and survived. On his worst, he could only admit that they had formed the oddest of alliances, the rules of which had never been spoken aloud.

The only thing he could say for certain was that he trusted this man more than any other at court, even though he suspected the friends Godfrey had would not bear too much scrutiny.

On the other hand, with a King who openly practised sorcery, who was to say Godfrey's friends were so bad?

'How long do you think they will bargain?' Godfrey stepped closer, keeping his voice low.

Osbert paused before replying, listening in to the exchanges between Kenrick and Ogiers, words about grain shipments, imports of cloth and wool. Even to his ears, the demands appeared hopelessly high, which, of course, would go some way to explaining the darkening expression on the young King's face.

'I don't know,' he replied softly, 'I understand Ogiers himself is not agreeable to the match. Kenrick will have to convince him before he can convince the girl's father.'

'Tirone is afraid of Kenrick.'

Osbert paused, glanced at Godfrey and let out a long breath. 'Yes, he is. Along with just about everybody else in this country. But Tirone is King of Mayenne and he's lost two of his three sons over the last few years. If he should lose the third, then he will need a strong alliance with Kenrick or Mayenne will be overrun, and alliance means marriage between Kenrick and Olivia.'

'She is a child of twelve! They are cousins,' Godfrey hissed with thinly veiled contempt. 'It is not right that Brome should consent . . .'

As Godfrey pulled up, Osbert had to suppress a smile. Godfrey had worked his way up to the highest echelons of the Church by virtue of his honesty, integrity and obvious intelligence. He had survived this long because he had an uncanny ability to keep his often outspoken opinions largely to himself. But every now and then, one would slip out.

'If you were in Brome's place,' Osbert replied, not ungently, 'would you have refused Kenrick his request for a dispensation?'

Godfrey didn't reply, leaving Osbert to return his attention to the long table set out before him, sitting on a thick woollen rug from Alusia. Ogiers sat at the opposite end, his secretary and lieutenants a step behind him. Ogiers was certainly a man equal to the task at hand. Lusara and Mayenne had been at odds for twenty-five years. It took a great deal of courage to travel across a land so openly hostile to meet a King whose father had once tried to kill you. But Ogiers was Tirone's man, loyal to the end. His skills at negotiating were renowned throughout the northern continent; Kenrick was not finding it so easy going.

At twenty-two, Kenrick was every inch his father's son. Tall, fair-haired, broad-shouldered, with a nasty scar on the left side of his face that had never been explained. Clever in a devious way, determined and wholly self-absorbed. He ruled Lusara with an almost vengeful hatred, giving nothing and taking everything. In so many ways, he made his father, the conqueror, appear soft and benign in comparison – a bizarre concept to any who had known Selar. Kenrick pursued his ambitions without appearing to have any idea of how he was viewed by those around him, by the people of Lusara, or Mayenne.

His council was corrupt, his advisors terrified and he relied far too heavily on a man whose name alone had the power to give Osbert nightmares.

And Kenrick was negotiating a marriage to the twelve-year-old daughter of an honest and noble King in order to further the ambitions of that man.

Osbert suppressed a shudder.

Abruptly Kenrick slapped his hand on the table and got to his feet. He gathered together the documents before him and thrust them towards Osbert, who stepped forward and took them quickly, ignoring the glitter in Kenrick's eyes, the heightened colour in his cheeks.

'You have given us many things to think about,' Kenrick began, addressing both Ogiers and the gathered courtiers. His voice was hard and clipped, giving away more than he probably desired. 'I pray you take rest and refreshment, Ambassador, while I consider your . . . requests. My Lord Proctor will play host.'

Osbert caught another flash in Kenrick's eyes before the King turned and left them, heading for his pavilion, his bodyguard close behind.

Osbert was not the only one in that gathering who sighed in relief.

*

Kenrick could only stand still a few moments once he gained the privacy of his pavilion. He could still hear voices from outside, his court relaxing their silence now that he had departed and, by the gods, the cooks and servants were ringing up a clatter in preparation for the feast he would have to preside over.

He had to get out, get away from that look, that glint in Ogier's eyes, that . . . that self-satisfied repulsion which had fringed everything the old man had said.

He should never have met the man face to face. He should have handled it all with his own envoys, clerks, priests and perhaps a personal visit from Osbert himself. Dealt with it all at a distance so he wouldn't have to see that . . . look.

Thank the gods that the only scar visible was the one on his face.

But what would he do if the marriage went ahead? How could he bed his new wife . . . with a body that . . . when she saw it . . .

Assuming, of course, Ogiers, and by extension, Tirone, would ever allow the match. Judging by the demands laid out in the marriage contract, they saw the entire proposal as little more than a joke.

A joke? He was a King! How dare they face him with such scorn?

Yelling for his guard, he strode through the pavilion to the door on the other side. There his men stood, a horse already saddled for him. Without pausing he swung up, gathering the reins and kicking the stallion before he'd even settled properly.

As he rode away from the gathering, he didn't bother looking back. He didn't need to see Ogiers' contempt in order to feel it.

The land enveloped him. Ancient rock peeked through dried and tufted grasses, fought with blackened heather, creating a patchwork quilt that looked soft but was, in fact, harsh. Here and there stands of moss-covered rock rose like towers, or tumbled down a grassy hillside like toys abandoned mid-play.

In the dips between, small lakes of brackish water collected, undrinkable, feeding what little life survived in this place.

Ransem Castle broke up this untrammelled wasteland with walls of rigid stone the colour of a blood-red rose withered with age. More than once, Kenrick had fancied that the place had not been built, but had risen from the moor, whole and complete, and yet rotten at its core.

He hated coming here. Hated having to.

Gates were opened for him, servants appearing from nowhere to attend his guard, take his horse. High walls surrounded him, square and fat; a tall round tower dominated each corner of this square. The moment the gates were shut behind him, the world outside ceased to exist and old, familiar fears once again rose up inside him, feeding him the energy he required to mount the steps to the hall, to stride through the door opened for him.

Lofty beamed ceilings shut out the daylight, leaving slim windows here and there to illuminate that which should be kept only in darkness. The room had changed little since he'd last seen it; fireplaces at either end of the hall gave out more heat than he required; chairs and a long table gathered at one end, giving the impression that this place hosted a warm and popular lord.

Samdon Nash was a master at deceit.

Before he could move from the doorway, the stench hit him.

Amazing how he always forgot the smell of this place, as though his memory had no desire to hold onto something so appalling.

'Good afternoon, Sire.'

He turned to look at the man who bowed before him. Taymar, one of the many Nash had Bonded to him, so that they obeyed his every order, so that their loyalty was to him alone, so that they would die for him if he said the word. The removal of individual will was replaced with slavery. The very sight of those dull eyes was enough to make him sick to his stomach.

'Where is he?'

Taymar waved a hand towards the far fireplace and a tall chair with its back to the rest of the wall. The table before it was covered in huge papers and three thick, weeping candlesticks.

The slave raised his voice. 'Master, the King is here to see you.'

Flames shifted around the fireplace, oily and slow, as though afraid of burning the logs too quickly. Kenrick kept his eyes on them, preferring to watch this perversion of nature rather than set his gaze on the man seated to his side, shifting distractedly through his papers.

'I take it you have not come here to report complete success.'

'Tirone asks too much.'

'Of course.'

'Things I can't begin to give him. He's doing it deliberately.'

'Yes.'

'He won't negotiate. I've tried.'

'You didn't also try to intimidate Ogiers, did you?'

Kenrick sighed, holding his exasperation in. It wasn't as though they hadn't had long discussions as to what he could say and what he couldn't. 'That would be impossible. The man barely stopped talking about the rumours and reports he'd had about lawlessness in Lusara and how I wasn't able to keep the peace the way my father could. And then he launched into tales of his noble master, the King, and Tirone's perfect children, their scholarly attributes, their achievements, how strong and healthy they are. How . . . flawless.' Flawless, yes. And unscarred.

'And he made you feel insignificant?'

Kenrick couldn't answer that, couldn't think about how it had felt to hear such things over and over without his skin crawling and a not uncommon desire to kill something almost overwhelming him. Ogiers had vexed his father. With luck, the bastard would die of old age soon and vex Kenrick no more. Or perhaps . . .

He stuck his chin out and changed the subject. It didn't do

to give too much of his thoughts away to this man. 'Well? So what do you suggest now? Have you had any further word on the remaining Prince?'

'I would have told you if I had.'

And not kept it secret, like he did so much else? Kenrick grunted, turned away from the fire and pulled a chair out from the table. He sank into it, sitting at an angle to Nash, keeping the man's face out of his line of sight. He didn't look at the papers and what might have been maps. He'd learned long ago that Nash was jealous of his knowledge and was prepared to enforce secrecy. 'So? What do I do now? We've removed two of Tirone's three heirs. The last one has been spirited away for safety – and your . . . your slaves, despite their Bonding, haven't been able to find him, leaving me with an intractable King, a stubborn envoy and a princess I can't . . .'

A creaking from the other chair warned him – but even so, he couldn't ignore the man as he stood up. The firelight did nothing to soften the hideous mess that face had become. One eye was permanently closed up, twisted and foiled into a chaos which blended horribly with his cheek, marring one side of his mouth into a permanent sneer. Wrinkled and bitter flesh flaked down his throat to thankfully disappear beneath dark cloth. The right arm still hung in useless abandon while the left gripped a walking stick with gnarled fingers.

So hideously maimed, so badly healed. Hard to believe that inside that rotting shell remained enough power to incinerate this castle, and Kenrick with it.

And all of it was damage done by the Enemy, by Robert Douglas.

Nash gave him something close to a smile, a hideous parody on that face. 'You're not contemplating something foolish, are you, my King?'

Kenrick stiffened. Why was it that no matter how hard he tried, his mind still leaked thoughts that this rotting sorcerer could pick up, like dead leaves in an autumn forest? Or was it that Nash knew him better than he would wish?

Nash leaned on his stick and hobbled his way to the other end of the table, where Taymar poured out wine into jewelled goblets. 'I'm sure you could indeed abduct the girl, marry and bed her before Tirone could find you – but would that really get you what you want? Mmn?'

The tone was half teasing, half contemptuous, making Kenrick grit his teeth. 'While we dance around Ogiers, Tirone could have his daughter betrothed and married off to someone else. His demands of me are exorbitant – but even if I could meet them, he'd find other excuses and you know it. Hell, if we had those kinds of riches, would we worry with taking Mayenne? And you didn't see his reaction to my scars! Why, why can't we do something about them *now*?'

'You know why.'

Kenrick threw up his hands and sat back. 'You didn't see Ogiers flinch when he first arrived. I could tell what he was looking at – and so could my entire court! You have no concept of the humiliation I have suffered – and more so with his stories about the perfect Prince and Princess! I'm the King. I insist you take this seriously.'

A single, baleful glare turned on him then, iciness leaking out of that dark gaze as though there had never been any warmth in the world, ever. Steeling himself, Kenrick refused to move, no matter how much his feet demanded it of him.

With something that was either a sigh or a hiss, Nash hobbled towards him, pausing close enough for the smell of rotting flesh to fill Kenrick's world, make his skin crawl with the effort to escape.

'This is little more than vanity,' Nash spoke, his voice soft and hard, edged with granite. 'And you have only yourself to blame. I have long warned you against experimenting with the forbidden side of your abilities until I was strong enough to guide and train you. You failed to listen to me and your body now pays the price. This is your mistake, yet you demand I fix it for you?'

'You said you would,' Kenrick almost winced at the whining tone of his own voice. What was it about Nash that brought this side out in him? 'You said it would not be a problem . . .'

Nash blinked at him. 'I have told you more times than I can

25

recall – neither I, nor any sorcerer alive, can heal a wound or mend a scar. To do so is to travel across a line not even I dare cross. I need blood to do as you ask. And powerful blood at that.'

'Then . . . then give me the means to regenerate, as you do. You promised you would when we became allies. We need Mayenne – and Tirone won't give me his daughter while I look like this!'

Nash grunted. 'You presume too much upon my patience, boy! You would have me give you some precious sorcerer, show you how to use his blood to remove a single scar from your face when I – *I* – require so much more before I can be whole again! The few sources I have been able to find over the last years have only closed up my wounds. And you want a few scars removed?'

Unable to move under that blistering gaze, Kenrick whispered, 'So what do we do?'

One side of Nash's face twitched, but the voice dropped low. 'I suppose we do want the same thing in the end,' he mused, frowning a little. He turned away then, but didn't go far. 'We cannot take Malachi or they will turn against us, but it's too soon for . . .'

Though there were secrets there Kenrick burned to know, he just sat and waited. The opportunity would come one day for him to learn more.

Nash shook his head. 'We have exhausted every possible avenue and yet they're still out there somewhere. We need to . . . find them. Now more than ever – but without bringing a battle down on us that we are not yet in a position to win.'

A burn of fear flashed in Kenrick's stomach; he almost flinched at what Nash was suggesting. He gathered himself, venturing the next necessary question, just to be sure. 'You're talking about the Salti Pazar, aren't you? But you've been looking for them for decades. We need sorcerers *now*. We can't wait for you to . . .'

'No,' Nash stiffened as though in surprise, sniffed in a breath and returned to his chair, sinking down with a short sigh.

When he spoke again, there was something calculating in his tone, as if of thoughts only just considered. 'You're right. We don't have any more time to find them. They're protected in some fashion by . . .'

'What?'

'That doesn't matter.' Nash fell silent then, but Kenrick didn't dare say anything. 'Perhaps we should . . . perhaps there is a way to draw them out in the open, where we can get at them.'

Kenrick frowned. 'The last time you tried that, we had a battle and Robert Douglas killed my father!'

'No, that's not what I mean.' Nash reached up and took the fresh cup of wine Taymar handed him, sipped and nodded to himself. 'Yes, I think that is definitely our very next step. Come here.'

Slowly Kenrick moved forward until his back faced the fireplace. Nash flicked his hand. As though from nowhere, a small black ball appeared and hovered in the air between them. Looking more closely, Kenrick saw the rough pock-marks over the surface, saw the dull ochre colour, despite the poor lighting. It was big enough to fit neatly into the palm of his hand. He knew what this was and his excitement, for a moment, almost overwhelmed him.

He dared not touch it.

'You know what this is,' Nash said, his tone almost bored. 'Use it only when you must. Let the blood flow freely into a calyx the first time you use it—'

'What's a calyx?'

'It's a . . . shallow bowl. Sit the orb in the bowl. Once the blood has gone, allow yourself a full day to absorb the power you have been given.'

'How?' Kenrick's whisper sounded loud, his gaze never leaving the orb as it hung in the air before his eyes. For so many years he'd wanted to know how to do this, how to prolong his life, to heal his wounds just as Nash had been doing for a century and a half – and now it was there, in front of him. His fingers itched to reach out and take it.

'Sleep with it between your hands, palms flat against the

surface. You will be tired afterwards, but . . . your scar will be gone.'

'But . . . it's so small.'

'Big enough for what you want. You're still young, you have no further need as yet. Later, I will show you more. Go on, take it.'

For a second, Kenrick's gaze flickered to Nash. Then he reached up and plucked the orb out of the air. It felt instantly warm and welcoming.

'Don't use it unless you're injured,' Nash added, settling back into his chair. 'And don't go killing Malachi to use their blood or they will turn against us and we will have an enemy we can't afford.'

'Then where do I find sorcerer blood to . . .'

That twisted half-smile returned as Nash looked up at him. 'Why, Salti of course. And, my King, you can do this part all on your own. In fact, I'm sure you will enjoy it.'

The heat of the early autumn night kept Osbert uncomfortable long into the banquet. He could not, of course, loosen any of his formal robes, but instead had to sit at the high table, by Kenrick's left hand, and continue to pretend that all was well, that this was a happy occasion and not one that might precipitate a war.

More than once he caught Godfrey's eye; he envied the Archdeacon his position beside Ogiers where he could at least be guaranteed some interesting conversation. Right now, however, the Mayenne Ambassador was engaged in dancing with a Duchess Osbert knew only by sight.

Long bench tables had been set up under the stars, a space left between them for tumblers and musicians and now, for revellers to join the formal dances. Ogiers moved in a gentle and stately manner, befitting his age, but the calm expression on his face betrayed to the Proctor his relief at no longer having to sit near the King.

There had been no bargain struck between them. Tirone of Mayenne had too many demands, was prepared to negotiate on too few of them. Kenrick, still needing to prove himself, had remained stubborn and the only thing the two men had agreed upon was to meet again in three months and review their respective positions.

Osbert knew Kenrick to be far too impatient to keep to such an agreement. He was more likely to find an alternative solution than to be content to let his ambition rest in the hands of others.

And yet, since his return that evening, Kenrick had been more quiet and thoughtful than anything else. His good humour had returned, making the celebrations a little easier to endure, and even now he sipped his wine rather than guzzled it, smiled a little at the dancers, tapped his fingers in time to the fiddle and drum and generally appeared to be enjoying himself.

So why did the sight of that send a fresh *frisson* of fear through Osbert? Was it because he'd seen the Baron DeMassey and his companion, Gilbert Dusan, enjoying the festivities? Was it due to the fact that those two men were so closely in league with Nash – or was it that Osbert had no doubts at all that Kenrick's disappearance today must have been in order for him to visit . . .

Osbert could not find words to describe the man who had turned Lusara into a quagmire of misery, although he had helped Nash to get where he was, unwitting of the danger, unmindful of the consequences.

And Kenrick served Nash as his father had before him.

'My Lord Proctor?'

Kenrick's quiet query broke into Osbert's thoughts and he turned with a carefully schooled expression. 'Yes, Sire?'

'What say you of Tirone's stubbornness? Do you think he will ever relinquish his daughter?'

This was the kind of question Osbert had to face on a daily basis, balancing what he believed was true with what he believed Kenrick wanted to hear – with little room for the harsh reality. If he voiced his honest opinion, the King would be pushed either to anger or to war. If he prevaricated too much, Kenrick would no longer ask him for his opinion, and any influence he might have, however small, would be eroded.

A real King, however, would listen without judgement, never condemning a man for his thoughts.

'I believe,' Osbert replied, holding up his cup to be filled by the boy waiting behind the high table, 'that given sufficient guarantees, Tirone will eventually agree to you marrying the Princess.'

'I know that,' Kenrick replied, his gaze not hard but almost quizzical, as though he held a secret, 'but how many of his guarantees can be dispensed with before he gives me the girl? I have already sent him a dozen shipments of grain to make up for the failure of his harvest – without, I might add, extracting an exorbitant price. I could have sold them to Budlandi for twice what he gave me.'

While still leaving his own people to starve their way through winter, Osbert added silently. He waited while the page filled the King's cup before replying, 'It is possible that in six months' time, his demands will change for the better. Or they might change for the worse.'

'So I should settle now?' Kenrick smiled and sat back a little, as though enjoying making Osbert squirm like this.

Osbert watched him for a moment, gauging mood and politics as though they were dancers on the floor below. Survival required sacrifices. 'Who is to say, within a year of your marriage, that Tirone will no longer be so adamant about your adherence to those guarantees?'

Kenrick's smile widened. 'So you're suggesting that I make promises now and break them later?'

'Rather,' Osbert's guts twisted at what he was saying, 'that you agree to them now and revise your position later. Conditions change, after all. If Lusara's harvest were to fail, would Tirone be equally helpful to us?'

'That's a very good point. And I could certainly use her dowry, that's without doubt.' Kenrick nodded, turning his gaze back to the dance floor. His brows drew together for a moment before he said, 'How many Guilde laws are there to govern the crime of sorcery? To punish it?'

Osbert blinked at the sudden change of subject. 'Fifty-six, Sire.'

Again, Kenrick nodded – and suddenly afraid, Osbert shot a glance at Godfrey, who was paying close attention to the entire conversation. Nobody else was close enough to hear over the noise and music.

'Only fifty-six? How many for murder?'

'Sixteen.'

Half of Kenrick's face lifted in an ironic smile. Then he said, 'How long would it take you to issue fifty-six law changes?'

His heart abruptly pounding, Osbert whispered, 'Sire? I don't understand . . . What do you . . .'

Kenrick sat back in his seat and turned a flat expression on him. 'I want you to reverse the laws against sorcery. I no longer want it to be illegal, nor punishable by death. Is that clear enough for you?'

Osbert could hardly breathe. What Kenrick was asking for was . . . impossible! Those laws had stood for more than five hundred years, created in the aftermath of the old Empire's battle. Osbert didn't have the power to reverse them! They could only be felled by majority consent within the Guilde – and such a debate would rage for years before any kind of agreement . . .

'Well?' Kenrick appeared to be waiting patiently for the desired response, leaving Osbert hanging over the edge of a cliff.

'Sire,' he began, urging the desperation from his voice, 'I would not wish to question your wisdom—'

'But you'll do it anyway?'

'Sire, you don't understand. I am not in a position to make such changes. Those laws are—'

'Treason.'

Osbert slammed to a halt, guts churning, heart fluttering with fears too long encouraged.

'Yes, Osbert, they are treason – for how can the Guilde continue to legislate against sorcery, to consider sorcery a great evil, to hold onto the sacred duty to eradicate all sorcery from the land, when your own King is in possession of such powers?' Kenrick's gaze narrowed. 'Why, neither you nor your fellow Guildesmen have done anything to arrest me – so you already know those laws are treasonous. If I am to marry, to produce an heir who might have these same powers, how would I appear to the rest of the world when I allow laws that could execute me to remain on your books?'

'Of course, Sire,' Osbert scrambled, but he was too late.

'I want those laws reversed, Osbert. You will begin preparing the papers tonight. I shall be sending letters to Bishop Brome to ask of him the same in respect of Church law. Now I think it's time I joined our honoured guest on the dance floor.'

Osbert rose to his feet as Kenrick left the table. A moment later and Godfrey was by his side. 'What are you going to do?'

Blinking the fog from his mind, Osbert glanced at his sometime friend and much-needed ally. 'What do you think I'm going to do? How can I defy him? He'd kill me and find a replacement to give him what he wants. Either way, those laws will change. I don't have a choice and he knows it.'

'You have other options,' Godfrey murmured, his eyes full of meaning, begging Osbert to ask the questions, to make a choice, to *do* something more than simply survive, to find the courage to strike back.

'No, Father, you're the one with the options. I'm the one with the responsibility.' Osbert's voice came out as leaden as his heart felt. 'But I wonder what you'd do in my place. I wonder how you would play it if in each hand you had an evil card and your choice only one or the other. If you will excuse me, I seem to have some work to do. Goodnight.'

No, courage had never been his greatest strength – but now was not the time for it to become a fatal weakness.

2

Damp leaves crackled softly beneath Finnlay's foot as he regained his balance. Still crouched low, he peered through the dense undergrowth, keeping his breathing steady and quiet, his movements to a minimum. Pale shadows streaked the forest floor before him, cast by a moon buried behind fine layers of cloud. His hands were cold, his boots dampened by layers of frost scattered about the ground. The rest of him was warm, heated by the chase.

He filled his chest with the evening chill, letting out the air against the curve of his elbow to hide puffs of steam which might give his position away. He absorbed the scents of the forest, individually and together, rolling them around in his head, identifying and discarding, picking carefully until he found the one he wanted.

Gentle sounds surrounded him, a subtle hum of forest life. Finnlay could have named each sound he heard, but it was all the more powerful – and infinitely more useful – to capture them as a whole, place the image of the forest within his Senses and let the intruder reveal himself against the familiar backdrop.

Shan Moss lived within him now each day, as it had done for the last eight years. This wide forest, almost bare in its autumn existence, had given him little joy and great heartache, seeds of sorrow and only one spark of hope. And now, after four days of tracking, he was nearing the end of his patience.

With one more casual sweep of his surroundings, Finnlay took a single step forward, listening with intent ears to the sounds he made, almost feeling the brush move to let him pass. Long tendrils of weeping pine glided across his face, a gentle caress, almost welcoming. There was still boy enough in him to smile at the fanciful thought.

Once more he came to a halt, concentrating. He waited.

He slipped the dagger from his boot, balanced the weapon and felt the hard horn handle, worn and well-used. Changing his weight from one foot to the other, he took in one more breath.

He sprang forward. In a moment he held his captive from behind with a blade to the throat, left hand twisting a sword from frozen fingers. With a dull thud it dropped to the ground and Finnlay breathed again, this time allowing the steam to fill the air around his prisoner's ear. He felt no satisfaction, only despair.

'Damn it, boy, what the hell do you think you're doing?'

The body relaxed slightly, a half-stifled sigh providing some answer. 'I'm sorry, Finnlay, I just didn't . . .'

Finnlay pressed the blade closer, let the boy feel the cold steel sharp against his skin. 'And what would you have done if it hadn't been me?'

The body stiffened with shock. 'I am sorry. I *was* trying, I just . . .'

With a grunt, Finnlay released him, putting the dagger away before picking up the sword. He tossed it to the boy with a casual gesture, denying himself the pleasure of acting on his anger and giving the boy a sound thrashing. 'Come on!'

He didn't look back as he began the long walk back to camp. He said nothing, but focused on the heavy footsteps trudging behind him, every now and then hastening to catch up.

If he left him out here on his own, perhaps then he might take this all a bit more seriously.

As though sensing his irritation, the boy spoke, his words punctuated by sharp breaths. 'Well, it's still early – can't we try again?'

'No.'

'But . . .'

Finnlay came to a halt and spun around. 'What's the point in trying again tonight, eh? We've been at this all day. You must be getting bored with it. I know I am.'

He could barely see the face before him, the dark shadowed shape, but he didn't need to. He knew the expression well enough. Hopeful, hurt that he'd done wrong, so very willing to make another attempt. 'But it is early, I mean, if we try again, I promise I'll do my best, really I will.'

'To what end? So I can catch you within fifteen minutes again? The longest you've lasted today was our first attempt – and that's only because I gave you a really big head start.' Finnlay spread his arms wide in the only gesture of frustration he would allow himself. 'Hell, Andrew, is this just some sort of game for you?'

'No!' Andrew looked horrified, blue eyes wide, mouth open in shock.

'The drill is we go out and you try to evade capture for an hour. Just an hour. That's all you have to do. Move silently through the forest without giving your position away for one tiny hour – and you still can't manage more than a quarter of that, even after four days of these exercises.'

'But you . . .'

'What?'

Andrew shrugged, turning away. 'Nothing.'

'What?'

'You're a Seeker,' Andrew mumbled.

Steeling himself, Finnlay stepped forward, deliberately towering over the boy. 'I don't need to be a Seeker to find you, Andrew. I could do it blindfolded with one leg missing, you make so much noise. You know I haven't once tried Seeking you – but it wouldn't matter if I had. How do you know the man who might some day be stalking you won't also be a Seeker? How the hell would you get away from him?'

'Nobody can evade a Seeker.'

'Oh? An expert now, are we?'

Andrew said nothing. His stance was one of such complete dejection, Finnlay's anger quickly began to fade.

'Come on,' he said quietly. 'The others will be waiting. Supper should be ready by the time we get back. You must be hungry.'

A slight nod was all he got in reply at first, then another mumble. 'I really am sorry, Finnlay.'

Such genuine remorse touched Finnlay deep inside, the way it always did. He felt the last of his frustration die away and with a sigh, he slung an arm around the boy's shoulders, urging him back along the path. 'I'm sorry, too. I don't mean to get angry, but I know you can do better.'

'What if I can't?'

Finnlay looked at the young face gazing up at him bathed in flashes of moonlight. He looked so much like his mother, it was almost frightening – and yet, something in his eyes gave his father away.

'What if I can't, Finnlay?' Andrew asked again. 'The others

can all do this, can't they? They can make their Senses work so they know when people are around them. What if I really don't have that power?'

There was a low note of desperation in the boy's voice and Finnlay felt suddenly guilty for pushing him so hard. If the boy's powers hadn't come through by now, after all that provocation, perhaps they weren't going to.

But Jenn was *so* certain Andrew had abilities. And Martha said she could Sense them as well. So if they were in there, buried somewhere deep, why couldn't Andrew push them up to the surface when he needed to?

'I can't be Salti if I don't have any powers, can I?'

'Are you worried about that? Honestly, it doesn't matter. Plenty of Salti have children who don't have powers. It happens all the time. It doesn't mean you don't belong.'

'Everybody I know has them. You've been working with the others. Do they keep failing?'

'Some of them, yes.' Finnlay stopped and faced the boy squarely. 'Look, I don't want you to worry about this. Your mother's abilities didn't manifest until she was seventeen, and you're still three years off that. The only reason we keep trying this is because of the time you spend at court, with Kenrick. And remember, these exercises aren't just about you developing powers – they're about you being aware with the normal senses everyone is born with. You can't go stumbling around a forest, making that kind of noise, leaving a trail a blind man could see. We want you to be as well-armed as possible, for your own sake, that's all. You're doing well in everything else – your mother's very proud of you, I know.'

A little smile lit Andrew's face. 'You must want to tear your hair out with me, sometimes.'

'Well, yes, that's true,' Finnlay agreed, deadpan. 'But you're not the only one. At least half my students have the same effect on me – and I can honestly say that you are, by no means, my worst student.'

'I'm not?'

'No.' Finnlay resumed walking, listening to Andrew walk behind, his step lighter now. 'I think you should also know,' he added, giving the boy a little hope, 'that I was the worst student of all.'

'Really?' Andrew's voice suddenly held a note of excitement.

'I drove everybody to distraction: parents, teachers and my brother.'

'Duke Robert?'

In the darkness, Finnlay grinned. It never failed. Every time he brought up the general subject of his brother, he would get plagued with questions. He just had to be sure he didn't do it within Jenn's hearing. Finnlay wanted Andrew to grow up with some knowledge of his father. Jenn, on the other hand, wasn't so sure that was a good idea – especially since neither Robert nor Andrew knew they were father and son.

'Finnlay?'

'Yes?'

'After supper, would you tell us about the Battle again? I'm sure Mother won't mind. It's just that, being here, in the forest where it all happened, makes it seem more real. Does that make sense?'

A little too much sense. Finnlay agreed, 'If the others are interested, then certainly. Now let's get a move on. I can smell the cooking from here.'

Finnlay found the clearing almost by smell alone. Something tasty and rich was being cooked over an open fire and his stomach reacted with odd noises. Andrew left him almost immediately and went to join his friends. They were on the other side of the clearing, gathered around Arlie, who was obviously trying to teach them something. Finnlay watched them for a moment, then headed to where Jenn was sitting by a fire, an open book on her lap. These days, she did little else but work, and there were times when he wished she wouldn't.

She looked up as he approached, a faint smile in blue eyes edged with a little tension. 'How was he?'

Finnlay sank onto a log pulled close to the fire and carefully framed his reply. 'About the same. What about you? How did the others go?'

Jenn frowned at his short response, then glanced across the

clearing, the dark blue eyes which were so like her son's narrowed with distracted speculation. 'They did well enough. Arlie's had them working on lighting fires for the last hour or so – hence the mess. They did prepare dinner, and that certainly smells good.'

'I noticed.' Finnlay leaned back on his hands and surveyed the clearing and the activity going on. They'd brought eight Salti children with them on this trip, twice the usual number, because it was getting late in the year. The youngest, at thirteen, was his own daughter, Helen. The oldest was Liam, turning eighteen next spring. So far they'd behaved well, experimenting with woodcraft and testing some of the other lessons they'd learned in the Enclave.

It was perhaps too little for them – but for a community living in a kind of prison, it was certainly better than nothing.

Right now, Arlie Baldwyn was demonstrating another technique to light a fire from damp wood – *without* using his powers. That, more than anything else, was the focus of these trips, teaching the young Salti how to survive in the forest, how to avoid capture, how to track and trace both game and human quarry, all skills Finnlay had learned as part of his normal education at home at Dunlorn, essential skills these children would have to master if the day ever came when they could live safely outside their mountain home – even if that day appeared as far away as ever.

'What's wrong?' Jenn's voice was quiet and as Finnlay turned to face her, she raised her eyebrows, putting the book on her lap to one side.

'Nothing,' he said. 'Just wondering how much use this is going to be in the long run. You know how bored they are at the Enclave.' Along with a few other people he could have mentioned.

'They've been fine while we've been away.'

'Exactly. But we're facing another long winter where any chance to get outside the Enclave will be limited at best. I can see more trouble brewing.' The last two years had been a trial on his patience. Some days he spent most of his energies keeping track of the children under his tutelage, just trying to keep them out of trouble. The truth was, he was tired of the responsibility, tired of training them for a life they were never likely to be able to lead.

Tired of the dead end his own ambitions had become.

He realised Jenn was watching him, but she said nothing for a moment. Her gaze drifted over the children at work, the horses unsaddled but hobbled at the other end of the clearing. Her expression was thoughtful, as though there were other considerations at stake here, things that even he didn't know about. She kept her silence as she began to tidy up her books and papers, packing them into the ancient leather bag by her side. Then, her voice quiet, she said, 'Do you have any other suggestions?'

Finnlay grunted. 'Like what? We're treating the symptoms of a disease we have no cure for. The Calyx is supposed to be able to tell us how to live outside the Enclave in freedom – but you can't get the Key to tell us where it is. Unless you can find some way to get rid of Nash and Kenrick, things are only going to get worse.' Those had once been his ambitions – to find the Calyx himself and to be at least a part of the battle to rid Lusara of the evil Nash had brought to it, the evil he'd corrupted the young King into.

'Is it really that bad?'

He looked up at her – really looked. At thirty-two, she was still young, still beautiful, with those fathomless blue eyes, rich dark hair and an expressive oval face.

The years had wrought little change in her; the past had done that instead. Tonight he would tell the children the story of the Battle, without mentioning how this woman had never really recovered from that day, had never regained herself in the wake of her actions. Instead, she held herself together with a dignity she didn't appear to believe in and a determination matched only by the man she had betrayed, his brother, Robert.

Like them all, she survived each year, considering hope, but not counting upon it.

Finnlay sighed. 'No, perhaps it isn't a crisis yet – but it will be one day. For five hundred years, Salti sorcerers have sheltered in the Enclave. We've trained them, then they've gone back out to live normal lives, returning now and then, sometimes permanently. Now it's too dangerous for any of them to live outside. Children born in the Enclave never have a choice. And,' Finnlay held up his hand to make his point, 'the only reason we can do this much is because you come along with us, using the Key to give protection nobody can Seek through.'

'Finnlay,' Jenn replied, her voice soft to keep her words from the children, 'I know they're restless, I know they're bored. But what else can we do?'

'Aye.' Frustration melted into weariness. 'What else indeed?' Finnlay climbed to his feet and grabbed his saddlebag. 'I'm going to the stream to wash. I just thought I'd warn you, though, Andrew wants me to tell the story of the Battle again tonight.'

He turned then, not wanting to see the look on her face, nor the shadow in her eyes.

With icy-cold hands, Jenn quietly lifted another log and placed it on the fire in front of her. She had quite a blaze going now, despite the fact that supper had been finished an hour ago. Even so, she couldn't quite stop the shiver that persistently ran down her back, no matter how many layers she wore.

Too many years spent living in the heated caves of the Enclave, no doubt: hard for her body to remember that she'd grown up in this forest, had run around here, winter and summer, from the age of three until seventeen when, chased by a squad of Guilde soldiers, she'd come across Finnlay and Micah and . . . Robert.

His quick thinking that night had saved her from punishment. His mystery had drawn her in much further, to the point where she'd lost the ability to extract herself. That story was still ongoing, even as Finnlay sat before the children, telling them of another chapter, one she already knew far better than she cared to admit.

He'd had a lot of practice over the years, telling this tale. He did so now with skill and patience, not minding the odd question thrown at him, carefully leaving out sundry details here and there – such as how the Malachi girl they'd captured had in fact been the same girl Micah had fallen in love with. How Finnlay himself had vowed to keep Jenn away from the battlefield, but that he had failed and instead, allowed Jenn to come between Robert and Nash, to stop them fighting, to prevent either of them dying that day.

And he said nothing of the hours after the battle, when Robert lay dying and when Jenn had saved his life with a lie.

No, Finnlay's story covered only the historical aspects of the battle: the men who'd fought, those who had been wounded and those who'd died. He told of how sorcery had been used and how well it had worked. He covered the strategy, the tactics and the tricks each army had played upon the other – and he could do none of it without talking about his beloved brother.

Jenn watched it all from a distance, keeping the distance inside her as well. The children, Andrew amongst them, listened in rapt silence, smiling, frowning, eyes wide as though this was the first time they'd heard any of this – but of course, this time they were actually here, in the middle of Shan Moss, though some distance from the actual battlefield. Somehow, hearing this story while surrounded by the same trees, breathing the same air, brought the whole thing to life.

Dreams of glory, of victory and freedom. She could almost see them in the children's faces – and it was impossible, at this age, for them to understand that the Battle of Shan Moss had been none of those things, but instead, a long series of mistakes – some of which had been hers.

She drew in a deep breath. Young Helen, Finnlay's beautiful daughter, sat beside him, head on his shoulder, his arm around her. Quiet, thoughtful, gentle and kind, it was hard to imagine that he had sired her: Finnlay, with his quick temper, his impatience and demands for instant results. No two people could be less alike – yet they were as close as father and daughter could be and it always warmed Jenn's heart to see them like this, quiet and at peace with the world, if only for a few hours.

On the other side of Finnlay sat the sixteen-year-old twins, Zea and Neil. Where Neil, like Helen, was a fairly quiet boy, Zea could be as demanding and impatient as Finnlay. Their parents often despaired of her ever settling down. Sitting behind Neil and watching everything with an eagle eye was Liam, at seventeen the oldest. Finnlay had wanted to leave him behind, but Jenn had insisted he come along. He, perhaps more than any other Salti child, chafed at the restraints placed on him by King and Guilde, by the circumstances which made their prison so much worse these days. He had a good mind, however, and with the right teaching, Jenn was sure he would grow up to be a natural leader.

Right in front of Finnlay sat Sayre, his freckled face and bright red curls reminding her perhaps a little too much of Micah – though his parentage was in no doubt at all. More often than not, his gaze would drift to Arlie's daughter, Damaris, who sat on her own a little, idly drawing something in a book she'd brought with her. Beside Sayre sat Andrew and his best friend, Guy. Andrew listened to Finnlay's story with a knowing smile on his face, which would have worried her if she hadn't seen it a thousand times before. This was his pleased look, where he'd done something that others had liked, and was enjoying it so much more as a result. It was hard to believe that he was already fourteen. Guy contented himself with listening, laughing along with the others, saving his questions for later, when he could be as blunt as he cared without getting into trouble. Andrew had once told her that was one of the things he liked most about his friend – that he could rely on getting the truth, no matter how grim it was.

And in another ten days, she would have to give him up again, have to let him ride down from the mountain with Micah, head back to his home at Maitland Manor for the winter. She would have to do it knowing that his powers had still not manifested, that he would go without the protection he needed, even if he didn't know it. Some days, that worry alone was enough to make her ill.

The noise rose as questions flowed from the children. One voice caught her attention. It was Liam.

42

'But, why did the army flee? Why did Kenrick turn and run from Duke Robert? They still had the advantage of numbers. With Duke Robert so badly injured, they would've had a good chance at victory. Kenrick would have known that – and yet he still ran. Why?'

Yes, indeed Finnlay was well-practised telling this story now – and he refrained from looking at Jenn. 'I don't know for sure, but I'd guess that, as a boy of fourteen, he didn't have the experience to fight a battle of that size. His father had been killed the day before and Nash, the man behind the entire thing to begin with, was also badly injured in the fight with Robert. I don't think Kenrick believed he could . . .'

'I heard,' Neil said knowingly, 'that Duke Robert did something to Kenrick some time before the battle. That he put a thought in the boy's head so that Kenrick would always be afraid of him. Is that true?'

Now Finnlay did glance at Jenn and she nodded. This was a truth they could give away without cost.

'Yes,' Finnlay turned back to the children. 'Though I have no idea how long something like that would hold.'

Jenn quickly looked at Andrew, wondering if he would react to this new knowledge; he was the only one here who knew the King. But Andrew's response was negligible, the barest blink.

'But,' Sayre leaned forward, 'if your brother is the most powerful sorcerer ever born, couldn't he make a fear like that last forever?'

Finnlay's gaze darkened then, and as though she sensed something was wrong, Helen shifted and snuggled closer to her father. In the silence, Finnlay paused, then said softly, 'Yes. Robert could make that fear last forever.'

Finnlay willingly took the first watch, leaving Jenn and Arlie to rest after the day's exertions. He said nothing to them, but the truth was telling the story of the Battle, answering the children's innocent questions, had left him feeling unsettled and unable to think about sleep.

He'd had plenty of nightmares in the days following the Battle, nights during which he'd recalled his own close

43

encounters with Nash, times when he'd almost died, when the feeling of helplessness had been so overwhelming, he'd almost welcomed death.

He'd been lucky – and so had Robert. It had taken Robert three weeks to get fit enough to travel after the Battle, and then, only on a litter. Finnlay had stayed with him the whole time, and for another month after that as he nursed him to the point where he no longer worried that his brother might die of either his wounds or some subsequent fever. Robert's injuries had appeared incurable then, the scar on his back still breaking open, the cut in his side weeping blood whenever he moved too much. By the time Finnlay had agreed to leave and return to the Enclave, Robert had been walking short distances for a few days only and it was almost impossible to believe that he would ever heal completely.

He had word every now and then about Robert: Murdoch worked with him all summer, then spent winter at the Enclave, when Finnlay would talk to him for hours about Robert's exploits, but quietly and secretively. Of Robert's health, Murdoch said nothing. Finnlay knew Jenn didn't want to know. Taunting her now was not high on his list of priorities.

There was something still left undone and his own rest-lessness was hounded by it. Despite what Murdoch told him, he really had no idea what Robert was planning.

The camp settled down in the usual manner, with fires banked, horses watered, beds made up and good-humoured bickering and some laughter until, long after the moon had risen, the clearing was silent of all but forest noises and the occasional shuffling of the animals.

Finnlay chose a comfortable spot just on the edge of the clearing, where a tree had recently fallen, giving him a trunk to sit on and a branch to lean back against. Settled, he closed his eyes and took out his *ayarn*, letting his power flow through the small stone, sending his awareness out into the darkness, testing the area for any dangers, Seeking for safety as his charges slept.

As usual, there was nothing and content, he opened his eyes – to find Andrew standing in front of him, wide awake, a blanket draped around his shoulders. 'Wouldn't you be warmer sitting by the fire?'

'Wouldn't you be warmer tucked up in bed?'

The boy looked over his shoulder at his sleeping friends then sat on the log beside Finnlay. He pulled his feet up and wrapped his arms around his knees. 'I couldn't sleep.'

'I gathered that.'

'Really, you could let Liam or Neil take a turn at night watch, couldn't you? Wouldn't that be good practice for them?'

'And if they fell asleep and we were attacked?'

Andrew's eyes crinkled up at the corners. The moon was very bright tonight, dusting the entire clearing in light enough to read by. 'I'll keep watch with you, then, and we can keep each other awake.'

Finnlay grinned. Andrew had an infectious smile, a way about him that made it impossible to dislike him. Despite the fact that many of the Salti children were envious of the freedom Andrew enjoyed living at Maitland, none of them openly hated him for it. Of course, Andrew was always happy to bring them gifts or books that they'd asked for and refrained from talking for hours about his exploits at court or other places. He lived in two worlds, this boy, and yet didn't seem to be at home in either of them.

'So,' Finnlay murmured after a moment, 'why couldn't you sleep?'

'Just thinking.' Andrew rested his chin on his knees and gazed into the darkness. 'About Nash and Duke Robert.'

'What about them?'

'What's the Word of Destruction?'

Finnlay blinked. 'Pardon?'

With a flash of blue eyes, Andrew grinned. 'No, I don't mean tell me the actual word—'

'Since I don't know it—'

'I mean, *what* is it? I know it was created centuries ago and given to the Key, and the Key gave it to your brother – but what is it? How does it work? Did Duke Robert ever learn more about it?'

Finnlay sighed. 'I can't tell you what he's discovered lately – if anything. As far as I know, he's only ever used it once, the day you were born. Having seen the effects, I'm not sure I want to see him using it a second time.'

'He was going to use the Word of Destruction to kill Nash, wasn't he?'

Suddenly wary, Finnlay said, 'Yes.'

Hesitant blue eyes darted to his and then away. 'Why . . . why did Mother stop him?'

Finnlay blinked in surprise. Hadn't Jenn explained enough to assuage his curiosity?

Obviously not.

Not waiting for an answer, or perhaps afraid of it, Andrew hurried on, his voice a sharp whisper, 'So Nash is still alive, which means Duke Robert still has to kill him – and that's what he's planning now, isn't it? Another war? Because he still has to kill Nash. Isn't it?'

'Have you been talking to Murdoch? What has he said?'

'Was I not supposed to? I'm sorry if I wasn't meant to know or something but . . . I just . . . well, I was curious and . . . Murdoch didn't say anything about a war. I just thought that might be what . . .'

'It doesn't matter,' Finnlay held up his hand. 'I take it you don't mention any of this to your mother.'

'No.' Andrew's voice came out short; there was tension beneath the surface. 'Why did she stop them? Didn't she believe in Duke Robert?'

By the gods, that was too much! How could she have told the boy so much and yet left him understanding nothing of her relationship with Robert? Quietly, Finnlay turned his full gaze on Andrew then, deliberately looking for the tiny signs of his father in the face that resembled Jenn's so much. 'Have you asked her?'

A shrug was the only answer he got.

'Do you think perhaps that if she wanted you to know, she would have told you already?'

'I don't know. It just seems like . . .'

'What?'

'Like she betrayed him in some way.' Andrew looked at Finnlay then, a little fearfully, as though he knew he'd said something he shouldn't.

Finnlay couldn't tell him the truth. It wasn't his story to tell. It had to come from Jenn, if anyone – and she could be a tyrant when it came to what her son was told and what he wasn't.

And she had held him to his promise never to tell Robert that Andrew was his son, a promise he had never stopped regretting.

He could, however, give the boy something to lean on. 'You know about the Prophecy, don't you? You know that the roles played by my brother, your mother and Nash were written down centuries ago?'

For a moment, Andrew didn't answer. Instead, his gaze drifted, floating to nothing in particular, leaving Finnlay with a perfect image of Robert doing exactly the same thing when he Sensed someone approaching. He waited until Andrew turned to him again, blinking a little as though nothing had happened.

Finnlay had to ask. 'What's wrong?'

Andrew shook his head a little, apparently unaware of what he'd just done. 'Nothing. You were saying about the Prophecy?'

Unsure how to interpret what he'd just seen, Finnlay decided it was best ignored for the moment. He couldn't get carried away with the hope that Andrew was finally developing Senses. It might be nothing at all. 'Well, it's just that you should be able to see whatever happens between them is going to be complicated. More complicated than either you or I can understand from the outside. I do know what she told me: that the Key had insisted that Shan Moss was not the right time for Robert and Nash to fight. Perhaps leaving it for another day meant Robert would have more weapons at his disposal, or more information. Anything beyond that is a guess – but I do know she had good reasons. Do you honestly think she would act in any other manner?'

'No!' Andrew's eyes were wide with horror at the mere

suggestion. 'I just wanted to understand and she won't really talk to me about it.'

'Well, perhaps she will one day, when you're a little older.'

'Maybe,' Andrew drew in a breath, 'maybe she's waiting until I develop powers.'

'Perhaps.'

'And . . . and what if I don't?' Andrew bit his bottom lip. 'My father didn't have any. I don't even have a House Mark, like you and my mother. Why should I have any powers?'

More questions Finnlay couldn't answer with total honesty. 'There's no proof that having a House Mark is directly related to sorcery – that's only a guess. But just because Eachern didn't have powers doesn't mean you can't. Your mother's blood is powerful enough.' Finnlay then allowed himself a smile. 'Just think how powerful you'd be if *both* your parents were sorcerers.'

That brought a shy smile to the boy's face then, easing away the worry.

Finnlay gave Andrew's shoulder a squeeze. 'Just sit still a moment while I do another scan.'

'Of course.'

Once more Finnlay closed his eyes, breathing deeply, sending his Senses out into the forest to Seek for any danger approaching. He found nothing in the immediate area, so he extended himself further, looking and Sensing and feeling and leaving those awkward questions, and even more awkward answers behind. On the last edge of his sweep, however, he paused.

Something. Something that shouldn't be there. Ten, perhaps twenty men, on horseback. Drawing further into the forest. Heading in this direction!

His eyes snapped open and he surged to his feet. Andrew stood quickly, his face already pale with fear. 'Go, wake your mother and Arlie. Now! We have to get moving!'

3

'We need to get closer. I can't see anything from here.' Finnlay frowned into the darkness, then glanced over his shoulder to where the others stood with the horses. He could see nothing in the way of faces, but the very stillness of the children, the restlessness of the animals, told him all he needed to know.

Jenn shifted beside him, pulling in closer to the shadows. The bright moonlight left the field before them open and bright, giving them cover within the forest.

'But what are they doing here? I've never seen Guilde soldiers venture more than fifty yards into the forest.'

'That's a search pattern,' Finnlay said, making out movement along the edge of the field: horses, men, somebody obviously in command, the familiar flash of Guilde yellow. On the opposite side, masked by younger, smaller trees, lay the Trade Road, the major route between Lusara and Mayenne which skirted the northern perimeter of Shan Moss. 'They're looking for someone.'

'Or something?'

There were two answers to that question, and Finnlay liked neither of them. He pulled in a breath. 'Well, we need to move. If we stand here all night they're bound to find us. We can try a mask, but the moment the horses move, we'll be given away and we don't have the firepower between us to fight off an attack from twenty or more soldiers.'

'Nor do we want to attract that kind of attention. If they search the children, they'll find *ayarns*, and that's a death sentence.'

'Oh, I do love being an outlaw.'

Jenn sighed, still watching the field. 'What do you suggest?'

'You and Arlie take the children east, but don't go too far into the forest. Sandy Gorge is too close and if they come after you, you'll get trapped. If we're clear of them by morning, we

49

can skirt around the gorge and go far enough into the forest they won't dare follow. After that, we head straight back to the Enclave.'

'I agree.' Jenn paused, then added, 'They can't be looking for *us*, can they?'

His stomach gave an uncomfortable clench at the idea, then he shook his head. 'I don't see how that's possible.'

'Very well. And what are you going to do?'

Finnlay turned back. 'I'm going to get a little closer to the soldiers. We need to know what's got them so fired up. I'll take Andrew with me.'

'No.'

Finnlay would have had to be deaf not to have heard the determination – and the fear – in her voice. 'Jenn,' he whispered, 'you can't protect him like this. He has to do these things, for his own good. You have to let him take the risks.'

'No!' Jenn grabbed his arm, a sliver of moonlight making her eyes glint. 'He's not ready.'

'But this is how we make him ready.'

'I won't have him taking risks without even a shred of power to protect him!'

'You honestly think I would allow anything to happen to my own nephew?' Finnlay stepped closer, desperate to make sure nobody either saw or heard them. 'Jenn, you have to get used to the idea that Andrew may never develop any powers at all. Robert had his when he was nine—'

'And mine didn't come until I was seventeen. We need to give him at least that long.'

'And what if the decision isn't ours, eh?'

She froze at that, then shook off his hand. 'Take Liam, not Andrew. We'll discuss the rest of it when we get home.'

Finnlay groaned, but there was no point pursuing it further. Shaking his head, he headed back to the horses.

Discuss it when they got home? Like they *hadn't* discussed it for the last eight years? What the hell was she trying to do, trying to hide?

He didn't know much about what she was thinking, what

she was planning any more, but he knew one thing: there would be no discussion once they got home.

It only took an hour for Andrew to develop a headache, trying to keep his horse quiet, listening so hard for noises that might mean soldiers were coming after them, peering into the inky shadows for pitfalls and signs of the ridge they were following. It was futile, of course. He didn't have Senses that would help him do something like that, and Arlie was a strong Seeker, even if his mother wasn't. And of course, all the others were doing what they could and would undoubtedly talk about it later, at great length, even knowing how inadequate it made him feel.

That didn't stop him trying, though. Didn't stop him wanting to succeed, to finally be able to show his mother that all her efforts hadn't been in vain, that something of what she and Finnlay had been trying to teach him had sunk in.

He didn't know what was wrong with him. Wished he did.

But he *could* feel something, though it was certainly nothing like what Finnlay had described. This was something else, something he knew, something that drifted on the edge of his awareness every now and then, perhaps once every five or six months. It wasn't a *thing* exactly, but more a . . .

What?

'Why hasn't Father come back yet?'

The fearful whisper to his left made him reach out until he could touch Helen's hand. She rode beside him, almost invisible in the darkness. 'I don't know, but I'm sure he's fine.'

'You can't know that,' Neil hissed from behind, but Andrew ignored him.

Zea was riding in front, her voice disembodied in the night. 'I don't understand why we're running. We've done nothing wrong.'

'We're Salti,' Guy replied. 'Isn't that enough?'

'But they can't know that, not just by looking at us. They won't be looking for us.'

'No,' Andrew shook his head, 'but *they* won't know that, will they?'

Zea turned to say something more, but her comments were silenced with a word from Arlie. Andrew returned to listening.

There *was* something out there, that something familiar he'd known for years – but he couldn't pinpoint it and he was no nearer to working out what it was than he'd ever been.

'Damn it, where have they all come from?' And what were they looking for? Finnlay held his tongue against further curses that might be heard and carefully steered his horse between the trunks of two dead trees. Silent in his fear, Liam followed, staying close, his eyes wide, his left hand keeping hold of his *ayarn* as though it were a lifeline.

Well, perhaps it was – though against an organised group such as this, it would not get him far.

With a frown, Finnlay twisted in his saddle and cast his Senses back the way they'd come. It had taken them long, dangerous minutes to circle around the soldiers, to sneak up on them from behind, just so he could listen in. He could only hope that Jenn would keep moving, taking the children away from this area.

For the moment, they were safe in these shadows. With a nod to himself, he swung down from his saddle and, not for the first time, wished he had the power to do one of those dimensional shifts Robert was so skilled at. Making himself invisible at this point would be useful indeed.

He handed his reins to Liam. 'Stay here. Count to five hundred. If I'm not back by then, leave my horse and go.'

Liam nodded, his fear held carefully at bay. 'How are you going to get closer? Can you do a shift?'

Finnlay had to bite his lip to stop himself from snapping, 'No, I'm not! And I wouldn't even if I could. I've told you a hundred times the dangers of using the forbidden side of our powers. Now do as I say and keep quiet.'

The boy opened his mouth to protest, but Finnlay didn't wait. He turned and strode into the forest.

Using every ounce of skill he had, he crept towards the soldiers, pausing when they paused, listening with his ears, extending his Senses to absorb everything he could. Only when he could hear actual voices did he halt his advance. The words themselves, however, almost made his heart stop.

Quickly he turned and made his way back. Liam smiled his relief and moments later they were on their way.

'This isn't supposed to be here!' Jenn jumped down from her horse and took two short steps to the edge of Sandy Gorge. The moon had moved, but there was still enough light to show the sharp drop, the flat ground below. The gorge stretched out left and right, carving a slice out of the forest, leaving them without a place to hide. Could she get nothing right? Even when lives depended on her, she made simple mistakes like this, in a place she was supposed to know better than anyone else. 'I must have turned in too soon.'

Arlie came up beside her, frowning down, then lifting his gaze to the other side, so close, and yet not close enough. 'We must have, but it looked right to me, too. Finnlay said there's no path down here.'

'So we either go back to where we turned off and keep going, or try to skirt around it from here.' Taking a deep breath, Jenn faced the others, gauging their reactions, how well they were holding up. So far, only Helen looked worried, but as her father hadn't returned yet—

Vibrations at her feet made her turn swiftly. Signalling the others to mount up, she moved forward, her hand flexing, ready to release whatever power was necessary to protect—

Two horses emerged from the trees, breathing heavily, slowing abruptly. Jenn allowed some of the tension to leave her body. 'Your timing is perfect, Finn. Did you find out anything?'

He nodded sharply, jumping down from his horse. He came close, keeping his voice low. 'The whole area is crawling with Guilde and there're more heading this way. There's been an ambush on the Trade road, a grain shipment heading for Mayenne. They think . . . no, they're convinced that . . . well, that Robert was behind it.'

Robert?

For a moment, nothing other than relief filled her. He was still safe, still alive.

Still fighting for what he believed in.

Thank the gods.

Swallowing quickly, she nodded, keeping everything from her voice. 'So they haven't caught him yet?'

Finnlay's gaze flickered and a brief smile flashed across his face. 'No.'

Uncaring, she matched his smile, then turned back to Arlie and the others. 'We have to keep moving, then.'

'Yes, only . . .'

'What?'

'How did you end up here?'

Jenn suppressed a groan and instead waved her hands in the general direction of the forest. 'Well, don't stand there gawping. Show us the way out.'

They moved in single file, Finnlay taking the lead, Arlie in the rear. After a moment's hesitation, Jenn rode behind Finnlay, watching him as he paused now and then to Seek for soldiers. Watching him for other things as well.

For the most part, Finnlay appeared happy with his life at the Enclave – but that was the problem: it was only for the most part. There were still, even after all these years, periods when he chafed at the bit, when a burning restlessness surged from within. If it hadn't been for Fiona and his children, Jenn didn't doubt that Finnlay would risk capture and leave the Enclave altogether, taking his chances with a life of freedom rather than the prison he was confined to.

Even after all this time, he hadn't realised that there were different kinds of prisons and his was the gentlest, the best he could hope for.

And now he'd had direct word of Robert; he might even be close by, was, even now, working in some way to help the people of Lusara, just as Finnlay had always wanted to do.

Just as she had once, a long time ago, before the Key had chosen her for Jaibir and her fate had been sealed.

As had Robert's.

Nothing had turned out the way they had expected.

There was so much of Robert in Finnlay, so much of that deeply embedded need to *do* something constructive. That's why Finnlay had started the Enclave Combat school in the first place, their very own D'Azzir to match that of the Malachi – and why he had suggested these trips out into the forest.

Why he was determined to *do* something about Andrew, regardless of the cost.

Abruptly Finnlay came to a halt, holding up his hand. There was a moment's pause, then he swung down with a thud.

'What is it?'

'The path,' he replied quietly, frowning at the ground, then at the trees standing close on their left. 'It's gone. Must have been a landslide since I was last here. We'll have to dismount and walk. The forest sits too close to ride. Get the others ready while I take a quick look around.'

Jenn passed the word back. As quietly as possible, they all dismounted, then stood waiting, the animals no longer restless but tired. They would have to rest at some point, but not until they were clear of the soldiers.

'Serin's breath!' Finnlay's curse came out resigned and Jenn moved to his side. He was just putting his *ayarn* away and he looked at her. 'There's another group of soldiers following us. They must have picked up our tracks.'

'Can we escape them?'

'Not on foot.' He frowned again, looking up at the sky. The moon was already past the tree-line, giving them more cover. 'There used to be a path going down to the bottom. It's not far from here. When we reach it, we'll set a false trail going down, and cover our tracks up here. That might be enough. Come on, let's get moving.'

Where are you, Robert?

Finnlay tried not to clench his teeth as he sent out the silent query again and again. Of course, it was a futile exercise; he'd never been able to mindspeak his brother; only Jenn. Even so, who was to say that it might not work one day?

He could already scent the morning on the air. In another

hour, the sun would begin to peek over the hills. They needed to be out of the forest by then. Out and away.

Damned stupid idea to come here in the first place. But they'd been doing it for years now and this was the first time they'd had any trouble.

They'd laid the false trail and it had worked, to a point. The soldiers had gone down into the gorge, but they were still following. It was now a race against time. If they could reach the village of Solmoss before the soldiers came upon them, they would be safe, hidden amongst the population. They were looking for Robert, for a band of raiders, rather than three adults and eight children – but one of those children was a Duke who frequented court, who knew the King. If Andrew were to be recognised – or himself or even Jenn, there would be trouble indeed.

Robert?

What was he doing? Leading an ambush? Feeding the people grain stolen by the Guilde? Making a tiny mark here and there when he, above all others, had the power to do so much more?

Was this all that the Prophecy had left him?

A cry from behind was quickly followed by a muffled thud. He whirled around to find the others rushing to the edge of the gorge. Leaving his horse, Finnlay pushed through, grabbing Andrew's shoulder.

'What's happened?'

'It's Helen,' Jenn whispered, falling to her knees to look over the edge. 'She slipped and . . .'

'Serin's blood!' He landed on the ground beside Jenn, his hand already reaching out to form a light – but she grabbed it to stop him. 'Damn it, I can't see her! Helen? Can you hear me?'

Terror caught in his throat, keeping his words quiet. The others were gathered around, but he couldn't think, couldn't do anything more than strain in the darkness, looking for a child he loved more than his own life.

Jenn's gasp was the only warning he had. 'Andrew, no!'

Andrew shifted his foot on the ledge, holding tight to the rock with both hands. At his movement, a handful of gravel scraped loose and skittered down the cliff-face, to be swallowed up by inky darkness.

His face was cold, pressed against hard stone moistened by dew. He could hear little more than the constant thud of his own heart and the muted sounds of voices from above. Specific words were lost to him, but his imagination could fill them in – along with too many other details, like how it would feel to lose his footing, how hard that ground below would be and how long it would take for those soldiers to come along and find him.

Carefully, he took in a breath and called out with a forced whisper, 'Helen? Helen, can you hear me?'

Straining, he looked as far around the rock face as he dared. In what remained of the moonlight he could see just enough into the crevice to glimpse a stretch of leg, pale brown boot attached at the end. Encouraged, he shifted his feet a little more, finding new hand-holds as he crept towards his friend.

'Andrew! Helen!'

He stopped, looking up to find Finnlay's face peering over the cliff edge. He was lying flat, but even reaching down as far as he could left him at least ten feet short of Helen's position.

'Is she conscious?' Finnlay hissed.

'I don't know yet.' Andrew inched his way along the ledge, feeling for each placement before he put weight on it. He couldn't afford to be afraid, couldn't spare the thought or the attention, because the moment he did, he would fall, he knew that. He would simply fall and then . . .

He gulped in another breath and paused, closing his eyes to shut out the sight of the drop below, visible in a vague wash of pre-dawn light. He couldn't afford to be afraid – but apparently that didn't stop the fear.

At least he'd had some practice climbing – not that it would help get Helen back up – but it meant he could get down here in one piece and avoid falling to his death. Hopefully.

Finally he rounded the corner of the crevice and reached Helen. She was wedged in firmly, one arm stretched above her head, the other jammed into the narrow rock. One knee was bent, most of her weight pressing on it, the other was free and it was this that Andrew reached out to touch.

'Helen? Helen? Can you hear me? Helen?'

She shifted, eyes opening slowly. She blinked a few times, then tried to move.

'Just keep still. You fell, but the crevice caught you. Finnlay's going to lower some ropes down, I think.'

'I'm fine,' Helen whispered, moving with a moan.

'Are you hurt?'

'I . . . I don't think so. Just a knock on my head.'

'Don't worry,' Andrew said, trying to smile, 'nobody will ever notice.'

Helen grimaced then turned her head to the side, enough to get an idea of the drop below. She froze.

'Helen? Listen to me.' When he got no response, he put his hand on her foot and squeezed hard to get her attention. 'Look at me!'

Helen looked up.

'You'll be fine,' Andrew said with every ounce of certainty he had. Fortunately, his own fear hadn't emerged in his voice. 'Finnlay and Arlie and all the others are up there. And . . . and my mother can help. She can probably lift us both out of here on her own, so don't go looking down and thinking about what might happen, because it won't. You know that, don't you? Don't you?'

Helen frowned a little, blinked a few times, then nodded slowly. 'What are you doing here? Did you fall as well?'

'No, I climbed down to help you.'

'Oh.'

A faint noise from above made him look up. Something slithered over the edge of the cliff, heading towards them. It looked like a rope. Slowly it descended, but he waited until it was level with his face before letting go his hold on the rock to grab it. More came down, to give him some slack, and when he looked up again, Finnlay was once more peering over the cliff, his face lined with worry.

'Can you tie it around her?'

'I'll try.' The walls of the crevice rose vertically around Helen. Andrew was perched on his ledge just outside the crevice, able to lean in, but that was about all. And of course, he had no idea what condition Helen's other leg was in because he couldn't see it.

He looped the leather strap around his wrist and repositioned his feet. Taking a good hold of the rock with his left hand, he leaned forward and slipped his arm around Helen's waist. He grazed his knuckles, but managed to wedge the strap between her and the rock. Then he withdrew and went in from the other side.

'Ow,' Helen grunted as he pulled the strap clear.

'Bruised or broken?' Andrew whispered.

'Bruised, I hope.'

'I need your hand to help tie this.'

Helen nodded and brought her free arm down. Awkwardly, their hands worked together, tying a knot firmly around Helen's waist, then doubling it. Done, Andrew refreshed his grip on the rock then gave the strap a good, solid tug. The knot held and he threw Helen an encouraging grin.

'You might be a bit more bruised by the end of this – but at least you'll be in one piece.'

'Or two, if that knot's too tight.'

'Then you'll be twice the trouble,' Andrew quipped back. He steadied himself on the ledge again and looked up for Finnlay. 'Try it now.'

The leather strap drew taut as those above began to pull. Helen started to pant as the pressure on her bruises began to increase. Andrew hovered, ready to give a hand if necessary, but for long seconds, it seemed like nothing was happening. Then, abruptly, Helen began to move, her hands scrambling for purchase on the rock before her. Andrew's hand shot out to steady her as she kept moving, up, until she was beyond his reach.

He didn't take his eyes from her until she disappeared, dragged to safety by welcoming hands.

Closing his eyes in relief, Andrew leaned back against the rock and took in a couple of deep breaths. As his heartbeat began to slow, he heard the rope slide towards him again – and something else.

He froze. Holding his breath now, he turned carefully, straining to hear what was going on below.

Horses. He could hear horses. And men. Voices. Tired and fed up.

Something flicked on his face and he nearly leaped off the ledge – but it was just the rope. He grabbed hold of it and stole a glance up. All he could see was the faint outline of Finnlay's face peering down at him. Everybody else must have moved back.

Shaking now, Andrew wound the rope around both hands. As it drew taut he let it take his weight, using his feet to climb up, one step at a time. He'd barely begun his climb when a warning note made him freeze once more.

'Wait!'

Heart hammering in his chest, Andrew carefully looked up. Both Arlie and Finnlay were there holding the rope and, with just enough light to see by, he saw Arlie mouth the rest of the warning.

'Soldiers. Directly below.'

4

In a flash of panic, Andrew turned his head, eyes seeking in the gloom beneath him for . . .

Five, six . . . no, more than that. Mounted and armed and . . . and he was fast losing feeling in his hands as the rope began to cut off his circulation. He couldn't move. If he put a foot down to shift his weight, they'd hear him; he'd probably dislodge some dirt or something and they only needed to glance up and they'd see him and Finnlay and Arlie and . . .

He closed his eyes and tried to breathe, but his chest was too tight and the pain was almost unbearable. He couldn't hold on much longer . . .

And that feeling came to him again, close now, so familiar, as though it could help him, as though it would save him from falling, from giving away the others as he plummeted to the ground, as though it was a balm against his terror.

And even if it wasn't, he held onto it, savouring it. Like the rope, it held him there, safe.

A shout, and his eyes snapped open. Shaking like a leaf, he stared down at the soldiers as word flew from one to the other. Orders were called out and they gathered together, pointing back the way they'd come, as though somebody had discovered something. With a triumphant cry, the animals were kicked and urged to a canter. Moments later, the entire squad had vanished from sight, the sounds of their retreat echoing around the hard walls of the gorge.

Gulping in air, Andrew let his body slide back down to the ledge. Huddling against the rock, he unwound the rope from his hands, blinking back tears from the crushing pain that made him dizzy, made his stomach turn.

It was a moment before he heard another voice: Finnlay, calling down to him gently.

'Take your time.'

Andrew nodded, swallowing. With his hands throbbing, he carefully tied the rope around his waist, then looked up to find Finnlay watching him with respect and admiration, giving him a smile from eyes lit by the first morning glow.

'Slowly and carefully. There's no rush. Those soldiers are gone for now.'

Inch by painful inch, Andrew climbed back towards the cliff edge. It felt like days since he'd gone down to help Helen. As soon as he drew close enough, Finnlay reached out and grabbed his arm, hauling him over onto the flat ground. They both lay panting for a moment, then Finnlay got up and helped him to his feet. As the others emerged from the trees, Finnlay reached out and pulled him close, his voice thick and gruff.

'Thank you, Andrew. Thank you.'

Long plumes of smoke rose up into the pine trees, losing shape in the furred branches and dark sky above. Jenn sat and watched them go, comfortable by Andrew's side, allowing the camp's peace to fill her now.

It had been a tough journey, steering clear of the Guilde. But Finnlay had led them out of the forest and into Solmoss without further incident. Now, with nightfall behind them, they made camp beyond the village, in woods she remembered all too well.

The river was close by; she could hear it rumbling beneath the swoosh of trees above her. Helen needed some rest before travelling again and this was as good a place as any to pitch camp. The ground beneath the trees was thick with dry, brown pine needles and it was warmer.

She could admit to herself now that she was tired. Still sleep eluded her and so she remained in the camp while the others went to their beds, her hand on Andrew's hair, simply listening to the peace.

Andrew lay at her side, curled up, one hand next to his face, fast asleep. He'd been quiet all day and into the evening, excused his usual chores because of his hands, saying little to the buzz of excitement which had greeted his act of courage that morning.

Jenn knew he was embarrassed, and that made her smile. So like his father in so many ways. So like Robert, to climb down after a fallen friend, stick with her until help got her to safety, to comfort her fear while ignoring his own.

So like him to pay for it afterwards.

But Andrew was not a copy of Robert. Instead, he was a lovely combination of the two of them, perhaps taking the best of the love that had conceived him, rather than the anguish which had followed.

Or rather, the Bonding which had conceived him. But which had come first, the love or the Bonding? Would one have survived without the other?

Andrew was a gentle soul, who cared genuinely and deeply for those around him. It was a gift he had no fear of showing. Often his thoughts were so clear Jenn could almost read them; he lacked Robert's ability to hide his feelings, his deepest thoughts – and sometimes that worried her, with the double life he had to lead, here and at court.

And yes, she did worry about the effect Kenrick might have

on him, though she'd seen no evidence that the King's evil had rubbed off on Andrew at all. Perhaps a miracle would occur and Andrew's good might do something for Kenrick.

She smiled again and looked down at her son. He was already taller than her, and filling out quickly. Soon he would be a man and quiet moments like these would be gone forever.

Silently she leaned over and brushed a kiss against his cheek. Then she got to her feet and wandered quietly through the trees towards the river. Cold air touched her then, driven upwards from the canyon below. She paused a moment, looking down, able to see nothing in the darkness, then turned to see Finnlay sitting on a rock, some distance away, his head lowered as though he were reading.

She walked towards him, giving him plenty of time to register her presence. When she came to a halt, he looked up and nodded back to the camp. 'How is Helen?'

'Still asleep. She's lucky she only has a few bruises.'

'Aye, very lucky. If anything had happened to her I . . .' Finnlay's gaze drifted down to the book in his hands.

'She's fine, Finn. She was following Andrew around from the moment we stopped to make camp.' Jenn sank on to a boulder away from the cliff edge.

And just as Andrew was like Robert, so those around him reacted in the same way they reacted to his father. Sometimes that scared her more than anything else.

'How is Andrew now?'

'Asleep. Feeling a little sheepish, I think.'

'Well,' Finnlay took in a deep breath, his head lifting again, gaze drifting to the other side of the canyon, 'he's Robert's son, all right.'

Jenn allowed herself a small smile. 'Were you ever in any doubt?'

Finnlay didn't answer that. Instead, he paused a moment, then said, 'They're cousins.'

'Yes,' Jenn breathed, admitting to something they'd never spoken openly about. 'But they're both still very young. We . . . don't know if it will ever be a problem.'

He let out a grunt at that. 'And what do we do if it is? Are you going to tell him then? Tell him that I'm his uncle instead of just some mean old man who yells at him when he does things wrong?'

Despite the dry tone, Jenn couldn't help smiling at this. 'You're not encouraging me.'

As though letting something go, Finnlay smiled too. 'Did you read the last letter from Patric?'

'Yesterday.'

'And?'

'Well, it certainly looks like he might be home soon. I can't believe he's been gone this long as it is.'

'He's had too much fun having adventures – he's forgotten why he was sent to Alusia in the first place.' Finnlay rested back on his hands. 'It will be good to have him home. I've missed him. All these hints in his letters are intensely irritating. I know he has to be careful, but . . .'

'You can't help wishing you'd gone in his place?'

For a moment, Finnlay said nothing. Then he pursed his lips and shook his head. 'No.'

No. Finnlay wanted to work alongside Robert, to free Lusara from the prison it had become, trapped by Kenrick, enslaved by Nash.

'I'd certainly like to go to Alusia one day, and Budlandi.' Finnlay shrugged. 'There is so much of our history there, lost over the centuries. Patric seems to have had a lot of fun, with one thing and another—'

'I don't know that having his ship attacked by pirates was all that much fun.'

'Or spending a year as a slave in a salt mine,' Finnlay added, half laughing, 'though none of what he's done surprises me at all. I just hope he gets back here in one piece. Did you get the same feeling I did, that he'd actually found something of real interest about the Prophecy?'

'Yes,' Jenn said. There had been so many veiled hints in the last few letters as though Patric was desperate to share some important news, but didn't dare trust it to a courier. With all her heart, she prayed that it was true, that he would finally be able to bring her back some hope that the Prophecy that had driven so many lives to desperation might, in fact, be wrong.

She got to her feet and stifled a yawn. 'Are you on first watch tonight?'

'As usual, yes.'

'Well, we'll be home in another three days.'

'Assuming it doesn't start snowing. I can't believe how lucky we've been so far.'

'Me too. Well, goodnight.'

'Goodnight.'

She turned and took a couple of steps away before Finnlay's voice stopped her. 'He did well today. He's not . . . as concerned about risks as you are.'

Jenn said nothing to that and, instead, continued on to bed.

She couldn't tell him that it wasn't the risks that bothered her, but rather, Andrew's desire to take them.

Andrew's aches and pains made it uncomfortable to ride for a whole day, but Jenn was worried about the weather and wouldn't call a halt. So he rode in silence at the back of the group, practising hiding his occasional wince when some movement from the horse shifted the wrong muscle the wrong way. Which felt like every three seconds.

They left the forest far behind as the trail took them up into the mountains. Slate rock covered the path and stunted trees sank their roots between, struggling to hold onto life in the most rugged terrain. Blustery clouds tore across the peaks in the distance, giving them patches of sunshine followed by long periods of dull grey. As they crossed the first pass, the air became noticeably colder and Andrew felt the muscles down the left side of his back tighten further in reply.

'Why don't you ask Arlie for help? You know he could get rid of the pain for you.'

He turned to Helen as she slowed her horse to ride beside him. She was looking at him with genuine concern in eyes that often held him mesmerised for whole seconds at a time. 'It's not that bad. You should be feeling worse. How is your knee?'

'Oh, I feel just fine.' She smiled smugly. 'Arlie deadened the pain for me. Is it your hands?'

'No.' Andrew started to shake his head, but his neck protested and he winced. 'Just a few pulled muscles. Didn't really notice it until this morning, and I didn't want to hold up our departure.'

'So you decided instead to suffer in silence all day, right?' Helen was laughing a little now. She had her father's dark eyes and hair, but nothing of Finnlay's temperament. She was undoubtedly one of Andrew's favourite people in the Enclave, one whom it was always worth travelling halfway across the country to see.

'Well,' he replied, happy to have a distraction, 'isn't that what heroes do?'

'Suffer in silence?' She pursed her lips, tilted her head to one side and laughed a little. 'I don't know – I mean, my father is a hero and when he's suffering, it's *never* in silence.'

Andrew laughed out loud at that, until a voice from in front said loudly and distinctly, 'I heard that.'

This only made Helen laugh more, though Andrew stifled his as much as he could. Finnlay would never kill his own daughter – but he might have something to say about Andrew's fate.

'Micah's taking you back home to Maitland in a few days, isn't he?' Helen said after a moment, this time keeping her voice low so the others riding in front wouldn't hear.

'That's right.'

'And when do you go back to court?'

Andrew tucked his reins beneath his thigh and stretched his arms above his head, trying to work the kinks out of his muscles. His hands were still raw, but wearing gloves cushioned them against the worst pain. 'Caslemas.' He glanced aside at her again and frowned when he saw her sombre expression. 'What's wrong?'

'Nothing. It's just what . . . well, what's it like?'

'What's what like?'

'You know,' she gestured with her hand, 'living out there. All the time. What does that . . . feel like?' She shot him a quick look then, so full of unsuppressed longing it nearly broke his heart.

He couldn't look at her then, not while answering her question. He had something she'd never know and yet she wanted to. Needed to. 'I don't have as much freedom as you think I do.'

'But you can go places, can't you? I can only guess what the sea looks like, and a city like Marsay? I just can't imagine it.'

'Marsay is about four or five days' journey to the north of Maitland. The city can be quite beautiful from a distance. It sits on an island hill in the waters of the Vitala River, close to the bank. There's a causeway which joins them. The Castle, Basilica and Guilde Hall all sit at the top of the hill; the rest of the city is cramped around them.'

Her eyes were alight with curiosity. 'It takes a week to get to Maitland from the Enclave doesn't it?'

'If we travel fast, yes.'

'And is it a beautiful country?' Helen asked this with breathless expectation.

'Yes, it is, very beautiful.'

She turned her gaze back to the mountains before them, the rocky peaks and barren cliffs, deep gullies and spindly trees hoping to survive the next winter. 'I wonder if I'll ever see it.'

Andrew smiled, 'You're like my mother was when she was your age.'

'Really?'

'She wanted to see the world. That's how she met Micah and Finnlay and Duke Robert.'

Helen smiled a little. 'Father has told me a little of what his life was like at Dunlorn, before he came to the Enclave. I can't imagine how it would be to live in a castle – I've never even seen one. Mother won't tell me much because she doesn't want me wishing for something I can't have.' Helen swallowed then, her gaze dropping to her reins. 'She says . . . she says my father wishes to leave because his heart is out there, fighting a rebellion that can't be won.'

'What rebellion?'

She looked up at that, giving him an impish smile. 'I don't

know. I suppose whatever rebellion Uncle Robert is planning. My mother just thinks it's all too dangerous. But then, she says everything outside the Enclave is dangerous. Is it?'

Andrew thought about his mother and the stories he'd heard about Duke Robert, his own life at court and the factions which till now, had played little part in his life, though that was more from sheer good luck than anything else. 'Yes, it can be dangerous. Especially at court.'

'Then,' Helen reached over and patted his hand, 'you make sure you're careful, won't you? And don't go falling into any more lakes.'

He took her hand and gave it a squeeze, doing his best to ignore the way her eyes danced and the effect that had on him. 'I promise I'll do my best.'

Finnlay couldn't wait to get back – he couldn't bring himself to say 'home' any more – because it wasn't his home, was it? His home was Dunlorn Castle, in the middle of his family's lands, six days' travel east of here, a place he hadn't seen for almost fifteen years, since before Andrew was born.

Some nights, when he slept, Dunlorn would creep into his dreams, dragging him back in time to when things were more peaceful in Lusara, when the only conflict was between him and Robert, over issues that were irrelevant now. But as he watched the path ahead, gazed up at the mountains around him and in particular at the Goleth peak which towered over him, he knew that he would never call this place home while Dunlorn still stood.

It was empty and deserted; that was all he knew. Neither Selar nor Kenrick had given the place to some lord they wished to reward. Why was that? It was certainly the custom to confiscate the lands and wealth of a disgraced lord and pass them on. Robert had not been disgraced, but he'd certainly committed treason.

But of course, Kenrick was afraid of Robert.

So the Enclave was as close to home Finnlay would get until either Kenrick was dead – or Nash – or someone finally found the Calyx and released them all from this prison.

Finnlay watched heavy clouds drape themselves low over the mountains with a kind of curious fascination. The higher they climbed, the darker and colder and windier it got. The entire vista was a vast collection of shades of grey, from the shale mountains to the sky so close. The air itself seemed equally uncommitted.

He was growing to hate this view.

At least they would be inside before it snowed, which would be soon. He just wanted to get off this horse, kiss his wife and get his daughter to safety. He wouldn't relax until then.

Tired but excited chatter grew up behind him as they turned the final corner in the path. The huge rock hiding the entrance to the Enclave loomed before him, pressed hard against the sheer face of the Goleth itself. With barely contained impatience, Finnlay led them inside the first tunnel, allowed the wash of the gate to pass over his skin and then he was out again, in the last threads of daylight, and dismounting at the edge of the open field hidden atop the mountain.

There were people waiting for them: Arlie's beautiful wife, Martha, and the parents of the other children. Greetings were called out, welcomes given with smiles and hugs. One by one the horses were taken away to the stables. As a group, they all began walking towards the heavy wooden doors that would take them below, and as he watched, Fiona emerged with a smile and a wave. Finnlay would have gone to her then, but Martha grabbed his sleeve.

'Finn, Jenn, wait.'

He turned to find her expression sombre. She checked to ensure she would not be overheard, then turned back to Jenn. 'I just wanted to tell you, before it becomes common knowledge.'

'Before what becomes common knowledge?' Jenn frowned.

Martha took her husband's hand and squeezed it for comfort, but there was clear worry in her eyes. 'I don't understand it at all – Osbert has made some radical changes.'

Finnlay raised his eyebrows. 'Osbert? You mean changes within the Guilde?'

Taking a deep breath, Martha whispered, 'According to new Guilde laws, it's no longer a crime to be a sorcerer. In effect . . . we're free to leave the Enclave.'

5

'Are you serious?' Jenn could barely keep her voice soft. 'How do you know?'

Martha's gaze remained steady. 'Men bringing up the last few shipments of goods before winter. They heard rumours and thought—'

'Rumours!' Finnlay interrupted. 'We can't go chasing after—'

'Hush, Finn,' Jenn put a hand on his arm to calm him before he could react too strongly.

In the silence, Martha continued, 'I asked Micah to go down into the valleys to try to get some confirmation. As official as he could manage without giving our interest away. We're expecting him back early tomorrow, but I can't guess what he will return with.'

Jenn nodded slowly, but couldn't dismiss the roiling discomfort seated deep in her belly. She *should* be greeting this as though it were good news, but her instincts were screaming otherwise. 'Call a Council meeting for the morning. Until then, try to keep this as quiet as possible – though I imagine that's going to be difficult. Still, I don't want people panicking or otherwise until we have some firm information.'

'So you don't think—'

Jenn held up her hand, looking pointedly at Finnlay. 'I refuse to form an opinion at this stage. We need some rest. And we need to keep clear heads. We'll know exactly what we have to worry about when Micah gets back, and not before. Now go and get some supper, and then get some sleep.'

For a moment, Finnlay didn't move; the others waited as though taking an invisible cue from him. Then he gave her a short nod, turned and put an arm around Fiona's waist, pressed a kiss to her cheek. He said a crisp goodnight and moved away, releasing the others – but leaving Jenn with the feeling that she'd just been silently rebuked.

Dark shadows swirled through her sleep, echoing some mournful cry barely heard but felt, like a tremor, or an ache bone-deep. Ancient time caught up with her, held her hostage and mocked her, screaming silent insults into her face that left her struggling against invisible bonds. She closed her eyes.

She could feel it, there, a little behind her, like a real shadow, solid and dimensional: the Key's presence. It was joined to her, as she was to it, as though they shared the same heart, the same blood, and it shifted between them, keeping them both alive, wounding one where the other hurt.

It gave her some comfort, this Key, soothed her, mellowed out the edges of the terrible dreams, but left her aching with another older, more impossible need, and it was the contrast between the two that woke her, left her gasping in air and fighting back tears.

He'd warned her. He'd tried to tell her that it was a mistake and now, once again, it looked like he was right and she, in her ignorance, in her determination to make something of her own life, had made the mistake once more of not trusting him, of not believing in him.

Swallowing hard, she threw the blankets back and swung her legs over the side of the bed. With angry hands she swiped the moisture from her cheeks and paused long enough to listen for early morning sounds.

She could hear nothing from Andrew's room, so she stood and dressed quickly, pulling her hair back from her face, ridding herself of its softness. Then, moving as silently as she knew how, she left her bedroom, crossed the living area and slipped out into the corridor before Andrew could stir and ask her what she was doing.

She gave no thought to the path to the great cavern. She could do it in her sleep, blind and deaf. There was something in the Key that warned her always where it was, even if it wasn't speaking directly to her. So she made the turns she needed, passing no others in the early morning until she paused upon the threshold, her gaze going out to the dais, and the shadows left by oil lamps hanging from the cave roof far above.

The Key. Always changing and yet never changing. It stood there alone, both innocent and worldly-wise: a bell hanging from a wrought-iron pyramid decorated in leaves or something. But when she woke it, the first miracle would occur and the bell would transform itself into an orb, glistening and shining as though wet, and she would speak to it, hear its replies whispered or thundered inside her own head, where nobody else could hear.

He'd told her it was their enemy, had said she should stay away from it, and had risked so much to keep her safe from it. But she'd come back here of her own volition, certain somehow, that he was wrong and that she – whose powers were so different and so much stronger than all but his – that she was the one destined to wield the Key as was foretold.

It came as little comfort to know Robert would feel no satisfaction to be proved right once more.

Her feet took her forward, her soft leather sandals scraping against the stone floor like a whispering reminder of pains long past. In her mind, she collected together the words, sorting and discarding, framing and building, putting all the effort she could into finding the exact combination that would extract the information necessary and prove once and for all, that she *hadn't* failed, and that she was indeed the one to wield the Key as was foretold.

I come with a question.

Then ask, the Key replied as softly as she.

Where is the Calyx?

And as always, the reply was only silence. Unsurprised, Jenn continued, *Do you know where it is? Can you tell me anything about it? What it looks like? What we are supposed to do with it? Can the Calyx truly show us the way to live outside the Enclave without fear and in safety?*

The Key paused before answering, as though it were pondering these questions she had asked so many times before. *The Enclave is safety. We keep you protected within it.*

Swallowing her frustration, Jenn took a step forward, but stopped short of the dais, not wishing to wake the Key properly and alert the entire Enclave to her continued failure. *Do you even know what the Calyx is?*

There was another long pause. She kept her silence, ignoring the room behind her, where the Council would gather soon, and where she would have to admit, once more, that she had failed them as Jaibir, that the Key had not chosen wisely when it had picked her to lead them.

All the records they had of the Key, and of the Calyx, said the same thing: the Calyx would free them – and the Key would tell them where it was, as long as it was wielded by the right person. Everyone – *everyone* had believed Jenn to be that person. But, eight years later, she was still asking the same questions, still getting the same non-answers.

She must have done something wrong somewhere along the line. There were, after all, no instructions on the use of the Key. Each Jaibir did the best they could – but Jenn had expected so much more of herself, and only Robert had had the wisdom to doubt.

Silence.

Damn it!

In a few hours she would have to face the Council, field questions, come up with ideas and provide leadership in a situation over which she had no control. *You do this deliberately, don't you?*

We answer your questions.

And yet you don't. You never tell me anything about the Calyx. Why?

Which question? We have answered everything you have asked.

No, you haven't! I've tried a hundred different combinations of the same question, but you refuse to tell me the one thing I want to know! Why?

There was another long pause. The response, when it came, was quiet and almost puzzled. *We can find no unanswered question. We do not always understand what you ask.*

Taking a deep breath for patience, Jenn clasped her hands together. *Very well. You know the word Calyx?*

Yes.

Do you know what it means?

A calyx is a shape, a cavity or receptacle.

So that's what we're looking for? A receptacle? Answer me!

You have not asked a question.

Are you protecting the Calyx? Is that it? Robert said you never meant us to have the Calyx. Is that what you're doing? Protecting it from us? Because . . . because we'd ruin it or something?

She came to a halt, squeezing her eyes shut against the answer she knew was coming.

The Enclave is safety. We keep you protected within it. You should not fear.

I'm not scared, damn it! Not for me! She pulled in a breath then let it out slowly, forcing herself to release the frustration, to turn away from the anger.

It would do no good. There was no point to her trying further. Whatever it was the Key was hiding, she did not have the ability to uncover it.

Do not worry, Little One, Ally. We are here.

The unsolicited comfort brought an ironic smile to her face. She turned, ready to go find some breakfast, only to discover Finnlay standing in the doorway, leaning against the stone, arms folded.

'Good morning.'

Jenn sighed. 'Please, Finn, don't start.'

He raised his eyebrows at her, neither hard nor mocking. 'I see. Is it something we can discuss over a cup of brew?'

It was still so early that the refectory had barely registered the new day. Fresh bread had been baked and Finnlay collected a few slices, along with honey and two mugs of minted brew. He brought the tray back to the bench table where Jenn sat and laid the things out. He didn't speak until he'd taken a bite of bread and honey, until he'd washed the night's cobwebs from his mind with the hot drink.

Where, in the name of the gods, had he finally learned patience from?

'I take it,' he said between mouthfuls, watching her, 'that the

74

Key was no more forthcoming on the subject of the Calyx than it has been in the past?'

Jenn pushed wisps of escaped hair back from her face and pulled a crust from the warm bread. Then, her eyes down and nibbling on the food, she recounted the conversation.

'I don't know . . . I can't help thinking that if I could just find the right combination of words. But it's so . . .'

'Childish?'

'Yes. And it never seems to change. You'd think now, after eight years of being joined to it . . . well, *I've* changed – why hasn't the Key as well? I just . . . I don't understand what it wants from me and sometimes I don't think it understands what I want from it. It's as though it . . . has this set of things it was designed to talk about, but anything outside that, it simply can't grasp the language or something.'

Her voice was full of anguish and frustration. Finnlay looked around, but they were almost the only ones in the refectory. 'Well, we know virtually nothing about who created the Key, or why, so anything is possible, I suppose. Since it was created using sorcery, it's likely that it can't be manipulated except by a set series of actions, in the same way that we use our powers.' When Jenn glanced up at this, her expression was sceptical. 'Look, I'm just saying that anything is possible – and therefore, you shouldn't blame yourself if you can't find the Calyx. It could just mean that it's not time for us to find it or something.'

'Except that it *does* seem to be time.' Jenn straightened up, sipping her drink distractedly.

Finnlay pulled in a breath and dived into the icy water. 'So, if Micah returns and tells us the Guilde *has* changed its laws, we have no way of knowing whether this has anything to do with the Calyx . . .'

Jenn looked up, hard, dark brows drawn together. 'We'll never be able to keep it a secret.'

'Do you think we should?'

'You're not going to tell me you don't think this is some kind of . . .'

'Trap?' Finnlay almost laughed. 'Of course it's a trap. And

75

the sooner everyone knows that, the sooner we can settle down again and . . .'

'And what?'

He paused at that, something of a warning prickling at the back of his eyelids. That wary-determined look was back in her eyes, as though she were daring him to say something about . . .

He snapped his mouth shut. No, not going to go near that one today. Not until Micah came back and the meeting was over. The subject of Andrew would have to wait.

As though she'd expected a fight, she waited a moment, then slowly relaxed. Abruptly she appeared more tired than she had before.

'I take it you didn't get any more sleep than I did?'

Jenn shook her head and produced what passed for a smile these days.

'You work too hard.'

'What? You're hardly one to . . .' She started to protest further, but Finnlay held up his hand.

'I don't work half the hours you do. Not any more. Not with three young daughters to run around after.'

She blinked at that and instantly looked away. Finnlay bit back a curse at his own clumsiness.

'Look, Jenn, I'm sorry. I didn't mean it like that. I know how much Andrew . . .'

'Do you, Finn?' She turned back to him, her blue eyes almost pleading with him. 'Can you understand what he means to me?'

Was it the responsibility for the Enclave which sat heavily on her, which gave her eyes those haunted depths? Or was it something else, something deeper and darker – something to do with Robert?

Sadly he shook his head. He could give her an honest answer, if nothing else. 'No. But I think I can guess. Now eat something more than a crust, please? You'll need your strength if we're to survive this council meeting.'

The flat field atop the Goleth Mountain had been covered

overnight by an inch-thick layer of snow; by the time Andrew stepped out onto it, the white had been trampled enough to completely ruin the scenic effect. Above, a bleak sky peered down at him, threatening more snow. What would his mother say if his leaving was delayed because of heavy falls on the trail into the valleys? At the moment, she'd probably barely notice, with the meeting and everything going on.

Not that she'd told him anything, though something important had obviously happened. She never told him anything voluntarily: everything he knew came from books, or as a result of pushing and nagging her until she relented.

Of course, there were reasons for her secrecy – he might not understand them, perhaps, but they were bound to be for his own good, or the good of the Enclave, or Lusara or . . . something. After all, didn't everybody believe in her? Even the Key?

So that was why she never told him anything.

He could hear voices raised in anger. He turned to find his friends gathered on the other side of the field, the huge rock wall of the mountain raised behind them. They'd set up the archery targets, but only Guy and Sayre appeared to be practising. Liam, Neil and Zea were waving their hands about while Damaris sat on a rock, her sketch pad on her knees.

He couldn't help liking Damaris. She reminded him sometimes of the way Micah looked at things, as though there were priorities about what he would get excited or angry about. Everything else could be handled with the same even temper.

With a sigh, he set off across the field, his boots sinking into icy slush and his face stinging with the morning cold.

'I didn't touch it!'

'Yes, you did!'

'I didn't! Why would I push at your stupid shot?'

'Because you can't bear the thought that I'm better than you!'

'But you're not!'

'How would you know? You won't let me prove it!'

Andrew came to a halt, watching as Neil and Zea yelled at each other and Liam tried to stand between them.

'Come on, that's enough!'

'Oh,' Zea rounded on him, 'and who are you to tell me what to do? Just because you're a year older than me? I'm a better shot than you, too!'

'Oh, I give up!' Liam threw his hands into the air and turned away. He picked up his bow once more and drew an arrow out of the box beside him. His apparent unconcern had a strange effect on Zea and Neil. They glared at each other, then picked up their own bows.

Andrew sidled away while he could, going over to where Guy was aiming up another shot. There were already three good ones on the target, though his friend was still squinting at the centre ring.

'Relax your shoulder,' Andrew said quietly, not wanting the others to hear. Guy didn't flinch, but the shoulder loosened a little. 'Now, relax your face.'

Instead, Guy's mouth came up in half a smile. 'I don't know what you're talking about.' With that, he let loose the arrow and it swooshed through the air to land with a thud very close to the centre of the target. Guy let out a soft chuckle, then turned to Andrew. 'See? I do listen.'

Andrew smiled smugly, 'Ah, but you were still squinting – and your shot missed the bulls-eye.'

'Oh, you're always talking big, little Duke.'

Andrew elbowed his friend aside and plucked the bow from his hands. He'd not used one like this before, but that didn't stop him. An arrow was placed into his palm, but Guy didn't step back to give him room. Instead, he tucked in close as Andrew took his stance.

'Now, relax your shoulder,' Guy began, 'and relax your face. You'd better relax your legs as well, and that back looks a little stiff to me.'

Andrew began to laugh and struggled to suppress it.

'Now, your fingers are awfully curled around that string, and you'll never fly straight like that so you'll have to relax those as well.'

Andrew was biting his lip, but he kept his eye on the target and did as he was told, releasing his fingers to let the bolt fly. It landed dead centre.

'I hate you.'

'Don't hate him, Guy,' Zea said, coming up to them. 'He cheats, just like the rest of us.'

'Oh,' Guy groaned, 'can't you leave us alone? Nobody cheats – and Andrew doesn't have the power to anyway. We're all supposed to learn how to do this properly, without nudging the arrows – you know that.'

'*We're all supposed to do this properly,*' Zea sneered at him. 'Serin's breath, just listen to you.'

'Try listening to yourself,' Liam grunted. 'Don't you have chores to do somewhere?'

'Oh, so it's all *my* fault, is it now?' Zea's cheeks turned pink. 'My brother deliberately cheats so that everyone can see it – and it's *my* fault? Damaris? You saw it, didn't you?'

Damaris looked up from her drawing. She raised her eyebrows and shrugged. 'I saw the arrow turn badly – but I don't know who pushed it.'

'Neil did,' Zea supplied, not without a note of triumph.

But Damaris hadn't finished. 'I just don't understand why it makes a difference.'

'You don't?' Zea rounded on her. 'Because it's not *fair*, that's why!'

As Neil began to laugh, Liam started to turn away. This pushed Zea too far.

'By the gods! If Neil did that to any of you, you'd punch him for it! But if he does it to me, it doesn't matter, is that right? He can be unfair to me because I'm his sister? Or because I'm a girl?'

'No,' Andrew murmured without thinking, 'he's doing it because he's afraid you *are* better than he is and you can't prove it if you get angry and storm off.'

'What?' Neil turned around, immediately towering over Andrew. 'What the hell would you know about it? Are you calling me a coward?'

'No, no, no.' Andrew raised his hands, backing away. His heart fluttered in his chest and he screwed up a hopeful smile from somewhere. 'Well, I . . . I was just thinking that perhaps . . . it . . .' An idea popped into his head and he grabbed at it. 'I was just thinking it was a good ploy. Worked perfectly, wouldn't you agree Guy?'

'Er . . . yes.'

'See?' Andrew carried on quickly, hopping from the fireplace into the fire and feeling the heat. 'It was obvious that Zea had already worked it out and was just playing along to see if she was right, isn't that so, Zea?'

Out of the corner of his eye, he could see her fold her arms and nod.

'Neil,' Guy urged, 'He's not doing you any harm. Just leave him alone.'

'Why?' Neil asked, taking another step towards Andrew. 'Can't the Jaibir's son stand up for himself? Will he go running to her for help?'

'He's never done that before and you know it.'

'Neil! Stop it!' Guy reached out and snatched the bow from the older boy. 'You are such an ass.' He went to move away then, but Neil reached out and grabbed his shoulder, his face red with anger.

'What did you say?' He drew his fist back to hit Guy, but Andrew pushed in between them, hands raised.

'Hey, he didn't mean anything. You know there's rules against us fighting.'

'And maybe I'm sick of obeying your *mother*'s rules!' Neil spat, but he did back away. He snatched his bow from Guy's hands and snapped it over his knee. 'And I'm sick of playing these boy's games as well! I'll leave you *children* to carry on.' He caught Liam's sleeve and walked off with him leaving the others to put things away.

Guy picked up the broken bow and groaned. 'My father is going to kill me for this. He spent days making this for Neil.'

'It's not your fault,' Andrew murmured, watching the departing boys. He turned back to Guy to find Zea approaching him, her dark eyes meeting his quizzically.

'Why did you do that?'

'Me? Oh . . . well, because . . .'

She came really close, her voice a hissed whisper, relieving all the anger she'd contained moments ago. 'Listen: I don't need any help to fight my battles, so next time, stay out of it.'

Andrew didn't breathe again until she picked up her bow and walked away, her head held high, her shoulders proud.

'You should know better than to get in between those two,' Guy murmured. 'They're a war in progress.'

'They're bored,' Andrew replied with a sigh. 'I'm sorry you had to . . .'

'Forget it,' Guy waved a hand.

'Thanks.' Andrew pushed his bow into Guy's hand and spun him back to face the target. 'So if they're constantly at war, perhaps you should learn how to defend yourself with more than a few words.'

One of the things Finnlay missed most about living in the Enclave was windows. Not that he'd ever been one for staring out of them for hours at a time; until circumstances had forced him into living here, he'd always taken them for granted. But there were no windows within the Enclave. There were only the caves below and the field above, and solid rock kept the two very much apart.

But this room, this chamber in which the Enclave Council was now gathered held the closest thing to windows he got to see nowadays. There, painted on the walls, was the story of the formation of the Enclave, more than five hundred years of those within – the Salti Pazar – all there in pictures. Over the years, he'd had plenty of time to study them, hoping to find answers in them, but even outside of their academic value, they were also quite beautiful, and always a pleasure to look at: the history of survival a triumph of will.

There was the story of the formation of the Enclave. When the Empire battled sorcerers, one small group had broken away, created the Key and headed to the northern continent. There the group had argued over the Key and split into two. On that day, Malachi and Salti had been born and the hatred between them flared and still burned brightly. He had no idea where the Malachi had vanished to, but the Salti had used the Key's protection and found this hideaway in the mountains.

These caves, this Enclave, had successfully hidden them from a world that had reviled sorcery for half a millennium. Could Lusara's fear of magical power ever end?

That was the heritage they'd been given, from those who'd gone before, and nobody, not even those who had studied most, had any idea *why*.

The clatter of footsteps outside the council chamber had Finnlay getting to his feet. He pulled the door open and stepped aside as Seamus and Martha helped the frail Henry into his room. As they got him settled, other councillors joined them; there was a subtle undercurrent of expectation, laden heavily with an ancient fear.

Fiona came in then, carrying a tray of cups and a huge pot of brew. She threw him a quiet smile, which warmed the cold inside him a little. Behind her came his mother. She smiled at everyone. Though she was not a member of the Council, she had an odd position of influence she very often denied. In a place that paid no heed to any title other than Jaibir, every person in the Enclave referred to her as Lady Margaret.

One by one they took their seats: Acelin, the librarian, Martha and Arlie, Seamus and Desta, Fiona, and Henry, whose age and ill health prevented him from doing much these days but offering opinions.

And there was Jenn, with a few words for each of them, enquiring after family and other minor events she'd missed while they were away. While not the natural charmer that Robert was, Jenn always sounded genuine and honest, a rare trait in a Jaibir.

She'd barely settled in her seat when she lifted her head a little, her eyes drifting to some spot on the table. 'He's coming.'

A hush of silence then, followed by abrupt scraping of chairs and conversations rushed to conclusion. He didn't need to listen for it, but he heard Micah's boots on the stone floor outside moments before the door opened. Micah Maclean was about Finnlay's height, with a shock of curly red hair. His normally sunny face and blue eyes were now grim and full of purpose. His cheeks were red with the cold and he moved like a man who'd spent too many hours awake and in the saddle.

'Well?' Jenn asked, coming to her feet. 'Did you find out anything?'

Micah stepped inside, closing the door behind him, and those simple gestures set a viper in Finnlay's stomach to coiling. The room was silent as Micah said to Jenn, 'I don't know whether it's good news or bad, but whatever you want to call it, the rumours *are* true.'

The knot of tension inside Jenn unravelled at Micah's words, as though it had been sitting there waiting for him to utter them. Keeping her expression schooled, she urged him to sit and, while Fiona poured him a cup of brew, he continued with his report.

'The countryside is afire with gossip and rumour.' Micah sipped from his cup and let out a small sigh of satisfaction. 'But I saw the notice with my own eyes, posted outside the Guildehall at Lochbear. There are no longer penalties for simply having abilities, nor for practising sorcery. Guildesmen are no longer authorised either to arrest or to detain sorcerers, and there is no death penalty.' Micah lifted his face then, his voice quiet. 'I'm afraid I just find it hard to believe that Osbert could do away with the Guilde's sacred duty just like that.'

A collective sigh rushed around the room.

'Well, that's that then,' Acelin murmured, first to speak.

'Really?' Henry sat forward, his hand reaching flat on the table in Micah's direction, his breathing a heavy rasp. 'Tell me, boy, was there any word of the Church's position?'

Micah shook his head. 'No. I asked Father Braden. Nothing so far – but I can't imagine that it will be too far behind. After all, what would be the point in changing one if not the other as well?'

'Wouldn't that depend on what Osbert wished to achieve?' Henry darted back.

'What makes you think this is Osbert's idea?' Finnlay ventured, his voice and expression tight. 'I know Osbert isn't the bigoted fool Vaughn was, but he's never had any love of sorcery. I have no doubt that this move has been forced upon him by Kenrick. This has to be a trap. There's no other reason for it.'

Desta frowned. 'To what end?'

Finnlay stared at her a moment, as though he couldn't believe she could ask such a question. 'To catch some of us, so that Nash can use our blood to . . . to regenerate. That's why he's been so quiet over the last eight years, because he's still healing from the wounds Robert gave him. That's what this is all about. Nash wants Salti blood. He's trying to flush us out into the open, by promising us normal lives in Lusara. Yes, I agree with Micah, I'll wager Brome is getting ready to issue similar changes to Church law, and there's nothing we can do about it.'

Jenn held up her hand to forestall further discussion for a moment and turned to Micah once more. 'Did you get a feel for how people were taking this change?'

'Largely, the people feel they've been betrayed – but Lochbear is a Guildehall town. How other people around the country are feeling, I have no idea. Does anybody know when Murdoch is due back?'

'Soon, I imagine, but there's no guarantee he knows more than we do, of course, though living out in the countryside all summer would make him a better judge of how the people feel about all this—'

'Damn it, Jenn!' Finnlay slapped the table. 'What does it matter how Lusara views this? We need to decide what *we* are going to do!'

Jenn tried to communicate with a look what she knew she couldn't say in front of these others. For a moment he held still and silent, then carefully and deliberately sat down, clasping his hands together on the table before him, almost entirely unrepentant. His frustration was almost palpable, but he was the only one in this room who had lived through the evil Nash threatened them with.

'I think it's important,' she began, equally carefully, 'that we know how the people feel about it, in case, for some reason in the future, we are *forced* to abandon our sanctuary here. We might not be able to stop this change, but—'

'I'm sorry, Jenn,' Desta spoke up, glancing to the others, 'but I don't see why we would *want* to stop it. Surely this is a change we've all been looking for, regardless of the true purposes behind it.'

'There's something else, too,' Micah added into the silence. He kept his gaze firmly on the table, his fingers wrapped around the cup for either warmth or comfort. 'Rumours are rife at the moment about the Hermit of Shan Moss. He's had another vision about an incarnation of Mineah coming to Lusara. I think that's the third or fourth this year. People believe it means her arrival is imminent – and it's very easy for them to assume it's connected to this law change. There's no real unrest at the moment, but that could change if the Church amends their laws as well.'

'Forgive me,' Seamus raised his hand a little before he continued. 'But we haven't considered the possibility that this might be real.'

'What?' Finnlay stared at the man.

Seamus leaned forward and looked around the table. 'If Osbert has put this change through of his own volition, then surely he has Kenrick's backing. Kenrick openly admits to his abilities. Surely any King would want to change laws that would execute him as well. And as for Nash – well, who of us has heard a word from him since the Battle of Shan Moss, eh? Robert wounded him very badly. How do we know he's not dead? Or permanently out of the picture?'

'And,' Desta chimed in, 'I know, Jenn, how you've worked to get the Key to tell you where the Calyx is – but what if *this* is how we're supposed to get free of the Enclave? For all we know, the Calyx might be behind these moves of Osbert's.'

Finnlay was on his feet in a second, but Henry beat him with bare outrage. 'Are you mad! Nash is the Angel of Darkness right out of Prophecy and until I see his body consumed in flames, I will believe he is alive! Anything – and I mean *anything* – that comes out of Marsay must, by definition, be tainted with the evil he was born from! How can you sit there and suggest that this is a prelude to peace? We don't need to be feeding our people those kinds of lies! We need to be asking ourselves why it's happening *now*!' Henry paused only to gasp in breaths that worked heavily in his chest, his puffy eyes watering with the exertion, ruddy face red and strained.

'Henry, please,' Jenn said, a hand on the old man's arm. Her Healer's Sight sent a dire warning through her, but he just shook her off.

'Damn it, answer me! Serin's blood, do you not take your Council responsibilities seriously?'

Jenn was on her feet now, Arlie moving as well. She could See it in Henry, see his body reacting badly to his outburst, to his anger and fear. 'Henry, calm yourself, please . . .'

'No, Jenn, I can answer.' Seamus got to his feet and faced Henry. 'You need to remember things have changed, Henry. We're a lot more powerful now than we were before Jenn became Jaibir. Finnlay's combat training has us all ready for a fight if necessary. But can't you see that we're all tired of this? Of living here, buried inside caves? We weren't born to this. Most of us were born outside the Enclave, and we want to return there some day. And we have a proud history. We come from a people who have the power to rule – so why are we hiding away in here? Kenrick is a sorcerer – and a King. There has never been a better time for us to move. *This* could be the Calyx – these very changes could be the exact thing our people have been waiting for all this time. We just need to have the courage to reach for our freedom. It might be the only chance we ever get!'

'You . . .' Henry gasped, his face red with fury, 'you would bring destruction down upon us all! You . . .'

'Henry!' Jenn reached out, but even so, she was too late. Henry's breathing stunted to several short gasps and then, abruptly, his eyes rolled back into his head and he collapsed onto the table.

6

One by one, Jenn folded and placed Andrew's clothes into the saddlebag. With tired fingers she did up the laces then placed the bag on the floor by the door. When she looked up, she found Andrew's eyes on her. He was already in bed, sleepy after a long day.

It had been a long day for all of them.

Troubled blue eyes blinked at her. 'Is Henry going to be all right?'

'I don't know.' Jenn moved to the side of the bed and he shifted over to give her room to sit. 'He has our two best Healers with him. They'll do everything they can, but we need to remember Henry is an old man.'

Andrew frowned a little. 'It wouldn't be the same without him here.'

'No.' Jenn could hear movement in the other room as Lady Margaret put things away after their supper. For reasons she didn't want to think about, Finnlay's mother had almost adopted Jenn and Andrew, as though she believed they didn't have enough family of their own – at least, not here at the Enclave. And in more ways she didn't want to think about, Jenn welcomed the friendship. She'd always felt a strong connection with Margaret, as though they'd each been thrust into a different world, both unknowing and unprepared.

'Do I really need to go to sleep now, Mother? I'm not that tired and I'd like to see what Arlie says about Henry.'

'I know, love,' Jenn leaned forward and kissed his forehead. 'But you and Micah leave very early tomorrow. You need your rest.'

She went to rise, but he caught her hand before she could move. 'You are still coming to visit next spring, aren't you? You promised to meet me at Elita so I can see it. I know Aunt

Bella would like you to visit at Maitland. It's been a year since you last came and sometimes . . .'

'What?'

'Sometimes she gets upset that you stay away so much.'

Jenn sighed. Her relationship with her sister had never been great, but Bella had taken in Andrew with open arms and loved him as her own; she had given him a home and the life Jenn, tied to the Key as she was, couldn't. But Bella knew enough about Jenn to disapprove heartily of what she was doing, though she'd never tried to poison Andrew's mind, as many in her place would have.

'I understand how she feels,' Jenn began gently, 'but *you* understand why I'm here, don't you? You know that I'd have you with me all the time if I could? You do believe that, don't you?'

He gave her a blinding smile, one which reminded her so much of Robert it hurt, but was also entirely his own. 'Of course I understand, Mother. I couldn't have a normal life if I lived here, could I? I miss you and Finnlay and everyone else – but I also like living at Maitland. Sometimes I just wish you and everyone else here could live like that as well, so that nobody had to live inside the protection of the Key.'

Jenn smiled and gave him another kiss. 'That's what we all wish, my love. Now you get some sleep. I'll send Lady Margaret in to say goodbye, as you'll be gone before she wakes in the morning.'

She rose then and went back into the main room, where a fire burned brightly and a lamp on the table gave further warmth to the room. Margaret was just pouring a cup of brew for them both.

'He's waiting for you.' Jenn picked up her cup as Margaret smiled and went into the other room. She could hear soft voices, but wandered instead to her desk and the pile of books she had stacked there. She'd barely had a chance to look at her work since Andrew had arrived for this visit, and with every-thing else that was going on, she wasn't sure when she would be able to get back to it, even though it called to her.

She would have to tell them about it soon.

The bedroom door clicked behind her and she turned to find Margaret smiling. 'That boy . . . I don't know where he gets his sense of humour from.'

Jenn didn't answer that.

'And are you going to tell me what's bothering you?'

Looking up, Jenn found a pair of deep brown eyes watching her. Margaret had aged beautifully over the years; getting older had only enhanced the person she was. Though her hair was peppered with white and the lines around her eyes clear, her smile, her openness and obvious caring only embellished her beauty. Finnlay had got his brown eyes from her – but Margaret had told her many times that both her sons favoured their father, Trevor, a man who intrigued Jenn, though he'd died more than thirty years before, killed fighting Selar.

'Well,' she answered with an attempted smile, 'I'm worried about Henry, and about this Guilde business.'

'And?'

'And what?'

Margaret picked up her mug of brew and drifted over to the desk. 'And you're worried about something else. I can tell. You've hardly spoken two words to anyone since the meeting. It's not good for you to keep things inside, you know that. You used to say as much to Robert.'

Jenn looked away at that.

It was impossible to escape him. It was impossible to forget that he'd been right, or that she'd lost him, or how much she still needed him, despite everything. It made her feel pathetic that even after eight years, such thoughts could still catch her like this.

Swallowing hard, she replied, 'I didn't handle that meeting very well today. I should have kept more control over the discussion. If I had, perhaps Henry wouldn't have had such reason to get so upset.'

'Oh, my dear,' Margaret put an arm around her shoulder, pressing a light kiss to her temple. 'You silly girl. You know Henry's been ill for a long time. His temper has never been good. You can't blame yourself for this.'

'Oh, I know he's been ill, but that doesn't excuse my

shortcomings,' Jenn said. 'I just don't think I'm very good at this leadership business. Some days I'm too cautious, others I'm too reckless. I feel so . . . uneducated, and so I read all the hours that I get and still there is so much I don't know, that I don't understand, and I need to.'

'Why?'

Jenn looked up. 'Because then, when days like this come, I would know what to do.'

The Enclave was quiet as Jenn stepped out into the corridor. Most people had gone to their beds, more than a few concerned about what the next day would bring.

She kept her footsteps even, listening to the noises she'd grown accustomed to over the years, things that marked this place as being so different to any other. Taking one turn in the passage brought her to the door of Henry's rooms. It was open and inside, sitting by the fire, was Finnlay, chin resting on his fist, ankles crossed carelessly, gaze buried somewhere in the flames. Micah sat at the table, paper before him, pen in his hand. One after another, he scratched words down, a small frown on his face, concentration focused on his task.

He was writing a letter to his family, who were now forced to live in Flan'har. Grant Kavanagh, Flan'har's independent Duke and true friend of Lusara, had welcomed them, and for the last ten years or so, Micah's five brothers, two sisters and both parents – not to mention a host of nieces and nephews – had resided in the peace and civility of that country. Exiles, perhaps, but at least they had not been executed because of their unwitting connection to Robert via Micah. These letters Micah wrote were his only contact with them, sending them via Enclave couriers his only safe means of delivery.

With a brisk movement, Micah finished the letter and signed his name. Jenn waited until he began to fold the paper over before speaking.

'I meant to ask how your father is now.'

Micah looked up, his pale blue eyes glinting with unhidden concern. 'My sister's last letter didn't elaborate very much. She says he's well enough – though I have no idea what that means exactly. She does insist that he's not at death's door and that I shouldn't worry.'

'But that doesn't stop you.'

He gave a wry shake of his head. 'No.'

Jenn glanced at the door leading to Henry's bedroom, then at Finnlay, who barely noticed that she'd returned. 'Is Arlie still with him?'

'Aye,' Micah said, putting his things away. 'We've heard nothing more since you left. Seamus and Desta have just gone to supper. Both feel a bit guilty, though Arlie assured them it wasn't their fault.'

Jenn sank into a chair opposite Finnlay. Slowly his gaze left the fire and landed on her; his face was framed by his dark hair and beard, and eyes which reflected nothing at all.

'Did you ask him?'

She said nothing for a moment, but didn't look away. Then, clasping her hands together on her lap, she shook her head. 'I told you I wouldn't.'

'Why not?'

'Osbert's actions have nothing to do with Andrew. I don't want him involved.'

'Isn't he already involved? Isn't he the best means we have of finding out what's really happening at court? Or are you unsure of where his loyalties lie?'

Jenn was not in the mood for another argument. 'You don't honestly think that—'

'I no longer have any idea what I should think. And it appears nobody would believe me anyway.' He looked back at the fire then, his gaze narrowing, his thoughts obviously elsewhere. 'Are you planning to bring him back here to live permanently?'

'No,' Jenn replied, a little surprised by the question. 'Why?'

'Just curious. I thought perhaps it might encourage his powers to develop. Forget about it.'

Jenn gently shifted the subject anyway. 'Besides, we do have Father Godfrey at court. I know we don't get direct reports from him, but Murdoch does. It's better than nothing.'

Finnlay nodded vaguely, as though there were matters of far more weight on his mind.

Micah left the table then, crouching down before the fire to put another log over the flames. He took a cup from a hook over the mantel and poured Jenn some of the brew simmering on a shelf within the fireplace. Curls of smoke drifted up into the chimney, heading for places Jenn couldn't begin to guess.

'Are we going to be able to keep it a secret?'

Jenn shook her head, knowing he wasn't talking about Henry. 'I don't know. Probably not, especially now.'

'It *is* a trap, you know.'

She looked back to find Finnlay watching her again. 'Yes, I know.'

He stared at her a moment, then let out an obvious sigh of relief. 'So, why now?'

'I have no idea – though Henry seemed to think the timing was significant. You know Kenrick's negotiating with Mayenne for a marriage. It might have something to do with that. Or . . . perhaps something important has changed.' She couldn't look at him then and instead chose to watch the twists of steam rise from her cup, feeling the eyes of both men on her. She knew they were both thinking about Robert, and about his absence from the Enclave since the Battle. Was he behind this in some way?

'Does it need to be something important?' Micah murmured eventually. Micah had been the truest friend Jenn could have had, especially the way he acted as guardian over Andrew. 'From what I've seen, each wave of this . . . thing has started with some small, inconsequential event. I'd hardly call changing laws inconsequential. Things are always changing.'

'Are they?' Finnlay grunted. 'It probably looks that way to you.'

Micah had a faint smile on his face. 'Things are changing here now, as we speak.'

The gentle barb drew Finnlay's brows together, but he said nothing more. The silence lingered this time as Micah drifted from the fireplace, wandering over to where Henry's formidable collection of books were arranged along shelves attached to the cave wall. Jenn watched the broad shoulders, read the underlying tension in them.

What was he thinking? Most of the time he was his usual easy-going self, ready to smile, as happy as he could be, considering the life he'd chosen. But some days, he seemed so . . . full of something, so overburdened with disappointment and some deep sense of betrayal.

And it was all because of Robert.

Micah had been only five when his father had sent him to Dunlorn to work for Robert's father, Earl Trevor. He and Robert had become the closest of friends, despite the seven year age difference, and from that time until the Battle of Shan Moss, Micah's loyalties had been firmly and wholly with Robert and his struggles for Lusara.

Then something had happened and, with Robert lying abed, clinging on to life, Micah had left as though banished from his side, travelled half the country to take up residence in a small cottage on the edge of Maitland estate. For the last eight years, he'd lived there alone, keeping watch on Andrew, accompanying him wherever he went, anywhere except court, and staying clear of anybody who might recognise him. He'd talked to the boy, taught him skills he'd learned from Robert, and not once given away the secret of Andrew's parentage.

The loyalty he'd once given the father, he now gave to the son, without question, without reserve – and yet, there was still something in Micah anchored to Robert, as though it didn't matter how many years had passed, he would still, at some point, want satisfaction, want . . . an answer. His open idealism hadn't changed a whit, despite the disappointments he'd faced.

They were all so bound up together in this, all equally trapped within the same spider's web. They looked to each other for answers, but after all this time, she wasn't so sure there were any.

With a creak, the bedroom door opened and Arlie emerged, looking tired and pale. Jenn got up and Arlie met her halfway.

'How is he?'

'It's bad, I'm afraid. It's his heart.' He ran a hand through his fair hair. 'It will be hours, no more. I've given him something to help him sleep and eased his pain. I'll be back shortly. I just need to get some air. Celia's in there with him at the moment.'

Jenn gave his arm a squeeze as he moved by her. As Arlie disappeared, Jenn turned to Micah. 'You should get some rest. You've got an early start, remember?'

Micah looked once at the bedroom door, then said, 'Call me if you need anything.'

As his footsteps receded into the distance, Jenn returned to her seat by the fire, picking up the book she'd brought in with her. Though she could barely concentrate, there were questions that needed answers and, for good or ill, she was the one expected to find them.

'Do you ever get the impression Micah's hiding something?' Finnlay was closely studying the cuff of his jacket, as though he'd just found something growing there without permission.

'Don't we all have something to hide?' she replied.

'Not me,' Finnlay said. 'I don't have time for secrets – at least, not my own. What are you reading?'

'*A Discourse on Arcane Origins.*'

'Ah,' Finnlay steepled his fingers together. 'Forfau's adventure into the philosophy of sorcery. I would have thought that kind of thing beyond your interests.'

'Hey, I'm still playing catch-up, here. I missed out on fourteen years of education, thanks to Nash.'

'Even so, this isn't the kind of thing you usually read, is it?' Finnlay was watching her, as though expecting her to take flight at any moment. 'I understood you to be researching the history of sorcerers and the Cabal. Why philosophy suddenly?'

Jenn put the book on her lap and laced her own fingers together. 'Let me ask you a few questions. Why can't Robert and Nash Seek each other, despite the fact that they've met, fought, and should know each other's auras inside out?'

'You don't know they can't.'

'Would they both still be alive now if they could?' Finnlay didn't answer that, but gestured for her to continue. 'And how does the Key's protection of the Enclave work, exactly? So that nobody can Seek somebody inside. Is a Seal related to that protection? When a Seal stops us from talking about the Enclave to anybody who is not also Sealed, is the Key operating that power from a distance, or has it been lodged within us?'

Finnlay's continued silence drew one final question from her. 'How complacent have we become because we have the power of the Key to protect us?'

One corner of his mouth lifted up in something of an ironic smile. 'You know, a few years ago, I wouldn't have thought twice about that.'

'But now?'

His gaze shifted back to the fire. 'Now I find that I wish Desta and Seamus were right. I wish I could ignore the existence of Nash and Kenrick, perhaps take my daughters to see Dunlorn, teach them about my part in their heritage.'

'But you've never been happy living here, Finn.'

'No.' Flames danced and haunted his eyes. 'But until last night, it never really hit me that I could be here forever. That I might . . . die here.'

A chill ran through Jenn at his words, but she refused to settle there, on that note. Instead, she shifted until she was comfortable, sipped her cooling brew and said levelly, 'Then let me give you another question to consider: what will become of us, of our ways, our schools and training, our history and traditions, when the day finally comes that we *can* live out there, in safety. What will we all become then?'

Finnlay snorted at that, but there was more humour in his eyes. 'Free, Jenn. That's what we become. Free.'

Inside his cave bedroom, it was so totally dark Andrew could see nothing, no matter how long he kept his eyes open. His mother had left no light on in the other room, so nothing crept under the door to give the shapes in his bedroom any identity. As a child, he'd had nightmares about the Enclave, dreaming of walls crushing in on him, of the roof developing cracks and of being buried alive. He'd asked and asked and lost count of the number of times he'd been reassured that the caves were perfectly safe – and yet, the nightmares had continued for years.

Sometimes when he came to the Enclave, he felt so at home he didn't want to leave again. And then there were trips like this one, when almost every word said to him reminded him that he didn't really belong here, no matter how hard he tried.

And not having any powers didn't help at all. At least the others would accept him then, instead of looking at him as though he were either a traitor for living outside, or some kind of spy for his mother.

Would there come a time when he wasn't welcome to come back to the Enclave? Isn't that what had happened to Duke Robert? He'd never been a sworn member of the Enclave, but he'd been welcome for twenty years, and then suddenly the Key had banished him. Was that why he'd gone on to become a rebel?

Oh, the questions he would ask if he ever got the chance. Like what did it feel like to use the Word of Destruction and how had he discovered he had powers as a boy and how had he learned to mindspeak and what had it been like to face Selar on the battlefield at the age of fifteen – and hadn't he been afraid to fight Nash at Shan Moss?

Hadn't he been afraid of anything?

Fear worried Andrew. A lot.

He rolled over, breathing deeply as Lady Margaret had taught him, willing his body to sink into the bed and draw him into sleep. Still the walls groaned under the weight of the mountain, just as they did in his dream. Now it was no longer the dream which kept him awake, but an aware, conscious feeling that something was wrong. Something terrible. Something was creeping along the dusty floors of the Enclave, seeping under doors the way the light should have.

Master Henry was ill, he knew that much, but this felt like something else, something . . . dangerous, as though he needed to warn somebody, as though . . .

He swore silently and closed his eyes. Then he focused on the darkness and the quiet, hoping that sleepy Senses would now awaken inside him and Seek out the wrong feeling.

The darkness of the room enveloped him, the air suddenly so flat and heavy it squashed the air from his lungs. He sat up, gasping, his heart pounding.

Definitely something wrong.

Something dangerously wrong.

He rolled out of bed, feeling in the dark for where he'd left his clothes. He dressed quickly and pulled the bedroom door open. Some white-crusted coals still burned in the fireplace, but nothing he could light a lamp with, so he made for the outer door, with no real idea of where he needed to go. Even so, the compulsion drove him forward.

The corridor was empty. He hesitated briefly about which way to go, but then turned to his left, walking carefully, leaving his fingers trailing along the stone wall, feeling the warmth and the cold and wishing he had just one hundredth of the Seeking powers Finnlay had.

Perhaps he should go for help – but how could he explain this unexplainable feeling? He had no powers to speak of, and therefore no way to prove that this wasn't just some fancy of his tired imagination.

He paused at the top of the gallery stairs leading down to the Great Cavern. Whatever he was looking for was in that direction – but he was forbidden to go anywhere near the Key, and that was where it lived. He would have to go around the long way.

Waiting long enough to listen for voices, he turned and took one twisting tunnel after another, sleep long banished from his mind. Only when he was sure he'd skirted the Great Cavern completely did he pause once more, hoping that something tangible would appear.

He was about to move on when he heard it: a small, almost faint whisper – but it was enough, it was exactly what he'd been looking for. He took the first staircase down, then another, and a sharp turn towards one of the school classrooms.

Without pausing, he pushed the door open, stepped inside then shut it firmly behind him. Three shocked faces turned towards him. Neil stood a little back, arms folded, a book open on the table before him. Liam stood alone in the centre of the room, his *ayarn* held in his left hand, the small stone dwarfed by his fingers. Zea, all innocence, sat on a chair before him, hands clasped together, as though she'd just been lecturing.

Andrew took all this in, in a single horrified glance. Then he strode over to Neil, grabbed the book and snapped it shut. He didn't need to be a sorcerer to know what these three were doing. 'Are you crazy?' he hissed, mindful to keep his voice down lest somebody hear *him*. 'How many times do you need to be told before you get the idea that this is *dangerous*!'

'Oh, bother, Andrew,' Zea was the first out of her shock. She sprang to her feet and crossed to the table, leaning forward and whispering urgently, 'How can it be dangerous? Duke Robert has done it a thousand times. And didn't Kenrick do it when he snuck into the camp to poison Princess Galiena? How do you think they learned to do it? It's just a problem of practising. Liam is strong enough and skilled enough to make a really good mask. Why can't he go further and try to make himself invisible?'

Andrew was thrown for a moment, then he rounded on Liam, ignoring Neil deliberately. 'You should know better. I thought you weren't going to let her push you into anything any more.'

'She didn't push me,' Liam replied stubbornly. 'I was very close last time, before Finnlay stopped me. I've got close tonight. Now unless you want to stand there and prolong this experiment, I suggest you be quiet and let me get to work.'

'This has nothing to do with you,' Neil added, holding out his hand for the book. 'Shouldn't you be in bed asleep? Won't your mother miss you? You don't want to get into trouble, do you?'

'You just don't listen, do you?' Andrew said, in frustration. 'There's a reason *why* dimensional shifts and all those other things are forbidden. Do you think that sorcerers over the *centuries* have just arbitrarily decided there are some things we're allowed to do and some we're not?'

'We?' Neil asked in disbelief. 'You are *not* a sorcerer! You don't know what you're talking about.' He turned his back to Andrew, shutting him out, dismissing him with a coldness that set Andrew's anger burning, making him throw his fear to the wind.

'I don't know?' Andrew tapped the book hard with his knuckles. 'Have you read this whole text? The last three chapters detail more than twenty experiments just like this that went terribly wrong.'

'Ah, there speaks the expert,' Zea muttered, not quite under her breath. 'Excuse me, son of our revered Jaibir, but *you* don't have any powers, no matter how many books you've read. If you don't want to be witness, then go back to bed. We don't want to keep you from your sleep. After all, your mother might come back and find you've been bad and then you'd get into trouble. We wouldn't want that, would we?'

Andrew could only stare at her. She – and the others – were impervious to any words he might utter, and threatening to go and find Finnlay or somebody wouldn't make any difference. For a start, they'd never speak to him again – and they'd just try it another time, again and again, until one of them got killed. And even if he did go for help, Liam would probably do more damage trying to do it quickly while he was gone.

The answer was obvious, though he wasn't sure he could bluster his way through it without any trouble. 'I'll stay. Neil, go and sit down over there, in the corner by the door. Pull a table onto its side and sit behind it. Zea, you go with him.'

'Are you giving orders now?' Zea almost shouted with indignation. 'We had this under control before you . . .'

'Have you read this book? From cover to cover?' When she didn't answer, he looked at both Liam and Neil. Neither offered a reply. Some part of him trembled at his own audacity. Hell, they were all older than him, more trained, and infinitely more experienced – and yet his words came out without hesitation. 'Fine, then yes, I am giving orders now. Go and get behind a table. If there's any backlash, get out and shut the door behind you.'

'If you do anything to ruin this,' Neil grunted, his face dark with anger, 'I swear I'll . . .'

The threat was never finished, but Andrew felt it all the same. Still he waited, the book in his hands, his expression carefully expectant. Inside, he could only pray this would work. For a moment, none of them moved. Neil and Zea looked to Liam, who in turn studied Andrew with a detachment that left a cold feeling in his stomach. Then, abruptly, he nodded. A minute later, they were all ready. Andrew positioned Liam in the centre of the room, and then stood before him. 'I don't understand why you're so determined to do this.'

'Well, you wouldn't, would you?'

'And why not?'

'You're a Duke. You've got lands and estates to your name and a place at court with your cousin the King. All *we* have is the powers we can master. We're not even allowed to use them properly. How much more do you need to understand?'

Of course they would see it that way, wouldn't they? 'Very well. How much of that book *did* you read?'

'Enough.'

'Obviously not, otherwise you'd have conquered this by now. Listen, just breathe deeply, twice, letting the air out nice and slowly. Close your eyes and focus on some point inside you. If you can hear your heartbeat, then use that. Count it if you like.'

He waited until Liam nodded before he went on. 'Now, imagine you've got somebody standing beside you, his arm close enough to touch yours.'

Another nod.

'Gather the power inside you and let it run through your whole body, right down to your toes, right to the ends of your hair. Feel it flow through the *ayarn* in your hand and into the person standing beside you.'

There was a long pause and this time Andrew could almost feel the power radiating off the older boy. Liam had been studying for five years, but he really didn't have the control necessary to make this work.

'Just take it slowly, don't force it. Don't let it overpower you.'

Another long pause and the ragged edges trimmed a little, leaving Liam with a film of sweat on his face. Eyes still shut tight, he gave another nod.

'Very well. Now, don't do anything until I say. When I give the word, I want you to think about stepping sideways and into the body of that imaginary person you've got by your elbow. When you do it, you will stop being where you are at the moment. Can you picture that in your head?'

Liam frowned a little, but nodded again.

Andrew looked at the others to make sure they were protected, then turned back, taking a deep breath of his own. The truth was, if Liam didn't control this, he would most likely kill both himself and Andrew at the same time.

'Are you ready?' he asked, keeping watch on the boy's face. When he got a final nod, he added, 'Very well. Do it. Take the step.'

He held his breath. For a moment, it looked like nothing was happening – and then, suddenly, Liam faded, right before his eyes. Faded, flashed back solid, then faded again. More transparent this time, but still determined to succeed.

Andrew had to stop himself reaching out. The distraction alone would kill them both. Even so, his own heart was hammering in his chest, as though desperate to get out and escape before it was too late.

'Look! He's doing it!' Zea hissed from behind him, but he waved a hand for her to be silent.

Liam let out a small gasp, but he was still there, only now a pale, washed-out shape against the backdrop of the classroom.

Andrew couldn't let this go on any longer. If it hadn't happened by now, it wasn't going to. He opened his mouth to call a halt – and Liam disappeared.

Instantly Andrew held up a hand, desperate now to stop Zea from yelling with triumph. Any distraction now would be too much.

'That's good, Liam,' he murmured, his eyes searching the room for any sign of the missing boy. 'Now, as soon as you feel the shift is stable, you need to take a step forward, towards me. You need to concentrate and hold the shift as you move.'

He had no idea how successful his instructions were, until Liam reappeared, a good two steps closer than he'd been before, but faint, growing more solid, and then faint again.

Time to stop this now. 'Liam, I want you to ease it back now. Just a little at a time. Ease it down until it's quieter inside you. That's it. A little more.'

For a moment nothing really changed, and then there was more form, more colour to Liam's shape. Then Liam's face twisted in pain and Andrew felt the power let loose with a surge that sent him moving so fast he could see nothing of his own actions. There was only Liam, the *ayarn* in his hand, pulsing with power, and Andrew, his hand clasping over it, frantic to contain the backlash he knew was coming.

The light blinded him. The force threw him to the ground, Liam with him. His ears roared, and then it was over and he was blinking and seeing things in the room again.

The first thing he noticed was Neil and Zea peering at him over the edge of the table. With a groan he rolled onto his back and sat up. Liam lay beside him, eyes wide open and a very stupid grin on his face.

'I did it.'

Andrew realised he had his own stupid grin in place. 'I guess you did. Congratulations. Can you get up?'

Liam turned enough to look at him. 'How did you do that?'

'Do what?'

'Contain the backlash.'

'I didn't – or hadn't you noticed that we're both on the floor when we were standing a moment ago?'

'Yes, I had noticed that.' With a grunt, Liam got to his feet, holding out a hand to help Andrew. Zea and Neil came forward then, huge smiles on their faces, matched by the one on Liam's.

'Are you happy now?' Andrew needed to know the answer to this, or he'd have to hide that book somewhere.

'I think so,' Liam nodded, putting his *ayarn* away.

'Then do me a favour?'

'Of course.'

'Go to bed. And next time you want to try this? Don't.'

Liam let out a short laugh and nodded. 'Who would have thought you'd be an expert on the forbidden talents, eh? Come on, it's late and if we're caught in here, we'll all get into trouble.'

Andrew followed the others out, turning out the lamp before he closed the door behind him. He watched as they headed for their rooms, then took his long circuitous route back around the Cavern. By the time he got to his mother's door, he'd already yawned three times, but he still didn't turn in. Instead he kept going until he rounded the corner and stopped before Henry's door.

The room inside was filled with the quiet hum of conversation. Finnlay sat by the wall. Jenn and Arlie stood talking by the bedroom door and turned as he entered.

'Andrew!' Jenn gave him a small, worried smile. 'What are you doing up so late? I thought you were asleep.'

'I . . . wanted to know how Master Henry was.'

Jenn's expression softened and she came forward, placing a hand on his shoulder. 'I'm sorry, love. He died a few minutes ago.'

'Oh.' Disappointment flooded through him as she pulled him in for a brief hug. 'How's Celia?'

'She's still with him, but she seems to be fine for the moment.'

Andrew looked up at her. 'I don't suppose we can afford to stay long enough for the pyre?'

'With all the snow we've had today, I don't dare risk you lingering longer. I'm sorry.'

'I understand.' Andrew gave her a small smile. 'I suppose I'd better go back to bed.'

'I'll be up in the morning to see you both off.'

Andrew's gaze drifted to the closed bedroom door before returning to Jenn. She looked very tired, her eyes a little red, her face very pale. On impulse, he leaned forward and gave her a brief kiss on the cheek. 'Goodnight, Mother. I'll see you in the morning.'

7

Quite deliberately, Godfrey chose to walk around the cloister to stay in the sunlight rather than hurry through the shadows on the opposite side. Even so, he could still feel the cold stone beneath his sandals and the end of his nose had already lost feeling. Winter had barely begun and already Marsay was cold enough to freeze over.

He must be getting old. Surely it hadn't been so long ago when a morning like this would have had him waking refreshed and ready for a full day. Now, despite his increasing duties, there was an unfamiliar desire to remain tucked up beneath his blankets and wait for the day to grow warmer before emerging from his cocoon.

But of course, to do so and miss morning prayers would hardly be pious, would it?

Godfrey smiled to himself as he hurried along. Despite the mess Lusara had become, it did his heart good to know he hadn't lost his sense of humour. He turned into the Chapter House to find his fellow Archdeacons, Francis and Ohler, in their usual seats. Francis was a man of little patience but, oddly enough, great wisdom. His bald head was kept warm in winter by his habit's cowl left permanently in place. Ohler was a pedant, from start to finish, and often mistaken for lacking in humour, which Godfrey knew to be untrue. Though several years older than both Godfrey and Francis, Ohler seemed to have stopped aging about ten years before, leaving only a little steel grey in his hair. Both men looked up as he entered, pausing in their whispered conversation until he could join them. He took up his seat against the wall next to them, his face turned towards the rest of his brethren, waiting for the day's Chapter meeting to commence.

'I suppose you've already heard?' Ohler murmured, his face giving nothing away.

'Godfrey is always two steps ahead of everyone else,' Francis replied, the humour injected into his voice taking offence from his words.

'That's because,' Godfrey whispered, glancing at them both before rising to his feet, 'I'm actually a mind-reader, Brothers. But whatever it is, can we discuss it after Chapter?'

When they said nothing else, Godfrey opened the meeting and gave his concentration over to the daily business, and then regained his seat as a chapter from the Order was read out to all of them. Then, as the cold from the stone seat began to sink into his bones, he closed the meeting and waited until all but two of his brethren had shuffled out. Only then did he get to his feet, stretch out the kinks of the morning and turn to the older men.

'What exactly am I supposed to have heard about?'

'You're the mind-reader,' Francis replied dryly.

Ohler tutted and shook his head. 'The Hermit of Shan Moss, Godfrey. Have you heard the latest?'

Only self-preservation stopped Godfrey from rolling his eyes. At one time in his life, he'd given serious credence to anything the Hermit might say. But there had been a Hermit in Shan Moss Forest for more than a century – the role obviously passed from one monk to another – and with some of the things that had emerged over the last few months, he was no longer sure he could take any of it with more than a grain of salt. However, the same could not be said of his Brothers, nor of the country at large, which absorbed whatever hope it could, while sliding down the hill of despair.

'No, I've not heard the latest. What have I missed?'

'You would do well to listen carefully,' Francis answered, noting Godfrey's scepticism. 'There are history books being written on the accuracy of this man's visions. Do you wish to be noted down for posterity as the priest who ignored the warnings?'

'I would be quite happy,' Godfrey sighed, 'to avoid posterity's notice altogether.'

Ohler held up his hands to silence both of them. 'The Hermit has seen her. Seen the incarnation of Mineah coming amongst us. Surely we should take that as a cause for celebration. That's eleven times this year he's seen her. I went back over the old records and there's never been that many—'

'Did he say where we would find her?' Godfrey interrupted, his mind on the work he had to get done today. 'Or what we should do when we . . . do?'

'No. Oh, come, Godfrey, you know his visions aren't that specific.'

'But they are that convenient. Is that all? I do have a lot of—' Francis was laughing at him. Ohler was frowning. 'What?'

Francis turned to his fellow priest, 'Godfrey is too busy to see the future for the present.'

'Doesn't it strike you as strange,' Ohler said, getting to his feet, 'that such signs and portents have filled this year? And now we have this directive from Kenrick?'

Godfrey froze, then made sure the heavy doors were closed. But Ohler continued without pause. 'And there have been other visions, those only communicated to the Bishop – and us. The Hermit has had recurring visions of the Battle of Shan Moss, of the fight between . . .' he shuddered, 'between His Grace of Haddon and the Guildesman, Nash. It is obvious to those who listen that all these disturbances lead to one thing: sorcery. What I want to know is, what you think we should do about it.'

'Do?' Godfrey's eyebrows shot up. Quite deliberately, he ignored his involvement with Murdoch and, by extension, Robert Douglas. He could not speak about it, even if he wanted to – which he didn't. 'I'm not sure we can *do* anything. At least, not unless we're prepared to declare a holy war against sorcerers – and may I remind you that our King is one of them, and since none of us holds the rank of Bishop, I would very much like to hear exactly what you *think* we should do. Personally, I'm all for getting on with our work and being ready to act when the time comes.'

'Spoken like a true patriot,' Francis laughed. He got to his feet and put a hand on Ohler's shoulder. 'But he's right. Let's just be thankful that Brome is indisposed and not likely to declare that holy war in a hurry. We don't want to hasten that day any more than necessary.'

Ohler's frown remained secure. 'I trust you will both take this a little more seriously when the crowds start banging on the Basilica door, wanting answers.'

'No doubt,' Godfrey said, 'I'll be out there with them.'

Osbert broke a last piece of bread between his fingers and dipped it into the milky porridge. There were pieces of apples and other fruits to sweeten the mixture and though many thought this was an invalid's breakfast, the truth was, Osbert preferred it to anything else.

As his servant refreshed his cup, Osbert popped the piece of bread into his mouth and sat back, pressing his fingers into a square of raw linen. Before him stood one of his most trusted men. He had too few these days, but still, five had to be considered a luxury. The man waited, travel-stained and weary, his poor clothing at odds with the sumptuous furnishings of Osbert's study.

Osbert swallowed and said, 'And Nash hasn't left Ransem Castle since then?'

'No, my lord.'

Nodding, Osbert waved a hand at his servant to give the man a cup of something hot. Then he got to his feet and wandered towards the window which faced the castle gate. Flags snapped viciously in the same wind which battered his casements and gave the room an edgy chill. Between the flags were stationed long pikes, upon which were spitted the heads of men executed over the last year for treason – or rather, men accused of treason, which wasn't the same thing at all.

At one time, to be accused of being a sorcerer would have brought such a fate – despite the fact that there had been no way to prove such a thing back then. Nowadays, a man could be a traitor without so much as a shred of evidence, and despite his protestations of innocence, the testimony of both friends and enemies, his head would still appear upon a pike, his fate to stand witness to further executions, his purpose to warn others against trusting the Crown.

Bitter lessons for a people trapped in a bitter season.

'Tell me,' Osbert continued, turning from the bleak sight back to the warmth of his study, 'What do you think Nash is up to?'

'I could not say for certain, my lord,' Lyle replied, 'So much of what he does we cannot observe, and what we can observe often makes no sense.'

'That's true, but is that enough to cause a rift between Nash and Kenrick?'

Pursing his lips, Lyle said, 'Alone, no. At least, not yet.'

Osbert nodded. He had no desire to plot against Nash – at least, not directly – but still, survival required that he keep tabs on the man who held his life in his hands.

'My lord, you do realise there could be some trouble over this change in our laws?'

'Have you heard anything I need to do something about?'

'Not exactly. However, I have heard many whisperings. Some about you, some about the King. Many of our brothers are unhappy with the situation.'

'As are we all, Lyle. You will keep me informed if you hear anything else.'

'Yes, my lord.'

'Very well,' Osbert waved his hand in dismissal. 'You may go and get yourself something to eat. Get some decent rest before you go back – and try to find something warmer to wear, will you? You'll be no good to me if you turn to ice while you're on watch. And return to me tomorrow. I have something I would like your opinion on.'

'As you wish, my lord.' Lyle bowed and left the room, closing the door behind him. Absently, Osbert returned to his window and gazed once more at the bodiless heads.

They'd all had ambitions to survive as well, hadn't they? They'd all believed in their own ability to remain one or more steps ahead of the King, sure that such a fate could not possibly befall *them*.

And perhaps that's why they'd all died. Osbert, however, believed exactly the opposite. In some part of his mind, he *knew* that fate awaited him, regardless of what he did to avoid it. The best that he could hope for was to ride the fear and put the day off for as long as possible.

He'd lived with the fear so long now he wasn't sure he could breathe without it.

Godfrey lowered himself to his knees and clasped his hands together, allowing his eyes to lift towards the trium high on the chapel wall. Against the pale stone the ebony was stark, the twisted frame of the triangle linked forever to the gods Serinleth, Mineah and the evil Broleoch.

Even thinking that last name made him shiver. Superstition maintained that to utter the evil one's name was to invoke his influence upon a man's life. There was just enough of the old soul in Godfrey to resist the temptation to try the theory.

Thick candles placed upon the altar flickered and danced, creating weird shadows on the trium, suggesting the carving could, given the right provocation, actually come to life. Incense drifted in the air, counterpoint to the gentle murmurings behind him as each of the Guildesmen finished off their private prayers before leaving.

Lately there had been more of them attending mass each day. While expected to be duly pious and respecting the Church, the Guilde had no specific rules governing individual worship. Even so, as Guilde Chaplain, Godfrey said mass every morning and prayers every evening and made himself available for confession one day a week. His duties in the Guilde Chapel had always been light – until recently. Now, fifty or sixty Guildesmen resident in Marsay would come to each service he conducted, more than twice the usual number. In their faces he could see concern, fear, confusion. He could only treat them with compassion. Their trust, their faith in the Guilde had been shaken to the foundations and too many of them floundered, not knowing where to turn.

Not that Godfrey had any answers for them. More than five hundred years ago, the old Empire and the Guilde had been allies with the Cabal sorcerers. Back then, times had changed too, bringing the sides together in a great battle on the plains of Alusia. The Empire had won and handed the Guilde its sacred duty to the people: to crush all sorcery, to put to death anyone found to have such powers. Sorcerers could not be trusted. Their powers were evil; those who would wield them, evil incarnate. Since that victory on the battlefield, the Guilde had lived up to its sacred duty, right or wrong.

And now that duty was gone, extinguished by a brush of ink upon vellum, propelled by the hand of the Proctor, Osbert, forced there by the King.

Godfrey could well understand the confusion of these men. He felt more than a little of it himself. Though he was under similar orders, so far Bishop Brome had procrastinated about abolishing Church laws against sorcery – an oddity itself, considering what a slave Brome had been to Kenrick on all other matters, and Selar before him. That was, after all, why McCauly had been imprisoned and Brome put in his place.

With practice born of many years, he framed words, let them fall silently from his lips, prayers to Mineah and Serinleth, prayers for peace, for calm, for wisdom. Prayers for those who could not be here, fulfilling the roles they'd been born to, those like Aiden McCauly.

Prayers for deliverance.

It must come, one day.

Whispering one final prayer for Robert's health and safety, Godfrey signed the trium over his forehead and shoulders, then got to his feet. Once again, he clasped his hands together, allowing his vestments to drop back into place. Only then did he turn for the sacristy. He could hear the men behind him climbing to their feet, the hum of conversation building as they left via the western door.

He could easily guess what they were saying.

'Archdeacon?'

Godfrey paused, feeling something itch across his skin. Taking a breath to ready himself, he turned towards the dark alcove whence the voice had come. A figure, framed in dappled light threading through the stained-glass windows above. The man stepped forward, a grim smile on his face, a veiled threat in his demeanour. Godfrey knew this man and his stomach clenched with fear.

'Good morning, my lord.' He was ridiculously proud of the way his voice remained steady as he drew himself up, prepared to face this new challenge.

This man was a Malachi.

Baron Luc DeMassey was around Godfrey's own age, and they were about the same height – but there the similarities ended. Where Godfrey had spent his life serving the gods and the Church, DeMassey had but one master: Nash.

'Can I help you?' Godfrey added, determined not to show his fear to this man. He could not be intimidated by the rich clothing and natural good looks and instead concentrated on the texture of the dark blue eyes, and how the light on his auburn hair turned it almost a blood-red.

Or was that just Godfrey's imagination?

'I hope that you can help me, Father.' DeMassey's voice was quiet and brisk. He came a step closer, then continued, 'I wish to make confession.'

Godfrey blanched and swallowed hard. DeMassey must have read his reaction correctly as he immediately held up his hand. 'Father, I have a need of your priestly services. I am *asking* for your help.'

'Are you telling me that if I refuse, you'll leave me alone?'

DeMassey raised his eyebrows in surprise, then slowly shook his head. 'I thought to ask you. I had believed it was your duty as much as anything else. Of course, the choice is yours.'

Since the Malachi said nothing else, made no other attempt at persuasion, Godfrey had no choice but to agree.

'But not here. I would be more comfortable speaking within the Basilica, if that is permitted.'

Not entirely sure what was being asked of him, Godfrey nodded again and turned for the door. DeMassey followed behind.

Godfrey picked up the taper and lit two candles standing on the prie-dieu. He signed the trium in the air once before turning to face the Malachi Baron, not believing for one moment that this was a genuine and penitent confession he was about to hear. Men had been known to use the confessional for their own purposes before, and the Malachi were not known for their overwhelming piety.

Of course, they might find other ways to show their devotion, ways that Godfrey wasn't aware of. Robert had told him too little about these people, only enough to ensure his survival. However, how much could Robert know when the Malachi were his sworn enemies?

Godfrey cleared his thoughts. He picked up the purple stole he'd left on the prie-dieu, kissed it gently, then placed it over his shoulders, symbolic of the seal of the confessional. DeMassey stood waiting for him, hands clasped together in front of him, no longer perhaps as arrogant as usual, but certainly not penitent.

'Very well, my lord. Do you wish to sit? Or kneel?'

DeMassey studied him for a moment, then shook his head slightly. He turned and waved a hand over the door in a gesture Robert had once explained was a warning. DeMassey would know if anyone approached.

The Malachi then reached inside his jacket and extracted a slim leather pouch, stiff-sewn up two sides and dressed in dark green wax worn and thick with age. Whatever rested inside was expected to last. Solemnly DeMassey laid the pouch on the prie-dieu before Godfrey, his fingers remaining on it until the last. Then his gaze lifted and he smiled a little.

'As I am sure you have surmised, I have not come to confess to sins I have never counted. Instead, I would ask of you a favour I have no right to. Please believe that I would not ask this if I had another, better option at hand.'

This comparative confession was enough to pique Godfrey's curiosity. He glanced once at the pouch and said, 'What is the favour?'

'If you receive word that I am dead, I need you to open this pouch, extract the letter within and carry out the task described with the utmost dispatch. And you must never, ever tell anyone at all that you have it, or that you have spoken to me.'

'Will you tell me what is inside the pouch?'

'I don't think that would be wise.'

112

'Then,' Godfrey kept his voice level, not liking the implications of this at all, 'how am I to know if I am prepared to carry out your instructions?'

DeMassey moved a few steps away, turning to the leaded window which drew in the morning light, but gave no view of the cloister. 'I know you will want proof, Archdeacon, but you are a man of faith, are you not?'

'I will not give you my solemn vow without knowing what it is that I am promising. Would you in my place?'

'I did,' came the quiet response. 'I can offer you nothing in the way of tangible proof – however, I may tell you this much: the man I . . . work for . . . is obsessed with the fulfilment of a Prophecy. The contents of that pouch may help you . . . pursue your own goals.'

Godfrey blinked hard, frowning before DeMassey could turn around and see. Was he honestly offering Godfrey a chance to foil Nash's plans? Could this be so simple? No, not simple, perhaps, for if it came to pass, then this man standing before him would be dead.

'I need you to promise.'

'But why me? You don't know me. You must know that I would oppose you and your kind if I could.'

DeMassey turned his head then, a wry smile on his face. 'Yes. But I also know you to be a good man, Father. And a good man is what this task requires. I could trust no other. If you were a man who did not care, or who served his own needs before those of others, then we would not be talking.' DeMassey came closer, his hands spread out before him. 'I have . . . treated the pouch so that the contents will dissolve if anyone but you tries to open it. I do not ask this favour lightly, Father. Believe me, if there were no need at all for such precautions, I would be a very happy man. However, I do need your promise. I dare not leave without it.'

Godfrey could not be blind to the soft plea, nor the open and genuine expression on this man's face. As far as he could tell, the Malachi was telling as much truth as he could. But as a priest, and as an honest man, Godfrey could not make any vow without meaning it.

'I promise to do as you ask, on the condition that . . .'

'No conditions, Father.' DeMassey held up his hand. His gesture, his stance, everything about him warned that any conditions he made would be broken. 'Instead, let me promise you something. If I am dead, you will *want* to carry out this task.'

'Are you sure?'

The Baron replied, 'Absolutely positive.'

And there was something in that simple response that Godfrey could not find it in him to refuse. He would probably regret it, but then, in the same way that he'd been around to help catch Osbert after his split with Nash, perhaps he could perform the same service here. It did not take a great man to form alliances, only one of faith.

'Very well,' Godfrey said, placing his hand on the pouch in benediction, 'I give you my word. I will carry out your instructions.'

DeMassey held his breath a moment, then let out a heavy sigh. He looked up at Godfrey once more. 'I hope it may never come to pass, but if it does, I will make sure you are quickly informed. And thank you, Father. You have given me . . . peace with this vow. I will take my leave.'

Long after dark, long after the shadows had melted into the night, DeMassey shifted in his bed once more and took Valena back into his arms. Her body remained stiff with anger, but he smoothed his hands down the soft skin of her back, soothing her fear and trepidation along with his own.

'Oh, Luc,' she hissed, not shifting away from him, but sharing her anger, as he needed her to. 'Why *him*! You know who he is! You know how close he is to both Brome and Osbert.'

'That's exactly *why* I chose him. He's kept Osbert's head above water for almost a decade now – and he doesn't do it for love of Nash. Godfrey is a man of integrity—'

'He knows what Malachi are, Luc! How is he to be our ally? You must take back the letter and kill him!'

DeMassey rolled them to their sides, cradling her beautiful

face between his hands. 'Godfrey is a priest. A man of integrity. He cannot reveal our secret – even if his life depends on it.'

'Even if *our* lives depend on it?' Valena paused, breathing hard. 'Integrity or no, if Kenrick or Nash tortures him, he will tell, and you know it.'

'And what can he tell Nash? That I asked him to do me a favour after I die?'

Her eyes widened then, her fingers instantly pressing against his lips, stilling his words. 'Don't,' she whispered, shifting closer, using her body as she always had, to tell him how much she loved him. 'Don't say things like that, Luc, please.'

He held her close for a moment, kissing her temple, feeling her warm breath against his throat. 'Are you saying you've changed your mind?'

'No,' she replied, her voice hopelessly vulnerable. He wanted to wrap her up, hide her and protect her and make sure nobody ever endangered her again. But she was who she was, and his protection would ultimately mean very little. And she wasn't anywhere near as vulnerable as she often made out.

But on this subject she was. Which was why they'd discussed it, why DeMassey had gone to such lengths.

'I know you don't want this,' he whispered into the night. 'You know I don't either.'

'No.'

He shifted onto his back once more, taking her with him, landing in the place they'd begun.

'I love you,' she murmured against his chest.

'I love you, too.' He kissed her head and closed his eyes.

8

By the time Godfrey reached the Bishop's Palace, enough snow had fallen outside to leave a layer of white on every flat surface. The grey sky had dropped, making it look like the roof of the world was coming down on them all. Wary, he climbed the stairs to the second floor and made his way unhindered along the Gallery. In the last crowded antechamber he was met by

Francis, who immediately took Godfrey's arm and drew him to the courtyard window, away from the others waiting in attendance.

'What's happened?' Godfrey asked. 'Is he dying?'

'Not that the doctors have said,' Francis replied, obviously tired. 'Still, you must talk some sense to him. Brome will listen to you. He . . . thinks he's being poisoned.'

'Is he?' It was hard to believe anybody would bother. Brome's health had been deteriorating for the last few years. How long he would last was anybody's guess.

'Well, he's certainly not getting any better – but then, I'm not a doctor. Even so, he's convinced somebody is trying to kill him.'

Godfrey looked at the closed bedroom doors. 'Anybody we know?'

Francis shook his head impatiently, almost dislodging his cowl. 'You must listen to me, Godfrey. He thinks he's dying and he's trying to make provision. That's why he wants to see you.'

Godfrey turned back to the priest before him. 'What do you want me to do?'

'You must decide according to the dictates of your conscience, Brother,' Francis replied, ominously. 'But whatever you do, make sure he agrees to change the laws.'

Shocked, Godfrey took a step back. 'What? But I thought you were completely against . . .'

'It doesn't matter what I'm against – what matters is the survival of the Church. For once in my life, I'm in agreement with that toad Osbert. He was right to make the change without hesitation. Do you have any idea how much attention Brome is getting from Kenrick at the moment? I wouldn't be surprised if Kenrick did poison him, just to give him a fright.'

Godfrey let air into his lungs slowly, hoping to ease the knot of tension. Some days he really wished he was somewhere else. Anywhere but here.

'He's waiting for you.'

'I'm sure he is,' Godfrey replied dryly, ignoring the response from Francis. It was all very well for his brother Archdeacon to hand him pat advice, but it was up to Godfrey to sell the idea to Brome in the end.

Almost the first thing Osbert had done when he'd returned to Marsay as Proctor after the Battle of Shan Moss had been to empty Vaughn's old study with his own two hands. He'd taken some of the furniture and most of the papers and installed himself in the larger room a little further along the corridor, where windows faced both towards the castle and across the square to the Basilica. His bedroom was immediately above.

There'd been a need in him to make some obvious change to the way he viewed the Guilde and his Proctorship, determined not to walk in Vaughn's shoes a single step further than he needed to.

Now his study had the appearance of order and calm, but also of comfort, with nothing of the gaudiness of Vaughn's taste. The oval table in the middle of the room had been made especially at his order, designed to be as unlike the King's Council table as possible.

He would *not* follow in Vaughn's footsteps. He would not make the same mistakes, commit the same follies.

Instead, he would make a host of his own.

He had each of the twin fireplaces blazing as the evening air descended on the city. He'd pulled the curtains as soon as he'd seen the snow begin to fall. It was too depressing to count how many months of gloomy weather would come before he dared step outside again without fifteen layers of wool between him and the world.

There'd been another reason why he'd cleared Vaughn's study with his own hands. Some of the papers he'd discovered had shocked him. Some of them hadn't surprised him at all. Even so, he hadn't found what he'd been looking for – and alone, he'd had to hide his relief from no one.

Vaughn had said to him, under the influence of a drug Osbert had given him, that the secret Guilde library, containing books dating back to the Empire, had been hidden in a

117

place where *none shall seek and none shall find*. It had been a great comfort to Osbert to know those books, as far as he could tell, were no longer anywhere within the Guildehall. Nash would never get his hands on them, nor put the sorcerous lore contained within to his evil use.

Osbert listened idly to the sounds of paper being shifted from one place to another. Lyle had returned and Osbert had immediately put him to work. It only remained now for the man to read to the end and give Osbert his honest opinion. He would trust no other.

He said, 'Will you be finished inside the hour?'

Lyle looked up. 'No, my lord. There are a few papers here that I would like to read a second time, to ensure I understood them correctly. Perhaps another two hours in total.'

Osbert nodded. He had an appointment with the King shortly. 'Have you found anything of value so far?'

Lyle glanced down at the piles of letters Osbert had received from Guildesmen all over the country over the last few weeks. 'From what I can see, the letters fall into three different categories. The first group feel wounded and hurt that you could make such changes to traditional Guilde law without following the correct procedure and consulting your brothers. While they appreciate your position, they still feel that proper respect was not given to them in the process and they feel an apology is due.'

'From what I've seen, those number the bulk of the letters I've received.'

Lyle continued, 'The second group are horrified that you've done such a thing. They are not only hurt that you didn't consult them, but that if you had, they would have done everything within their power to stop you. Their trust in you as Proctor has been sorely tested and there is a hint there that any future radical changes you intend to make will be met with the strongest resistance wherever possible. I would call this group the troublemakers.'

'I would as well,' Osbert felt thoroughly vindicated at asking for Lyle's opinion in the first place. The man was a soldier, experienced in subterfuge, spying and gathering of information. If any man could recognise a genuine threat, it was Lyle.

'The final group are what I would call fanatics. These are men who were at the Battle, saw the sorcery with their own eyes and feel that not only should the laws *not* be changed, but that you should increase the punishments tenfold. They are quick, I might add, to assure you that they don't believe the King is a sorcerer—'

'Though he admits it openly,' Osbert added dryly.

'— in an attempt to avoid propagating treason. However, any number of curses are called down upon your head and each one demands that you either reinstate the old laws or resign your position as Proctor. Many of the letters are unsigned. A man who is not prepared to accept the responsibility of his own words is doubly dangerous in return. You were right to be concerned.'

Concerned indeed. There had already been trouble over the last five or six years, mostly in outlying towns and villages. So many little insurrections here and there, certain to have the Douglas involved with them somewhere – and Guilde soldiers were always involved in keeping that peace. And now these dissenters. To many, it would appear that the Guilde had given up completely, that the powers of darkness, of evil – of *sorcery* – had finally claimed their victory.

There would be more trouble, there was no doubt at all. He would have to send word to all his Halls to put on extra guards as this news travelled further, as the full import was felt.

Pursing his lips, Osbert reached for the cloak he had thrown over the back of a chair. He swung it over his shoulders and turned back to Lyle. 'Do you think these men would have written these letters if Vaughn had still been Proctor?'

'I doubt Vaughn would have changed the laws.'

'That much is a given. Even so?'

Lyle rested his elbows on the table and folded his hands together. 'Even so, Vaughn largely kept our brothers in check by use of fear. For the most part, the brethren were terrified of him. They don't have the same fear of you.'

'This has to be a secret between you and me. I have no desire for the rest of the Guilde to learn of such dissent within the ranks. I should be back in two hours.'

The moment Godfrey stepped into Brome's bedroom, the smell hit him, as it always did. Brome's bed dominated the room. Four tall posts were draped in rich red velvet, the floor entirely covered in rugs of green, blue and gold. An enormous fireplace to his left hosted logs blazing brightly while the window to the left was draped with curtains, shutting out the bleak dusk. A table was covered in potions and dressings and two doctors leaned over the bed where Brome lay, his static bulk enlarged by layers and layers of bedding.

Godfrey gathered himself. 'You sent for me, Your Grace?'

Two red eyes turned towards him and a hand waved the doctors away. 'Godfrey? Come.'

Deliberately breathing through his mouth, Godfrey came to a halt at the bedside. Through years of overindulgence, Brome had whittled away the natural health he'd been born with. He'd not moved from the Palace for almost two years, from this bed for more than six months. His breath came out as a wheeze when he shifted his position and Godfrey had seen the blackened sores which were rotting away the flesh on his legs.

But was he being poisoned? By anything other than his own greed? Or was the sickness now reaching his mind, clouding it with fake realities?

'Godfrey, you must talk to these doctors.' Though ill, Brome's voice still had the hand of command to it. He'd not won his position by skill or piety, but through subservience to King Selar. As a result, he'd spent the last fourteen years living a life of luxury, making decisions for a Church that had never wanted him as its Prelate. And all the while, Aiden McCauly, the man rightfully enthroned in that role, had lived the life of a rebel, in exile and in constant fear of his life.

McCauly would never have abused his position so. On the other hand, McCauly, had he been allowed to keep his mitre, would probably have been dead by now, executed for defiance.

As Brome was likely to be soon. Who would have thought the man would find courage so late in the day?

'Your Grace, the doctors are well-skilled, the best in the country. I am sure they are doing all they can to help you.'

'Send them out, Godfrey, now!'

Suppressing a sigh, Godfrey nodded to the doctors. He waited until they were gone and the doors closed again before he turned back to Brome. 'I beg Your Grace to remain calm. You need your rest.'

'Godfrey, you're the only one I can trust.'

'Your Grace?'

'Sit. Sit.'

Godfrey drew a chair by the bed and sat. How was it that it was always he who ended up with these tasks? Was it some curse? Or perhaps retribution from the gods for the double life he led?

'Godfrey,' Brome wheezed, turning to face him, his flesh a sickly grey and rolled around his chin like a fresh-baked pastry. 'Kenrick demands I provide him with papers by the end of the month. I have put him off as long as I can but I fear he will wait no longer. I . . .'

There was a pause while Brome lifted himself a little, sitting so he could face Godfrey better. He coughed a little, dabbed at his mouth with a pristine lace cloth. He looked as if he had a list of things he had to say, prepared long before. 'You must understand, he is determined to change the very fabric of the Church, and in doing so, will destroy us all. Proctor Osbert has already succumbed to the pressure and has made the necessary changes to Guilde Law – but I fear I cannot do the same.'

Godfrey was torn, deeply. The priest in him longed for the power to stop Kenrick forcing such a radical change on a Church so ill-prepared. The man in him, the Lusaran hoping for help from those very quarters, longed for Brome to give in and change the laws, allow Robert even the smallest amount of help.

'Your Grace, if you are sure you wish to . . .'

Small eyes darted to him, almost buried within a face overwhelmed by fat. Red blotches had grown here and there, turning Brome into something young children would run away

121

from. 'Have you heard the news from Shan Moss? About the Hermit?'

'Yes, Your Grace.' It was all Godfrey could do not to sigh. He had a pain developing at the back of his neck.

'Then you must be able to see that Mineah will soon walk amongst us again, perhaps even does so now. When the day comes, we will be ready to fight alongside her and extinguish the evil of sorcery once more. Once, the Guilde took on this sacred duty. Now it has fallen to us.' Brome reached out to grab his sleeve. 'We must be ready when she comes, Godfrey. You must . . . *you* must be ready!'

Godfrey read the urgency. 'What do you need me to do?'

A frown appeared on Brome's forehead. 'I have heard a whisper of an attempted assassination. I am sure Kenrick is poisoning me. If I don't give him the new laws by the end of the month, he will make sure I die, and then put another man in my place who will do his bidding. Godfrey, I want that man to be you.'

Godfrey froze. For terrible seconds, he couldn't muster the will to breathe, let alone move. Then Brome's grip on his sleeve shook him a little, forcing his gaze down to the ringed, pudgy hand where new sores had begun to open up.

Bishop? Godfrey?

Sweet Mineah, no, anything but that!

'You must do this, Godfrey. You must write the new laws. You have the mind to do it, the wit to outsmart Kenrick and his sorcerer cronies. Write the new laws for us in such a way that their meaning is inoffensive to the gods and can easily be overturned. Give Kenrick as little as you can and keep the rest back for the day when we can return to our former glory.'

'Your Grace, you must change the laws yourself!' Godfrey leaned forward, his mind made up. 'You have provided as much opposition as you could – far more than Osbert mustered. The gods will understand. By all means, I will help you write the laws, but let it be your hand which signs them. Let Kenrick see you are worth keeping alive.' Was he more afraid for Brome's life, or of taking his job once he was gone? And what kind of priest was he to be asking such a question?

Brome laughed a little, closed his eyes and leaned his head back, 'I am dead, whether Kenrick kills me or no. But my conscience wears me down. I have . . . wronged . . . my predecessor. I wish to make amends now, before I submit my soul to heavenly judgement. I cannot give Kenrick what he asks.'

Godfrey almost swore aloud at that. It was fine for Brome to think about his immortal soul now that he was on his deathbed, was happy to consign Godfrey's to hell in order to avoid a little dirty work.

Just as he'd learned to expect from this man. No, Brome had not learned courage; instead, he'd reformed cowardice.

He would help all he could, but he would never be Bishop, not as long as McCauly lived. No matter what Brome wanted, the title of Bishop had far more meaning than Brome had ever understood. Godfrey had no desire to sully the sanctity of the primacy simply to fill in where Brome's courage had left off.

Besides, he wasn't worthy.

'Promise me, Godfrey. Vow that you will stand in my place when I'm gone. I have already made letters up, informing our brethren that there will be no election to replace me. I have nominated you as my successor. You have only to give me your word and I may die in peace. Will you swear?'

Godfrey closed his eyes, aching inside at what he was being forced into. This was so very wrong. He was not made to be Bishop. He was too selfish, too rebellious to hold such a position of responsibility. He had enough trouble caring for his own soul; how should he care for those of every Lusaran?

He should have gone with Robert when he had the chance, to spend his days working alongside McCauly for the freedom of Lusara. Instead, he had to play the hypocrite, placing his feet in shoes he had no desire to wear.

And the terrible truth was if *he* didn't do this, somebody else would. At least if he agreed, he would have some control over what happened next. It would be his hand which framed the new laws and not another self-serving Brome.

Assuming Kenrick approved the appointment.

'Well? Damn it, Godfrey! Will you promise?'

With a sigh of deep dread, Godfrey said, 'Yes, Your Grace, I promise.'

Brome dismissed him then, and Godfrey, relieved to at least be free of that room, emerged into the antechamber to find Francis waiting for him. Before Godfrey could even open his mouth, Francis held up a cloak for him, his expression dark.

'I'm afraid your day is not over yet. Kenrick has sent for you. He's expecting you directly.'

This time Godfrey successfully refrained from swearing. It appeared superficial expressions of dissatisfaction were only irritating the gods, and he was being held to account. He tied the cloak laces at his throat and headed for the gallery. Francis kept pace at his side, saying, 'Well? Are you going to tell me what happened?'

'He won't make the changes,' Godfrey said without preamble. 'He thinks he's dying. He intends to leave his reputation intact and hand the issue of the changes to his successor once he's gone. His decision is, of course, tantamount to suicide.'

'Oh, by the mass,' Francis groaned. 'And who is his successor to be?'

Godfrey didn't pause at the staircase. He just put one foot in front of the other, determined to get to the other side of this day with his patience and sanity in one piece. 'Me.'

There was an escort waiting for him outside the Bishop's Palace – just two footmen with pikes, wearing Kenrick's livery, but their presence alone was enough to set his teeth on edge.

He would spend tonight in confession and then on his knees in prayer. Every ungenerous, selfish, untidy and insensitive thought he'd had today would need to be accounted for. How in Serin's name could he call himself a priest and still react and think the way he did?

He was ashamed. And so, with his face burning a little in the cold evening, he marched towards the castle, a footman on either side of him, keeping silent, but making the pace quick and brisk.

He passed into the castle, taken through the main courtyard

and hurried up into the long gallery which faced the river. Normally the view below would be filled with river boats lit by colourful lanterns, splashing life against the dead of night. But these days, people had trouble trading safely on the river and so spent less time docked around Marsay. Instead they came to the island city in daylight, exchanged their goods, then headed back downriver, where it was safer.

Godfrey wanted to go with them, because it wasn't safe here any more. He wanted to go someplace where his life didn't depend on him saying a word wrong here, or looking at the wrong thing there. Where the people he loved and trusted weren't outlaws and rebels. Where his very thoughts weren't infected by the secrets he needed to keep, and wounded by the guilt of keeping them.

Being a priest had turned out to be so much more complicated than he'd ever thought possible.

'Come, Father,' a guard motioned to him to hurry. 'You're late. The King is impatient.'

Some small creature of defiance in Godfrey stopped his feet from hurrying. Instead, he kept his pace steady as he was led along the gallery to the other end, determined to assume the dignity of a priest, even if he didn't feel it. He passed tables and chairs, where young men of the court played at dice, and young ladies watched and laughed, generally entertaining themselves without an eye to their country's future. Those older folk who would normally provide some balance here were either dead or banished – or too afraid to come to court for fear of what would happen to them.

'Archdeacon!' The King's voice sliced across his awareness like a sword drawing blood. 'I sent for you an hour ago. Why have you kept me waiting?'

Godfrey clasped his hands together so they wouldn't shake. Kenrick stood with his back to a blazing fireplace, looking none too happy. Osbert was there also, his expression bland, hiding a wealth of fear beneath it.

'Forgive me, Sire,' Godfrey bowed low, showing as much contrition as he dared. 'I was summoned by the Bishop. He wished to give me instructions.'

Kenrick's gaze narrowed, as though figuring this into finely balanced calculations. He lifted his chin slightly and said, 'Instructions on changing Church law, I trust?'

For a moment, Godfrey's throat closed up, refusing to let him answer. But then, from the corner of his eye, he saw Osbert's hand clench, and from somewhere, Godfrey found the strength to both lie and tell the truth, to betray Brome, and keep his faith. 'Yes, Sire.'

'And?'

'There are difficulties, Sire.'

'I'm not interested in difficulties.'

'No, Sire. Only, His Grace suffers very poor health . . .'

'I take it, then,' Kenrick watched Godfrey now like a hawk with talons ready to strike, 'that the Bishop is too unwell to compose the law changes?'

If Kenrick knew there would be no answer from Brome, then the Bishop was a dead man. His only hope was for Godfrey to buy him some time – the time they would need to make the changes. 'I would not expect his health to allow him such work for some weeks yet. His doctors attend him, but their best advice is continued rest.'

'Oh, I can arrange a *very* long rest for him, if he wants it!' Kenrick sprang forward, bristling energy and a loathing that almost soaked into the plush rug at his feet. His words echoed around the hall, making everybody else look up with the same flash of fear in their eyes.

Godfrey waited, trying not to hold his breath.

'He's doing this deliberately! Can you gainsay me that, Archdeacon? Can you?' Kenrick glared at him. 'You can tell that Bishop of yours that if I don't have those laws repealed within the week, I'll have him arrested for treason. We'll see how long his poor health keeps him alive when I throw him into the same cell where his predecessor rotted for two years. I doubt there would be too many men in the country willing to rescue *his* putrid carcass the way they did McCauly!'

Godfrey raised his hands, as though in prayer. 'Forgive me, Sire, but even if he started this night, it would take more than a week to change those laws in such a way as to make them legal.'

'Very well,' Kenrick snapped, his fury only abated, not extinguished. 'How long *will* it take?'

Swallowing hard, Godfrey answered. 'To make the changes would require at least two weeks. In order for them to be legal, they must be distributed to every church, abbey and monastery in Lusara, with a fixed date noted therein.'

'Therefore?'

'The laws could be in place by Caslemas, Sire.' He couldn't help it. Though he choked on the last words, there was still some part of him which rejoiced in the capitulation. Did he want the responsibility taken from him? Did he want to be forced into this, so his conscience wouldn't plague him in his old age?

Or was that part of him rejoicing because he'd consented to undoing an injustice that had stood unchallenged for over five hundred years?

Kenrick saw only his own goals. 'Very well. Caslemas it is – and no excuses. Osbert, when Brome's documents are ready to go out, I want you to send a letter with them.'

'To what end, Sire?'

The King paused, his gaze drifting off towards the other end of the gallery for a moment as a small smile graced his scarred features. 'You will write on my behalf. Since it will no longer be illegal to possess sorcerer's abilities, I wish to welcome to my court any man or woman who has such talents.'

'What?'

Godfrey stared, but Kenrick didn't seem to hear Osbert's strangled response, nor see the way the man's face flushed clean of colour.

'Word it as genuinely as you can,' the King continued, gesturing to a waiting serving boy to bring him some wine. 'I want it clear that any sorcerer wishing to enter into my service will be well rewarded. What's wrong, Osbert?'

'Sire . . . I . . .' Osbert's mouth opened and closed, sounds issuing forth without form.

Kenrick took the wine brought to him, sipping on it.

Osbert's rapidly contained shock was little more than a momentary inconvenience. 'Look at your maps, Proctor. Go back to your library and pull out maps of the golden era of the Empire. Back then, every petty Prince, every King, every Guildehall had its own sorcerer. We lived together in harmony once before; I don't see why we cannot now – especially as I am in a perfect position to bring about such peaceful agreement. Or would you deny me the opportunity to make Lusara as great as any Empire?'

Osbert's expression might have been carved out of a block of wood. 'No, Sire. Of course not.'

'Good. You'll write the letter and have it to me by tomorrow night. We will send copies with the same couriers who will deliver Brome's law changes to every town in the country. That way, nobody will be able to say I am offering positions at court to sorcerers without the blessing of the Church. I charge you, Archdeacon, with ensuring the Bishop carries out my instructions. That is all.'

Osbert had bowed and backed away, turned and fled down the gallery before he realised he'd been holding his breath. At the bottom of the stairs, he turned and said to Godfrey, 'Serin's teeth!'

Godfrey didn't react immediately. Instead, he looked back up the way they'd come and began to walk. His stance, his rigid shoulders spoke of a man close to the end of his tether – the exact opposite of the impression he'd given in front of Kenrick. Osbert knew this could only mean trouble, but within Kenrick's castle was not the place to discuss it.

Glad to be out of it, Osbert walked alongside Godfrey as they wound their way through the castle and out into the main courtyard. There, Osbert's guards awaited him. By the time they were clear of the door, the two men had fallen in behind and Osbert finally regained the power of speech.

'Brome still refuses to make the changes?'

'You're asking me about Brome when you've just been told to betray the entire Sacred Trust of the Guilde?' Godfrey said in disgust.

'And what do you suggest I do to stop it?'

'Hah! You sound like you don't want to – which we both know is a lie.'

'If I don't give him what he wants, he'll just find another who will.'

'And you can still ask about Brome as though you care about his fate?' Godfrey snapped back.

Osbert waved his arm towards the Sunset Tower, a black gash against the night sky, buried within the depths of the castle wall. 'Look around you, Godfrey. Up there in cages hang the remains of good men arrested for no good reason. Do you think I want to see *any* more suffer the same fate?' Osbert dropped his voice to a whisper. 'He's refusing to make the changes, yes?'

'That's right.' Godfrey replied, his voice hard, his face set.

'How are you going to get around that?'

'Why? Have you a suggestion?'

'Forgive me, you're right. Church business is Church business. But I am curious. I recall, many years ago, a Guilde Governor in the depths of trouble, and a careful priest who offered the comfort of a listening ear. That Guildesman would now like to offer the same in return.'

Godfrey grunted in something that sounded like bitter laughter. 'As I remember it, that Governor chose not to reveal his problems to the priest.'

'Have we not come some distance since then?'

'You know as well as I do what will happen if those laws are not changed by Caslemas. You heard the King. You saw what—'

'Then my advice, if you care to take it, is to use whatever means necessary to ensure Brome begins work tonight.'

'And what if I am not able to convince him? What then?'

Osbert waited until they'd passed through the castle gates before putting his hand on Godfrey's arm, halting the priest in his stride. 'The King's Council has no power to halt this. Kenrick has deliberately stacked the numbers so that he has absolute control, so there is no level of appeal. You have no choice. The laws against sorcery *must* be changed.

Forget Brome's safety – Kenrick has now made it *your* responsibility!'

Godfrey looked at him with an unreadable expression.

Osbert wanted to laugh – would have done, if the entire subject didn't make him sick to his stomach. 'I find it amazing Brome has held out so long.'

'Why? Because you thought yourself so much stronger and yet you gave in without a fight? Just as you did tonight?'

'What do you want from me? Do you want to see me sacrifice my life for the sake of a principle?'

'What would you have done if Vaughn had still been alive today, in Brome's position? You know what a harridan Vaughn was on the subject of sorcery. With Kenrick breathing down his neck, Vaughn would have refused to make the required changes and dared the King to do something about it. So if Vaughn was still alive—'

'We don't know he's dead. He vanished, remember?'

'But if Vaughn was here and he was asking you for guidance, what would you tell him? You hated him. Would you let him die, or advise him to capitulate?'

'I would have told him to make the changes. Just as you have done with Brome.'

'You don't know I told him that.'

'No?' Osbert pulled in a sharp breath. 'Just as I don't know that you secretly hope for the Outlaw to bring an army against Kenrick one day, destroy Nash and relieve us all of this problem once and for all?' Osbert paused to watch the expression on Godfrey's face change so subtly, nobody else would have noticed. Then he went on, 'I received word last night that one of my grain shipments headed for Mayenne was waylaid somewhere near Shan Moss, vanished into thin air. I can only assume that the Outlaw had something to do with it – but I dare not go to Kenrick with my suspicions. We can wait all our lives for Robert Douglas to do something. I don't know what he plans or how soon he intends to act. I can tell you the people will be behind him – they always have been, damn them. But what I would really like to know is, why is he taking so damned long? When we are being forced into one terrible position after another – and you and I are arguing about something we agree on?'

'Do we agree?' Godfrey's voice dropped to a murmur and, for the first time, Osbert became aware of the fact that they were standing in the middle of the square and another light drift of snow had begun to fall. None of that disguised the fact that Godfrey was expecting him to answer, to decide once and for all whether he was prepared to take the Douglas's side or not.

But how could he, when he had no more chance of survival at that man's hands than with Nash?

Instead of replying, he held up his hands, beginning to feel the cold. 'I'm sorry, Godfrey, the issue remains the same. You must convince Brome to change the laws. I strongly urge you to go now and do exactly that.'

Godfrey opened his mouth to speak, but an enraged voice from behind them bellowed, echoing through the stone square. 'Traitor!'

Stunned, Osbert could not move in time to avoid the blow that fell towards him from his own guard, but Godfrey could. With one swift shove, Osbert went flying. By the time he scrambled to his knees, he caught a flash of steel, three bodies engaged in battle and a dark lump sprawled close by. Scurrying towards it, Osbert carefully reached out a hand to roll Godfrey over. His face was too pale, but after a moment, the eyes flickered open.

Another bellow of rage and Osbert looked up. His two guards were fighting with a third man, an expert swordsman by the look of him, except that . . .

'By the gods,' Godfrey said as he scrambled to his feet, reaching to Osbert for a steadying hand. Even as they watched, one guard stumbled and fell. The other quickened the pace of his blows, but their saviour had weight and skill on his side. With a sickening thud, the second guard fell to his death. In the silence, Godfrey spoke again. 'DeMassey?'

The man turned slowly. He knelt down and wiped his blade on the cloak of one of the dead guards. 'I heard them talking of assassination before you came out. I wasn't sure if they were serious or not and thought it best to follow them.' DeMassey got to his feet, his gaze flickering over Osbert, to pause on Godfrey. 'I suggest you get to your apartments now, my lords. Some nights these streets aren't safe.'

With that, DeMassey sketched a short bow, then turned and headed back towards the castle.

'In Serin's name, what is *he* doing saving our necks?'

'I don't know,' Godfrey murmured, still watching the man as he walked away. 'But I can make a good guess. You do realise he heard every word you said?'

Osbert swallowed hard. 'I . . . oh, hell!'

'There's your door, Osbert. Go inside and start looking to your own advice.' Godfrey began walking towards the Basilica.

'What are you going to do?' Osbert called after him.

'I'm going to bed,' Godfrey replied, without pausing. 'It's been a very long day.'

Godfrey got inside the door of his room, turned the key in the lock and rested back on it, drawing in breaths deep and cleansing – or at least, that was the plan. In reality, they did nothing to ease his fright, nor the worry which now coursed around his insides like a whirlpool, stirring up too many troubles he'd hoped never to see again.

These were the times the Church needed a man like Aiden McCauly as its Bishop. His courage, his intelligence, his character was something the Church lacked terribly, and try as he might, Godfrey knew he was not the man to step into that breach.

But McCauly was not here. He was somewhere safe, over the border, where Kenrick couldn't find him and execute him. Some place where he worked alongside Robert.

What would McCauly make of this dilemma? Godfrey had raged against Osbert for his path of expedience – but wasn't *he* demanding Brome do the same thing, for much the same reasons?

So much for all his grand principles now.

Godfrey's gaze drifted, for comfort, over the simple furnishings in his room, the clean lines and plain designs he had chosen deliberately for their ability to help him think without clutter. Finally, as though directed there by some unknown force, he found himself looking at his desk, at the pile of books on one corner, the papers on the other, the ink stand and the chair behind.

Without thought now, he went straight to it and sat down. He pulled a sheet of fresh paper towards him, dipped his pen in the ink and set about writing a letter to Robert.

By Caslemas, Kenrick had said. By midwinter, the King planned to start gathering young sorcerers from around the country, offering them gold and a place in his court in exchange for their skills to be at his service. What Kenrick would want with them Godfrey could only imagine – but he knew it couldn't be anything good.

His only hope was that he could get a warning to Robert in time for him to do something to stop it.

9

Bishop Aiden McCauly remained kneeling as the last notes of the *Te Deum* floated up into the roof of St Julian's Chapel. Light flooded through the smooth-arched windows high above, but it was more the ancient stone of worn rose red that gave this place its atmosphere of welcome. Soft incense still hung in the air and despite the winter chill, this place held a warmth he hadn't found anywhere else.

He'd been made to feel very welcome by the Brothers here. The Abbot of St Julian's had given him his own apartments, allowed him access to libraries and scribes, and accorded him all the respect due his rank. It didn't seem to matter to the Abbot that Aiden was not a native of Flan'har and would one day – hopefully – return to Lusara. In return, the Abbot merely asked that Aiden not make any attempt to sway the monks on the touchy and sometimes volatile subject of sorcery. So far, this request had been easy to fulfil.

Of course, Aiden knew he was here largely because Flan'har's Duke, Grant Kavanagh, had insisted upon it. Even so, Aiden had only ever felt at home in this place, and every day said prayers of thanks that he'd been so fortunate in his exile.

As monks filed out of the quire in solemn procession, serene in their quiet, dignified faith, Aiden's gaze followed them. Had he once appeared so sure? Had he once been so arrogant?

A private smile creased his face and he turned into the aisle. A few steps along and the smile faded completely. He'd lost his arrogance a long time ago – roughly about the same time he'd met Robert Douglas.

It was so frustrating not knowing what to do! He'd spent hours in prayer, asking for guidance. He'd talked and listened, spending much time with the Lusaran refugees who struggled across the border. He listened to their stories, their woes; heard the strength and the despair in their voices – and yet, even with all that tumbling together in his mind, he was still no closer to an answer.

Already tired with the day, he stepped out of the church. He could see the bleak sky, outlined by the compact cloister roof. On the ground inside the square, small headstones were layered in icy white from snow that had fallen the day before. There would be more today.

Tucking his hands beneath the folds of his habit, he turned and headed for the refectory, following after the other monks. The moment he stepped inside, the flavour of the air changed and he could smell fresh bread baked that morning. A low and familiar voice murmured his name.

'Good morning, Father McCauly.'

Aiden turned, then smiled in genuine welcome. 'Why, Sir Alexander Deverin! How are you?'

The big man came closer, his own smile refreshing the lined face and greying beard. 'I am very well, Father. And you?'

'Fit. Very fit. I wasn't sure what day you would be arriving.'

Deverin spread his hands. 'I was entirely dependent on the weather, Father. There are heavy drifts of snow in the south, around Bleakstone. I could not leave for two days or I would have been here sooner. I would ask a favour of you, if I may?'

'Of course,' Aiden gestured to the cloister door. 'Let's walk.'

Deverin followed him out into the cloister, wandering amiably with his hands behind his back. As Master at Arms to Robert's father, this man had been largely responsible for teaching Robert about all things martial and, to this day, remained faithful to the House of Douglas, despite all the hardships of the last ten years. Aiden had often wondered how Robert would have fared without the invaluable support of men like Deverin. Like himself, Deverin was showing his age, his thick beard almost white now, his face tanned and lined, yet his eyes still sparkled with determination and though he carried his share of battle scars, his body remained fit and healthy.

'And how is your wife?' Aiden began. 'Have you finally settled into married life again?'

Deverin chuckled deeply, 'Matilde is wonderful, though she has so much energy, she picks me up and sweeps me along with her. For a man my age, I'm not sure that's so good.'

'Well, you should have thought of that before you married her.'

'Aye, I should,' Deverin grinned. 'Which brings me to the favour I wanted to ask. I'll be moving Matilde and the baby to St Julian's in the next few weeks. I expect I'll be away much over the coming months, so I was wondering if you would perhaps keep an eye on them. My boy will likely be coming with me, but he's well old enough to look after himself. It's Matilde and the baby that worry me. She hasn't ever been through this with me before.'

'Of course. I'd be delighted to.' Aiden accompanied this with a smile, but he wished he could give this man more. Playing guessing games without Robert around was a tiring business.

Aiden chose a door in the passage leading from the cloister to a gate. Beyond were the monastery gardens sitting alongside the village of St Julian's. The small house he used as his own looked out over the same gardens. He pushed the gate open and tried to find some hint of sun somewhere in the sky.

'Have you seen any of the others?' Deverin kept his voice low, aware of the lay brothers who worked in the vegetable patch a stone's throw away. 'I saw Lord Daniel arrive late last night.'

'And Owen?'

'He travels slowly these days. I don't expect him until tomorrow.'

'Payne should arrive this evening, but with the weather the way it is, I hope he arrives sooner or the roads may be blocked.'

'And Robert? Any word on when he might return?'

Aiden replied, 'Soon, that's all I know. He keeps the specifics of his trips from me, so I can't give a better answer than that. You know what he's like, especially these days.'

'Aye.' Deverin paused before the village gate. The common stretched out before them, ringed on the east side by huge oak trees now bare of leaves. Beyond the common, the village jumbled together, tall houses and brown thatching covered in snow, chimneys belching smoke into the morning. 'Has he talked to you?' Deverin sounded like a man afraid he was committing treason.

'A little.'

'I have no wish for you to give out confidences,' Deverin rushed to assure him, 'but . . .' he paused, obviously troubled, 'I have concerns I dare not voice to his face.'

Aiden's eyes widened and he turned to the big man. Deverin was a soldier, a warrior at heart, but a man who loved peace and was willing to risk his life to achieve it. 'What concerns?'

Was Aiden not the only one who felt like this?

'Has he told you what he plans?'

'He's not yet explained the goal he wishes to achieve. I believe that's why he's called you all here now.'

A little relief flashed in Deverin's eyes, but the hard core of concern overwhelmed it. Deverin looked away, his gaze tightening, his jaw set. 'He's changed.'

There was so much in those few words, enough to send new ripples of fear through Aiden. He couldn't pretend not to understand what the man was talking about. 'Yes, he has changed.'

'I must see to my men, but I will attend mass in the morning. Until then, I will take my leave of you, Father.'

Deverin gave him a small bow, then pushed the common gate open. He was three long strides away before Aiden spoke, his question surging forth against better sense.

'If you're so unsure, why are you here?'

The soldier paused, turned and came back. 'Why are you?'

'That was not my question. Have you not served your time with Robert? Will he not allow you to retire in comfort, to enjoy your new family?'

A genuine smile spread across Deverin's face. 'Those were Matilde's very words to me when I left to come here. But you know it's not Robert who asks this of me. My honour demands it. Much as I love Robert, I would give the same loyalty to any man who had the power and the will to free Lusara. We all know Robert is the only man who can do this.'

The open honesty in the man's eyes was more refreshing than the cold winter's morning.

'And my concerns are nothing,' Deverin continued, 'in the face of the destruction of my country. I'll follow Robert until Lusara is free or until I die.' With that, Deverin turned and began walking away once more, his final comment floating on the clear air.

'And so will you.'

By dusk, thick wretched clouds had covered the sky, drowning the sunset and warning of a bad night to come. An hour after that, the first snow began to fall, wiping out texture and feature until Aiden could barely see across the courtyard to the infirmary.

Feeling the chill in the air, he got up from his desk and put more wood on the fire, watching as the flames danced around it. The room warmed slowly, but the light was good, rich and golden, bringing colour to the simple furnishings, round table, three chairs, tall bookcase, desk and rug on the floor. Across the windows were his one luxury: heavy drapes to keep in the heat, a deep green which suited any season.

He wandered to the window, pushed the cloth aside a little and peered out into the swirling snow. He spent too many hours looking out of this window, across the gardens and the common, over the roofs of the village and in the direction of Lusara. Of course, the border was a day's ride away, and though he would never see it from here, it was always in his mind: that line between danger and safety, between good and evil, between life and death.

He'd spent the last eight years enjoying the comforts of St Julian's. He'd been able to work, to write his letters and books; the physical demands on his body were minimal. He was in excellent health for a man of sixty and felt little of the infirmities he should, by rights, be suffering from – but a large part of that was because he walked each and every day, and ensured he took his turn at drawing water from the well and chopping wood for the kitchen fires.

A few of the monks, he was sure, thought he was crazy for doing work that could easily be done by others, but two years locked in a prison cell had taught Aiden that there was a joy to be had in any task that was performed in freedom.

Some commotion from the courtyard intruded on his thoughts. He quickly picked up his cloak and swung it over his shoulders. Collecting the lamp from his desk, he hurried down the stairs and outside.

The night air bit with a vengeance. Huge flakes of snow almost blinded him, but he could see shapes moving through the abbey gate: people, two horses and a small cart.

More refugees.

Without hesitation, Aiden headed towards them. Already some of the brothers had arrived to see to the people, their voices rising above the noise, calming, reassuring. Aiden did his best to help, urging tired and terrified children indoors where it was warmer, issuing instructions for the animals to be taken care of, all with that same deep well of something he might have identified as despair if he hadn't already determined never to tread that path.

So many people now, fleeing tyranny.

There were some twenty of them in all, the last still struggling through the gate, some limping, some carrying meagre possessions. And behind them, a figure he recognised with a sudden mixture of delight and overwhelming relief.

'Robert!'

The curtain of snow almost parted and Robert emerged, his dark hair damp around his shoulders. Tall, powerful, his cloak muddied, in his arms he carried a child; his horse bore a woman.

He looked a little hunched with exhaustion, his steps almost stumbling. The dark gaze flickered to Aiden, full of pain. A flash of a smile spoke silent greeting, and then he attended to his charges, handing the child over to a monk before helping the woman down from his horse.

Aiden lost sight of Robert after that. Some of the refugees were sick, others were wounded. As they settled, some in the infirmary, some into the guest quarters, a familiar quiet fell over them, one Aiden had been witness to before. This was relief, this was thanksgiving, but it was also the sadness of people displaced and dispossessed, who wondered what their lives would be from this day forward.

He spoke to none of them at length. The time for that would be later, perhaps tomorrow, or in a week, when the shock had worn off, when they would have most need of whatever words of comfort and counsel he could offer.

It tore him apart to do this work. It tore him apart that it *needed* to be done.

And then the church bell tolled midnight and he emerged back into the courtyard with Robert following close behind. He paused long enough to get a good look at the man, framed as he was in the flickering light of a row of torches along the walls. 'Come into the house. You look about ready to collapse,' he ordered.

'You've convinced me. I've been travelling through snow since I left Shan Moss more than a week ago. I could almost believe it's been following me deliberately.'

'And what were you doing in Shan Moss?'

'Is Deverin here yet? And Owen? I lost track of time. I thought I'd be here two days ago, but I got delayed.'

'The refugees?'

'Yes.'

Aiden didn't question him further; the story would emerge

soon enough – or at least, the parts of it Robert was prepared to share. He led Robert inside and up the stairs into the small bedroom he kept for these visits. Leaving Robert to settle, he went into his study to retrieve some coals to start a fire. By the time he returned, Robert had dropped his cloak over a chair and collapsed on the bed. His eyes were closed, his breathing gentle and even.

With a smile, Aiden set the coals in the fireplace and waited long enough to make sure they had caught. Then he spread a blanket over Robert and left as silently as he could. He had prayers to say before bed, and not just for those poor people across the courtyard.

The morning brought a gloomy half-light which spread over fields thick with snow. Every flat surface on the monastery matched that grey-white, leaving only damp stone corners here and there to mark occasional features. The walk back from morning prayers froze Aiden's nose, forced the air out of his mouth in dense clouds and made him fear he'd lost his toes completely.

Without pausing, he pushed his door open and headed upstairs to his study – where he stopped at the door.

Robert stood there, naked from the waist up, holding a dressing to a wound in his side, while a monk from the infirmary wound a bandage around his middle. The monk smiled a greeting and Robert raised his eyebrows in the closest thing Aiden was likely to get as apology.

Why, in the name of the gods, hadn't he said something last night? More to the point, why hadn't Aiden noticed that Robert was injured?

'Good morning.' Aiden stripped off his cloak and hung it up, moving to build up the fire so Robert would at least avoid freezing to death. As he turned back, he noticed something sitting on the desk that hadn't been there last night. 'What's this?'

'It's for you,' was Robert's reply.

Frowning, Aiden moved towards the cloth-covered bundle and lifted the wrap away. Beneath was an exquisite book stand,

140

carved and detailed like the woven threads of a bough of ivy, solid and strong. Sitting on the sturdy ledge was a small soft-leather pouch. Gingerly Aiden opened it and slid a silver-bound disk of polished glass into his palm.

'I don't understand,' he murmured, looking up to find Robert watching him with thinly veiled expectation.

'They're a gift for you.' Robert said with a little smile on his face. 'You shouldn't have to squint or get a sore neck when you read. That's all. It's nothing.'

Aiden was overwhelmed. The book stand was heavy and would have been a trial to carry; the glass was very fragile. 'Thank you,' he said, the words inadequate.

Robert thanked the monk and waited for him to leave before pulling on his shirt and flashing Aiden one of those famous smiles. 'I was about to come looking for you. We have to talk.'

Robert Douglas had always been a force not easily refused. At forty-three, it seemed his energy, his passion and determination were never to age; his looks were those of a man ten years younger. He still had the power to dominate any gathering by virtue of his personality, his confidence, his smile and dry humour, but in a room as small as this, the walls strained to contain him.

But Deverin was right – Robert *had* changed over the last eight years.

'How are Murdoch and the others?'

'They're all well, off to their winter homes as usual.'

'How did you get injured?'

'It's nothing,' Robert waved a hand, pushing his arms through his jacket sleeves. 'Just a brief argument with some of Kenrick's men.'

'Oh? In the same place where Selar wounded you?'

Robert finished getting dressed and failed to reply.

'By my count, that's the fourth time you've been wounded in the same place.'

'It happens.'

'Does it? I wouldn't know.' Aiden swallowed down the fear that rose in him again and tried not to sound like a petulant fishwife. 'Are you . . . dropping your guard on that side? Or favouring it? There must be some reason for—'

When Robert didn't reply, Aiden said nothing until Robert had no choice but to meet his gaze. 'You don't make it very easy for me, do you?'

Robert spread his hands. 'What do you want me to say? I got injured. It doesn't matter.'

'It matters to *me*.'

With half a smile, Robert turned to the fire and took a copper pot away from the heat. 'But it doesn't matter to me. Not in the long run. I'm still here, aren't I? Still alive? I can still fight. Does it really matter if I get injured now and then?'

'I'm not going to win this one, am I?'

'Stop worrying, Bishop.' Robert turned back to him, taking his hand and putting a warm mug into it. 'I made some brew. Drink. The morning will seem the better for it.'

Aiden gave up. When Robert turned back to the desk, he deliberately changed the subject. 'Did you find everything?' Aiden had laid out the letters and other documents last night after Robert had fallen asleep. 'Are there any problems I should know about?'

'No, you've done your usual excellent job, Bishop.' Robert pulled a single sheet of paper from the piles, unfolding it slowly between distracted fingers. 'You manage my investments as well as any Guildesman could.'

Aiden made a rude noise and Robert smirked in response.

'Take that as a compliment, Bishop. It appears my finances will keep us for another year.'

Another year? Aiden successfully suppressed his reaction to that. Robert had lost his lands at Dunlorn and elsewhere, but he had managed to rescue his family's possessions outside of Lusara, which, for reasons Aiden had never been able to fathom, he left in the hands of a renegade Bishop who knew too little about finance to do more than hold on to what he'd started with. However, for their purposes, it appeared to be enough.

But another year? Could Lusara last that long? Could Robert?

He turned towards the window where the drapes were open to allow in the meagre light. As casually as he could, he said, 'And the letters? Anything I should know about?'

'Nothing too exciting, I'm afraid – though I haven't got to the bottom of them yet. I haven't seen one from Patric.'

'No. But that might just mean that he's already on his way back.'

'Aye, it might. We can only hope. What's this?'

Aiden turned to find him turning a sealed letter over and over in his hands.

'Oh, that arrived two, no, three days ago. I don't know who it's from.'

Robert went to open it, but then stopped himself, as though he didn't want to get distracted. Instead, he took the sheet he'd picked up earlier and handed it to Aiden without fanfare. 'Read that.'

Frowning, Aiden took it, read it, stared at the words with eyes that couldn't absorb such wild news.

The Guilde . . . reversing laws . . . sorcery? This had to be some sort of joke!

'I take it,' Robert said quietly, 'that you'd not heard?'

'No! But are you sure it's true?'

'That's an official notice I took from a Guildehall.'

Aiden read the paper a second time. Impossible – and yet, there they were. 'On the surface, it looks like a piece of insanity.'

'How do you think Brome will handle it?' Robert wandered to the fireplace.

'Brome hasn't been well over the last year.' With abrupt disgust, Aiden tossed the notice onto his desk. 'He'll probably bluster – but the chances of him putting up any kind of opposition are very slim indeed. He'll either do it, or he'll die and some other fool will do it in his place. Either way—'

He came to a halt when he realised Robert was laughing softly.

'What?'

'Oh, Bishop. So many years and I thought I'd successfully convinced you. If I have failed here, what hope have I left?'

'What are you talking about?' Robert's laughter dried up, leaving behind a flash of pain and disappointment. 'Am I missing something?'

'So much, and yet, nothing at all,' Robert replied obliquely. 'Are you really so horrified that, after almost six hundred years, my kind are no longer anathema, at least according to the Guilde? That it will no longer be legal to hunt us down like vermin? To burn us alive at the stake? Is that really so terrible? If it is, I wonder why you've been writing books about just such things for the last eight years.'

Aiden grunted, seeing all too well. 'And I suppose you see nothing wrong in the peremptory and illegal manner in which centuries-old laws are being overturned without regard to the proper process and the will of the people.'

Robert raised his eyebrows in disbelief this time. 'The will of which people? *My* people, the Salti Pazar – *sorcerers* – get murdered and you talk about proper process? By the gods, Bishop! Where has your sense of justice gone?'

'Apparently the same place as yours.' Aiden turned to the sideboard and pulled the stopper out of the flask of ale he kept there for Robert's visits. He poured out two cups and handed one to the Duke. 'There is a reason things are done the way they are. Those laws – and hundreds of others – are there to protect the people. Surely you can appreciate that.'

'Certainly,' Robert's voice came back with that same hard edge. 'But Osbert has just given us something we've all been working towards for years, you more than anyone else. This is a free gift. According to you, Brome will do the same. So what if the change isn't entirely legal? Does it matter? Surely the death of oppression is good in any form.'

'By the gods, man, are you blind all of a sudden?' Aiden snapped, determined to pound sense into him. 'You know full well the reason the people trust the Guilde and Church is because of those same laws, because there is that process to be followed, because that process protects them against upstarts and usurpers. If those laws can be changed like that,' he clicked his fingers, 'what other laws will soon follow? The people of Lusara have already lost faith in the Crown. They will also now lose faith in both Guilde and Church – and where will that leave them? Without an anchor and without hope. How then will they view sorcery? The gift from the gods you claim it to be?'

Robert stared at him for a moment, then, abruptly, he looked away. 'I never said that. And those laws didn't protect them against Selar.' He paced away a little, reaching the desk and pausing there, one finger tracing the edge of the notice, his stance rigid and uncompromising. 'You don't understand what it's like to be born with something that you're told is inherently wrong, to find the pillar establishments legislate against something you have no choice in being.' He paused, lifting his head enough for Aiden to see a glitter of hatred in those green eyes. 'Even if I'd never once used my *gifts*, I would still be called evil, still executed. You have written your books because to you, there are intellectual questions to be answered, an imbalance of understanding about sorcery, and you seek to redress that. For me, on the inside, losing these laws is something to rejoice in – regardless of how much a trap they are. I have spent so much time trying to release Lusara from a much lesser tyranny, all at the expense of the Salti, who have nobody to champion their cause. Perhaps if I had paid more attention to it then . . .'

Robert didn't finish that thought. Instead he turned, his expression unreadable. 'So you see, proper process means little to me and to others born like me. No matter Osbert's reasons for doing this, no matter if the laws are overturned in six months – for *this* time, I am not an abomination, and my people, however trapped in history they may be, are, for a moment, honestly free. Can you understand that much, Bishop?'

He could understand – and was touched. He had rarely heard Robert speak so eloquently and so freely. He offered up a smile of understanding. When Robert gave him one of his own in reply, Aiden sipped his ale and said, 'What do you mean by it being a trap?'

Robert's eyes hardened. 'Kenrick or Nash have obviously issued an instruction to Osbert, and probably Brome. I have no doubt that the whole thing is designed to draw Salti out into the open.'

Aiden swallowed loudly, choosing his words carefully. 'Should we be sending a warning to the Enclave?'

'If I can see it, they will.'

'Even so, we need to consider how the people are going to react to this. Up until what, about sixteen years ago, sorcery was little more than a myth. I would think the people are very confused about the entire issue.'

Robert nodded absently as he turned his attention to the sealed letter in his hands, forgotten until now. He broke the wax and unfolded the paper, reading quickly. For a moment, he froze.

Fathomless green eyes gave nothing away, though something of an old vulnerability filtered through the unguarded gaze.

'What is it?' Aiden frowned, worried.

Robert blinked and his gaze cleared a little. He took a breath and continued, as though nothing had happened, 'Confused? Yes, I suppose they would be.' He slipped the folded letter inside his jacket, then turned back to Aiden with a face that held no expression at all. 'I heard Deverin and Payne have arrived. Owen is expected this morning some time. Could you send word for them to come here, discreetly? This afternoon? I . . . need to go out for a while.'

'Of course. They've been waiting for such a . . .'

'So have we all.' Robert's gaze fractured then, drifting once more out of the window to rest on some place far in the distance. Perhaps he was looking at and imagining that same border, that same boundary between one state of being and another.

And then he was gone.

It was the strangest feeling, riding through the snow, riding back into the past. As the white-sheathed landscape was draped by fresh veils of falling flakes, Robert could almost imagine that same powerful sorcery was pushing him back through the years, to the last time he'd seen David Maclean, one of his most influential, and yet powerless enemies.

Micah's father.

There had once been a time when he'd spent hours framing words he could use on the man, to change his mind, to convince him that in taking a seat on Selar's Council, Robert had not been committing an act of treason against his people. He'd seen the sorrow in Micah's eyes, understood how hard it was for him to reconcile the father he loved and the friend he believed in. He'd stood by and watched that huge family almost split apart from taking sides in an argument that should never have happened in the first place.

Long after he left St Julian's, he rode down into a still valley where a dozen winter houses sat close by each other for company. A tiny church stood to the east of the hamlet and he stopped only when he reached the shadows of its tower.

He didn't pause. Instead, he ignored the pulling of his wound and swung down from the horse, tying it to a post. With his feet crunching into iced snow, he entered the church-yard.

Rough grey stones stood up from the white ground in eager rows, small fences between this world and the next. He walked without direction and yet, unerringly, his feet took him to the right place, where fresh-turned earth scorched the placid ground, where the dead warmth was almost visible.

'Good morning, Your Grace.'

Robert didn't turn, but there was a thread of the familiar in that voice. He let out a sigh and wished he hadn't. 'When did it happen?'

Footsteps came towards him, carefully, stopping at his side. 'Four days ago. The end itself was swift.'

'He'd been ill for a long time, hadn't he?'

'Aye, for the last year. He . . . hated it.'

'I'm sorry.'

'We know.'

'Do you?' Robert turned then, facing the man who stood there. Light blue eyes, some fine lines around them, wavy red hair and the shadow of freckles. Tall, fit, tanned. A gaze open with truth and without fear.

So like Micah.

'I'm Durrill Maclean, Your Grace. Next youngest after Micah.'

'Yes,' Robert murmured, 'I remember.' And he did, perhaps too well. 'How is your mother?'

'Sad, but well enough, considering.'

'And your brothers? Sisters? Is there anything I can do?'

A frail but genuine smile lit the familiar and yet different face. 'Thank you, Your Grace, but no. All that could be done is done. My father died as he had lived. He . . . he spoke of you, on his last night.'

'I'm sorry.' Apologies seemed all he could offer now. After all, the Maclean family had been settled and prosperous once, until he had revealed himself as a sorcerer, until he had waged war against his own King. Then, by deed of proximity, by virtue of the fact that his closest friend was this man's brother, the entire family had been forced to flee for fear of reprisal. They'd settled here, buying a modest farm with the small resources they'd brought with them. They'd done well, but nothing would replace what they had lost.

Just like so many others.

'He could never forgive you.'

Robert looked up again.

'My father.' Durrill shrugged, as though the act of indifference was holding him together. 'There was some stubborn mark in him that wouldn't allow it, no matter what you did. He said you didn't have it in you to be ruthless enough. He said you didn't deserve forgiveness. Micah always said that it was not for my father to judge, either way.' Robert looked away from the truth in those words.

The younger man stood in silence for a moment, then spoke again, words flowing from him in what sounded like a prepared speech. 'When you move, Your Grace, we . . . my brothers and I, we would like to go with you. To help in what way we can. There are only five of us and though we've fought no battles, we are trained well enough.'

Robert's eyes widened, turning on the man before him. 'With your father not a week in his grave? He hated me! And you would fight alongside me?'

Durrill raised his eyebrows, an easy and relieved smile belying his age. 'It is not our place to judge you.'

That simple-voiced faith ran through Robert like cold water. 'Thank you.'

Durrill took a step back. 'We will be ready to leave whenever you send word.' He gave Robert a slight bow, then turned to walk away. Robert didn't allow him more than two steps.

'Have you sent word to . . .'

'Micah?' Durrill faced him once more, his smile gone, replaced by the shadows of mourning. 'Aye, we have.' He paused, as though preparing his next words. 'My lord, we know nothing of why he left your side. However, we . . . we would all welcome whatever reconciliation might be achieved in time.'

Each word landed hard inside Robert and he felt the blackness seethe and bubble for a moment, soaking up that sentiment. The demon took what nourishment it could get.

Reconciliation? With Micah?

Yet this man watched him with hope in his eyes, as much as Micah had ever done. 'Please pass on my best wishes to your mother.'

Durrill smiled, turned and walked away. Soon even the sounds of his footsteps were gone and Robert was alone with the ghost of David Maclean.

10

'They told us the land didn't belong to us any more and that it was best that we leave. Papa didn't want to go and Mama wanted to stay and fight them. But Papa and me, we'd seen them, how many there were. We saw the swords and the lances and the looks in their eyes. They just marched into the house and started throwing our things out onto the snow. They only let us take one horse and a cart. When Papa tried to take the other horse, they put a knife against his throat. Then . . . when one of the soldiers . . . got Mama, my brother ran to help her. They . . . they killed him and his blood went all in the snow.

Mama cried. They laughed at us. We filled the cart with things they let us keep and then we left but we stopped when we got to the woods because Mama was crying and Papa had some cuts that needed binding. Mama was angry with the soldiers and the King. She wanted to kill them. I think Papa did too, but he didn't say anything. He just had this horrible look in his eyes when he looked out of the woods, back at the house. I . . . was scared.

'Then Papa said he'd rather burn the house down than let the King have it, that a man was better dead than disowned. Then this . . . man came out of the woods towards us. He was riding this big roan horse and he carried a huge sword. Papa was ready to fight but the man he . . . he . . .'

Aiden sat forward, reaching out with a gentle hand to the boy's shoulder. Soothingly, he stroked until the wide eyes looked up again. 'Go on.'

The boy continued, 'The man said that Papa shouldn't throw his life away when the King wouldn't even notice. He said we should leave and go with him. He said the soldiers would look after our farm because the King wanted money from it. The man said that we should go with him, to where it was safe, and then he promised we could go back home soon. Please, Father, are we safe now?'

Swallowing a lump in his throat, Aiden glanced from the boy to the young girl sitting silently beside him, perched on the wooden bench as though she'd just been placed there. She hadn't said a word, but watched him and her brother with enormous haunted eyes.

'Yes, you're safe now.' Aiden wanted to promise them that everything would be all right, but the words stuck inside him.

Looking down at his sister, the boy asked, 'What will happen to us now?'

Aiden sat back in his chair. This was the inevitable question that was always so difficult to answer – especially for a child who understood nothing of politics and for whom a power struggle was limited to seeing his mother in full flight against a man he knew nothing about. Gathering himself, Aiden forced a smile onto his face, making sure it was genuine. 'You and your family can stay here and rest as long as you like. The monks will look after you. Then, when your parents have recovered, you can find a new home for a while, until it's safe to go back to Lusara.'

Both children looked at him then, still a little wary, but the boy offered a slight grin and that was enough. Then their gazes shifted as the door behind him opened. Aiden turned in his chair and gave a smile of welcome to the man who entered the infirmary, though he looked uncomfortable, as he always did when walking around inside a house of the gods, as though he had sins to be forgiven that he could keep from them if he tried.

Aiden got to his feet and the man came towards him. 'Good afternoon, Father. I see you're working hard as always.'

Everard Payne, Earl of Cannockburke, exuded charm, bestowing it on the children before him while looking around at the effects of last night's arrival. 'Deverin told me Robert had brought in another batch of refugees. Have they settled in?'

'They appear to be comfortable, given the circumstances. There are a couple of injuries and a bad fever between them, but nothing dangerous.'

'Excellent.' Payne said as he caught Aiden's elbow. 'Could I speak to you for a moment?'

'Of course.' Aiden took his leave of the children and allowed the Earl to usher him outside. The air was cold and damp, the sky still heavy and grey, as though St Julian's had been cut off from the rest of the world.

Payne began quietly, keeping his voice low from the others working or passing through the courtyard, 'Do you know where Robert has gone?'

'He just said that he had to go out.'

Payne ran his hands through his short fair hair, then put them on his hips, a gesture of impatience and some irritation. 'You know David Maclean is dead?'

A wash of something flew over Aiden then. 'Sweet Mineah!' he breathed. This was not something Robert needed right now – and poor Micah . . .

151

'So Robert said nothing about it?'

'No.' But there was little doubt in him that Robert had gone to see the Maclean family.

Payne pursed his lips, his gaze penetrating. 'This can't go on much longer. We need to get moving, damn it!'

'Please,' Aiden whispered, 'keep your voice down!'

'Father,' Payne moved closer, dropping his own voice. 'We need to make Robert see what's really going on here. He used to have so much support, but he's taken so long to move against Kenrick, there are men who think he's past it, or that he's become too involved with the sorcery issue – or worse, that he's become unhinged in some way. One of the major reasons Robert held so much support was because he was trusted to only ever do the right thing, but you must agree that eight years is too long for any man! The things I've heard are . . .'

'What?'

'You know what they call this, Father? The Silent Rebellion, because nobody's talking about it. And nobody's talking about it, because there's nothing to talk about! What is Robert waiting for?'

Aiden wished all Payne's concerns were unfounded – but he'd heard the same things from others, here and there. Had Robert? He received so many letters while he was away. Surely there would be some mention, some word of the danger further delays would bring.

But he'd called a meeting. Because of Osbert?

'I don't think we'll be waiting too much longer,' he murmured, sending up a prayer that he wouldn't be made a liar with that statement.

Payne took it in his stride. 'No? Good. Well, Deverin, Daniel and Owen are waiting in your study. Now all we need is—'

His words were cut off by the clatter of hooves entering the courtyard. They turned to find Robert riding in, his dark hair flowing behind him. He gave Payne a nod, then met Aiden's gaze with only a hint that not everything was as it seemed.

Aiden silenced his thoughts, his questions. Yes, he would

soon have some answers, but now he wasn't sure he was going to like what Robert had to say.

The cold hemmed him in on all sides. Though the ride was over, though this room was lit with torches and firelight, though the stone walls were strong and stout, the cold still penetrated, accompanying him wherever he went, a shadow even the brightest summer could not chase away.

Robert stood before the fire, his eyes closed long enough to ease the sting of the night air. He sipped again from the small bottle he carried with him, hoping the drug would keep the pain at bay as long as he needed it to.

Only two things would make a difference to this future. Either Patric would finally return, bearing news of the Prophecy. Or – and this was the most useful but the least likely – Robert could try finding the Calyx.

He was certain the Calyx held a lot more information than previously believed. If he could just find the damned thing, he might be able to find the real Prophecy, or at least get a context for this one. He could learn if there was text missing from it. And, of course, it was Salti legend that the Calyx held the way for them to live outside their prison, though how they could ever manage that in the present climate, he couldn't begin to guess.

He took in a breath and held it, summoning up the power easily. Out he went, sending his Senses along the road, Seeking west, turning to avoid a hill. Further and further he travelled, over the border, back into his beautiful Lusara, picking up faint traces here and there of living things, people, animals, birds and others. He knew them all, ignored each one and moved on further again, travelling north now, into more darkness, until he found what he was looking for.

So different to the aura of any other sorcerer, and so familiar, after all these years. Unscarred, and yet strong, very strong.

He couldn't stop the smile creasing his face. At least this felt good, in its own way.

With a sigh, he let out the breath he'd been holding,

withdrew carefully and opened his eyes again, peering out into a night filled with evil weather. It would be hard travelling tomorrow, but it would get even worse if he left it much longer.

A door behind him opened, letting in other noises, voices, footsteps, the unmistakable sounds of men moving into the room. Only when silence fell did he turn around and face those who had gathered here.

At the table sat one of his oldest friends, Lord Daniel Courtenay. As boys, they had fought with sticks under the watchful eye of their fathers. With his fair hair thinning on top, his girth expanding a little more each year, Daniel's appearance belied his fighting ability – but like so many of his kind, Daniel had a carefully buried streak of toughness deep inside him.

The next man would see none of the fighting, unless from a safe distance. Deverin had served Robert's father faithfully for many years, had fought Selar on Seluth Common and at Nanmoor, had taken up his sword again at Shan Moss and now walked with a limp from a wound that had healed badly. Beside him sat Owen Fitzallan, the patch over one eye testament to his efforts at the Battle of Shan Moss. Like Deverin, he had spent most of his life in the service of the Douglas family and now, in his later years, he still strived to serve as he could.

Opposite, his hands laced neatly together as though he were not impatient, but calm and composed, sat Aiden McCauly, rightful Bishop of Lusara, a man whose loyalty to his own people had never once been in doubt. Despite imprisonment and exile, Aiden had refused to move too far from the border, not wanting to be more than a day's ride from the soil he wished one day to be buried in.

The last man at the table looked out of place with these would-be rebels, even though, deep down inside, he was as much of their ilk as anyone. Everard Payne had been handsome as a youth and as a young man. Now almost forty, he still carried his looks well. Perhaps not as rich as he'd once been, his clothing maintained his customary air of casual elegance; he looked under no illusions as to what was to be discussed here, nor of the costs involved.

A serving boy entered the room, placing a tray of wine and cups onto the table before Robert. Another boy followed, bringing food: sweet yellow bread and cold sliced bacon, onions and radishes and fruit tarts that left a lemon scent drifting in the air. Robert waited until they were done, then shut the door behind them. He waved his hand over the lock, setting a warning.

Slowly, he walked back to the end of the table, his gaze drifting to the heavy chest he'd brought up from its hiding place downstairs. He came to his chair and placed his hands on the back, before looking up into the first pair of eyes which met his: Aiden's.

'I'm sorry,' he began evenly. 'You've all had to wait a long time for this. Still, you're here now and for that, I thank you.' Robert could hear something in his own voice that sounded terribly final. 'Before I go any further, I want you to be clear on something. I won't have any of you travelling across the border to help. This time, there won't be an army, no battle and no war. At least, there won't be if I can help it. There's already been too much bloodshed in the name of this cause. However, I do need your help.'

'You know you have it, Robert,' Payne replied firmly, echoed around the table.

'Aye, I do know. And for that, you have my thanks, poor though they might be.' This was greeted with smiles he matched by habit. Being around these men had never been difficult and seeing the hope in their eyes did something to him.

Gathering his thoughts, he swallowed and gestured behind him to the heavy wooden box he'd brought up from downstairs. Then he said, to no one in particular, 'In this chest, you will find all the documents, letters, maps and everything else you will need. I'm the only one who can open the lock. However, if I'm gone, go ahead and break the thing apart.' Robert took another mouthful of ale and wandered towards the fireplace. His eyes on the floor, he continued, 'If I don't survive, you must work together to ensure that my plans come to fruition. Everything you need to know is in that chest.'

'If you want us to do it,' Daniel asked quietly, pushing his empty plate to one side, 'then why not show us now?'

Robert gentled his words with a weary smile. 'This is not a matter of trust, my friend. Rather, perhaps I trust you all a little too much.'

'Being cryptic is not going to get you anywhere,' Aiden grumbled, shifting in his seat.

'Cryptic?' Robert asked. 'In plain words then, I don't want you having access to all this right now because I'm afraid that if you do, if you have all the evidence in your hands, if you see the mechanics, the strategy all laid out for you – you'll do your best to stop me – and I can't afford to make enemies out of *all* of you in one night, can I?'

Aiden snorted at that, but both Payne and Deverin chuckled dryly.

'Feel free,' Robert added, again walking around the table, 'to look all you want once I'm gone. You'll need to be familiar with it all.'

'So, my lord,' Owen leaned his elbows on the table and looked up at Robert, 'what is it you would have us do?'

'No, Owen,' Payne shook his head. 'The question you should be asking, is what Robert plans to do?'

'I plan,' Robert replied, completing his circuit around the table, 'to put Andrew Ross Eachern on the throne of Lusara.'

Even as he spoke, Robert watched the men around the table.

Payne was first on his feet, disbelief on his face, almost stuttering with shock. 'Andrew Ross? When did you get this idea? Have you talked to him? Spent any time with him? Told him what you're planning?'

'You're the first to know.'

Daniel started shaking his head, getting to his feet as well. 'This is insane, Robert. Absolutely insane. Do you honestly think the people of Lusara will accept a *boy* as King – after what they've gone through with Kenrick? You know the rumours that abound about Andrew's mother, how she must have killed her husband in order to escape, how she didn't die—'

156

'Yes,' Payne interrupted, pointing at the air. 'Too many people saw her at Shan Moss! Nobody believes she died in that fire. And if they saw her at Shan Moss, they'd know she was a sorcerer!'

'Just like me.'

'Robert,' Daniel held up his hand, 'don't pretend it's the same thing. You're a hero revered by the people. You proved yourself twenty and more years ago, long before they found out about your abilities. They trust you. How are they going to trust Andrew? He's unknown, untried, his mother is under a black cloud and his father was one of the most hated men in the country! And . . . and . . .' Daniel broke off, glancing guiltily at the others.

'What?' Robert asked quietly.

'I still have friends at court. Enough at least, to hear a little gossip now and then and, well . . . you have to know that Andrew is close in with Kenrick. One of his favourites. They're cousins, damn it! Robert, you have to rethink this.'

'There is no other option.'

'Then we have to find one!' Payne shouted.

'He's just a boy, Robert,' Daniel agreed. 'How old is he now? Twelve? Thirteen?'

'Fourteen.' Before they could find more objections, Robert turned to Deverin. 'What say you?'

The big man toyed with his fork before carefully placing it on his empty plate. 'I think it largely depends on the boy himself.'

'Why?' Payne asked.

'I remember Robert at the same age. Fate shaped him, as I'm sure Andrew will be. Success in this venture will rest on how strong he is, how passionate, how disciplined.'

'Oh?' Payne moved forward. 'And what if he's been corrupted by Kenrick, eh? What then? Does Robert have some sorcery that will turn a boy's heart from black to white? If so, why doesn't he just do that to the King and be done with it?'

Robert left the questions unanswered, turning instead to Owen, oldest of this group. Scratching the side of his chin,

Owen pursed his lips a moment. 'I think you could have a lot of trouble.'

'See?' Daniel began, but Owen continued, as though uninterrupted.

'But I also think . . . that he's the right one to choose. Actually,' he added with a wry grin, 'I think he's the only one.'

'And why is that?' Payne demanded.

'Largely for the same reasons you've just held against him. His father, Eachern, was Selar's maternal cousin, giving him a claim on that score alone. He is Lady Jennifer's only child, and her grandfather four generations back was King of Lusara. Andrew is the last of our old royal family. Though his mother might have killed her husband to escape, Eachern *was* hated, and to many, her actions would have been seen as justifiable, and certainly courageous. And,' Owen leaned forward, warming to his subject, 'he *is* young. He can be moulded, shaped to be the King Lusara both wants and needs. Yes, he may be a sorcerer – but the people don't need to know that, do they? Selar had no powers and yet Kenrick admits to them. And there's one other thing you need to take into account.'

'What's that?' Payne asked, his temper somewhat soothed by Owen's simple reading of the situation.

Owen nodded towards Robert. 'The quality of the man placing him on the throne. Most people believe that Robert could take the crown and nobody would be able to stop him. How powerful an idea is it then, to find that man is placing another above him? If Robert is as revered as you say, then surely the weight of his own reputation must play in favour of the boy. No, I agree with Deverin. In the long run, the viability of this plan lies mostly with Andrew himself.'

Robert wanted to smile, would have done, if Aiden's face had regained some colour after his announcement, if that level gaze had looked at him with something other than ill-concealed shock. His skin crawled under such scrutiny, but he asked the question anyway. 'Bishop? Do you have anything to offer?'

Seconds drifted by without a word. Then, slowly, Aiden sat back in his seat, mouth firmly closed.

Robert was no fool. The actions, the silence, the look: the Bishop's opinions would be given later, when they were alone.

Very well. So be it.

Robert picked up the second jug of ale and moved around the table filling their cups. When he reached Payne, he put a hand on the man's shoulder, gently urging him to sit once more. 'I understand and appreciate your objections. I myself have gone over every one and many more like them. For the last six years, I have pushed and prodded my tired brain, trying to find another solution – but there is none. And there's no point in your insisting I take the throne. In order to wrest Lusara free from her chains, I must fight Kenrick, the Malachi and Nash – most likely, all at once. I have tried to plan for most contingencies, but in all likelihood, I will either not survive, or I will be in as bad a state as I was the last time I fought Nash.'

Payne looked at him then, as did the others. He let them remember a moment, what it had been like the first few days afterwards. Then he continued, 'Which is where you all come in, along with that chest of documents. I have set the seeds for rebellion in certain spots all around the country. Specific places, crucial posts and the like. Nothing will happen at all without the proper signal, leaving each man and woman free from danger until the right moment – and that signal won't come unless you give it.'

'Robert,' Payne tried one last time, a valiant effort, 'even injured, you could still assume the throne . . .'

Robert shook his head, unable to explain the further reasons why he needed Andrew as the pivot to this plan. 'When Nash and Kenrick are dealt with, you will all cross the border and take up your roles as Andrew's provisional Council. He'll need men such as yourselves, with your experience, your loyalty and your dedication. Even as you've given these things to me over the years, I would ask that you transfer them to him.'

He looked away then, but he felt the eyes of five men on his back. 'And . . . whether you like the idea or no, the simple and unavoidable truth is, that throne belongs to Andrew Ross

Eachern – and I will make sure he sits on it, if it is the last thing I do.'

Breaking the ensuing silence was the noise of a single chair scraping against the wooden floor. Then footsteps, a key turning in the lock and the door opening and closing.

Robert didn't need to be a sorcerer to know Aiden had just walked out on him.

If he lay still and listened carefully, he could almost hear the ice forming in the courtyard. Though it was still dark outside, Robert rose from his bed, washed and dressed in warm clothes, ready for his journey. His feet trod upon boards newly put back in place, hiding the wooden chest and all it contained. The chances were he would never see it again.

Leaving his cloak to one side, he pulled his saddlebags up onto the bed, packing his meagre belongings carefully, wrapping the box with the silver rod and placing it at the bottom, where it would be most protected.

With everything packed, he took his bags out into the hallway, listening for a moment. The house was silent. Aiden had not made an appearance again last night. Instead, Robert had left his last instructions with the others as he'd detailed their removal to the castle at Bleakstone, in the south, with an armed guard. It was much easier to defend than this abbey – plus, when and if Patric ever arrived back, he would go there first. It had taken hours and much discussion, but in the end, he had achieved a consensus and gained their agreement.

He couldn't help but be relieved that that part, at least, was over. However, the Bishop's continued silence both worried him and hurt.

Robert opened the front door and slipped outside. He crossed the courtyard and found the stable in darkness. He went directly to his horse though, his sight enhanced more by will this morning than by his powers.

With deft fingers he saddled the animal, strapped the bags on and led him out. He tied the reins to a ring in the wall, then headed back to the house to collect his cloak and to write a note for the Bishop.

He picked up his cloak from his bedroom, then stealthily climbed the stairs. Making as little noise as possible, he turned into the study and found pen and paper on Aiden's desk. As he dipped the pen in the jar of ink he noticed the familiar shape standing by the window, the curtain pulled open before him.

Robert paused. This was not the time for him to break the silence.

'You never stay more than a couple of days,' Aiden said, his voice even and soft. 'It took me until last night to understand why.' Suddenly it all makes sense, and I'm so . . . annoyed with myself that I let you distract me.'

Robert tried not to hold his breath as the next words were formed. 'You said you had not spoken to the boy. So you haven't asked him how he feels about your plans?'

'No.'

'And of course, you won't have spoken to the boy's mother, will you?'

Robert flinched at that, but he wasn't surprised. 'You know full well what's at stake.'

'Do I? All I know is that you want to make that boy into a King. You've said nothing, however, of how you think the Prophecy will be affected by your pursuit of that goal.' Aiden paused, turning his head a little, so Robert could see his flat expression in profile. 'Or are you now ignoring the Prophecy altogether?'

'We don't have a single shred of evidence that the Prophecy is real.'

'What about Nash?'

'What about him? Where does it say the Dark Angel will be called Nash? Why can't Nash be unrelated to the Prophecy? Isn't it just possible that evil can rise on its own? After all, nobody saw the rise of Selar – or of Kenrick, for that matter. There's no requirement for the Prophecy to be involved.'

'Except that you're mentioned in it.'

'So? Does that make it real?'

'Very well, what about the Bonding?'

Robert shook his head, waving a hand in dismissal. 'The Bonding was nothing.'

'But Jenn—'

'We had *nothing*, Aiden. Nothing at all.' Robert drew in a breath, begging patience. 'If we'd never heard of the Prophecy, we wouldn't have spent all this time worrying about it. You know damned well much of my hesitation about helping Lusara has come directly because of my concerns about making the Prophecy come true.'

'And I know you'd do anything, say anything necessary, to deny that there is any truth to the Prophecy.'

Robert, frustrated, said, 'Why are you so committed to it?'

'I'm not,' Aiden murmured steadily. 'You are.'

'Before Shan Moss, when Jenn and I were in Budlandi, she said something about the Prophecy. I didn't really understand it at the time. She said that I was looking at the Prophecy the wrong way, that it wasn't the question, but the *answer*. The answer to who we are and why we must do what we do.'

'But that boy isn't part of the Prophecy. Why involve him? Simply because he isn't?'

'Aiden, this isn't about the Prophecy. It's about—'

'Everything you do is about the Prophecy. Don't lie to me, Robert, I won't stand for it!' Slowly Aiden turned until he faced Robert squarely. His voice lowered, both menacing and timorous. '*By your very means, that born unto your hands alone, you will be the instrument of ruin. In the act of salvation, you will become desolation itself, destroying that which you love most.*'

'This isn't about the Prophecy, damn it!' Robert repeated, taking a step closer. 'It's about freeing Lusara. That's the mistake I made all along: forgetting where my real responsibility lay. It was always there, right in front of me. Losing Jenn taught me that. You talk about being distracted from the truth? Well, that's exactly what I've done for the last thirty-five years and it has to stop! Now! Serin's blood, Aiden, I would have thought that you, of all people would understand. I would have thought that you'd be glad that—'

'That you were hurrying to your own destruction? And what happens if you fail this time as well? Will you leave the fate of Lusara in the hands of a bunch of old men and a fourteen-year-old boy enslaved to the task? What kind of King will that make him? Can you be sure you won't *turn* him into the kind of monster Kenrick is by the act of placing him on the throne? And if you're right, and you do die in the process, who in Serin's name should we get to save us from *him*?' Aiden blinked, tight fissures of tension fluttering around his eyes. He paused a moment. 'Promise me you will ask him.'

'I cannot.'

'Then you are indeed no better than—'

'Nash?' Robert raised his eyebrows. 'That's no more than I have told you all along.'

'Then you would force the boy to a fate he has no say in, just as the Key did to you! Don't you see that you *must* have his consent? Otherwise, it will all have been for nothing.'

'I can't afford to give him the chance to say no.'

'But you can afford to put him on the throne, to ask us, and indeed, the entire country, to respect him as our King – and yet you would not grant him that same respect.' Aiden's gaze narrowed. 'Yes, I do understand all too well. I know what the others will never see.'

'What? That I would . . . still, despite all my reasons, my arguments, do all this only because I am determined to defy my fate? Am I really so pathetic in your eyes, Bishop?'

Aiden stared at him a moment, hard and unchanging. Then slowly, he shook his head, his gaze softening a little. 'No, Robert. But for good or ill, you have put me here to say these things to you, even if you are determined to ignore them.'

Robert swallowed hard against words that were too close to the truth, then took a step back. He swung his cloak around his shoulders, fighting to find words that might mean something this friend could hold onto. His voice came out softer than he intended, and suspiciously husky. 'I have to go. I . . .'

'Still, I beseech you, ask the boy. Give him the choice you were denied.'

Robert gazed at him a moment longer. 'Farewell, Aiden. Take care.'

With his heart heavy, he turned and left.

11

Night after night Robert travelled through a tumbling waste-land devoid of feature but for the blackened trunks of trees wet from frost. He tried not looking and not seeing the wilderness his beautiful country had become. While towns managed to hold onto a semblance of prosperity, villages struggled, main-taining little more than an air of survival. Daylight hours saw him passing league after league of empty fields unploughed for winter, of vacant farms and burnt-out houses.

He stayed clear of them all, both for safety's sake and to deny the demon.

But he did not head north immediately. Instead, he turned due west, making for a place that haunted his memory. Just before dawn on the eighth day, with a *frisson* of anticipation, he turned off the road and headed across a hilly pasture grey with new frost. No bitter thoughts intruded on him now; they never did when he approached this same place. He was, for a moment, emptied of doubt and recriminations, of hesitation and self-loathing, leaving him with the closest thing to peace he'd known in eight years.

Home could do that to a man.

He took his time now, giving the horse a rest as he walked alongside it, allowing the sun to peek beyond the horizon before he crested the last snow-strewn hill. And there it was: Dunlorn.

Lost amidst a field of overgrown brush and abandoned weeds, blackened ice and fresh-fallen snow were the familiar walls, the towers he'd grown up with, the doors and windows now empty and forlorn. This had once been the centre of his world, the people within, ready to die for him, as he'd been for them. He'd married Berenice here, and here she had died by his hand. His father was buried within the chapel, along with ancestors going too far back to count. This place was the heart of his journey and the remnants of all his House stood for.

And now it was empty.

The tightening in his chest loosened as he drew in a breath of something like relief. With the sun at his back, he walked forward, his gaze sweeping over battlements and fine stone while his Senses stretched to the maximum, just in case Dunlorn castle was not as empty as he hoped.

Once sure there was nobody else around, he approached the gates. Tall and bleak, these had kept out many a foe, but were no barrier to him now. With one hard push, they opened and he ventured through the barbican and into the inner ward. There he came to a stop, simply listening.

It was always the silence of this place which both welcomed and overwhelmed him, as though it was nothing in reality and only something of his dreams; that the moment he woke, he would find the place teeming with activity the way it had done years before, when he'd returned from his exile, before he'd weakened and allowed himself to become involved in his country's fate once more.

For all that it had been deserted for fourteen years, there was nothing of decay about the place. It seemed, for some strange reason, that though the rest of the country was crumbling to ashes, Dunlorn was to stand fast and act the silent witness.

He led his horse into the old stable. He removed saddle and bags, then emptied out the sack of oats he'd brought with him, letting the animal eat while he brushed it down. Finished, he took his things and ventured upstairs to the guardrooms. He had been here enough times over the last years to know he could not bring himself to wander into the main keep, to walk in spaces that held such weight of expectation and failure. Coming to Dunlorn was a necessity, but there was no need to make things worse.

In the main guardroom, he knelt down to pull up floor boards and removed things he left here each time; blankets, enough firewood to start with, a few candles, some dried figs and nuts. In their place he left a heavy bag of gold pieces, ready for when he needed them. He made himself comfortable, kicked off his boots and settled down to sleep.

The silence hid his multitude of sins.

He dreamed again. Drifting in the icy winter night. Cold and hard. Yes, he knew this place. Knew it too well.

He ran, stumbling, blind and wounded. Nash ran before him, laughing, immune to Robert's power. Shan Moss shook and trembled around him, echoing horror. Too exhausted now, Robert chased Nash out onto the battlefield.

They were alone. Their armies had vanished, and one look in Nash's eye told him this had been his doing.

But how could he win the battle without his army? How would he stop Selar without loyal men at his back?

Loyal men forced to fight their own countrymen. Forced to bleed and die. To starve. To vanish as though they'd never existed.

He gathered together all the demon had bred in him, all the anger and fury, frustration, hatred, fear and self-loathing. He pulled it all together inside him, knowing what it would do – but now it was tenfold, glowing bright like a whole evil sun inside him. His own Angel of Darkness, to battle the one standing before him.

This was what he'd been born for. This was his true destiny. To destroy. He thirsted for it, lusted after it. He hungered for it, needing it to fill his empty soul.

His hands caught the fire within him, trembled and tingled with the all-consuming power of the Word of Destruction. They rose before him, ready to unleash hell.

'Go ahead and use it,' Nash called out to him. 'Say the Word! Say the Word and crush me, Enemy!'

The Word rose in him, perched upon his lips, a heartbeat from being spoken—

She was there, standing in front of him, her eyes full of sorrow, and by the gods, how he loved her, how he needed her, how she filled his soul and starved the demon of breath.

But she did not come towards him. Instead, she moved back and he could hear Nash's laughter, echoing on the wind.

And the demon inside flooded forth, making him gasp for air, driving balance from him. He fell to his knees, unable to look away as she walked to Nash, unable to shut out David Maclean's words.

But David Maclean was dead. And Nash was no longer whole.

And Jenn?

He woke, his eyes staring at the ceiling, listening to the empty wind, the cold night and the parts of him that would soon wither and die.

Robert threw off his blankets and paced a path up and down the guardroom as though he could drive the past beneath his heel and leave it there forever. Outside, the wind rose once more, but beneath it were new noises that drew him to a halt, heart thudding in his chest.

Voices.

Leaving his boots, he padded silently to the window and looked down into the courtyard. Low, black clouds hung like a warning in the sky, promising more snow for tomorrow. The wind pushed them around, drove them together and buffeted the three people struggling into the courtyard.

Like a thief, he sank back into the shadows, careful that no glint of fading daylight catch his face. Instead, he held his breath and strained to hear what they were saying.

Two men and a woman. One of the men was older, his hair salted with white and he walked with a limp. The other man was younger and bore a scar on one side of his face. The woman might have been his mother. Her shoulders looked strong, but rounded with years of heavy labour. She carried a basket in one hand, the other raised to keep her cloak in place.

They seemed to be arguing. Robert followed them from window to window, but could hear only the voices, not the words. He watched as they climbed the stairs to the main keep, opened the door and disappeared inside.

In a flash, he had his boots on. With quick strides, he ducked through a doorway and up a flight of stairs. Following a long corridor, he crept up another flight of stairs at the end and gently pushed open the door at the top.

He emerged into hushed light and echoed noises. This was the lord's peep, a room which looked down into the great hall with long narrow slits where guards could aim arrows from. Extending enough power to hide his footsteps, he reached one arrow slit and found the people below.

For a moment, he assumed he had to be still asleep and dreaming this, but seconds later, too many things fell into place. The two men, under the direction of the old woman, set about with brooms that had come from somewhere. Keeping up a steady flow of conversation about nothing in particular, they all worked to clear the hall of dust and dirt that had blown in over summer. They swept down cobwebs and knocked free birds' nests. The boy went outside and drew water from the well. He returned and scrubbed the empty hearth clean.

Only then did Robert see that this was not a new thing. He looked around the room he was in, remembered back to the guardhouse and the stable – even to the weedless state of the courtyard.

Damn fools! What were they doing? If they got themselves caught by soldiers he knew patrolled this area then they'd be tried for treason, all so they could tend to something nobody cared about any more. Idiots! What right had they to do this? To trespass upon his lands! Couldn't they see this place was dead? That it should be left to rot?

He should scare them away. Make out like he was a ghost or something, ensure they never came back. But he couldn't move. Their bent backs, their steady flow of conversation, their earnestness whispered to him, and he had no choice but to listen.

When finally they finished, he watched them exit the hall and close the door carefully behind them. In the silence, he wandered back to the guardhouse, then down to feed and water his horse again. The people had gone, closing the gate behind them, and as night fell he returned to his room and lit a fire.

He ate simply. Done, he sat down opposite the fireplace and listened to the wind rattle through the battlements, snapping at the window casings and creeping under doors.

There was something about Dunlorn that drew him back here, year after year. He could still hear Finnlay's voice as a boy, chasing after Robert, complaining that he'd been cheated in a contest of archery. He could hear his mother issuing a stern warning for them both to behave. And he could hear – and almost see – his father striding into the courtyard, looking so much like Finnlay did now, but more stern, more threatening. He had been a formidable man, but Robert's other memories of him were the quiet moments, the lessons learned, the stories told. He'd tried too hard to live up to that image, but for a long time now, he knew he'd failed.

But this time, he would not fail. If he had learned anything from his father, it was that success never came from giving up . . .

Are you there?

With a start, Robert sat up, his eyes snapping open, his heart pounding, foggy sleep clouding the dream until he couldn't tell if it was a nightmare or . . .

No, she wouldn't . . .

Please, Robert. Can you hear me?

Yes. The word was out and sent to her before he even thought about it, chased by a thrill of joy to hear her voice . . .

In the darkness, he scrambled to his feet and deliberately slammed his hand against the stone wall. He needed the pain to remind him of who this was and that joy had no place in his dealings with her.

He could not afford to be fooled again.

Yes, Jenn, I can hear you.

12

It had always amazed Nash to find the world so over-populated with beings who thought themselves superior to the average fool. And, of course, the old adage required that they not become aware of it until it was too late. More than once, at such a moment as this, Nash had been tempted to issue a warning to that effect, but what would be the good of it, when this particular truth was buried in a host of his other lies?

Still, Nash mused, sitting back in his chair to study the man before him, it might be interesting one day to actually say something, to add a little variety. Sources of genuine entertainment these days were few and far between, and his body's infirmities dictated too many of his activities.

On the other hand, here was this man, this young and bristling Malachi, fresh and ready, passionate about his ambitions, determined in his means to achieve them. How was Nash to prick that bubble of arrogant enthusiasm with the sharp edge of reality? Especially since, in the long run – and for that matter, short term – Nash would be much better served to use this man as originally intended and let the truth die the lonely and bitter death it deserved.

He smiled into light brown eyes and lifted his hand generously. 'Come closer.'

Hiding his wariness, the man took another step towards the desk, his shoulders squared, his chin raised in defiance of a fear he was trying to ignore.

Here against his better judgement, unless Nash missed his guess. 'Your name?'

'Chiel.' The voice was confident and yes, perhaps a little arrogant. It echoed in hollow fashion along the length of the gallery. 'What do I call you? Carlan?'

Nash waved his hand again; ultimately, names did not matter. 'If you wish – though if you pledge yourself to work for me, you will call me Master, like the others.'

The young man couldn't stop the crease of a frown marring his unscarred forehead. 'But those that call you Master are . . . Bonded to you, are they not?'

'Indeed they are.'

'Then I'll have none of that.' Chiel almost puffed out his chest with pride. 'I've no wish to be losing control of my own mind to you. I'll work for you, yes, but my soul's my own.'

'Your soul?' Nash let out a light laugh, enough to scrape a fraction of the tension from the Malachi's shoulders. 'And why would I be interested in your soul? What I want is obedience.

170

Obedience and trust. If I cannot trust you, how can I have you work for me?'

Chiel tilted his head at that, eyes on the floor, thinking it through. Nash turned, giving him time, and gestured towards Taymar waiting at the other end of the gallery, just returned from Marsay. His faithful servant came forward with a tray between his hands and the scent of hot food drifted towards him, bringing alive the air in the overheated gallery. Crystals of dust floated in the thin sunshine that almost reached the floor from windows spread along the length of the room. Nash kept his back to them, using the bleak winter sun to his best advantage.

As Taymar placed the tray on one side of the desk, Chiel spoke. 'I would not have come here if I wasn't ready to offer you my obedience. I can be trusted as well as any man.'

Nash barely glanced at him. 'And any man can be induced to betray a trust. A man can even betray himself, with the right . . . persuasion.'

He looked up to find Chiel watching him with some element of fear combined with an interesting thread of determination. The young man took a deep breath, 'Why Bond me? You have fifty and more Malachi working for you who do so without such . . .'

'Nobody,' Nash returned his attention to his meal of fish and vegetables, 'works closely for me any more unless they *are* Bonded.'

'Those Malachi . . . they're Bonded to you? Even De-Massey?'

'No, not him. He keeps his own men. I have mine and yes, they are Bonded.' The spices in this dish had been brought all the way from the southern continent, from Budlandi, a gift from a Prince eager to gain his attention. The scent reminded him of so many things, going back more than a century, and he breathed them deeply, closing his eyes to all else for a moment, merely to savour a time before plans and schemes and Enemies and Allies had not driven his life, when his body had still been his own. A time when he had not needed men such as Chiel, who were willing to betray oaths made to their own people in favour of finding a short and glorious path to success. Not one of them understood the overwhelming value of true patience.

Why was every Malachi so determined to wrest the Key from the Salti? And what, in the name of Broleoch, were they intending to do with it afterwards? Put it on a dais in the domed hall at Karakham so they could look at it?

It mattered not. Though he would admit it to no one, Nash had no intention of ever letting a Malachi get his hands on the Key – but it paid to make them believe he would.

Matters of faith were always so easy to manipulate, given the right perspective.

Promise to give them what they want. If necessary, give them little pieces of it, to make it look more and more like the whole, all to the end of keeping control of them. This basic principle had worked wonderfully so far. No reason not to continue. Nash swallowed a mouthful of fish, allowing his tastebuds to wallow in decadence while he formed his reply for the Malachi standing before him. Swallowing, he collected the wine Taymar had poured, then leaned back in his seat and looked up once more.

'You have a reputation for disobedience.' A faint flicker in the young man's eyes encouraged Nash to continue. 'Did you not expect me to enquire about you before I allowed you this close to me? You are Darriet D'Azzir, specially trained in combat, with years of discipline behind you, following the dictates of the Baron Luc DeMassey – and yet, I understand he despairs of you ever mastering what he has tried to teach you. You are impatient, antagonistic, making more enemies than friends, and you question every order he gives you to the point of insolence. As a D'Azzir, that, above all else, is rigidly frowned upon.' Nash paused long enough to sip his wine, then continued, 'And your support for my plans to seize the Key from the Salti is well-known. Whether you like it or not, you have already alienated yourself from your own people. Where else can you turn but to me? What price have you already paid to keep your own soul, as you put it?'

Chiel's gaze narrowed. He sniffed in a breath and pointed sharply at Taymar. 'I won't go around looking like that, with that dull colour in my eyes. I won't go on living without a say in what I think.'

Nash allowed himself a small smile. 'I have . . . improved upon the Bonding process since Taymar joined me. Nobody will ever know you are Bonded.'

'And how do I know that? If you Bond me, what do I do if I find out the truth afterwards? I cannot go back on it, can I?'

'No. A Bond is for life, I will grant you that. But you overestimate my abilities.' Nash swiftly took another sip of wine to hide the incipient laughter. 'Taymar and his like have no talents as you do. Therefore, my control over them is total. With you, as a Malachi, I cannot, by definition, exert anywhere near such control.'

Again, Chiel made a gesture of impatience. 'How am I to know that? How am I to trust *you*?'

For the first time, Nash allowed a thread of hardness to emerge in his tone. 'If you can not trust me, why are you here? I can do nothing without your consent.' Nash uttered this bitter truth without rancour. Though he had worked hard to develop and strengthen his perversion of the ancient and sacred ritual of Bonding, there was no way to guarantee it lasting more than a few minutes without the element of consent. It was unfortunate, but of course, there were ways to *get* consent, and he'd learned over the decades more than a few of them.

Including the one he employed now.

Nash grabbed his walking stick and carefully came to his feet. He leaned as heavily on it as he could, keeping the illusion of frailty to him as the shield it was. One step after another brought him around the desk. Chiel resisted the temptation to move away as Nash approached, suppressed the desire to shudder at Nash's appearance, made more unholy by his increasing proximity.

'You have come to me,' Nash began, stripping his voice of all pretence, 'because you desire something that I can get for you. You do not understand the nature of desire, do you? How it hounds you, breathes into your blood, makes you alive and

173

dying at the same time. But though you have no words for it, still you feel it, do you not?'

Chiel stared at him, his mouth open. Nash reached to where his own desire dwelt, peeling back the layers to use as he needed. 'Your world is not what it once was. Aamin is old and no longer the strong leader Karakham needs. You have only men like DeMassey and Gilbert Dusan to follow – and still they don't speak to the fire in your heart, do they? They don't see the need you feel to push and push hard, to take in the centuries of shame the Malachi have worn and use it to burn all who would stand in your way. Your family, your friends, they don't know either. They tell you to calm down, to trust your leaders, that what you want can be achieved if you would only learn to exercise patience but—'

The young man's breathing was shallow, his face pale, but his eyes glittered.

'You don't want to wait, do you? You want it *now*.'

Chiel nodded once.

Nash sensed Taymar come to stand beside him, ready through years of familiarity. It was nice to know there was always somebody around who didn't doubt his abilities. There was such perfection in this kind of obedience. It was a thing of beauty.

'You cannot lose your soul,' Nash whispered, watching, feeling the thudding heart in the man before him, the conflict between desire and sense, the need, so dreadful, so desperate, to have something so terrible, to give up something more treasured than anything else. But it was there, in amber eyes fixed on his, there in the faint pulse at the temple and throat. Yearning, wanting to give it up and yet, still terribly afraid of that one single desire. 'You cannot lose your soul,' Nash repeated. 'It already belongs to me.'

Chiel didn't move as Nash held his hand out for Taymar to place an ancient dagger in his palm, the blade fresh and sharp. The young man's gaze drifted down slowly, fascinated, horrified and yet drawn to it, as though it was something he craved even as it repelled him. And there, in that space between, this Malachi, like so many before him, offered up his permission.

Hunger flooded through Nash, burning in his gut, bellowing in his ears with a lust he could barely temper.

He grabbed Chiel's wrist, held it palm up between fingers that shook with contained rage, a love and a hatred that so frequently threatened to consume him. He placed the tip of the blade at the root of the thumb, ready, waiting for that whispered word, that permission – and the waiting filled him, drew out each moment with exquisite pain and impossible joy.

More a slave now than he would ever be later, Chiel's entranced gaze rose slowly, as if anticipation alone now drove his actions, as if he shared that lust, as if his entire existence had whittled down to this one moment. 'Yes.'

The breath had barely left his body when Nash slashed the blade across the palm, drawing blood instantly. The young man hissed and stiffened. Heart pounding, Nash held his ring to the blood, catching one drop, then another. Every muscle in his body vibrated with the power as it surged across the connection, making the red stone in his ring hiss and smoke, grow darker until the blood was absorbed completely. He covered the wound with his own hand, setting it, making it forever, and still his reality flew with the moment, soared so far beyond anything else he'd ever known.

Bonding a sorcerer was the ultimate perfection, the ultimate slavery. Absolute perfection. The ultimate triumph.

One day, he would Bond with *her*, the Ally, Jennifer Ross. When he did, he would be invincible.

A wall of dizzying exhaustion smacked into him and he staggered back, dropping Chiel's hand. It didn't matter now. It was done. The boy was his.

Taymar caught him, steering him back to his chair with smooth efficiency. A cup was put to his lips and he swallowed, gathering himself, holding the tiredness off long enough to give Chiel his instructions. He would have time to recuperate later.

He opened his eyes to find Chiel swaying on the spot for a moment, a frown clear on his brow. His eyes opened then and absently he brushed one palm against the other, as though

175

removing a little dust. There was now no mark of the blade, no remnant of blood. The man who watched him now did so with a patience he would never have understood an hour ago.

'Chiel,' Nash began, emptying his wine, 'how do you feel?'

'Well, Master.'

'Are you ready to begin work for me?'

'Of course, Master.'

'Do you have any concerns you wish to voice?'

'No, Master. What concerns could I have?'

Nash allowed his body to sink back into the welcoming arms of his chair. 'Who owns your soul, Chiel?'

'You, Master.' There was not a hint of worry in that young voice now, no suggestion of anything other than content.

Another perfect conquest.

'Very well. You will go with Taymar now. He will show you a room where you can rest. After that, you will behave in every way as you have done to date whenever anybody else is around. No one outside this room will know that you are now Bonded to me unless I ask for your obedience.'

'Yes, Master.'

'I will give you full instructions later. You may go and rest now.'

'Thank you, Master.'

The sun had come out again by the time Kenrick called a halt by the edge of an iced stream where the land dropped sharply into a bowl populated by a village. One of his men jumped down and kicked a hole to allow the horses to drink. They stood by bare trees, black with damp, white ground surrounding them, a washed grey sky above.

No colour anywhere he looked.

He could see people emerging from their houses, looking up the hill, watching with trepidation, ready to run and hide if they needed to. But such an easy target was beyond him – and besides, he was too close to Ransem Castle, and Nash would hear of it.

How was he to get what he wanted without throwing it all away in the same moment? How far did Nash trust him?

Always the same questions, the same problems. How could he move forward when the consequences were so terrible?

Of course he was afraid of Nash – how could he not be? But fear kept him healthy, alive, ready to fight the next battle.

Even so, he couldn't wait any longer.

With a grunt, he pulled his horse away from the stream and kicked it into motion. His men followed behind and once more they resumed their journey towards Ransem Castle.

Rest had done Nash little good. Bonding always stretched his energies thin, but in his current condition, it took so much longer to recover. Taymar had let him sleep a little, then wakened him, helping him to ready for Kenrick's imminent arrival. Then there had been another meal and while he ate it, Taymar reported on his own recent trip to Marsay, an odd combination of good and bad news that had little effect on his appetite.

'And you have found no other evidence? No proof of what DeMassey is up to?' Nash asked between mouthfuls.

'No, Master. He is skilled at evasion. I have tried to follow him when he leaves Marsay, but I lose him after half a league. He goes in a different direction each time and I don't have your abilities to . . .'

'No.' Nash sniffed and tore a piece of bread in half, almost wishing it were DeMassey's neck. 'Anything else?'

'Only what I have already told you, though I cannot guess what it means.'

'And you're sure of what you saw?'

'Yes, Master. I was but yards away.'

'He's up to something, I know it. I can almost smell it on him whenever he comes near me. So,' Nash continued, sinking his teeth into the bread, 'what is the Baron DeMassey doing in the company of Archdeacon Godfrey?'

'He was with the priest more than a few minutes. I did not dare get close enough to listen to their conversation.'

'And then once Godfrey had left the King's chamber that evening, DeMassey saved the priest's life by killing the two traitor Guildesmen?'

'Yes, Master – though I have no doubt the Proctor was the first target.'

'Interesting.' It was indeed very interesting. But why would DeMassey be consorting with a priest, of all people – or was it that priest in particular? 'What can you tell me about Archdeacon Godfrey?'

Taymar formed his thoughts carefully. 'He appears to be very loyal to the Church. He works with Bishop Brome on most things and has been instrumental in keeping things running while Brome has been incapacitated. From what I hear, he is the one who is busily rewriting the Church laws rather than Brome. For the most part, Godfrey stays out of trouble and manages to offend nobody.'

'An accommodating man, by the sound of it.'

'Perhaps. He also appears to be the only person at court who has any kind of relationship with the Proctor.'

'Osbert?' That made Nash sit up. He knew Osbert of old, had placed the man in his current position, but he'd long ago stopped trusting him. Ever since his failure to find the secret Guilde library, when he'd shown Nash the empty hiding place filled with the ashes of fifty books. He'd never quite been able to believe that Vaughn would have willingly destroyed what could have been the only real weapon available against sorcery – but then, even searching on his own, Nash had never found a trace of it. Circumstances had forced him to assume Osbert had been telling the truth.

But it was wholly out of character for him to develop a friendship with Godfrey – or any churchman, for that matter.

'So Godfrey is a good man, but he's allied himself to Osbert for some reason.'

'It appears so, Master.'

'And now DeMassey has become friends with Godfrey as well. My, that priest is very popular. I wonder if it would be worth . . .' No, taking Godfrey in for interrogation would get him nowhere. In fact, all it would do would be to scare DeMassey off. This was the first shred of evidence he'd been able to obtain for years about what that man was up to. DeMassey had no honest business dealing with a priest. Nash couldn't afford to destroy this first opportunity to get what he needed.

Abruptly restless, he pushed himself to his feet, leaving the walking stick leaning against the stone wall. He walked around the desk with only a little of the limp he normally showed. It had paid him well to feign continued weakness; so many people had underestimated him because of it.

And one man in particular would be looking for signs of an impending recovery. Nash had no intentions of revealing his returning strength until he absolutely had to.

Time. Up until now, it had been his greatest aid, but for the last few years, it had played against him. Though he was stronger than most thought, he was by no means ready to face the Enemy, Robert Douglas. Nor could he face *her* in this state.

Still, there *were* options he could explore, despite what he'd told Kenrick. 'Taymar, I think I will go to the springs this afternoon. The Envoy can meet me there.'

'Yes, Master.'

'Have Chiel accompany us. Prepare to leave as soon as Kenrick has gone.'

Taymar didn't answer immediately. Instead, he went to the window and looked out. 'I believe he comes now, Master.'

By the time Kenrick appeared at the door, Nash had resumed his hunched posture. 'Good morning, Sire.'

Kenrick looked like he was in a hurry. As usual, his clothes were of the highest quality, rich without being gaudy. As he strode into the gallery, Nash was momentarily reminded of the boy's father: the same fair hair, the same tall and warrior-like bearing, though the eyes were brown rather than blue. But the resemblance was fleeting. For all that Kenrick looked like Selar, he had none of his sire's canny ability to read people, to understand complex political situations.

A failing that Nash had only encouraged.

When Kenrick looked at Nash, his gaze narrowed, as though to hide his surprise. 'You're . . . you look terrible.'

What was it about this boy that irritated him so much? Nash could see himself crushing Kenrick between his fingers like a green bug; he found it difficult some days, to find the will to stop himself.

Necessity was what kept this boy alive, nothing more.

'Thank you for your words of concern for my health, Sire,' Nash began, taking a mouthful of wine and keeping his expression neutral. 'How many Malachi have you at court now?'

'Twenty, the same as last time.'

'And you used the Bresail to check?'

'Of course,' Kenrick's tone was one of weary resignation. 'You ask me the same question each time. I check on a different day every week. It never seems to occur to you that I want the answers as much as you do. If you distrust the Malachi so much, why do you insist on working with them?'

'They have their uses.' And he needed to keep track of those men who served DeMassey, those who were not Bonded to Nash.

'As do I?'

Nash ignored the petulance and continued, 'Do you plan to winter at Marsay this year?'

Kenrick wandered along the gallery, fingering idly the long tapestries which hung from the wall opposite the windows. 'No. Ogiers has confirmed his return visit – but he refuses again to meet me within the safety of the city. Instead, he's chosen a site near Cewyll. I leave in two days and will be back in Marsay in time for Caslemas, unfortunately.'

Interesting that the Mayenne ambassador was prepared to meet in winter. Perhaps Tirone was starting to take the offer of marriage for his daughter a little more seriously?

'And how is our little Salti hunting expedition going? Caught any sorcerers yet? I notice that horrible scar still mars your cheek.'

Kenrick stiffened, his face abruptly suffused with red. He opened his mouth, but pulled himself back before he could do irreparable damage.

Nash wanted to laugh, but refrained. It appeared they were both learning restraint. The thought of that depressed him beyond measure.

'Well?' Despite the needling, he *did* want an answer. Kenrick might need his face mending, but Nash needed Salti blood more than anything else at this moment.

'No, no luck yet,' Kenrick grunted. 'With all this snow, it could take weeks more for word to filter around the country. And have you heard the Hermit of Shan Moss? He's prattling on about the incarnation of Mineah and everybody thinks it's because of me, that she's going to come back and strike me down because I've dared to change the laws. You're nicely out of this, Nash. I'm the one who has to face the crowds – so don't you start going on about how much time it takes!'

Nash considered how little time he really had. His last full and complete regeneration had been twenty-eight years ago, just after the battle that won Selar the throne this foolish boy now sat upon. Even though he'd had to repair wounds since that time, this body would cease to function if he did not refresh it completely before it was thirty years old. Though he was surrounded by Malachi, both Bonded and not, to use one would risk his alliance with DeMassey and, in turn, risk all that he would achieve.

'Of course.' Nash got to his feet, reaching for his walking stick and leaning on it heavily. 'I am trusting you to find me a sorcerer I can use to heal these wounds – or don't you want me back to full strength?'

Kenrick blinked, his expression as flat as an ice-lake. 'I will get you what you need. But you have to remember that it will take time.'

'Of course. But the longer it takes, the longer everything else takes. Are we not supposed to be allies?'

'Allies?' Something hard and belligerent burned behind Kenrick's eyes. 'You tell me nothing of what you're really up to – and yet, I must come here every two weeks to report to you on what *I'm* doing. You mention useless things like the Key and the Enemy and the Ally and you *know* they mean nothing to me. You promised to teach me to use my powers, and yet you give me each grain of information as though it were gold dust, keeping me from developing enough so that I can kill you! Oh, yes, we're great allies, Nash.'

Kenrick turned then, as though it was the only way he could stop himself from striking out. 'You know how many times I've heard about that stupid Hermit and his damned visions? Have you any idea of the speculation I have to endure about whether Jennifer Ross's appearance at Shan Moss has anything to do with it? After all, she was supposed to be dead – but there she was, between you and Douglas, and I've been asking you for the last eight years to explain to me what that's all about and yet you say nothing.'

Nash dropped all pretence of subservience. 'I tell you all you *need* to know. Have you not done well enough on what I've given you so far? Why bother with things that ultimately do not concern you?'

'Robert Douglas killed my father!'

'Yes,' Nash snapped back, 'and as a result, you became King. Now, you tell me, which would you rather?'

Kenrick stared at him a moment, then looked away, still stubborn, though snubbed into silence.

Satisfied now, Nash moved back towards his desk.

The truth was, he didn't need Kenrick anywhere near as much as the boy thought – and if he really had to, he could use his replacement, though the mechanics would be awkward. He had one waiting in the wings already; somebody who, if placed on the throne, would probably have the gods writhing in cosmic irony. To make Andrew Eachern, Duke of Ayr, King would be a piece of arrogance he would definitely enjoy, especially as the boy's mother was the Ally herself. Especially since the boy carried his father's name of Eachern, a man the entire country had hated.

Of course, they hated Kenrick too, didn't they?

But he knew Kenrick, and for the moment, he remained controllable. To make a change merely for his own entertainment would be foolish, especially at this stage.

Kenrick stared at the floor, leaving the silence for Nash to fill. He did so as little more than an afterthought.

'Enjoy your meeting at Cewyll.'

Kenrick grunted and stalked out.

*

Kenrick rode halfway back to Marsay before stopping with his men at a village with a good tavern. There he invited them to drink, have a meal, to enjoy themselves for a few hours. He stayed with them until nightfall. Then, pretending to go upstairs with one of the serving wenches, he slipped out into the stable, saddled his horse and rode back towards Ransem Castle.

His approach took him wide, down into a gully that sheltered him in what was something of a blind spot for the Castle's defences. He still had fifty and more paces to make across clear land, but under cover of darkness, and using one trick Nash *had* taught him, he knew he could do it easily.

There were lights burning in selected places all around the Castle, but Nash was no longer there. Nor was Taymar. Kenrick had lingered in the stable long enough to learn of the visit to the hot springs. Nash would not be back until tomorrow.

So this was his opportunity, perhaps the only one he would ever have.

Dismounting, he secured his horse to a withered bush in the small icy gully, then straightened up, concentrating on his breathing. When all inside him was as peaceful as it ever got, he pushed hard, taking the mental dimensional step sideways that would make him invisible to any who looked in his direction. With a grin at his own temerity, he set out across the moor, Ransem Castle in his sights.

There was almost nothing to mark the area as being any different to that a league distant in any direction, bar the guilty twists of steam which rose from the lake's surface. Along the edges, strange, ghostly shapes formed in the heated water, some spongy and tantalisingly rough, others hard and dangerous.

There were legends about this place and its springs, stories of gods emerging from the water, of almighty battles being fought over this land, of a flaming body thrown into its depths, to leave the lake bubbling and steaming for eons. The water certainly helped soothe the aches which bled deep into Nash's bones, and the shorter, sharper pain he lived with each day. He was certain it aided his recovery, little by little – and any help was worth the effort.

Nash ignored Lake Finiah itself and instead let Taymar lead him into a wooded area nearby, where stunted trees let out branches gnarled and twisted and the land rose enough to create odd-shaped caves that a man had to crawl through. The largest of these opened out, holding a pool of water hotter than any in the lake. The air was different here as well, thick, clinging, almost tangible. With the roof so low and spiked with lion's teeth, and the area so full of legend and make-believe, Nash had found little difficulty in keeping the locals away. So he had the place to himself.

Already his body tingled in anticipation.

Kenrick sneaked into Ransem, stepping around people to squeeze through opened doors, climbing up to slip through a window, flattening himself against a staircase wall to avoid a dozen soldiers marching down.

And he had to be silent. Invisible he might be, but if he made a noise, somebody would hear him. In this place, they'd soon guess what was happening.

His heart raced; his breathing was no more than a stunted gasp as he stole closer and closer to his goal. A thin, dangerous nausea threatened his stability and he had to pause and press his forehead against cold stone before it would go away.

This had better be worth it.

He came out at the top of the staircase and put a hand on the door before him, the one leading to the gallery. He could hardly turn the handle. What if Nash were still here? What if those stories of Finiah Springs were just a trap set for him, to test his loyalty. Kenrick had been here only a few hours ago; nothing had changed. Nash might very well be on the other side of this door, waiting for him.

For a moment, the desire to flee almost overwhelmed him, but then, almost without his own volition, his hand turned and the door creaked open. He peered around it and found the gallery empty. Sick with relief, he slipped inside and closed the door silently behind him.

He was alone and, with relief, he released the shift. He gulped in air, letting it out steadily, trying to calm down a little. He wiped sweat out of his eyes and looked around. What was it about this place that made his skin crawl? Even without Nash in residence, there was some quality in the air that made him clench his teeth, even when he consciously tried not to.

He listened carefully for a moment, then started off towards the other end of the room.

Eight years ago, when he'd been a child, he'd been tempted enough to agree to an alliance with Nash, believing that he was clever enough and powerful enough to rid himself of Nash once he'd received the training he needed. But as a child, he hadn't known enough to understand that Nash would *never* train him to be so strong that he could destroy his own teacher.

So he'd been forced to experiment on his own, to play with powers he knew he didn't really understand, and the results so far had not been positive. Nash knew about the scar on his face, but not of the other scars on his body, the other . . . damage he'd caused in trying to heal it.

There were two doors before him. To the right was Nash's bedroom. He pushed the door open and stepped inside.

It was too dark to see anything of use. He closed the door behind him and conjured up his own light, just enough to identify a candle standing on a table at his left. With a flick of his fingers, he brought it to life.

The room was big, wide and fit for a lord of noble birth and esteemed lineage. An enormous bed was draped in rich thick comforters; there were rugs on the floor and other furnishings of great quality. This was, undoubtedly, the bedroom of a very wealthy man. But, like everything else about Nash, it was hidden away here, out of sight, where nobody could learn anything from it and use it against him.

There were books on the desk, ancient yellow pages and worn and threaded leather bindings. Kenrick picked up one after the other, blind excitement filling him now, and flipped through each book before putting them aside. The worst part was, he didn't really have any idea what he was looking for, or whether he would know it when he saw it. For all he knew, it was something totally innocuous – but all that talk of the Ally and the Enemy, that had to be something written down, he was sure, and more likely than not, it would be old.

Forcing himself to slow down, he looked through the books more carefully, pausing here and there when he found a page of illumination or a note on a separate sheet. Very little made much sense to him, as most of the books were written in languages he was unfamiliar with. The candle had burned down a whole inch by the time he finished, none the wiser. There were no other notes on the desk, nothing else to look at.

Picking up the candle, he began behind the door, poking into crevices and behind pieces of furniture.

He was halfway around the room before he found a small alcove, underneath one corner of the bed, shunted into the wall as though by accident. There was nothing different about it, except that it felt a little warm compared to the rest of the wall.

Pulse rising in anticipation, he placed his hand against the stone, feeling with more than his flesh for something that might give. Abruptly, the stone shifted. It moved back, then swung inwards, leaving a hole in the wall where a leather pouch sat flat against the stone.

His heart leaped a beat, then settled down to a steady pounding. He lifted the pouch out and sat on the floor, setting the candle down by his knee.

There were five sheets of paper inside, one of which was obviously a scrap of something else, something larger. He scanned each one but could read far too little. Just the odd word here and there – until one leaped out at him.

Prophecy.

Taymar, the ever-present, the ever-useful, the ever-efficient, had outdone himself. By the time Nash emerged from the pool, rested, invigorated and ravenously hungry as he was at no other time, his efficient slave had organised a pavilion erected, a cot bed put together and a light meal laid out on a table under the wan stars. With his skin still tingling from the spring waters, Nash allowed himself to remember what it had felt like to have a whole body, to have all his power at his fingertips. A pleasant memory, touched with a bitterness that ate away inside him, an acidic hatred.

It had once been so easy for him to move about, to pursue his goals, to subdue his opponents with little more than a thought's worth of effort. Now he had to rely so heavily on Taymar, on his Bonded Malachi – and on men such as DeMassey and Gilbert Dusan, whose loyalty was always to be split between Nash and Karakham. These visits to the springs and the pale power of those sorcerers he'd bled over the last few years had served only to seal up wounds, not heal him. He needed the blood of another sorcerer to become at least able-bodied again. A strong sorcerer would return him to full power, to the point where he could face both Enemy and Ally.

And if he found the one he wanted, the one he *desired*, the one whose blood-power would sustain him forever, then . . .

He had so little time left. Perhaps a year, no more. The Enemy had done so much damage, and yet, so little, in comparison to what *she* had done, how she had betrayed them both.

But he would make her pay, even as he loved her, he would make her pay. He was weak, but he was not dead yet. He just needed to regenerate fully and then Robert Douglas would meet his match.

And if the Prophecy came true, if he found the one he was looking for, then he would need no more regenerations, he would find the Key, take the Ally, incinerate the Enemy and blow away his ashes in triumph.

Prophecy.

'You bastard, Nash,' Kenrick breathed into the cold air. He looked at the other pages and saw the same word on all but the scrap.

He had to find someone to read these for him, to figure a translation, but he couldn't take them or Nash might find out and if he did, Kenrick would be dead before he even had time to think about it.

But at least he'd finally found something! And so easily, too. Just sitting there, in that little . . .

His heart stuck in his throat and he choked for air.

Found so easily. *Too* easily? Had Nash made things easy for him because . . . because there was some trap here? Or had Nash some means by which he could tell that Kenrick had been riffling through his private things . . .

A wave of dizziness made him stumble. He fell against the desk and tried to breathe. He felt sick, horribly sick.

Nash. Nash had done this to him, hadn't he? Afraid Kenrick would grow stronger than he. Afraid Kenrick would take over—

His nausea eased and his dizziness faded. He straightened up a little, to find the candle burned halfway through. Beside it rested twenty books, some open, some closed, other notes and things he'd already gone through. Invaluable things he couldn't read due to his ignorance.

He began to laugh.

No. Nash would never go to the trouble of protecting all this with subtle traps and signs to alert him of intruders, because he believed in himself too strongly. He would never believe Kenrick would have the courage to do something like this – and who else would come here, knowing this was the place to look?

The fear and its side-effects fell away from him. Quickly now, he picked up the pages and candle and returned to the desk. He drew out paper and pen, dipped it into the ink and began to copy.

By the time the candle was burning an inch from the bottom, he was finished. He left his copies on the desk to dry and put the originals back in the pouch and then into the wall. Slowly now, he checked around to make sure he had disturbed nothing else, then he gathered up his treasure, folded the sheets and slipped them inside his jacket. He put the candle back on the desk, blew the light out and set about his escape.

By the time he reached his horse, he was laughing with triumph.

*

His Malachi guards built the fire up high; Nash was in no mood to sit inside his pavilion. Nor was he, thanks to his dip in the pool, inclined to sleep. Instead he sat, a rug over his knees like the old man that he was, and listened to Taymar reading aloud the reports sent by his Bonded spies, from Mayenne, from Karakham, from Alusia and Budlandi – and, of course, from Flan'har.

Especially there. Where else would the Enemy hide?

Of course, he wasn't dead. He had the power of the Key to keep him alive, no doubt. But still Nash puzzled over *what* Robert Douglas was doing. Nowhere in these reports was a single whisper of an army being formed, of supplies being amassed, of any other sign that full-blooded rebellion was at hand. Could it be that the Enemy had *not* yet recovered from his wounds, was, even now, in a condition similar to Nash?

A slow smile drifted across his face. He could hardly think of a more delicious punishment. All that tall, elegant warrior's power, the stubborn good looks that would turn any head – all twisted and warped and maimed and ravaged?

He couldn't afford to think along those lines, for he would be too disappointed to find he was wrong.

Nevertheless, the complete absence of Robert Douglas from Lusara was intriguing – and made his need to regenerate more urgent: for the longer it took the Enemy to come, the quicker that moment would arrive.

And this time, he had to be ready. *This* time, Nash would end it, once and for all.

A movement to his left and he looked up. Shapes were emerging from the darkness, shifting amongst the twisted trees, heading towards the light.

'The Envoy, Master.'

'So I see,' Nash nodded. 'Put those papers away and see if you can find another chair for him.'

The windswept plains of Budlandi were visible in the eyes of the man who faced him. Dark eyes, like his own, surrounded with fine white lines, of sun damage more than age. This man had travelled far. His patience, like Nash's was unbounded. He sat in his chair, his body arranged in lines of elegance rather than comfort. His robes of cobalt blue and ochre red were apparently unable to keep the northern winter at bay, and yet, this Envoy seemed wholly and completely at home.

Nash could only respect such discipline. It would be a challenge to Bond one such as this – and perhaps he would, one day in the future. For the moment, however, there were pressing matters of business to attend to, matters of gold and property, and funds to cover the costs of his growing operations. And matters of hidden spies.

The desire for control was a hunger never fulfilled.

He waited until wine had been poured for them, until attendants had moved back to a discreet distance. Then he asked the first, necessary question. 'Is your Prince prepared to pay my price?'

'He is, on the condition that you can prove the quality of the goods before he buys them. I'm sure you can understand the position he is in. This is not only a matter of security for him, but one of great pride. His ancestors will bestow divine favours upon him if he is able to restore his family to their former glory. If however, the goods are inferior – or . . . fake,' a smile accompanied this, 'then his shame will be only equalled by his anger.'

Nash matched the smile, and he took a moment watching the expression on the other man's face as he did so. 'I am a great believer in ancient traditions,' he said evenly, 'in regaining a man's rightful possessions, in fulfilling a destiny he was born to.'

'I rejoice to hear you say so.'

'The gold?'

The Envoy gave no outward sign, but two of his men moved forward, carrying a chest between them. The lid was opened to reveal sacks of gold and silver. That was all the promise Nash needed. This had become so much easier than he could ever have hoped. He smiled again and turned to his right.

'Chiel?'

The young man emerged from the shadows with barely a sound. 'Yes, Master?'

Nash watched the Envoy, saw the eyes widen in speculation, and some degree of greed. 'You will go with this man, do all that he says. When you arrive at your destination, you will pledge your allegiance to the Prince and give him your whole-hearted loyalty. You will perform whatever actions he deems fit and do all you can to esteem the honour of his family. Do you understand?'

Nash waited then, listening carefully for the rehearsed pause, the faint question in Chiel's voice. 'Master?'

Then Nash turned, giving Chiel the benefit of his full attention. These orders must be believable, or the Envoy would never convince the Prince. 'You will do as I say. Do you understand?'

Chiel looked at Nash. 'Yes, Master.'

Nash got to his feet, leaning on his stick. 'Take him now, before I change my mind. Tell your Prince he has what nobody else in the world has: his own private sorcerer.'

13

Andrew pushed his cloak hood back and peered up at the sky. All day the clouds had tumbled together, different layers of them, gathering as though for a storm. It was entirely possible that the heavens would open before they could reach Maitland.

He risked another glance at Micah riding silently beside him. The older man didn't look particularly perturbed, but then, he rarely did. Not only that, but he hadn't made any measuring glances upwards, had spent no time at all turning his face into the wind and not once had he sniffed the air, all of which Andrew had done at various different points during the day. This could mean one of two things. Either Micah already knew what the weather was going to do to them, or he believed that they would reach Maitland before it could matter. Or both.

With one final look up, Andrew settled and placed all his chances on one bet, putting all his certainty into his voice. 'Snow.'

'Nope.'

'Damn it, Micah,' Andrew swore. 'How do you do it? Are you sure? If it's not snow, then what is it?'

Micah smiled but didn't look at him. 'Sleet. Later tonight.'

'Once we're home.'

'That's right.'

'I'm never going to get this right, am I?'

'I don't know, are you?'

'There's something you haven't told me about it, isn't there? Some other trick to telling the weather that you're keeping to yourself. Isn't there?' He couldn't keep the note of frustrated hopefulness from his voice and he knew Micah's smile was widening, even though he refused to look.

'No, I've told you all I know.'

'And I'm still wrong.'

'I'm afraid so.'

'And you're never wrong.'

'I wouldn't say that.'

'No, you wouldn't.' Andrew sniffed. 'I would.'

'My lord,' Micah continued evenly, 'it's not just a process of learning the signs. It has just as much to do with experience as anything else. It took me years to gain the skill, and I made plenty of mistakes before I did.'

Andrew asked carefully, 'And who taught you?'

'My master,' came the quiet reply.

'Duke Robert?'

Andrew didn't need to see Micah's face to know there was no particular expression there. Micah wasn't so good at hiding what he was thinking and for the most part, it was easy to guess. But whenever the subject of Duke Robert came up, Micah got this look in his eyes, this set to his face that meant he wasn't going to be drawn.

They crested a wind-blown hill and caught the full view before them, laid out like a tapestry in muted colours. This country was all so familiar to him, within a day's journey of Maitland. In all likelihood, he could travel through here blindfolded if need be, and not make a wrong step. The hills continued on eastwards, barely stopping before they reached the border with Flan'har. To the north, another few days' ride

192

away, was Marsay, where he would be headed in a few short weeks, and to the south, the land stretched out before rising into mountains that overshadowed his family's ancient home of Elita.

He'd never been allowed to see it. Bella and Lawrence had forbidden him to ever go there, had instructed Micah that he was never to take Andrew, despite his pleas. It hardly seemed fair, considering Andrew had been born there, moments before Duke Robert had destroyed the castle with the Word of Destruction.

Oh yes, he'd heard the story. Many times. Why, even Micah had added his few details once. So he knew there was little left standing beyond the main keep, and at this time of the year, the barren stones would be covered in snow. All the same, he longed to go, to just get a glimpse of a place that had so many legends attached to it.

But his mother had promised to take him when she next came to visit. Though she'd admitted that there was some danger for her to go near her old home, she had relented. A brief visit would do little harm. So Andrew now looked south, imagining the bluff of mountains as they would look now.

'How do you think the Enclave will fare now Henry's gone?'

'They'll survive. It's a strong community. The death of one cannot force the death of the whole.'

Andrew smiled. 'That sounds like something Henry would say.'

'I wouldn't worry about your mother, either.'

'Oh? Why not?'

'Because I've found that worrying about her has little effect on her fate.'

'And you've had practice?' At Micah's nod, Andrew added, 'So who should I worry about?'

This made Micah grin, openly, his expression lending itself to sunshine. 'Worry about your lessons. Worry about your own future, my lord. Count your blessings while you can. Enjoy the life you have.'

'Ah, now that really *does* sound like Henry.'

'And learn to be respectful to those who can thrash you

193

without so much as blinking.' With that, Micah kicked his horse – but Andrew was quicker. He raced away, laughing all the way across the valley.

Micah counted the trees. One after the other, along a well-travelled lane between two fields. He knew exactly how far he dared go, how close he could risk going to Maitland and how far back he had to remain, at least until nightfall.

Andrew rode in front of him, tiring now that he was minutes away from home. He had his hood pulled back, his cloak draped over his shoulders, as though the winter was something only other people had to worry about. One of the benefits of being young. Dark hair was pushed about by the wind, a little longer than usual – but by no means as long as his father's, assuming his father still had long hair.

Micah frowned. It was getting harder and harder to hold to the lie. Each year, as Andrew grew older, his mind expanded, his interests encompassing so many things Micah was hard-pressed to keep up. But the boy had *always* had an interest in anything and everything to do with Robert. Why was that? Because somewhere, deep in his bones, he knew the man was his father? Or was it simply because Andrew was a boy, growing up in a country that had so few heroes left, wanting to emulate the best of them?

One day, Micah was going to slip. He knew that. One day, when Andrew asked another question, or pressed him for more detail, or rekindled feelings he would rather forget, he knew he would slip and say the wrong thing, giving rise to more questions, making the boy unsure of what was real in his life and what wasn't. Making him doubt who he was and who he could trust.

Jenn had never made Micah promise not to tell Robert, had instead, asked him not to say unless asked directly. But he'd never been asked and now, fourteen years later, he wasn't so sure he'd want to tell.

'Are you staying for Caslemas?' Andrew asked. 'Or are you going to visit your family in Flan'har?'

'I'll hardly have time, will I?' Micah replied levelly. No point in giving the boy something else to worry about. 'At this time of year, I'd barely get there before I'd have to come back. You won't be at court for more than a few weeks this time.' And Micah stayed with him every day that he wasn't. Stayed and watched, guarded and guided. Played the servant and the brother, teacher and student.

Did whatever was necessary to ensure this boy would survive and grow. Did it because . . .

Whatever his reasons had started out, they'd changed over the years as he'd grown to know and love Andrew.

'Are you going to come up to the house?'

'Not tonight.'

'But it will be dark in a few minutes. You'll be sheltered.'

'I'd rather get home and start a fire before the snow begins. The place will be damp and freezing after so many weeks away.'

'I'll come by tomorrow and help you clean up if you like.'

'Thank you.' Micah smiled. How could he not like this boy, this son of Jenn and Robert, this child who was to be the best of both of them, without their scars? He could only hope and pray, as he had done for every one of those fourteen years, that Andrew would not be cursed in his life the way his parents had been.

He counted the last of the safe trees and pulled his horse to a halt. Andrew paused and turned, giving him a smile. 'You go on home. I'll be fine from here.'

'I'll watch as always, my lord,' Micah replied, matching the knowing smile with one of his own. These ritual games they played were as important as any other part of their relationship. 'Go on. Your aunt and uncle will be waiting for you, with, I'm sure, a big fire and a hot meal. Think of me as you eat and climb into your soft clean bed.'

'I'll do my best to feel guilty, if it will make *you* feel better.'

'It will, my lord, it will. Go.'

Andrew nodded. 'Thank you. I'll see you in the morning.' He paused a moment longer, then turned his horse and trotted along the rest of the lane. From there the path opened out into a field which dropped gently towards Maitland Manor. Micah could watch the remainder of Andrew's progress without hindrance or observation. He had to stay back, had to pretend he wasn't even here. People knew his name; some, years ago had known his face, known him as friend and aide to Robert Douglas, the rebel. So he stayed back in the shadows of his last tree and watched a rebel's son return to his home in one piece. Saw the forecourt gate open wide to greet him, saw people wave to him as he rode in, saw the gate close behind him, ensuring his safety as much as anything else. Only then did Micah release himself from his duty and turn for his own home.

'Andrew!'

He was barely down from his horse when he was swept up into a hug. Aunt Bella was not normally a demonstrative woman, but she allowed herself these small indulgences whenever he returned home, no matter where he'd been.

'You look cold!' She frowned. With her hands on his shoulders, she stepped back to take a better look at him. 'And pale. Any problems?'

The question was so carefully phrased, even after all these years. Andrew just smiled and shook his head. He could never mention the chase through Shan Moss and Henry's death, and worry about Osbert's law changes would mean nothing to her. 'No, we had a good trip back. Not too much snow.'

'I'll bet you're hungry. Come inside and get warm.' Bella turned and led him into the hall of Maitland Manor. Familiar warm wooden panels shut out the winter's evening. A full fire glowed from one wall, while the other was decorated with three lit torches. Exactly as he remembered.

It was good to be home.

Bella gave him only a moment to absorb the scene. Then she put an arm around his shoulders and steered him towards the huge staircase set along one end of the hall. She walked with him as she continued, 'Lawrence should be back shortly. You'll see him at supper. I ordered a bath for you when I had word of your approach. I think you've grown another inch since you went away.'

Andrew laughed, looking once behind them to make sure

they were completely alone. 'Finnlay says I'll be as tall as him by the end of summer.'

Bella's smile froze a little at that, became noticeably less easy. Andrew said nothing about it. He'd long grown used to her reaction to anything to do with his trips to the Enclave. If she'd had her way, he would never mention them at all – she would much prefer it if he never went, and made do with the infrequent visits his mother made to Maitland under the deepest secrecy.

'Well, I'm sure you will be,' Bella replied at last. Her resemblance to Jenn was remarkable, though she had more height to her and now, a little more weight. She had the same startling blue eyes as his mother, the same rich dark hair, though Bella had a patch of delicate silver at each temple, which sometimes looked more a decoration than anything else. She could be hard and uncompromising, but Andrew loved her all the same, even if she did seem to see everything from only one viewpoint.

They arrived at the landing where two corridors turned away to the east and north wings. There Bella paused, her hands smoothing back her hair, then the skirt of her grey winter gown. 'And how was your . . . mother?'

This question always came sooner or later; sooner if Lawrence was not around. 'She's fine. Looking forward to coming for her visit.'

Bella looked at him then, her gaze measuring and a little fearful. Her next question came with a voice pressed and guarded. 'And did anything . . . else happen while you were away?'

Anything else?

Oh.

Andrew couldn't look at her. Instead, he stared at his feet, some parts in him twisted in shame, others doing the same with relief. If only he could work out how he really felt about this. 'No. Nothing. I . . . I think Finnlay has given up on me.'

'Oh?'

Andrew continued, whispering himself, 'You don't have to

worry, Aunt Bella. I don't think I'm ever going to be a sorcerer.'

Her silence sat heavy inside him, drawing his eyes up once more to see her expression giving nothing away. Then she murmured, 'Would that be such a bad thing?'

Andrew shrugged. He wouldn't have much choice either way.

'Go ahead and wash up. We're having supper in the winter parlour. Come down once you're changed. We've all missed you. Welcome home.' With that, she gave him a brief kiss on his forehead, then turned and left him.

He headed down the passage towards his bedroom. The door was open, candles lit and another fire crackled to warm up the room. A thick blue rug lay on the wooden floor before the fireplace; the curtains were drawn to keep in the heat and fresh clothes were laid out on his bed.

Home.

He shut the door, pulling off his jacket as he walked across the room. He kicked his boots to one side and stretched his toes, moving more slowly now. He came to a halt by the north window, his hand on the cloth, feeling it between his fingers.

He waited and listened, an old, familiar and not unpleasant excitement building inside him.

Nobody came. Nobody knocked on his door. He had a few moments alone, at last.

Quickly he pushed the curtain aside to reveal the stone window embrasure. The night killed any view he might have had, but he was here for something else entirely. With deft fingers, he felt along the wall to his left, edging out a piece of stone that, to the eye at least, appeared to sit perfect and flat with its neighbours. Little by little he loosened it until he could get a better grip. Then, his heart in his throat against disappointment, he slid it out completely to reveal a small cavity in the wall, a place, he was sure, nobody but he knew about.

Or rather, nobody but himself and one other, whoever he was.

Pulling up his bottom lip, Andrew reached into the dark, cold space and touched his fingers upon a smooth, flat surface.

His heart leaped and a grin poured over his face. He gripped the book and brought it out carefully – sometimes these gifts were quite old and a little fragile. This one, however, looked newer and very sturdy.

Pausing only long enough to listen again, he turned so he could hold it up to the light, allowing the curtain to shield him from the window. He opened the cover of the book and removed a single sheet of paper. He unfolded it and read:

> *As always, once you have finished with this, place it back in the alcove. Do not leave it lying about as it would raise too many questions. This book you hold in your hands is rarely seen outside a Guildehall. It's called a Shamar and contains the oldest Guilde laws in existence. When you read it, consider the evolution of the Guilde and how these laws became those we have today. Consider how each successive Proctor has interpreted such laws and used them to his own purposes.*
>
> *In answer to your last question, no, I don't believe the war between the Empire and the Cabal could have been prevented. The power the Cabal wielded was always going to be a threat to the Empire. While the Empire had a sorcerer in every court, it appeared the situation was under control. The moment that changed, war was inevitable. Power must always have its balance. Nature demands it. Perhaps that was why, despite its obvious advantages, the Cabal was unable to defeat the Empire on the battlefield – because for the Cabal to rule in such a manner would have allowed no balance of power. Corruption is a simple child's step away.*
>
> *Read and read carefully. Learn what you can.*

It was unsigned, as always.

Andrew sank back against the wall and sighed. The leather binding felt warm in his hand and already he itched to read the words chosen so carefully for him. Even so, he would like to know who it was who left these books for him, who answered his questions so neatly, who posed questions of his own not so easily answered.

His stomach growled. Even his endless curiosity was not a sufficient replacement for food.

He put the book back in its hiding place, to be read later. He replaced the stone, set the curtain straight and began stripping off his clothes. As he sank into the bath, he put his head back and breathed deeply. Delicious smells rose from the kitchens below and his stomach protested loudly once more.

Even so, he relaxed and listened, tried to feel the air for that . . . essence he usually felt after a book had been left – but there was no trace. He'd been gone two months. Perhaps that was too long.

Or perhaps he was just imagining that part of it. After all, if he wasn't a sorcerer, how could he Sense anything?

The air was damp by the time Micah approached his home. For all the arguments and fights he'd had to endure from both Bella and Lawrence to him staying there, they had, in the end, allocated to him a woodcutter's cottage, hidden in a narrow copse over which hung an ivy-strewn cliff. Now and then he would have dreams of the cliff falling down on him as he slept, but apart from that, the place was both comfortable and discreet, considering he shouldn't even be here.

Of course, not all of his fellow rebels had been blessed with such a fate. Most of the men who had survived the Battle of Shan Moss had been forced to leave Lusara. So Micah was not unaware of the precious position he occupied. Neither Bella nor Lawrence had ever fully sanctioned his presence, despite the help he'd been over the years. They still believed that his being here, for whatever purpose, endangered Andrew as much as it protected him. Micah couldn't help but agree with them.

But still he stayed.

As the ground began the gentle climb up to his cottage, he dismounted and completed the journey on foot. With his weary horse trailing behind him, he reached the small clearing, blinking in the darkness.

Something was different.

He dropped the reins and silently drew his sword. It was too dark to see footprints in the snow. With his hand on the latch, he pulled in a breath, ready to sprint forward.

The latch turned without his help and the door swung inwards, revealing nothing but darkness—

And a scent sweet and unpredictable.

'Sairead?'

The whisper barely breached the air when she emerged from the shadows, a flash of smile on her face and then she was in his arms, warm and close, delightful, burying her face in his shoulder as he held on.

It felt so damn good holding her again. He breathed her in deeply, letting her essence fill and sustain him, warm and complete him. Minutes drifted by uncounted and then she was clasping his face between her hands, her breath warming his skin.

'I've been waiting for you for hours. I thought you'd never come home. Do you have to leave again tonight?'

'No,' he replied, a smile growing from inside him. Two long months and he still hadn't seen her face. 'You?'

'No. I can stay until tomorrow.'

'Good.' He wasted no more words then, silencing further questions by kissing her deeply.

He didn't notice when the sleet began hours later.

Andrew sipped gingerly on the spiced wine. The aroma alone was almost enough to make him sleepy. A week on horseback crossing the country, then a hot bath and a wonderful meal had all worked their toll on him. He wanted to slip under the table, curl up with the dogs and go to sleep.

Lawrence, however, had other ideas. He sat at the end of the table, talking in his quiet way, explaining all that had happened at Maitland while Andrew had been gone. No small detail was left out, no lost sheep forgotten, nor fallen branch unaccounted for. Lawrence had a good mind for such detail.

His uncle ate his meal in a methodical manner, sipping wine every three mouthfuls of food. This spring would see his fiftieth birthday and Andrew and Bella had planned a small party in honour of it. Brown eyes watched everything Andrew did in silent judgement, his bald head making soft features seem harder than they were. For all his lack of humour, Lawrence was a gentle man. He did not, however, approve of Jenn, nor of Andrew's continued involvement with anything to do with sorcery.

Bella also sat at the table, contributing only a little here and there. Seated opposite Andrew was the faithful Father John. He'd been Jenn's chaplain at Ayr and had come here with Andrew after his father died. Though neither Bella nor Lawrence knew, John was Salti, a sorcerer of modest but determined power – though he exercised those abilities rarely.

John was his teacher, his tutor, his companion, but most of all, his friend; someone he could talk to about anything. Right now, however, John was watching him with a smile in his serious eyes, waiting for him to answer a question he hadn't been listening to.

Andrew sat up straight and drew in a deep breath to wake himself up more. Turning to his uncle, he offered a smile of apology. 'I'm sorry, Uncle, I'm afraid I was daydreaming. What were you saying?'

Lawrence raised his eyebrows. 'I know you're tired, son, but you really do need to know about this. The situation could deteriorate at any moment.'

That woke him up. 'Situation?'

Lawrence drained his wine and pushed his plate away. 'I don't know how else to deal with it. I try to find work for them, but it's never enough.'

'Refugees?' Andrew frowned and looked at Bella. 'Has there been some trouble?'

'I'm afraid so,' Lawrence replied. 'A barn on the south ridge was burned down two weeks ago. We've had grain shipments attacked with stones, fishing nets emptied. I know there are sheep missing, but I can't prove it until spring – and what would be the point anyway? I know our neighbours are in a worse predicament.'

'That's because they make no effort to help these people,' Bella added, obviously annoyed. 'But even helping them makes no difference. I'm sorry, Andrew, but I think you need to speak to them again.'

'Of course I will.' Andrew turned back to Lawrence. 'But are you sure it will help? I mean, the people may remember who my mother is, but they'll also remember who my father is, won't they? And they hated him. Why should *I* be able to talk to them when you can't?'

Lawrence sat back. 'You're young. The sins of your father are forgiven in you. I don't know that you'll be able to do much good, but I doubt it will make the situation worse.'

'I'll ride out tomorrow afternoon.' He opened his mouth to say something else, but was besieged by an enormous yawn.

Father John chuckled. 'I fear His Grace needs some sleep before he can contemplate such weighty matters further. Come, my lord, I will take you up.'

Andrew looked to Lawrence for permission, his uncle waved him on. 'Get your rest, son.'

'Goodnight.'

John opened the door for him, a hand ready at his elbow in case he should stumble from tiredness. Andrew laughed a little and, speaking softly though they were out of earshot from his aunt and uncle, said, 'You think I'm ready to fall over?'

'I think you'd *like* to fall over, yes, my lord. Come, be careful up these steps.'

Andrew pulled himself together and made it to his bedroom without incident. Father John followed along behind him, shutting the door with a gentle hand before turning to face Andrew. 'How is your mother?'

'She's well. Very well indeed. She gave me a letter for you. I'll get it in a moment.' Andrew perched on the edge of a chair and pulled off his boots. 'Is the situation with the refugees really so bad?'

'I wouldn't call it a crisis at this point. These people come because they know your uncle will not turn them away. They stay as long as they can find work and food – and then they move on.'

'I know. Micah and I saw more on the roads as we came

home.' Barefoot now, Andrew crossed to his bed and pulled the sealed letter out from under his pillow, handing it to John.

As John turned the letter over in his hands, he said, 'I should warn you, my lord. When you head off to Marsay, I shall be heading east.'

'East?' Andrew's eyes widened. 'To . . . Flan'har? You're going to look for Bishop McCauly?'

'That's right.' Something like pride flashed in John's eyes then, making Andrew grin. 'I just wanted to warn you, it may not be safe for me to come back for a while. It will depend on the situation, where he is, and how involved he is with Robert.'

Dumb with envy, Andrew sank back onto his bed. John was going off on his own adventure, following the trail of refugees across the border, without any idea what he might find. 'Do you know where to start looking?'

'I have a few ideas – but of course, I dare not go around asking without caution.'

Andrew stood once more. 'Please be careful.'

'Of course.' John reached up and traced the trium on his forehead. 'Now you get some sleep. We have a lot of work to do before I go. I can't allow you to be the worst-educated Duke in the country, can I?'

Knowing he was far from that, Andrew chuckled. 'We can't?'

Father John growled. 'Get some sleep, my lord. That's an order.'

'Has it stopped snowing?'

Micah shifted and lifted a corner of the curtain. Outside, the morning whiteness was dazzling against a sun only recently appeared. He could even see flashes of blue here and there amongst the barren tree tops, promising better weather to come. The ground was frozen with a thick layer of snow, burying both his trail and hers beneath it.

Satisfied, he laid down again, taking Sairead into his arms once more. She hadn't opened her eyes yet, but kept her head on his shoulder, the blankets around them, only moving long enough to wave some encouragement at the fire.

Micah moved to look at her properly. Her golden hair was a mess – mostly his fault – and strewn half across the pillow, framing her face with an innocent halo. There was nothing innocent however, about the smile which played across her lips, nor the faintly tanned face. Her eyes, when she finally opened them, were a soft crystal blue that turned ice-green when she was angry.

She made no comment about his watching her. She did her own share now and then, her fingers dusting over his face as though touch were an equal part of memory, necessary to keep warm the long months when they had to be apart.

'You travel more and more each year,' she said eventually. There was no question involved, merely a statement of fact. They never asked each other such questions, for answers were forbidden them.

'Yes,' was his only reply.

'I came by two weeks ago, but I missed you.'

'I'm sorry.'

She smiled. 'I know. I worked that out last night.' She slipped her hands around his waist and tried to get beneath his shirt. He made no effort to stop her, but her fingers were cold enough to make him shiver. He'd risen early to stoke up the fireplace and feed the horses, then climbed back into bed with her. Now she wriggled against him, beautifully naked and tempting him all over again.

Who knew how long it would be before she could come back – and whether he would be here when she did?

A sudden wave of fear washed over him and he caught her hands, pulling her close. She easily read the tension in his body and fitted herself to him, stilling instantly.

'I wish,' he said.

'So do I,' she replied. 'I love you.'

'I love you.'

And then they were silent again, immersing themselves in what they had.

Micah started when a log fell in the fireplace, reminding him that the day had begun – and that he was desperately hungry. 'You want something to eat?'

'I brought bread and cheese with me, both fresh. There's also some ale, but it's not very good.'

'Shall I bring it over?'

'Not for me. I'll have to get dressed.'

She said nothing about leaving soon, though he knew those words were inside her. He brushed his lips against her temple, then released her. Rolling out of bed, he pushed his feet into boots, tended to the fireplace and pulled out the bread and cheese from her bag. He would have to go into the village today to get his own supplies for the next few weeks. After that was the journey north with Andrew as he travelled to Marsay for Caslemas. Micah would wait outside the city and come back with him when he returned . . .

Andrew!

Micah dropped the knife, even as the sounds of footsteps crunching through snow reached him. Without a word to Sairead, he dashed to the door and pulled it open. Quickly he moved outside, closing the door firmly behind him. He was just in time.

Andrew was wading his way through the fresh snow, breath coming out in great clumps of steam. He wore a smile of triumph and lifted high a bag full of food.

'Good morning! Thought you might like some breakfast.'

Micah had to stop him, had to get him away before he could notice.

'What are you doing out here without a cloak?' Andrew almost laughed at the silliness of the idea, but Micah could think of no reply, impending doom sitting about him almost as effectively, and certainly more heavily. 'What's wrong?'

Andrew came to a halt only feet away. His smile was gone, replaced by a frown – which progressively grew deeper.

It was already too late.

'Micah?'

He could see all too clearly the progression. See the faint warnings Andrew would be feeling at the edges of his awareness, the vague unsettling something in the air he could not name – and yet it was undeniably there, and he couldn't ignore it. All a product of the Seal which protected all Salti, warned them of just such moments.

Micah gave it one try. 'My lord, thank you for the food but I think you should . . .'

Andrew stiffened, his eyes widening. 'You have . . . there's a Malachi inside, isn't there?' His gaze turned to the house, remained fixed on the door until, slowly, it opened. Andrew took a step back, then halted, his gaze flickering from Sairead to Micah and back again.

The cold suddenly bit into Micah's flesh, making him shiver. Almost all his worst fears had just come to life. Sairead came forward and placed a cloak over his shoulders. Her touch was enough to make him move, though his voice emerged rough and unkempt. 'Sairead, may I present His Grace, Andrew, Duke of Ayr. My lord, this is Sairead . . . my wife.'

Andrew froze for a moment, then, barely blinking, he reached out and took Sairead's hand. He brought it to his lips and didn't shudder with the courtly greeting. Then he straightened up, his eyes blank. He handed Micah the bag of food. 'Forgive me for disturbing you.'

Before Micah could say anything, Andrew spun on his heel and walked away, treading the snow he'd already trampled down on his long journey here. Breathing heavily, Micah turned to Sairead, searching her eyes for acceptance, though he knew he could never have it. 'Wait for me, please.' Then he was running after Andrew, as much as the snow would allow him.

'My lord, wait!'

Andrew pushed his body harder, picking his way between the trees where the snow was more shallow. Micah ran to catch up with him, nearly falling as he reached out to grab Andrew's arm.

'Andrew, let me explain!'

The boy turned and faced him, panting, air coming out in sharp jabs, hot and angry. 'Why? What is there to explain? Why you didn't tell me before? Well, I'm sure you've got a very good explanation, but since I wasn't supposed to know, I don't think there's any point in you telling me, is there?'

Andrew twisted his arm, trying to get away, but Micah held on firmly.

'You don't understand. It's not what you think.'

'Oh?' Andrew stopped struggling, his eyes opening wide, his eyebrows rising in an expression that was far too like his father's for Micah's comfort. 'You know what I think? I think I've been taught all my life that Malachi are a mortal threat to Salti, that Malachi work hand in hand with Nash, that they fought alongside Selar at Shan Moss and tried to kill a lot of people I care about. I know that the Malachi would do anything to destroy the Enclave and kill my *mother* to get the Key so don't you *dare* tell me that I shouldn't be angry, Micah or so help me . . .'

'I'd never tell you not to be angry.' And he wouldn't, by the gods, he wouldn't! Yes, too much of the father in this boy. The father who had exiled him without a word raised in question. The father who had turned his back on more than twenty years of friendship for the sake of that single question. And now he was about to get the same from the son.

Andrew's gaze narrowed as he struggled to regain control of his feelings, doing the same thing his father had done all his life, suppressing his anger. Though Micah could see it happening, he could do nothing to stop it.

'You should have told me,' Andrew pulled his arm free, but didn't appear ready to run off again.

'And what could I have said? Would your reaction have been any different?'

'Does anybody else know?'

Micah nodded. 'My mother knows I married, no more.'

Andrew searched his eyes. 'Could you not have told *me* that much?'

'I did not dare.'

For a moment, Andrew stared at him. Then he turned and took two steps away, his gaze dropping to the colourless ground. 'I can't believe you . . . married a Malachi, Micah. I mean, after everything you went through with . . . with Duke Robert. I know you're not friends with him now . . .' Andrew stiffened, his head coming up. 'That's it, isn't it? Why he banished you from his side? Because of Sairead?'

'Because I didn't tell him about her when I could.'

'And that's . . . that's why you hate him?'

Now it was Micah's turn to stare, to remain frozen to his place, trapped, as he had been for eight years, between two worlds that would never meet in peace. Could he say the words now? After so much time had passed?

'Tell me, Micah,' Andrew pressed, moving closer. 'Do you hate him?'

'Yes,' Micah breathed, releasing something in the process, though it made him feel no better.

'How can I trust you when he didn't?'

'But he should have.' Micah pushed his voice to communicate as much confidence as he could, all that he felt. 'Sairead is no threat to you.'

'No? How can you be so sure?'

'Because I know her. We've been married nearly seven years. Don't you think that if she'd wanted to betray me, she would have done so before now? She knows why I live here, she knows who you are. I've told her nothing – as she's told me nothing about her people. We see each other only every few months, for a few precious hours. That's the only way we can do this, until . . . until it's all over. Please, my lord, don't distrust me because of her. She won't harm you.'

Andrew remained unblinking throughout this plea. Then his gaze drifted over Micah's shoulder, back in the direction of the cottage. Abruptly, he took off for it, leaving Micah to once more hurry after him.

Sairead was waiting for them inside, her bags packed, the fire blazing to dry the building out after months of winter emptiness. Andrew waited on no formalities this time. He just walked up to her. There was wariness in her eyes, but she didn't spare a glance for Micah. He could only stand there and watch the exchange.

'You are Malachi, aren't you?'

'Yes. How did you know?'

'I can't answer that any more than you can tell me where your people come from.'

'The same place as yours, I believe.'

'So where are they now?'

'You must be Salti in order to ask that.'

'Micah says you can be trusted.'

'I will not betray my people.'

'But will you betray him?'

'Never! He is my husband! I have pledged my heart and soul to him.'

'Then will you betray me?'

'Why not? What are you to me?'

Micah took a step forward, 'Sairead . . .'

But Andrew held up his hand, silencing Micah. He'd never seen the boy like this before and while a part of him trembled at the sight, another part of him rejoiced.

'She's lying, Micah. I can see that much.'

'You can tell I'm lying? How?'

'I think I've already told you enough.'

'I'll say you have. More than I've learned about Salti in all my life. A little foolish, don't you think?'

'So?' Andrew shrugged. 'Better I test you now with only my life at risk, than discover later that you have lied even more – and to Micah.'

'But you won't kill me, will you, Salti Duke?'

Andrew kept his silence for long, terrible moments. Then he shook his head. 'No. I've never killed anyone. I don't think I could start with Micah's wife. Besides, he wouldn't let me, would you?'

Micah didn't get the opportunity to reply. Andrew turned and left then, only pausing once he got outside the door. His shoulders squared, Micah prepared to hear the verdict.

'So, what have you decided, my lord?' He swallowed hard against the inevitable. 'Will you banish me as your . . . as Robert did?'

'She stabbed him, didn't she? Before he fought Nash.'

'She was trying to protect me.'

'Of course.' Andrew didn't turn around. He just kept walking.

'My lord?' Micah called after him, but stood his ground. 'What will you do?'

Andrew kept going, but his words echoed around the clearing and up to the cliff above. 'I don't know, Micah. I really don't know.'

14

The constant slow tapping of steel against stone rang around the lower caves. Martha found it difficult not to pace her walking to the rhythm, nor to hum a tune along with it. These days, it was a constant within the Enclave, almost a new and vibrant heartbeat to the underground community, even if it did stop at nightfall and gave the air to the lower levels a distinctly dusty smell.

'How much more work have they to do?' came Jenn's voice from behind her.

'They've almost completed this cave – but there're another three to be done,' she finished as she reached the open doorway where the noise was loudest. Lady Margaret, Fiona and Jenn crowded beside her, looking in.

Two men looked up at their arrival, smiled and continued on; the tapping resumed. Chips of stone fell to the floor from an alcove the older man was working on, while the other set iron pitons into the wall, from which would hang shelving. The cave still had furniture to be brought in, rugs for the floor and a bed built into the alcove. But once done, it would be as comfortable as any other couple's dwelling in the Enclave, even if it was three levels further down than the rest of the accommodation.

'How much of this was here before they started?' Jenn said clearly over the noise.

'Most of what you see. The stonemasons refine the caves enough to make them livable. They Sense into the stone a little way, to make sure the support structure is strong, before doing any enlarging. Most of the Enclave caves are natural.'

'Natural for what? Who put them here in the first place?'

'I have no idea – although some of them were caused by water and gases. About half the tunnels between the caves were added later, by our ancestors.'

'And where are the new caves?' Jenn asked, stepping back. Martha gestured down the corridor and led the way.

Here the ground was rough. The natural tunnel had been partially widened to allow the workmen access, but it was far from complete. It came to an unsteady halt, leaving a drop of six feet or so. There was a temporary stepladder down, which Jenn took without hesitation. Margaret and Fiona stayed with Martha at the top.

This cave was bigger: wide and a little flat, one end coming to a halt in a stubborn wall of rock, the other tapering down until there was barely enough room for a man to crawl through.

Jenn inspected it thoroughly, running her hands over the rock, bending down to look at the dark crevice where shadows formed by the workers' lamps did not reach.

'We can't put a family in here,' she announced finally. 'Not unless we wall that area off. Children would find it too tempting. It looks like somebody has already been playing around here as it is. Has anyone followed the crevice along? To see where it goes?'

'These lower caves were surveyed about ten years ago.' Fiona replied, her tone as ungraceful as it always was with Jenn. 'I don't think it goes anywhere useful.'

'How far are we from the fire pools here?' Jenn stopped her inspection and faced them with her hands on her hips.

Martha let Fiona answer. She knew these caves better than anyone. Fiona pointed towards the opposite side of the cave. 'About twenty feet in that direction, another level or so lower.'

Jenn looked around again, as though for inspiration. 'And these are the best we have left?'

'The best we've discovered,' Martha spread her hands. 'Until we organise another survey party to go lower, then yes, this is all we have left.'

'It's not enough.'

'No.'

A silence folded in around them then, set to the constant rhythm of the workers. Then Margaret shifted her footing, going closer to the stepladder. 'This cave could be divided with a wall. We'd need to bring wood up from the valleys, but it could be converted into a school room, or library – then we could use the existing library as housing.'

'It's not big enough for the library,' Fiona replied, her tone much more gentle with the older woman. 'And we have no idea of the strength and stability of the rock this far into the mountain. We don't dare start enlarging these caves as we have done others further up.'

Martha looked at her, at her handsome face and careful, watchful eyes. There had always been some degree of conflict between Jenn and Fiona. They'd never become friends and, for the most part, appeared only to tolerate each other because of their respective connections to Finnlay. Lately though, there was a deeper undercurrent.

Margaret continued, 'Are you sure we can't build on the field? There's plenty of room. I know we'd need to get more materials – but we have to do that anyway, don't we?'

'Can you see anyone willing to live up there when the mountain gets snowed in for the winter?' Jenn asked. 'Even if we could spare the grazing land, we'd have to bring in far too much fuel. No,' she sighed, 'I think we need to consider the possibility that Salti have finally outgrown the Enclave.'

'What are you saying?' Fiona said.

'I'm saying that since Vaughn created a Bresail, it's been impossible for any Salti to live in Lusara without being in danger. Now more than ever. As long as Nash and Kenrick are in power, and the Malachi want the Key, our people need to stay here – only we have no more room here. So . . .'

'So?' Margaret asked, smiling a little.

'So,' Jenn continued, her tone speculative, 'perhaps we should look at finding another home.'

'What?' Fiona's voice echoed around the harsh walls. 'We couldn't possibly find a place bigger than this, or move everyone without drawing attention and what about the Key . . .'

Jenn raised her eyebrows and her hands at the same time. 'I didn't say we should all move – but why not found a second Enclave somewhere else? I know we'd have to consider how the

Key protects us – but there might be a way we can duplicate that. I mean,' Jenn smiled a little, including them all in her glance, 'Haven't you ever wondered why those Salti, six hundred years ago, decided on the Goleth as a likely spot to live?'

'No,' Fiona said decidedly. 'What difference does it make how they found the place?'

'So, you believe they just climbed through the mountains, heading for this peak, saying to each other, I'll bet there's some juicy caves we can settle in up ahead?' Jenn could barely keep the disdain from her voice. She made for the stepladder and climbed swiftly up to their level. 'I also think it might pay us not to have everyone in the same place. After all, the Key only protects us against being discovered – not against being attacked. So if somebody *were* to find out where we were . . .'

'Why?' Fiona snapped back, the flare in her eyes giving away more than she knew. 'Are you planning something we don't know about?'

'You know that's not what I said. And what if we lost the Key's protection? Wouldn't it be good to know we had another place already organised?'

'And wouldn't we be splitting our strength if we divided ourselves so? And—'

'Jenn! Martha!' Arlie emerged onto the small landing, sparing the new cave only the most superficial glance. 'You have to come. Finnlay and I . . . we've found something.'

Margaret walked a little slower than the others these days, so by the time she got to Henry's rooms, they were already all there. Finnlay, bless his enthusiastic heart, could hardly contain himself, and Arlie looked like he had the day his youngest baby had been born; awfully pleased with himself and trying to pretend he wasn't.

She looked around the room, at the space that had once been Henry's. The heavy bookshelves were almost empty now, their contents already deposited in the library. Most of his personal possessions had been removed over the last two weeks by his niece, Celia. And although there was still a faint air of Henry's character to these rooms, what remained was . . .

'What a mess you've made!' Margaret exclaimed. The table had been pulled away from the wall and was covered in notebooks, sheets of vellum, scrolls and boxes. The three chairs and parts of the floor were equally draped, leaving the place looking like a whirlwind had passed through recently, and none too kindly.

'Close the door, will you, Mother?' Finnlay flashed her a smile, then darted back around to the other side of the table. Once she'd shut the door, he gestured towards the chaos before him.

'Celia asked us to go through Henry's papers, to make sure there wasn't anything to do with council business we might need. We haven't finished yet—'

'But we found something very interesting—'

'Yes,' Finnlay nodded, tapping his hands on a pile of papers. 'Very interesting indeed.'

The women standing before them looked at each other with expressions so plainly patiently indulgent, Margaret almost laughed. Instead, she carefully moved a box of papers from one of the chairs and sat down.

'So, what have you found,' Jenn began, 'that's got you both excited as a pair of schoolboys?'

'And why,' Fiona added, 'do we need the door closed?'

'Ah,' Finnlay's enthusiasm faltered a little then. He paused, shot a measuring glance at Arlie and then replied, 'Well, it's just that, Henry never told anybody about this. The notes I've found so far suggest he didn't think people would take it very well but . . . well, until we've discussed it . . .'

'Finn,' Jenn sighed, 'please, just get on with it. We don't have all day.'

'Right, well . . .'

Arlie grinned at Finnlay's dithering and began crisply, 'Henry appears to have been working on a project for the last five years or so. Possibly longer, but that's as far back as we've got so far. He's been studying the children born at the Enclave, comparing the numbers to our historical records dating as far back as they go – which is to the Enclave's founders. What he's found is—'

'Incredible!' Finnlay finished for him, his enthusiasm now back in full flood. 'I have no idea why he started all this, but I can't believe nobody else noticed what's been happening, right under our noses.'

'For pity's sake,' Fiona groaned. 'What?'

'Well . . .' Finnlay began, but Jenn held up a hand and pointed to Arlie.

'No, you stay quiet. Arlie can tell us.'

Finnlay scowled, but kept his peace. Arlie, suppressing a smile, continued, 'Henry had trouble getting complete proof for all this because of the gaps in our library – but we all know that sorcery rarely followed a family line. When the Enclave was founded, fewer than one family in twenty had children with abilities. It didn't seem to matter whether one or both parents were sorcerers. Before that, inside the Cabal, it was even less frequent.'

Arlie paused, glancing down at the notes before him. 'Fifteen years ago, a family with one parent sorcerer had a one in three chance of having a sorcerer child. For both parents, it was one in two.'

Margaret frowned and looked at Jenn, but her gaze was fixed on the Healer as though she'd already guessed what he was about to say. A grey light glinted in her eyes, but she said nothing.

'Henry had no idea how or why it's happened, but today, in a family of one sorcerer parent, two out of three children will have talents – and when two sorcerers marry, *all* of their children will possess abilities.'

'All?' Jenn murmured, staring at him.

'And,' Finnlay added, determined not to be left out of this completely, 'with so many of us living here permanently now, each year we produce more and more sorcerers. I mean, our Seekers hardly find any nowadays, even when they do go out.' He looked to Fiona to confirm that, as she was responsible for coordinating their activities.

'Yes,' Fiona nodded, frowning. 'We're only finding children too young to take. Are you saying this is connected? For all we know, the Malachi are out there Seeking . . .'

'They never have before.'

'That we know of.' Fiona's voice came out hard, with an edge of disappointment to it – but Jenn held up her hand.

'Let's not get ahead of ourselves, please. Are you saying that if this trend continues, within a generation, or perhaps two, every person in this place will have abilities?'

Both Arlie and Finn nodded.

'But does he give any reason for this?' Martha asked. 'Is there nothing in his notes that suggests a theory as to why this is happening now?'

'He did seem anxious about the timing of these law changes,' Arlie shrugged. 'But he said nothing to us after he collapsed.'

'But we're still going through all this,' Finnlay's enthusiasm hadn't dropped at all. 'We need to check it all more carefully, and go through the rest of his books and papers, to make sure we didn't miss anything.'

'Well,' Fiona murmured, her gaze on the table, 'it's a pity we don't have any records of Malachi traditions. For all we know, all their children are born with abilities, and we're the ones lagging behind. Or,' she looked up at her husband, her eyes narrowing, 'perhaps they *are* taking all those our Seekers would normally pick up.'

'But the Malachi don't have the Key,' Finnlay waved his hand, dismissing her comments without even looking at her. Instead, his gaze was on the notebooks before him, his fingers tracing the edge of papers that held secrets from him. 'What happens to them doesn't have any relevance here. We need to start thinking about what this means, how we're going to deal with twice and three times the number of sorcerers within our midst. As it is, we have a problem with the children getting bored – how much worse is it going to be—'

'And where,' Martha added quietly, 'are we going to house all these people? If anybody with abilities is vulnerable to the Bresail . . .'

Margaret listened to all the arguments, but her eyes were on Jenn. There was something very odd going on beneath the surface, something almost a little frightening.

Abruptly, Jenn looked up, taking in a sharp breath that almost turned into a shudder. 'Henry *was* very concerned about the timing of the new laws, as though . . . Did he leave *any* theory behind at all?'

Finnlay met Jenn's gaze and the fine hairs on the back of Margaret's neck rose. It was almost as if a whole conversation was carried out in those brief moments, something weighty and hard and not at all pleasant to either of them. A battle of wills, almost.

'His last notes,' Finnlay replied after only the briefest hesitation, 'pinpoint the change to the year Andrew was born.'

Jenn's eyes widened fractionally. 'He actually mentions . . .'

'Andrew, yes.' And there was nothing in his voice. 'The last child without abilities was born two days before Andrew. Since then . . .'

Jenn paled a little, swallowed hard, then dropped her gaze to the table once more, but her eyes seemed to bore right through it.

Margaret felt compelled to fill the silence before it could become too difficult to ignore. She cleared her throat and said, 'Have we heard anything more from Patric? If he's due home soon, perhaps he'll be able to shed some light on this.'

'Yes!' Finnlay took off again. 'He had a reference to an obscure prophecy, centuries old. It predicted something would happen about four hundred years ago and . . . Henry's notes suggest a similar increase in sorcerer children at about the same time. As though . . .'

'What?' Fiona asked flatly.

Finnlay spread his arms wide. 'As though Salti were getting ready for something. Something that was supposed to happen!'

'That's ridiculous!' Fiona snapped. 'This is all guesswork! This is just because we have more Salti living here than before. It's natural that Salti will marry other Salti . . .'

'But the number of children born with abilities for each couple has increased,' Finnlay began to argue, but Jenn held up both hands, ordering silence.

'Henry was an old man when he died.' Jenn's voice came out

level, quiet, determined and quite unlike the way she usually sounded. 'He hadn't been well for a long time.'

'What?' Finnlay stepped towards her, enthusiasm ready to redirect to anger if necessary. 'Are you going to say he was feeble-minded? That he was imagining things?'

Jenn's gaze snapped to his – and again, there was that secret communication between them. Everyone in the room noticed it, including Fiona.

Jenn continued as though nothing had happened, 'Henry was a sick old man, trying to do the right thing. But we can't just take his word for this, he could be wrong.'

'How can you say that when—'

And in the blink of an eye, Jenn's expression changed completely, along with her voice. Both gaze and tone came out much harder than Margaret had ever witnessed before. 'Don't argue, Finnlay! I refuse to examine this question further until all this work is verified. I won't have you spreading the word throughout the Enclave that there's something strange going on. We have enough problems at the moment without that kind of reckless speculation from someone in your position.'

'Oh, what, so you're just going to *pretend* that none of this is true? Is that it? By the gods, Jenn, you're a fool!'

Abruptly the air was full of a physical tension far greater than the other. Margaret held her breath, waiting for Jenn to turn her full wrath on Finnlay, but nothing happened. Instead, Jenn just shook her head at him, and whispered, 'No.' With that, she turned and walked out, closing the door gently behind her.

'Serin's blood!' Fiona muttered into the ensuing silence, her anger more contained, but equally focused on Finnlay. 'When are you going to leave her alone?'

'Leave her alone? But you know what . . .'

'I know that you're obsessed with that . . . with that *boy*! To the exclusion of me, of your own daughters, to everything else where you just don't have the energy to even smile at us any more. But anything to do with Andrew, and you're right there, aren't you? Well, I don't care if he *is* your . . .'

'Fiona!' Finnlay stepped around the table in warning. 'We'll discuss this later.'

But his words had emptied his wife of her anger. Instead, she gazed upon him with sadness. 'No,' she murmured, 'we won't. And that's the problem.' She moved away from him then, and left quietly.

For a moment, Finnlay stared at the door, indecision clear on his face. Then his eyes narrowed and, without a word, he left. Margaret already knew which direction he was going in.

A gentle hand touched her shoulder and she turned to find Martha watching her, a faint, slightly resigned smile on her face. Arlie put an arm around his wife's waist and pressed a kiss to her temple.

'You're not worried about them, are you?'

Margaret resisted the urge to look at the empty doorway. 'No more than usual.'

'I think I might go and see how Fiona is,' Martha disengaged herself. 'Arlie could probably use some help working through all this, if you're interested?'

With a look at the tall man, then at the table, Margaret felt a crooked smile form across her face. 'Strangely, though I wouldn't have said so before, now I find a strong curiosity in me.'

As soon as Martha left them, Arlie pulled a chair up to the table and sat her down to work.

It was with a cautious hand that Martha knocked on the door to Fiona and Finnlay's rooms. A single word was called out and she entered, immediately peering around in case the girls were inside.

'They're out. All of them,' Fiona's voice came from the bedroom. 'I have no idea where and right at this moment . . .'

Carefully, Martha moved to the bedroom door and paused. Fiona was sitting on the end of the bed, feet on a wooden chest, winding spun wool from a skein into a ball. She appeared quite calm on the surface, but it was a good thing the wool was strong.

Martha dived into the mire. 'You know he can't help it.'

'Yes.'

'And he doesn't do it deliberately.'

'No.'

'He would never intentionally hurt either you or the girls.'

'Of course he wouldn't.'

'He's a good husband and father.'

'I could not possibly have asked for more in a man.'

'Except?' Martha posed quietly.

'Except . . .' Fiona's hands came to a halt. Her eyes shifted to the floor before her and she added, 'loyalty.'

'He loves you.'

Fiona said nothing to this and Martha moved forward. Shifting her skirts, she sat on the end of the wooden chest and turned to look at the other woman. 'He does love you, Fiona.'

'I'm not sure that even matters any more.' Fiona blinked a few times, as though her eyes stung. 'He was once prepared to defy Robert in order to marry me – and now, he runs around after . . . and she smiles at him and shares her secrets with him and loans him her son so he doesn't feel as though he's . . .' Fiona clamped her mouth shut, forcing further words back into her throat.

'Have you talked to him about this?'

Winding the wool once more, Fiona shook her head sharply. 'I've lost count of the number of times I've spoken and he's not listened. He just says, how can he not watch over his own nephew?' Fiona swallowed hard, her bitter words almost too much for the soft wool. 'The sainted Robert and his sainted Jenn. You don't know how close I've come to hating both of them!'

Fiona slapped the wool down on the bed and placed her hands either side of her, rocking back and forth a little, doing what she could to contain the confusion and frustration that leaked out of her with every gesture, every word. 'And you just watch them. Watch her. You'll see. It will all start up again and then he'll go off and be a hero once more because his damned brother is too damned noble for his own good. Those people out there,' she waved her hand, indicating those beyond the walls of the Enclave, 'they can't be saved because they don't want it. They've been conquered, for twenty-eight years. Most of them can't even remember what it was like before. What is Robert trying to prove? And why, why does he have to involve my husband in it? Why can't we just . . . just be left alone this time?'

Martha said nothing. Fiona didn't want answers or pat comforting responses that meant little in the light of her reality.

'He blames himself, you know.' Fiona added after a moment, her voice dropping to a whisper. 'He doesn't think I know. But I sleep with him. I hear his nightmares. I know about the . . . fears he has for Robert and Lusara. I know it means a lot to him, I understand that, I just . . .'

'Just what?'

'I just didn't think it would go on for so long. I thought . . . I thought by now he'd have a little . . . a little peace. But it's not going to happen, is it? Not now. Perhaps never. Can you tell me I'm wrong?'

Martha reached over and patted her hand once. 'I wish I could, my dear. I honestly wish I could.'

Finnlay didn't dare go straight to Jenn's rooms. He *wanted* to – but he simply couldn't trust his anger. Instead, he strode down one corridor after another, wasting minute after minute, sure he would calm down – but still, sooner than he expected, he was outside her door.

For once he didn't knock. He turned the handle and pushed the door open, but the room was dark and empty. He hovered on the threshold, still angry, then stepped over, into the shadowed space where he wouldn't have to pretend any more.

He left the door half-open, giving himself some light. It would be wrong to do this and burn candles at the same time.

She just had no idea. She was too close to the problem, and couldn't see it like he could. And turning her back on this new evidence was a piece of blatant stupidity.

His feet took him to the corner where she had her desk. It was piled high with books and scrolls, things she was working on.

She was always working. She never stopped. Even when they went to Shan Moss, she took work with her – but he had no idea what kind of work it was.

Frowning in curiosity, he checked the titles of some of the books, but those only increased his curiosity. These were all commentaries on a variety of different religions from all around the world. Some were holy books he hadn't even known were in the library. Many of them were open, and more than a few had little tags of paper stuck in them at various different pages.

What was Jenn doing here?

He flipped open a notebook that sat on top of everything else, skimming through one page after another, through scribbled quotes and their origins, and small but private notes beside each one. Little scraps of prophecy, jumbled words promising something or other, but nothing familiar, nothing that looked the same as Robert's Prophecy – but there was so much of it! And all had come from these holy books Jenn had been studying, as though . . .

One quote in particular jumped out at him, holding him still and steady against a host of possibilities. *And one shall be born to raise his armies, increasing his faithful by tenfold, to bring them unto the new world.*

He felt rather than heard her come up behind him. Her silence darkened the room. Inside it, he closed the notebook and laid it down on the desk. There was something horribly inevitable about the shadows.

'What else are you hiding?' he began.

'Nothing.'

'Why don't you trust me?'

'Perhaps because you break into my rooms, read my private journals – as though I belong to you in some manner. As though I owe you something and you're determined to get it, no matter what.'

Finnlay spent a moment listening to the words, and another moment listening to the deep silence. Then he turned. She looked too small, too fragile for this work. Too close to failing and too close to success.

'Tell me about Andrew.'

Jenn shook her head, her eyes fixed on his. 'This doesn't have anything to do with Andrew.'

'You can't keep protecting him.'

'He's a *child*.'

'Yes, and I have three daughters younger that I don't protect as much.'

'Three daughters who aren't subjected to anywhere near the dangers Andrew is.' Jenn turned away, waving a hand to the candles for light. She closed the door and rested her forehead against it. She looked tired. 'For pity's sake, Finn, Andrew spends half of every year at court. Nash knows he's my son.'

She closed her eyes, shutting out Finnlay and his demands, his anger and his truth. 'Every time Andrew leaves here . . . I wonder if it will be the last time I see him. It would be so easy for Nash to just take him, to use him against me, force me out into the open – but he hasn't.'

The answer was all too obvious. 'He's not ready. He's not strong enough to face you.' Forming a frown of his own, Finnlay moved forward. 'But he's never shown any interest in Andrew, has he? He can't know Andrew is Robert's son . . .'

Jenn moved away from the door. 'Please, Finn, just leave it alone, will you?'

The denial snapped something inside him. 'Mineah's teeth, Jenn, I'm the closest thing he has to a father! Don't I have a right to know? Don't I have *any* say in his life, in his future? What are all those books about? And why did you dismiss Henry's work with barely a look?'

'I didn't dismiss it,' Jenn began – but Finnlay opened his eyes wider, seeing something he'd entirely missed before. He raised his hand and pointed at her, the fullness of certainty swelling through him, guiding his words.

'You're afraid Andrew is also involved in the Prophecy. That's it, isn't it? That's what this,' he waved his hand at her desk, at the books and scrolls piled there, 'is all about, isn't it? That's why . . . By the gods! *And one shall be born to raise his armies* . . .' He had to stop then, to swallow hard, unable to stop the patterns forming in his head, struggling to voice them all as they came to him. 'That's what the . . . the Bonding was all about. Why you and Robert . . .' Shame made him pause then, forced him to choose his words with propriety.

He looked up. Jenn was staring at him with open horror in her eyes. He wanted to stop, wanted to go on as she had and pretend that none of this made any sense. It would be so much easier to pretend.

'You and Robert were Bonded so you would conceive Andrew.' The certainty in his own voice both startled and scared him.

'No,' Jenn breathed the word and looked away, her chin tightening as he continued.

'You said . . . you said it was a compulsion, to be with Robert that night before your wedding. That he . . . felt the same compulsion—'

'He didn't force me.'

Finnlay dropped his voice, moving closer to her to put his hands on her shoulders. 'He loved you – but he knew there were powers at play there. That's what sent him away afterwards. That's why he felt he'd betrayed you.'

She was silent then, her gaze on the floor between them, as though the truth were something that scared her more than the future.

'You have to tell him.'

'Oh, Finn, what good would it do him to know his father . . .'

'No,' Finnlay interrupted quietly. 'I mean, you have to tell Robert. You have to let him know there's another factor to the Prophecy he doesn't know about.'

Her head shot up. 'I can't do that.'

'Not even if it might have a bearing on his survival? On Andrew's?'

'And how can you possibly know that – when Andrew isn't even *mentioned* in the Prophecy!'

'Neither is the Word of Destruction and yet, Robert is haunted by it!'

'This has nothing to do with Robert!'

'Andrew is his son!'

'No!' Jenn held up her hands, her voice strong and determined, her eyes alight. 'I am so sick of hearing that from you! I swear, the next time—'

'But he *is* Robert's son!'

'Only to the extent that Robert sired him! Beyond that?'

'What do you mean?' Finnlay frowned, stumbling in this sudden change of direction.

'I mean,' Jenn replied, her expression hard, 'that Robert had plenty of opportunity to ask me. I even saw the thought cross his mind – but he never did. He couldn't bring himself to ask because he didn't want to know, Finn. He still doesn't.'

She turned away then, her profile hiding much of what she was feeling. 'He never wanted to love me in the first place. My having his child would only have . . .'

'Made things worse?'

He stopped when she turned her full gaze on him, the depths in her blue eyes silencing him.

On impulse, he reached up and touched the side of her face, soothed cool skin and brought a tiny shudder to the rest of her.

His breath caught in his throat and he stepped closer, not thinking about what he was doing – and determined not to. He kissed her, and knew immediately the answer to the first question. He'd always known he would do this one day.

And when she kissed him in return, he knew she could read his mind. When they parted, they clung together just long enough to be sure. Then he stepped back, his hands on her waist, his eyes on hers.

She was smiling a little. 'I guess we know now, huh?'

'I guess we do.'

He took her hand and squeezed it. 'I'd better go and see my wife. Are you coming down for supper?'

'Later.'

As the silence grew between them, he murmured, 'If Andrew *is* a part of the Prophecy, there is nothing we can do to stop it. You know that.'

Jenn smiled a little. 'You never give up, do you? The three of you, all Douglas men to the last. You simply refuse to give up.'

226

'Well,' Finnlay said, 'we all have our little faults.' Andrew's of course, was that he stubbornly refused to develop powers – and his mother's determination that he should was abruptly clear.

There was more of that smile in her eyes. But it was not – and never would be – the smile she'd once given his brother.

He left quietly, walking along the lamp-lit corridors drained, tired and ragged along his own edges. All this talk about things changing and Prophecy and Kings – and really, nothing had changed at all. Perhaps nothing ever would.

He found himself in the doorway to his rooms. Fiona stood at the hearth, pouring water from a heavy jug into a pot over the fire. She knew he was there and yet she didn't turn. Just blew a strand of hair from her face, one of many that had escaped the tiny braids she had laced that morning.

He moved forward, took the weight of the jug and let her guide the last drop into the pot. Then he placed the jug on the table, reached out and pulled her into his arms. She felt stiff and unyielding, but that didn't matter.

They would always fight. They always had. It was as much a part of their lives as their children. She was afraid for him, afraid for their future. How could he not love the passion with which she fought for them?

'I'm sorry,' he whispered.

'I know,' she whispered in return, relaxing in his embrace a little. But Finnlay knew that did not mean either forgiveness, or retraction.

'I love you.' And he did, with something that filled his entire being.

'And there are days when I almost wish you didn't.'

He turned and placed a soft kiss on the lobe of her ear. 'I know. But I wish you wouldn't worry so. You know . . .'

She moved, placing her hand over his mouth and looking into his eyes. A heartbeat later, she murmured, 'I can live with it. I won't fight it. But please, Finn, don't promise me everything will be all right? Not until it's all finally over? Please?'

'Yes. I can do that.' And he pulled her close again, resting in her, where he belonged.

*

Jenn let the shadows grow long across the floor of her bedroom as the candle burned low. Of course she should have been working, but even now, hours after Finnlay had left her, the echo of his words still clamoured around her empty rooms, showing up their emptiness, making her too aware of the depth of that emptiness.

Silliness, all of it – she should be used to feeling lonely by now.

But work was not the distraction it had once been. Henry had blown all that away with a few well-chosen theories.

Another violent flash of fear twisted across her belly and she took a breath, sitting up to swing her legs over the bed.

This was stupid. Fear alone wasn't going to get her baby hurt, was it? But communicating her fear to him, making him think there was something to be afraid of, making him wonder if she'd failed him, or not told him something, that she'd betrayed him . . .

As she had his father.

'Damn it!' She stood, brushing her skirts down, reaching up to smooth her hair back to where it was bound up.

She couldn't let this rattle her. There was still absolutely *no* evidence that Andrew might be involved in the Prophecy and, worse, no way of proving he wasn't – short of asking the Key. But then, the Key never answered direct questions about the Prophecy anyway, so there wasn't any point.

'Jenn?'

The call was followed by sharp knocking on her door. She went out into the sitting room and pulled the door open. Martha stood there, her face pale with worry.

'You need to come. There's been some trouble. Some of the children – they've gone missing.'

The press of people within the council chamber was nothing compared to the pressure Jenn felt behind her eyes, the dull ache inside that told her she had failed. Nevertheless, she worked as quickly and as efficiently as she could, given the degree of near-panic the news had engendered. Everybody was talking at the same time and the level of anxiety was almost painful to her ears. Already three small groups had begun searching lower tunnels and disused passages. There were Seekers straining to find some sign of the children, but so much rock – and indeed, the protection of the Key – hindered such efforts.

It was going to be a long night.

A friendly face came towards her through the crowd and Jenn almost sighed with relief to see Martha's smile. Murmuring apologies, she pushed her way through to Jenn's side. Only then did Jenn see who was following behind her.

'Guy?' The boy could barely raise his eyes to look at her. Instead, he stuck close to Martha and seemed to shrink under the tension in the council chamber.

Without hesitation, Jenn raised her voice and called for quiet. Seconds later, she perched on the edge of a chair in front of Guy and took his hand in hers. She deliberately ignored everyone else and instead, concentrated on the fact that this was Andrew's best friend.

'You know where they've gone, don't you?'

Guy nodded. He swallowed loudly, then his eyes flickered up to hers. 'Neil said that if I told anyone . . .'

'Neil isn't here,' Jenn replied gently. 'And I wouldn't let him do anything to you anyway. Tell me where they've gone, Guy. If they're in the new caves below, they could get trapped, hurt or killed. I need to know.'

'They wanted me to go with them but I said what they were doing was stupid and it is. They've . . . they've left.'

'Left?' A faint shuffling in the room made her hold up her hand, but she kept all her attention on the boy. 'Left the Enclave?'

'Yes. Last night. They took horses and clothes and . . .'

But Jenn didn't hear the rest as the entire room erupted. Still ignoring them, Jenn leaned in close to Guy. 'Do you know what direction they headed in?'

As he shook his head, Jenn squeezed his shoulder and stood, keeping hold of him as much for his protection as anything else. Once more she raised her voice, forcing them to listen. 'We need two mounted search parties, one to head east and one west. Recall the searchers from the lower caves. Murdoch will lead the party heading east, Arlie going west. Martha, Desta and Seamus, gather the people you need and sort out a plan of evacuation just in case we need it.'

The noise exploded again, fear, horror and determination. Jenn added, 'We don't have time to ask why or how. We need to get those children back. Now.'

Murdoch, Arlie and others helped then, drawing worried parents out of the room, issuing orders of their own. At the movement, Jenn turned back to Guy. 'Do you know how many went?'

'Neil and Zea, Liam and Sayre and . . .'

'Jenn!' Finnlay's voice cut through as he himself was pushing through the last of those leaving. He held a piece of paper in his hand, his face white as snow, his eyes wild. 'I have to go with Murdoch. Helen's gone with them!'

Finnlay ignored the wind as he brought his horse out of the stable, even ignored the icy brush of snow as it slapped against his face. He could only focus on getting out there, following Arlie's men through the gate and rushing down the eastern path through the mountains.

It was all his fault. Entirely his fault. If he'd never suggested taking the children out into Shan Moss, if he'd never given them a taste of freedom, this might never have happened. And now there were five of them and his own dear, sweet Helen, all out there on their own, with no real knowledge of the world, thinking that Osbert's laws would save them. They had no real understanding of the Bresail, how it could Seek them out and betray them to either King or Nash. They simply couldn't comprehend the danger they were in from a country terrified of what they were.

Damn it, they'd been *told* the law changes were a plot! How could they think it was safe to leave?

Fiona was right: he was too wound up with Andrew and Jenn and Robert; not spending enough time thinking about his own family, his own daughter. He should have seen her desire to go, should have found some way to stop this before it happened.

He couldn't Seek her. Jenn had reminded him, made him promise he wouldn't try. If he did – out there on his own without her protection – and Nash was paying attention, then he would be found and . . .

No, he couldn't think about that either. So he wouldn't Seek her, but he would find her, he had to.

Murdoch called out to him, his words whipped away by the wind, his face almost invisible in the darkness. How long had it been now? A day and a half, perhaps? How far could they get in that time?

'We can't go out in this, Finn! We'll get blown off the mountain!'

'I'm going on!' He began to lead his horse across the field, already ankle-deep in snow. Of course the children had taken their opportunity, hadn't they? When the snow had cleared for a few days, when getting down off the mountain was possible; a brief opening in the winter for them to escape into.

Murdoch stumbled after him, grabbing onto his arm, forcing him to stop. 'We have to wait until this calms down! What good are you going to be to Helen if you get killed? Now come inside!'

'I can't leave her . . .'

'I'm not asking you to! We just need to wait a few hours, that's all.'

'A few hours might be too late!'

'Not if we get some help!'

Finnlay stared at the man, into dark eyes framed by greying hair made whiter by sticky snow. The pause allowed him to remember who this was. A moment later, he let Murdoch drag him back to the stable, left his horse in the care of the others, then followed him back into the caves where the air was warmer but his heart was colder.

Murdoch's stride was long and purposeful. The door to the council chamber was half-open, only a few people still inside. The big man wasted no time. He walked the length of the room, carefully caught Jenn's elbow and drew her into a corner where the lamplight drew strange shapes against the painted walls.

'You need to mindspeak Robert.'

Jenn's eyes widened and her mouth dropped open. She looked at Finnlay, standing by uselessly and frowned. Finnlay could almost see the thoughts flashing across her mind, but she restricted herself to just one word. 'Why?'

'Because we can't get down off the mountain at least until morning, possibly longer. That will give the children almost two days' head start. If they have gone east, they could be anywhere by then – and if they have been picked up by . . .'

'By Nash or Kenrick?' This was barely breathed, but instantly, Jenn's mind was working along the same lines as Murdoch's.

'I know where Robert will be now. He's close enough to meet up with us – and he's almost as strong a Seeker as Finnlay. He can find the children no matter how strong their shielding. If you mindspeak him now, he can be Seeking them, while we're waiting for the storm to stop. He might even find them by the time we get down into the valley.'

Jenn said nothing for a moment, then said, sharply. 'You're right. I'll get my cloak. It will be easier if I'm outside.'

15

The solid walls of Dunlorn Castle protected Robert from the outside world, but not even that dense stone could silence the voice inside his head. He pressed both hands against the guardroom wall, feeling the ancient and the familiar, the close and the near; concentrating on keeping the past in this present, remembering whose voice was speaking into his mind eight years since he'd last heard it.

Robert? Where are you? She sounded worried, quiet and yet urgent, but with no personal inflection in her silent tone.

Robert swore, a muttered curse, even as he was preparing words to send back to her, carried on a breath of fear. *I'm at Dunlorn. What's wrong? Is it Finnlay – or my mother?*

No, they're both fine. Murdoch said I should contact you. Some of the children have left the Enclave. They've run away. We've sent a search party west, into Shan Moss, but the Goleth is besieged by a snowstorm at the moment and the eastern search party can't get away until it stops. Can you help?

Robert was already moving, packing up his few things, storing the others away beneath the floorboards. *How long since the children left?*

A day and a half now. Murdoch and Finnlay are ready to go, but . . .

Finnlay? Why?

He could almost taste the hesitation in her voice.

I can't stop him, Robert. Helen has gone with the others.

Helen too? His own niece? And why would they run away? *How many in all?* He'd reached the stable and was saddling his horse, yet his eyes saw nothing in the darkness, only the memory of Jenn's face as he'd last seen it, her beauty no reflection for the shadows within him.

Five. They think it's safe with these law changes. I should have . . . And he could hear her drawing herself together, turning from self-recrimination to determination in one swift step.

That step brought a smile to his face, even as the memories sifted around inside him. Without a word, he brought his horse out into the empty courtyard and swung up into the saddle.

She had been to Dunlorn once, in secret, aiding the Queen's escape. She'd seen nothing of the place and he'd sent her away, already afraid of how he felt about her, knowing that there was all some terrible purpose behind it, but desperately wishing there wasn't.

With a kick to his horse, he brought his thoughts back to her in this time, back to these problems here and now. *Are you prepared in case we don't find them in time? Or in case they're followed back up to the Goleth?*

We're already packing in case we need to evacuate.

Do you have somewhere to go if you do? The naked pause at this made him curse. Before she could provide him with some hasty lie, he said, *Head into Shan Moss and stick together. If I can, I'll come and get you – if not, as soon as the weather calms, go south to Aaran. Take a ship to Flan'har and make directly for Bleakstone. The Bishop will be there and there's enough room to keep everyone safe for a while. Just don't go unless you have to.*

Of course not. Jenn paused and when her voice came back, it was as though the last eight years had never been. *The Key said we should stay, no matter what.*

Robert rode through the gate, closing his eyes in what he knew, deep down, was defeat. *The choice is yours, Jenn. You're joined to the Key after all, and bound to do as it says. All the same, if you head to Bleakstone, you will at least have the luxury to argue that I'm wrong.*

I know. That voice was small – but then, abruptly, she returned, as strong and as indomitable as always. *Let me know when you meet up with Finnlay. I don't want him mindspeaking me, just in case Nash can trace him that way as well. Good luck.*

I think we're going to need it. And with that, her voice was gone and the feeling of being alone faded with it.

Helen shivered, a rattle that made her bones ache and her teeth snap together. She'd lived her whole life on top of the highest mountain in Lusara and yet she'd never felt this cold before.

She could hardly see anything in the gloom. Thick fog surrounded the wood, soaked into the tree trunks, seeped into the ground, leaving her skin, her clothes, her boots, everything, damp and cloying. One of the boys had tried to light a fire just after dark, but it had never grown into the blaze they needed, never did much more than emphasise just how dark the fog really was in the middle of the night.

But she refused to be sorry, to wish she'd not come. Perhaps they should have waited until spring at least, but nothing bad had happened to them so far, and they *would* go home in a little while anyway.

She gave a determined sniff. Mother and Father would be worried, that was true. But she had left a note, so they would understand at least. Hopefully they wouldn't worry too much. She gave another sniff and batted aside the twinge of guilt. It only made the cold worse.

It was her turn to keep watch. She sat with her back to a

rotting trunk, blankets wrapped around her, arms hugging her knees, trying not to jump and call out at every noise in the night. She could smell dawn on the air, but it was still a long way off. The others were all asleep, as close to the meagre fire as they could get, in their own blankets, with their own nightmares, with their own share of the cold.

Liam had given her the opportunity and she'd taken it. Neil had made it all sound so exciting, so possible, and she'd believed him. Sayre had got the horses for them, Zea the food, all without the adults knowing. They were going to see Lusara at least once in their lives, do it on their own for once, without Father, or the Jaibir, or anyone else saying where they could go or what they could do. No more stupid rules to follow or punishments for breaking them.

Just . . . freedom.

It had sounded so good. And the gods seemed to be with them, giving them a break in the weather, a passage into the hills between layers of snow. But every time they turned south, they found soldiers riding the roads, more men in Guilde yellow, a stark warning despite the fact that the laws had supposedly changed in their favour.

She shivered again, pulling the blanket over her head, shutting out the soft slithers and gentle quakings of the winter forest. She did want to go home – but not yet. There was still more to see, perhaps a thread of sunlight on the hills, or better still, the ocean.

That's what the others wanted, though they were careful not to show the fear they felt whenever a Guilde squad rode nearby or when they had to find some empty building, away from villages or farms where they could take shelter.

She knew, without asking, that she was not the only one who wanted to go home.

The horse stumbled and Robert jerked awake, blinking rapidly, his Senses reaching out from instinct, looking for trouble. Alert now, he looked around, feeling more than seeing, but for the moment, he was alone on the road. It was his horse who was in trouble.

He pulled up, swung his leg over the animal and slid gingerly to the ground. His legs felt stiff and his feet tingled with the sudden movement. An icy winter sun bled down through patchy clouds, giving no warmth and none too much light. He glanced up at it, trying to guess how much of the day was left, but his head ached with the angle and a moment later he pressed his forehead against the warm neck of the horse, both giving and receiving comfort.

He was getting too old for this.

A dry chuckle rattled inside him. He didn't feel age, not physically. The Key had seen to that. He was forty-three, but looked and, on a good day, felt ten years less than that. Only this wasn't a good day. Nor had the three previous been as he'd raced across Lusara looking for Salti children and his foolish, stubborn brother. He needed sleep, and so did his poor horse. It stood panting beside him, too well-trained to move, too brave to just settle where it was and take the rest it needed.

'Don't worry, my friend. Not too much further to go.' He gave the animal another pat, then collected the reins and began walking, letting the horse follow at its own pace.

The exercise would do him good, wake him up properly. Dozing in the saddle was fine if he wasn't alone, but out here, on this exposed ridge, travelling one of the better-made roads west was not a good idea. The dirt beneath his feet was wet with vanished snow, the fields north and south still covered in patches of it as though waiting for the next downfall.

As a child, he'd loved winter, loved the differences it would bring to the land, knowing that spring would come along eventually and change everything back with a kind of hope that was almost tangible.

It had been a long time since he'd felt that way.

The land around him was silent, with only a faint breeze in his ears and the steady clopping of the horse to keep him company. This was as good a place as any to try again.

He came to a halt, gentling the horse with soft words and hands. Then he closed his eyes, held his breath and sent his Senses out. West from here, further. South a little, and there,

236

there was Finnlay, his aura bright and so easily distinguishable, others with him, travelling now, moving slowly.

Robert carried on, beyond to where the hills were flatter, to where trees grew only in stunted copses and where sheep and cattle picked what they could from the iced ground. South further, scratching around, going back and forth, pushing and yet trying not to, trying to make it come as it would, to make his power work itself without direction because that was the only way he could find her, his own niece, a child he barely knew.

A shadow. A faint shifting of colour on the hazy landscape of his Seeking. He couldn't guarantee it was her, but there were tones to it similar to Finnlay's, similar to Fiona's – and it was the closest thing he'd found in three days of trying.

So, she was still alive, at least. Were the others? And they were still heading south, perhaps three days from the coast. Did they mean to stop there, or keep going? And what, in the name of Serin, had possessed them to leave the safety of the Enclave in the first place?

He opened his eyes. A wave of dizziness almost made him stagger against the horse. Rest he needed – and a hot meal.

He resumed his journey, his feet hurrying as much as his exhaustion would allow. By tonight, he would meet up with Finnlay and the others. Perhaps tomorrow, if they were lucky, they might come upon Helen and her friends.

So it was to be tonight, then. Meeting up with Finnlay again for the first time in eight years. Having, for once, a little more than the detail-filled stories Murdoch would give him each spring, when they began the new year's work together. Robert tried not to ask, but Murdoch supplied regardless, understanding his need to know, to partake in his family's life, however vicariously.

But tonight he would see Finnlay himself. See him and remember how much he'd missed his brother, find out if he in turn had been missed.

And whether he'd yet been forgiven.

As each day drew to a close, Finnlay's patience thinned a little more and he could do nothing to stop himself pacing up and down in whatever spot they'd camped in for the night. Always hidden by trees, in some copse or gully; always where it was sheltered and where there was no traffic on the road, nor people who would find them by accident. Always in a place where the Guilde was far away and where the snow was settled deeply until spring.

It was worse than being blind, not being able to Seek. Never before in his life had it meant so much to him to try – and yet, he didn't dare. Risking his own life was one thing, but he could not risk others as well.

In the shadow of a barren elm, he crouched down onto a raised and knotty root exposed above the snow. He leaned his back against the ancient trunk, deliberately preventing further pacing. He knew it bothered the others, knew it did no good, but he had all this urgent energy he needed to burn up, as though he were once again a young man.

Everyone else was asleep, except for Murdoch keeping watch by the outer line of trees. But Finnlay couldn't sleep, couldn't forget that they still hadn't found the children.

Some moments, Finnlay could hardly breathe with worry. Not only that, but he missed Helen. With the exception of the time he'd spent at the Battle, he'd not been away from her more than a day in her entire life. She had become as essential to him as living. Now, there was just this ache inside him, black with frustration and anger, directed entirely at himself.

He should have been paying more attention. How could he not have noticed that his own daughter had been gone almost a day? How had the other parents made the same mistake?

Because they'd all grown accustomed to the safety of the Enclave, become complacent. Because they knew the children were restless and sought to give them whatever freedoms they could have by not structuring their days too much, nor demanding to know where they were every minute. Because everybody had been warned, in the strongest possible terms, that regardless of the Guilde, it was still hopelessly unsafe for any Salti to go wandering around in Lusara.

Because they'd all thought that fear would be enough. But to children young and fear*less*, warnings meant too little and had been given much too late. After all, hadn't he – and Robert, for that matter – gone and done similar things at the same age? Had their adventures been any less foolish?

So why did his own fear almost paralyse him?

Because this time, he was the father, and this time, his beautiful Helen was in danger.

The itch in his hands burned. From reflex, he flipped his wrist, bringing his *ayarn* out so that he could just look at it, perhaps even imagine that it was safe for him to try Seeking and hope that Nash wasn't paying attention and would find him. After all, it was still possible that Robert had succeeded in killing him, that the reason everything had been peaceful over the last eight years was because the man was dead.

It *was* possible, wasn't it?

'What do you plan to do with that?' Murdoch asked, approaching from the fire.

'Trying to remember what I'm supposed to be doing with it,' Finnlay replied, hearing the heavy irony in his own voice.

When Murdoch stopped before him, he said, 'I certainly don't envy you, I'll admit that much. But for the moment, I wouldn't worry about it.'

'Oh? Why not?'

The big man turned and peered into the trees. 'Because Robert's coming.'

Finnlay sprang to his feet, but before he could do so much as take a step forward, Robert appeared out of the gloom, his horse trailing behind him. The darkness gave little away, but Finnlay could still make out the broad shoulders, the power and strength in a stride he knew better than his own. When Robert stopped in front of him, his smile said it all.

'Thank you for coming,' he blurted out. Robert watched him without saying anything. Then, weariness reeking from every line of his body, Robert reached out and pulled him close. The embrace lasted little more than a moment, but its fierceness lingered much longer. Then Robert let him go, turned and looked around at the sleeping bodies, his face catching the flicker of firelight, the green eyes Finnlay remembered so well lined with exhaustion.

'They're heading south,' Robert said quietly. 'I've been Seeking them for the last few hours. I wasn't sure . . . Helen was five when I last saw her.' He turned back to Finnlay, pausing long enough to make him worry again.

'What is it?'

Robert handed his reins to Murdoch and began to unsaddle his horse. Murdoch took it and set it with the others. 'We could have a problem finding them.'

'Why? You just said you'd managed to Seek Helen.'

'Well, at least I hope it's Helen – but that's not the problem.' He took the cup of ale Murdoch brought back for him and drained it in one swallow. He murmured thanks then drew them away from the others so as not to waken them. 'You should know that your search parties have caused something of a stir in the area. I've heard a dozen different references to groups of men searching the countryside for a group of wayward children. Nobody knows who you are, nor where you've come from – and that's the problem.'

'Why?'

Finnlay was glad Murdoch asked this question when he heard the answer.

'Because I know Nash – and if he hears of this, if he's trying to draw us out into the open, then he will know what's going on here. He'll send in Malachi to pin us down. We don't have much time. But . . . if we push it tomorrow, we might find Helen and the others by nightfall.'

Finnlay stamped on the rush of relief at those words. Still, it was good to hear Robert speaking with this much confidence, even if there was reserve in his gaze. Then again, it *had* been eight years since they'd last seen each other. 'You need to rest.'

'I've actually forgotten the last time I slept. Not a good sign, I'm afraid.'

'I'll bet you haven't eaten, either.'

'Food? What's that again?'

Finnlay couldn't help grinning. 'Necessities, Robert. You taught me that.'

'Too tired for food now. I'll eat in the morning. We'll need to be away before dawn. Can you manage that?' Robert appeared about ready to drop where he was and sleep for a week, so Finnlay just nodded, unable to stop the smile which woke his cold face up like nothing else.

Eight years and finally Robert was standing before him, fit, well, just as bloody-minded, stubborn and determined as he'd always been.

Finnlay laughed a little, and felt no shame in it. 'Come, put your bedding by the fire. I'll get your horse settled. You get some sleep.'

Robert looked at him again for a moment, something odd in his eyes. Before Finnlay could pinpoint it, Robert had turned for the fire.

'You were at Dunlorn?'

With barely a pause, Robert nodded.

'How was it?'

Blankets were pulled out before Robert gave his soft reply. 'Empty.'

Helen could smell something different in the air. Zea and Neil were riding and arguing as usual, but they didn't seem to notice.

They were getting close to a village. She could hear faint noises in the distance, the scent of baking bread. Enough to make her stomach grumble.

She let her horse slow and looked around. They were traversing the side of a gentle hill, where boulders grew green with moss and where patches of grey ice stuck between them. Dark swathes of heather crouched on top of the rise, but she could see nothing over it. To the south were more hills and the silent promise of the ocean beyond.

Her stomach growled again and soft laughter from behind made her blush. She turned to find Liam smiling at her, not unkindly.

'Do we take this as a hint that it's time to find some food?'

Helen looked away, but he drew alongside her anyway. 'We have a little flour and some salt pork left. Not enough to make a meal out of, so buying some more food would be a good idea. Aren't you hungry?'

'Me? I never get hungry.' Liam raised his eyebrows, as though such a thing was utterly beneath him. The expression on his sombre face was comical and he knew it. Helen couldn't help smiling at him.

'Well, I'm glad you said that,' Helen countered, 'because it will be easier to find food for four people rather than five.'

'So you're volunteering?'

His eyes were smiling at her and she couldn't help it. She nodded, wanting more than anything to have the opportunity to visit a real village – even if only to buy bread and vegetables. So far the boys had refused to allow either her or Zea near the towns they'd passed, though the risk was the same for them all.

'Liam,' Neil objected, intruding on the conversation, 'We can't let her go. If anything happened to her, Finnlay would kill us – literally. We talked about this before. There are too many Guilde soldiers around, and those others with the red livery. I've seen at least twenty so far today. We could be close to a Guildehall or something. Finnlay's an outlaw. What if somebody recognises her as his daughter?'

'But I want to go,' Helen said, ignoring how Zea rolled her eyes and looked away. Sayre kept his silence as usual, watching the contest before him.

'Don't worry, Neil,' Liam waved his hand, dismissing his friend's objections. 'I plan to go with her. There's no reason any Guildesmen or any other soldier would stop us. All we're doing is buying a little food.'

Something of Helen's elation vanished then, but Liam grinned at her in a way that excluded all the others, and the elation returned.

She was finally having her own adventures – the way Mother and Father had, when they'd been younger. It was a Douglas tradition, wasn't it? To go out and meet the world on its own terms? To pit your wits against whatever trials might come your way? Well, it was her turn, and she was going to take it.

'See that stream down there, winding at the base of that hill?' Liam pointed for the benefit of the others. 'We'll meet you there in an hour. See if you can get a fire going. We could all do with a hot meal.'

When Liam turned back to Helen, there was the same light of adventure in his eyes. 'Come on, let's go.'

The full screech of the birds above the field drew a gasp of appreciation from the men watching. Kenrick looked once at them, then back up to the birds in time to see the larger eagle swoop and dive at its smaller opponent. The clash was inevitable. Halted mid-flight, both birds plummeted towards the ground, but pulled apart in time to glide away. A handful of feathers fluttered down, some with a splash of red blood upon them.

'That grey is a demon fighter. Did you train him yourself?'

Kenrick turned to the man beside him, seated upon a roan stallion of immeasurable value. Ogiers, Duke of Quels had dressed for the occasion. His shirt was of the finest silk, his brocade jacket sported pearls laced into the collar and his cloak was lined with sleek black fur Kenrick guessed hadn't come from a bear. The trip from Mayenne didn't appear to have tired the Envoy. Rather, he seemed brighter than ever, more alert, interested in any information Kenrick might let slip.

But there was still the marriage to negotiate, young Princess Olivia to woo and win. Moreover, there was the wealth of Mayenne to plunder and a multitude of other riches to enjoy if he could manage to impress this man enough.

He put on his best smile. 'I trained *her* from the moment she was weaned from the nest. I plan to breed from her next year. I'm sure her brood will be just as talented as she is.' Kenrick paused only a moment before adding, 'If you like her so much, I can send you one of her chicks, trained or not, depending on your wish.'

Ogiers squinted up at the birds now circling the field. The lines about his eyes grew deeper as he shook his head. 'I think not. I would be unable to give such a creature sufficient work in Mayenne. I'm afraid we have grown out of the habit of sporting with animals. Thank you, however, for your kind and generous offer.'

Kenrick bit his tongue and turned away, his blood boiling. He could almost feel the man's contempt oozing out of every pore, soaking the air between them.

It was always the same. Ogiers was Tirone's most trusted Envoy – but the man did little more than spend his time making Kenrick feel inferior, uncivilised – and the last man likely to be chosen to wed the Princess.

Of course, once the Princess was heir to the throne, Tirone – and therefore Ogiers – might be singing a different tune.

But that required Nash to find the last Prince and see to his end.

As his eagles squawked above him once more, Kenrick's attention strayed to where his courtiers watched the fight, along the edge of the field. It was a smaller court than he usually travelled with, because of the winter, and the cost of moving so many people this far from Marsay and keeping them all warm in winter pavilions. Even so, it was enough to keep him in state – even if a dozen of those men were Malachi, led by Nash's ally, the Baron DeMassey. No matter where he went, Kenrick could hardly move or breathe without having his actions reported by the Baron. It was an open secret between them. Of course, DeMassey was also his bodyguard – and having a man of such talents watchful of his safety had to be considered an asset.

But right now, DeMassey was watching as Osbert chatted idly with other courtiers. Beneath his jacket, Kenrick could feel the leather pouch almost burning him with curiosity. He had but to hand it over to the Guilde Proctor for translation and he would have some answers. But was he ready to commit himself to such a dangerous venture? Osbert had once been Nash's creature, ready to do his bidding. What was to stop him running to the old man with news of Kenrick's betrayal?

He couldn't do it. Not yet. Not until he'd had time to think about it more.

A violent screech from close by snagged his attention. He turned just in time to see the fighting birds swoop away from the trees, towards the field, heading straight for him.

No – heading straight for Ogiers. Instantly, Kenrick's

defences rose, his hobbled power surging through him before he could stop it. Wings flapping wildly, screeches deafening, feathers bloody and fluttering, the birds came on. Ogiers tried to get out of the way, but it was too late. Even as he ducked, Kenrick's power shot out. A burst of flame, meagre in reality, but stunning enough to incinerate both birds, left their dying carcasses spinning and tumbling to the ground before the Envoy.

A shocked silence followed, then Ogiers' guard moved forward to assure themselves of his wellbeing. The court remained distant as always, and in that second Kenrick hated them.

'Thank you, Sire, for your timely intervention,' Ogiers gathered himself with frightening speed, his voice cold with disdain, even as his words were of gratitude. 'Though I fear the destruction of your favourite bird hardly worth my ancient bones. I mourn too, the loss of her much vaunted brood. Do you have another to take her place?'

Kenrick met the man's gaze, seeing far more there than he was supposed to. And if there hadn't been so much depending on keeping this man alive, he would be dead by now – for his subtle taunts if nothing else. 'Yes,' he lied smoothly and efficiently. 'I have a dozen such birds as talented as this. This one was nothing compared to your safety, my lord.'

As though he were accepting a genuine compliment, Ogiers bowed in his saddle. Quickly Kenrick gathered his reins together, the bubbling in his veins already warming him to the danger level. He would have to take care of it before he saw this man again, or there would be blood of a different kind spilled on the winter ground.

With a nod to Ogiers, he turned his horse and rode away, knowing his Malachi guard would follow.

It was time for some real sport.

With a shudder, DeMassey staggered into the passage, breathing hard and deep and trying to make it shallow. The stench . . .

He swallowed hard, forcing bitter fluid back into his tight

throat, his hand coming up to wipe the flash of sweat from his face.

In the name of the gods, what was that boy playing at?

Flat noises echoed along the slimy stone walls of a ruined and abandoned abbey. The building had stood solid for a handful of centuries until the Guilde had taken over hospice work from the Church, appropriating large swathes of land along with it. This place had been empty for ten years, stripped clean of materials by a desperate people unable to afford the luxury of keeping a sacred building intact.

Kenrick had seen the ruin in the distance, something fit to be used for his . . .

Could he honestly call *that* entertainment?

The gorge rose in him again, his stomach churning as his mind pictured again what he'd seen in the small room behind him, a room that a decade ago had housed a pious monk. He bit his lip hard, forcing the pain to make him concentrate, to draw his thoughts from that poor . . .

He couldn't even tell if it was a man or woman!

He took two steps further along the passage, drawing in thin, cold night air, hoping it would be enough to steady him. He'd been around Kenrick a long time, seen too many of these . . . incidents – but this was by far the worst. This went beyond the bounds of anything DeMassey ever wanted to see again.

It was his job to get rid of it, he knew that. He also knew that he would rather do almost anything than go back into that cell.

He closed his mouth, moistening it, tasting the bitterness and the vileness that was Kenrick. Then he straightened up. Deliberately, he brought forth a memory of Valena, her bright eyes, her glowing beauty as he'd last seen her, just a few weeks before. He kept it before him as he turned back to the doorway, held it as the beacon he needed while he gathered a fistful of power and unleashed it, setting all in the room on fire.

Barely blinking then, he turned and strode down the passage. Away.

'Are you sure this is going to be safe?' Helen leaned forward a little further, hoping to see more of the village from the safety of the wood in which they were hidden. The afternoon sun was glistening down on the snow-scattered field. A muddy road ran close by, leading into the village, and the spires of both Church and Guildehall were clearly visible.

Unfortunately, also clearly visible, were a grave number of mounted soldiers, idly wandering through the village, or riding in squads around the outskirts, as though on patrol for some desperate enemy.

'I don't know where they've all come from,' Liam frowned alongside her, using his body to shield her close to the tree. 'I hadn't expected these numbers – not here, so far from the cities in the north. I thought if we headed south, nobody would notice us.'

'Well, there's no reason anyone *will* notice us,' Helen replied, opting for a smile of encouragement. 'I mean, how can they tell what we are?'

'Without a Bresail, they can't.'

'But you still don't think it's going to be safe?'

Again Liam frowned, then looked back up the road, as though he could guess what lay beyond the hills. 'I don't Sense any Malachi nearby. Do you?'

'No. Should I?'

He looked at her and she laughed in response. 'Well, what do you want to do? Chance it – or move on and find somewhere quieter to buy supplies?'

Helen shrugged, turning back to the village. 'I think we should chance it. After all, who's to say other villages in the area aren't equally thick with soldiers? And not only that, but they would assume Salti wouldn't go anywhere near them, wouldn't they?'

Liam was already chuckling. 'So we bluff our way in?'

'Unless you don't want to . . .'

Liam turned for his horse – and froze. Helen looked behind them and her heart leaped into her throat. A dozen soldiers, mounted, swords drawn, were eyeing them with amusement and open hunger.

'So, boy,' the leader spoke roughly, 'I'm eager to know what this bluff is all about. Planning to steal something, were you? Or maybe you have already. This one's a little young for you, isn't she? Nothing more than a child. I wonder what her parents would say if they found her out in the woods with you, eh? Eh?' He gestured to his men. 'Take them.'

'No! Wait!' Helen surged forward, to put herself between Liam and the soldiers, but he pushed her behind him, his hands already going into position to combat with his powers. But to do so would guarantee their deaths. Frantic, Helen turned to him, 'No, Liam, don't! You can't or we'll . . .'

He twisted away from her, bending enough to career into a soldier approaching. The man tipped backwards and Liam grabbed the sword from him. Helen rushed to help, but she was snatched from behind, something cold and sharp pressed against her throat. A clash of steel rang out through the wood as Liam tried to fight off their attackers. Tall and strong, Liam had learned all her father had tried to teach him. He held the men at bay for precious moments, but soon it wasn't enough, their greater numbers overwhelmed him.

She barely heard his stunted cry as he stumbled to the ground. She could hardly see him between them. But she could smell the blood, saw how it soaked into the snow, trickling towards her.

'Liam!' She struggled, uncaring of the blade against her throat or of the threats made against her for the same dire fate. She needed to see him, to know he was going to be . . .

The soldiers stepped back, regaining their horses. Even as she was dragged away, she saw him, lying on the ground, two huge wounds in his chest, his heart no longer beating, his eyes gazing at the sky, unblinking and still. So very still.

'Liam!' Helen screamed once into the deadly silence, and then again. After that, a dirty rag was stuffed into her mouth and her sobs were drowned out by the pain inside.

16

Sayre wasn't too good at many things, but he could keep time better than anybody. He knew exactly when the hour was up, knew exactly when another had expired and Liam had still not returned. Of course, by then both Neil and Zea were restless, tossing bare-peeled sticks into the fire they'd carefully built.

Fearful and resolute, he got to his feet. 'I think something's wrong.'

'How in Serin's name can you know that?' Neil asked, standing. 'You can suddenly mindspeak? Is that it?'

'No. But they've been gone two hours now and it's going to be dark soon. If we don't try looking for them now, it will be too late.'

'Fine! Go and look for them! You know as well as I do what they're probably doing!'

'Neil!' Zea thumped his shoulder for that. 'Unlike some people, Liam is a lot more honourable than that. Helen's only thirteen. Not everybody has thoughts as disgusting as yours.'

Sayre stopped listening after a moment. Usually he didn't much care for their incessant bickering, but right now he was worried. He turned for his horse, tightened the girth strap and swung up into the saddle. 'Are you coming?'

'Yes,' Zea replied immediately. She mounted up without looking at her twin. Only when they were about to leave did Neil finally give in. He kicked snow over the fire, paused long enough to watch it melt a little on the coals, then climbed onto his horse, all the while showing his utter boredom for the whole search idea.

Sayre ignored him. Instead, he headed through the sheltering woods. He took out his *ayarn*, held it in his left hand and tried Seeking – but he'd never been very good at it, and Zea and Neil were even worse. Still, he followed the trail through the snow, hoofprints left by two horses.

Glimpses of the village showed through the trees, and he could hear horses on the road ahead. But then something else caught his eye. The dark stain of red blood against white snow.

'Liam!' He fell from his horse and scrambled between the brush to land beside the still body of his friend. He reached out to touch, but Liam was colder than the winter.

'Where's Helen?' Zea turned and turned, looking in the growing shadows. Neil stayed on his horse, his expression empty in shock.

'The horses are gone as well,' Zea added, coming to a halt beside Sayre. 'Come on, we can't stay here. They might come back.'

'Who?' Sayre stood, swallowing hard, unable to absorb the horror, still struggling with the terror. 'You think . . . they'd come back for us?'

'I don't know!'

'But what about Helen? We can't just leave her. We don't know who's got her, or why? We're in this together, aren't we?'

'Don't be an idiot, Sayre,' Neil suddenly joined in the argument, pulling his reins up ready to leave. 'You go into that village and you'll end up like Liam, bet on it.'

'I hate you!' Sayre spat. 'You're a vicious coward, that's what you are! You don't give a damn that your best friend's lying there dead. You only care for your own safety. Well, fine! Go ahead and run away. But I'm going to help Helen.'

'How? By getting yourself killed?'

'No,' Sayre looked once more at Liam's stiff body, then swung back into his saddle. 'I'm going to get some help.'

Helen tried to keep track of where she was taken, tried to count each horse pace into the village and beyond, tried to measure each turn, each new direction, but she could hardly see a thing from the horse, her vision blinkered by the arms of the soldier who held her. Her hands were bound behind her back, her feet at the ankles. She couldn't begin to think about what they wanted from her. She'd heard enough in their ribald comments about getting her back to their barracks, about sharing her and what they would charge for her, and the only good thing about it was that they obviously didn't suspect her of being a sorcerer.

She *should* have let Liam use his powers. If she hadn't been so quick to stop him, he might have still been alive. If she'd thought to use her own . . .

Another sob welled up inside her and she shut her eyes, unwilling to let it loose. She had to think. She had to concentrate, or Liam's sacrifice would mean nothing.

She could feel her *ayarn* beneath her sleeve. If they stripped off her clothes, they would find it, though they might not know what the small stone was for. Even so, she had too little time left before she would lose it. But what could she do? Burning through her ropes would only expose her as a sorcerer, and she simply didn't have the power or the skill to fight more than one of them at a time. But if she didn't make an effort to escape . . .

Louder noises surrounded her now and she opened her eyes, twisting her head beneath the soldier's arm to see a huge encampment spread out across the bottom of a valley. They hadn't seen anything of this as they'd travelled! Even as the sky darkened, she could see dozens of fires lit, smell food being cooked, voices raised enough to conjure the picture of a living city, here in the middle of nowhere.

The soldiers made no fuss of her passage through the camp. In fact, if anything, they went to some lengths to keep her presence hidden from their comrades. Aching in every limb, she was manhandled down from the horse and hustled into a small tent. There, a hissed discussion regarding her immediate fate gave her some element of hope – only to be dashed a moment later, when the leader of the dark band announced that he was going to enjoy her first, and the rest of them could wait in line.

The men chuckled at that, leering at her with evil eyes and stinking breath and she felt so sick she knew she was going to throw up – but with the rag stuffed in her mouth . . .

She breathed deeply through her nose, willing the nausea to leave her, willing her strength to stay – but all she could see was

Liam before her, still and dead, his body growing cold even as she watched.

Hands drew her back further into the tent, tossed her onto the ground where some filthy blankets lay in the semblance of a bed. There was some muted discussion about the wisdom of using this tent, but the soldiers were far too preoccupied to worry about it much. And then they moved on her, holding her down while their leader ran his hands over her body. She began to shake, closing her eyes so she wouldn't remember this, hoping they'd let her live long enough to worry about it. She knew she was crying, but she could hardly feel the tears leave her eyes. She tried to think of Father, of Mother, her sisters – even of the courage of Uncle Robert, but nothing made those touches go away. She heard the men laughing at her tears, heard them pass a bottle around between them as the leader's touches grew more intimate.

She bit her cheek, trying not to shudder at the touch. She couldn't bear to show any fear – but by sweet Mineah's blood, she *was* scared! She was, and there was nothing she could do about it. Nothing at all . . .

Something changed. For a moment, she hardly dare open her eyes for fear of what she might see, but then the hands touching her withdrew abruptly and the men around her scrambled to their feet, leaving her bound on the floor of the tent.

And then she heard it. Voices raised in surprise, orders being shouted, booted feet moving in this direction. The men again whispered between themselves, but this time with open fear.

Hope once more surged within her, but she couldn't find an explanation that would fit. She could have no allies within this—

The tent door was ripped open and the men instantly snapped to attention. A barked order had them part and suddenly she could see. Two men stood there. One, a soldier of some rank, the other with fair hair, dark eyes and dressed more richly than she had ever seen before. In his hand was a glass bowl, filled with some half-glowing liquid that rattled at the back of her memory without giving up any answers.

'Well,' said the fair-haired man, his scarred face moving into a wide smile. 'Look what I found.' He glanced around the tent a moment, then back at the soldiers who had murdered Liam. 'Get her up off that floor. Find a chair from somewhere. And have these men flogged while you're at it.'

Helen could hardly spare a glance for her attackers then as they were pushed outside. She couldn't take her eyes from the man who stood and watched her carefully. The one the others called Sire.

She knew who this was – and now *he* knew who she was as well.

'Robert! This way! Quickly!'

He turned, saw the others gathered at the bottom of the gully and swiftly made his way to them, slipping and sliding on the icy ground. Already it was getting dark, a thick fog falling just when he needed it to be clear. They were too close to the village, too close to what was sitting on the other side.

Finnlay was waiting for him. 'Three of the children have found us! Young Sayre thinks something has happened to Helen but I can't . . .'

Robert gripped his shoulder, offering a scant second of comfort before making his way to where the three were being fussed over by parents too scared and relieved to scold just yet.

'Can you tell us where Helen and . . .'

'Liam,' Finnlay supplied.

'Where Helen and Liam are?'

All three children looked up at him, wide-eyed, as though they were looking at a ghost.

'Liam . . . is dead,' said one of the boys. Sadness filled his voice. 'They were going to the village, to get supplies. They never came back. We found Liam's body by the road. Helen just wasn't there when . . .'

'Did you try Seeking her?' Finnlay demanded.

'I . . . I . . . I'm sorry.'

'Damn it, Sayre! You left my daughter—'

'Finn!' Robert took his brother's arm and pulled him back a little. The boy had obviously told them all he knew. Turning,

Robert found Murdoch. 'Get everyone back to the Enclave. Don't stop to rest, or to eat. Just get on the road now! Use any means necessary to get up to the Goleth. If the path is unpassable, ask for sanctuary at St Germanus Abbey. They'll take you in, no matter what you might be. Either way, don't stop until everyone is back in safety. Do you understand?'

'Of course. Good luck.' Immediately he began ordering the others to move, herding them towards horses, leading them out into the night. Robert watched only until he was sure they were on their way. Then he turned back to Finnlay, who was watching him with wide eyes.

'What now?'

'Now,' Robert replied, turning back towards the hill, 'now we find Helen.'

'I don't like the look of this at all.'

Finnlay didn't argue. Just looking at the patched landscape below them made him physically ill. The village, the royal encampment, the lights, the fires, the moving shadows of horses and soldiers. All too much and all at the wrong moment.

He looked aside at Robert. 'Are you sure she's still down there?'

Robert frowned up at where the moon would be rising if there wasn't so much cloud around. 'I told you, I'm not even sure I'm Seeking Helen's aura. I *think* she's down there, but there are so many Malachi around the village, it's impossible to tell where she is exactly. Damn,' he swore softly, taking a step back from the top of the hill. 'This would be so much easier if you could Seek her yourself. But of course, for all we know, Nash might be down there with Kenrick and . . .'

Robert seemed to be talking to himself. Finnlay watched his brother in silence, knowing that Robert would have an idea they could start with. At least, he *hoped* Robert had an idea, for Finnlay was fresh out of them. Instead, the bleating pulse of urgency rattled through him, insisting he just get on with it, just go out there and get her to safety, without any idea where she was – or with whom.

Of course, Kenrick had to be here as well, didn't he? Silently,

he prayed that Kenrick didn't have her. That she was somewhere else, in relative safety. Silently, he begged the gods for
some mercy and equally silently, he watched his brother.

'I don't think Nash is down there.' He stared at the village,
his head tilting this way and that, a frown on his face, his left
hand raised a little, as though he still used an *ayarn*. Then, his
voice oddly confident in the darkness, he said, 'You remember,
years ago, before Nash got his claws into you – you were
playing with a form of . . . what did you call it? Tandem
Seeking? Where you tried Seeking through another person's
ayarn?'

'Yes. That's what I was doing when Nash caught me.'

'And you were Seeking with Fiona, but she was a day's ride
away from you, wasn't she?'

Finnlay's eyes widened, understanding all too much. 'You're
not serious! But . . . I mean, how . . .'

Robert's expression was about as grim as he'd ever seen it.
'We don't have time to search the whole camp ourselves. I
need to know exactly where she is. Once we have a location,
I can get her free – I hope.'

'But tandem Seeking won't disguise my aura from Nash.'

'No – but just as I can't Seek Nash, he can't Seek me. If you
Seek through me, use me as your tandem link, my presence
should shield you. She's your daughter, Finn. You'll need only
a glimpse.'

Finnlay was already nodding in agreement. Before Robert
could say another word, he reached out and took hold of one
strong wrist, feeling the lifeblood pulse through, warm and
comforting. With his other hand, he brought forth his *ayarn*
and steadied his breathing.

By the gods, it had been a long time since he'd done this. A
long time since it had been safe for him to try. But he had not
forgotten.

The power rose in him like a mighty wave, gushing forth to
be used as he saw fit. Almost reeling with the familiar joy of it,
he focused on Robert's aura, since he had no need of an *ayarn*
of his own.

Then he let go.

A split second and he was there, in some tent, surrounded by soldiers, their faces grim and full of distaste. The picture came clear and sharp, the way it only did with tandem Seeking.

She was still alive! She was right there, in front of him, her eyes filled with fear. A faint movement under his hand brought his rampant panic under sudden control. Instantly, he swung around, looking further and further until he caught a glimpse of—

Cold air strangled his throat as his eyes snapped open. Robert was looming above him, holding his arms, steadying him.

'Why? Why did you stop me?'

'You went too far, for too long.'

Finnlay tried to wrench himself free, desperate to go back and see her, make sure she was . . .

'Stop it!' Robert shook him, his voice loud on the empty hill. 'Calm down, Finn! It's all right! I saw her, too. She's still in the camp. We have to get moving.'

'But Robert, she's with—'

'Kenrick. Yes, I know. Now let's go!'

'Now what possible harm could come with you telling me your name, eh?' Kenrick kept his voice sweet. She was such a young thing, barely into her woman years. He didn't want to scare her any more than necessary – at least, not yet.

She sat on her chair, her arms pulled behind her, her huge dark brown eyes watching him, sensitive to his every move, his every breath. Just being a part of such scrutiny was addictive. If he'd not had other plans for this child, he might have considered keeping her as a pet – tightly leashed of course.

He tossed the stone up into the air, catching it where she could see. She had fought him, but eventually he had taken it from her, and now he knew she could do nothing to stop him getting what he wanted.

'Your friend,' Kenrick continued, enjoying the sliver of hunger gripping his belly. 'The one you were with when my men captured you. He's still alive, you know.'

'Liar! I saw him die.'

'Child, you don't know what you saw, do you? He fought with my men, they took him down and carried you away. When I realised what you were, I sent men back to that spot in the woods. They found your friend and took him to my surgeons. He still lives, though perhaps not for much longer.'

'What have you done to him?'

'Stopped his bleeding, nothing more. I could, of course, be so much kinder to him, if you'd just tell me your name.'

He could see her debating with herself, trying to work out if he was lying or not. She had no way of telling that the squad had yet to return either way. Of course, if the wounds were as his men had described, the boy would indeed be very dead by now. But would she take the bait?

'Helen,' she murmured, her pretty face crumpling at the idea of giving in.

'Helen what?'

Her gaze shot up to him and he prepared to rephrase his threat when she added, 'Douglas.'

And there, between one breath and the next, was the answer to his heart's desire. He could not have stopped his smile had the safety of his realm depended on it.

'Guard! Get her a horse and bring mine around here. I'm going out to the monastery – and try to keep DeMassey and his men from following me!'

The glimpse had been enough. Just that awesomely powerful splash of aura against his Senses, supplied by a brother unaware of just how gifted he was. But then, when the brother is desperate to find his daughter, he can be forgiven such tiny flaws.

Robert kept Finnlay close. It felt too good to be doing this with him, familiar and comforting for them both to be fighting on the same side again, after so long. Robert determined to enjoy the peace for as long as it lasted, and prayed the reward would be to find his niece safe and alive.

Each step he took, however, brought him closer to another battle, one he'd hoped not to face so soon. Kenrick was around here somewhere; the man who had murdered his own sister,

Galiena, Robert's new bride. And Kenrick now had Helen. The man who had chosen evil, chosen to follow Nash.

With each step, Robert's fear rose. What if he couldn't control the demon? What if seeing Kenrick and rescuing Helen was enough to set the demon alight – how would he scramble back to safety?

But he could feel it rumble inside him, with every thought of Helen and the monster King.

They stole through the camp, moving from one shadow to the next, doubling back, using what cover they could and doing without when they had no choice. Robert could have crossed the dimensions and made himself invisible, but Finnlay had never mastered that trick, and it was far too dangerous for him to start learning now.

But fortune denied them. They took too long getting to the place and they found it empty. Only Robert's strong grasp stopped Finnlay from letting loose his rage. Within the cover of the blackest shadows, Robert settled down and let his Senses roam as fast and as thoroughly as he'd ever done.

'She's not far,' he whispered, offering his brother all the comfort he could in a few seconds. 'And she's still alive. There's a building south of here. Let's go.'

The stone walls glittered black and shiny, lit by the candles he had set up inside the ruined chapel. The roof had long since gone, leaving a gaping hole to the heavens and rubble at his feet. Faint patches of ghostly blue appeared in the sky as the moon tried to force its way through, but the clouds were stronger, overcoming the light with thicker darkness, blanketing what he was doing, increasing the safety.

He carried her in, draped across his arms, her will to resist pinched between small powers he had mastered with a little of Nash's help. She was beautiful and pale and white in the candlelight, still and safe in his grasp.

He'd debated only a moment before setting her down on the stone altar. Nash, of course, would have done it that way deliberately, *wanting* to make some silly symbolic point, but for Kenrick, it was simply practical. He planned to drain the blood from her body and he needed her elevated in order to do it.

Carefully he arranged her on the hard stone; her dark eyes watched him with unbridled terror now. All the defiance had gone now that she had lost control of her own body and he shuddered violently with the thrill of it all.

This was what power really was. This was true control.

And she was a Douglas; if not the Rebel's daughter, then certainly related, with looks like that.

Happy with her position, he picked up one hand, holding the wrist, pushing the sleeve of her gown up her arm, baring fresh skin almost translucent in this light. With his eyes on hers, he bent his head to the curve of her elbow, tasting the sweet skin, feeling the blood pulsing beneath.

He shuddered again as his own heart pounded. He was daring to do this, to perform an act of blatant sacrilege, using techniques centuries old, twisting them to his own purposes. He could barely contain the rush of excitement along his nerves; he strained his Senses to pick up every single fluctuation in the air around him, and especially in her.

On impulse, he bent forward and placed his lips on hers, feeling her immobile struggle to escape. His hands moved up her body, feeling each subtle curve, each signal of her growing womanhood, and the revulsion that flowed from her burning gaze.

This was torture at its greatest. He need do so little to generate so much.

For a moment, he was tempted to do more, to play with her as he played with his other toys, to spend the night revelling in who she was and what she could give him – but the bloodlust was too strong, the desire to see if this magic would actually work, too overpowering.

And more than *anything*, he wanted to be rid of these cursed scars.

With a final obscene kiss, he ignored his arousal and stepped back, leaving her bare arm dangling over the side of the altar. He brought forth the bag he'd carried in and extracted a smooth, polished wooden bowl and the orb Nash had given him. The surface made it feel like stone, but it felt too light. He'd spent hours examining it, but knew no more now than before.

He placed the bowl on the floor beneath her hand. He pulled out a dagger from his boot and pressed the sharp edge against the soft skin of her arm. His breath shortened, harsh and shunting, and he had to swallow hard to bite down on the sudden fear which almost consumed him.

Once he'd done this, there would be no turning back. He would be like Nash, doomed to seeking healing and regeneration in this manner for the rest of his life—

But it would be a *long* life.

The blade flashed down, cutting deep, drawing blood instantly. He kept the cut short, so as to control the bleeding and then, before any could be lost, he placed her arm so each drop could fall into the bowl.

A brush of dizziness dimmed his senses for a moment, but he shook his head and it disappeared. Then he had to force himself to stand back and not touch, to just watch the thick trickle of black liquid pooling in the bottom of the bowl.

Anticipation clawed inside him. He would be whole again. His scars gone, his mistakes wiped clean.

Unable to stop himself, he took out the orb, held it between his hands, warming it, and then took a step forward, wanting to put it in the bowl now, to see the blood being absorbed by it. A flicker of movement from her eyes stopped him. She was gazing at him without blinking, her eyes boring into him. And then she did blink and her focus shifted slightly, to his shoulder, his hands and the orb. Each breath came slowly, laboured, each a fight for survival she could not win.

How long would it take? How long until her last breath was drawn?

A faint breeze, almost imperceptible, drifted into the chapel. He took a step back—

And froze.

Something hard and sharp and uncompromising dug into his back and at his ear, a breath, a voice that commanded, a voice he would never be able to refuse.

'Move back very slowly. Do not attempt anything foolish.'

No.

Nonononono!

The blade shifted, released him a little. 'Step back, *now*.'

More power in that voice than he'd ever heard before, even around Nash at his worst.

He knew who this was.

Another flash of air and the invisible figure behind him stepped forward, turning and facing Kenrick for the first time.

Stark, unreasoned terror flooded through him. The black-lit eyes of a demon struck into his soul, the promise of torment beyond his imagination, the face he'd hoped he'd forget, now whole and healed, clashing with his nightmares, bringing them all back to life, the man who had murdered his father, who had come so close to killing Nash . . .

Robert Douglas. The name echoed inside his head a thousand times before the demon in front of him shut it off.

17

'What have you done to her? By the gods, she's lost so much blood!'

Robert didn't dare turn and watch as Finnlay tended his daughter. He had to keep his entire attention on the King before him, a man who, just a short time ago, had been a boy – a boy Robert had almost killed. He had to keep his attention on himself, to suppress his desire, his almost overwhelming, bone-deep urge to pick up this monster and slam him against the wall, to tear his skin from him a piece at a time. The hunger burned through him, rattling against his reason. To kill this man now would be insane. To kill him like this would be murder . . . revenge . . .

Sweet. Too sweet to take this life, to use it up, to swallow and spit it out like the filth it was. But he wanted it with every ounce of him. This was what the demon had been born to do.

The old pain in his side stabbed at him, quickening his breath, snapping him alert and aware.

He gritted his teeth against the pain, against the demon. He'd failed before to control it, but he had to now, had to get Helen to safety. 'How bad is she?' Robert half-listened for the reply, his Senses slipping beyond the chapel walls to the fields outside, back towards the camp. They would not be alone for long. The edges of his nerves warned of Malachi approaching in numbers. They had minutes, no more.

'She'll live, I think,' Finnlay's voice was ragged as heartbreak and rage battled inside him. 'But she's barely able to move.'

Robert took a step closer to Kenrick, deliberately powerful, letting the demon leak out through his eyes. The young man gazed up at him, blinking rapidly, with his mother's eyes set in a face that belonged to his father and yet held a wilful selfishness all its own. 'Whatever hold you've got on her, release it.'

Kenrick, almost shaking with terror now, flicked his hand. Immediately Finnlay caught Helen in his arms, helping her from the altar. Her bound arm lay limply across her belly; she was almost transparent, she was so pale, but she was breathing and that was all that mattered at that moment. 'Can you take her?'

'Yes.'

'Go. I'll be out in a moment.'

'Robert . . .' The note of warning almost tore Robert's gaze from Kenrick.

'Don't argue, Finn. Get Helen on that horse. Malachi are on their way.'

Finnlay picked up his daughter and vanished behind Robert.

The silence was broken only by Kenrick's forced breathing.

'Tell me,' Robert murmured, 'Did Nash do this to you? Did he make you into his image – or was it your father?'

Kenrick blinked rapidly at him, his jaw clenching as though he would spit. 'Don't . . . what are you going to do with me?'

That fear in the King's eyes. Was that alone from what Robert had put there? Or were there more ghosts haunting him now he was older, more seasoned.

Robert was wasting time. He would find no answers now. He stepped back, sheathing his sword. 'Where's Nash?'

'Nash?' Kenrick grunted, the sound of thick gravel. 'Why would I know where he is?'

'I don't have time to get it out of you. But you should be far more scared of him than you are of me.'

'Oh? Why?'

'Because he will destroy you – whereas I would only seek to save you.'

'Save me?' Kenrick said. 'From what?'

'Robert!' Finnlay called from beyond the walls. 'Come now!'

Robert grabbed the bottle of wine sitting on the floor and poured it over the bowl full of blood. He then took a candle to it.

'No!' Kenrick almost howled. 'Leave me the calyx at least!'

Robert froze. 'What?'

'The bowl. Leave me that blood at least. What harm can it do—'

'What did you call it?'

'The bowl? A calyx.'

A calyx? This bowl?

And where had Kenrick learned such a word from?

With the demon cold inside him now, he touched the candle to the wine and stepped back as flames flashed light into the ruined chapel. He didn't dare use his own powers. Such a release would be enough to give the demon permission.

Then, not hesitating a moment, he stepped forward and snatched the orb from Kenrick's fingers. The King flinched as though struck, then Robert was backing away. 'Has Nash regenerated yet? It's my guess that he hasn't. But when he does, your life won't be worth a grain of sand. He uses you while he needs you. Just like he did with your father. Just remember that. When I come back for you, remember what Nash did to your father.'

'*You* killed my father!'

Robert paused in the doorway, the stone beneath his feet rumbling a little with the pounding of horses approaching. 'Nash sent him to me to die. Remember!'

Then he turned and ran, skidding down the passage until the ruined wall opened to the night air. Finnlay had Helen on the horse in front of him, Robert's animal dancing around urgently. Robert leaped onto the horse's back and kicked hard.

Even as they raced across the night-black fields, as the sound of approaching horsemen thundered in reply, the demon clawed at his back, demanding he return and finish the monster off for good.

No, he told it silently, never. Never set it free.

Finnlay rode and rode, deep into the night, unready to stop, reluctant to look back, unwilling to let go his precious bundle for even a moment. But hours stretched into the night and the horse beneath him grew weary. Robert vanished as Finnlay kept going, returning through the dark fog with fresh horses trailing behind him. Finnlay didn't waste words on asking where they had come from.

But he had to stop long enough to change saddles. Robert stood there looking up at him, his expression open, understanding filling his eyes. Slowly Finnlay gently lowered Helen into his brother's waiting arms. Then he dismounted and took her back, settling on the ground to leave Robert to work with bridle and saddle.

And sitting on the damp forest floor, the night as silent as death around him, Finnlay finally felt tears fill his eyes and cascade down his face, unable to lift a finger to stop them. Again and again, he pressed kisses to his sleeping daughter's forehead, holding her as tightly as he dared.

And then Robert was done. He turned and sat beside Finnlay for a moment, bringing forth a flask of something which he offered up. Finnlay had no choice but to drink, each swallow coming hard.

'Thank you,' he whispered.

He felt Robert's nod, and an arm around his shoulders, squeezing for a brief moment. Then, 'Let's keep moving. I can't Sense any pursuit, but I don't want to take any chances.'

'No,' Finnlay said, standing carefully. 'No more chances.'

Only now, helpless in his relief, could he acknowledge that he'd never in his life been more afraid than when he'd found Helen with Kenrick.

Kenrick plunged his hands into the bowl of hot water, ignoring how it seared his flesh. He needed to feel the pain at this moment.

He dried his hands on a cloth held out by a page, then turned and snatched up the cup of wine offered him. His senior courtiers stood around, looking helpless, half-asleep and mostly useless. It was all Kenrick could do to stop the shivering inside being visible to all of them.

Never. Never again would he let something like that happen.

He barked out orders to break camp, ignoring protests that it was the middle of the night. He took his Chancellor to one side, giving crisp instructions as to what the man was to say to Ogiers, the apologies and the excuses of matters of state, all built up to create an image of a dynamic King willing and able to respond to the smallest danger.

DeMassey appeared once, briefly, long enough to tell him his skilled and well-trained Malachi had so far been unable to find a trace of the Rebel and his brother. Of course, he was also full of reproach that Kenrick had gone off on his own, making DeMassey believe he was in some danger. And Kenrick wouldn't have lost the orb if he hadn't been on his own. With a grunt, he dismissed the Malachi, knowing only too well there would be no result to the search, and not entirely sure he wanted one.

Then, alone with the noise of chaos all around him, he called for Osbert. The Proctor arrived already wary and Kenrick could clearly see the fear in the older man's eyes. It had been there for a long time, probably put there by Nash.

Kenrick swallowed down the nausea that filled him. His own fear still coursed through him, like a plague, destroying everything in its path. By the time it was done, he would be no more than an empty wasteland.

He'd been terrified, in the chapel, after the Rebel had gone. Unable to move, like a . . . like a child before a giant. Frozen to the spot until his men had come for him, shaking his shoulder as though he'd been standing there asleep. That was all. Just a few terse words and that had been his entire defence against a man who had taken not just the girl from him, but also the orb. Nash was going to kill him.

But Robert Douglas had stolen something else from him, something he'd not noticed until it was gone.

He *had* to get it back.

Without another word, Kenrick took the pouch from inside his jacket and placed it on the table. Keeping his eyes on Osbert, he slid it across, his hand not leaving it until the last moment. 'I want this translated.'

Osbert looked at the pouch briefly. His eyebrows raised in question, he said, 'Translated, Sire?'

'Yes.' Kenrick said, not sitting back, not relaxing, but watching the man before him in the light of a dozen waxy candles. The thick yellow light did nothing for the Proctor's complexion, giving his grey eyes an almost green hue.

Robert Douglas had green eyes.

Kenrick's fingers abruptly itched and he clenched his fist to prevent himself snatching the pouch back—

But he needed to know, needed as he needed to breathe. The Rebel had warned him, had said Nash would destroy him. Kenrick needed weapons against both of them.

'Translated,' Kenrick continued, as though he'd not just had a battle with himself. 'By your hand alone. Show it to no one. Discuss it with no one. Bring the results to me yourself. Do I need to say what will happen if you don't follow my instructions to the letter?'

Osbert pursed his lips and shook his head slightly. 'No, Sire. May I look now?'

Kenrick nodded. As Osbert fiddled with the pouch lacing, Kenrick rose and refilled his cup. He drained it again in two large swallows, but stopped then. Wine was not going to give him back himself. Osbert frowned.

'What is it?'

'Nothing, Sire.' The frown vanished as Osbert pushed the papers back into the pouch, absently tying the laces once more. 'I will begin work on it as soon as I get to Marsay. This language is ancient and a little beyond my expertise. I do have books at the Guildehall that would assist me—'

'Fine! Go to it! And remember, not a word to anyone!'

Osbert bowed deeply, the pouch held stiffly between his hands. 'Yes, Sire.'

The moment Kenrick was alone again, he began to shake, hard, until he closed his eyes against it.

Never again would he let the Rebel get so close. From now on, he would keep the Malachi within shouting distance, not close enough to spy on *all* that he did, but near enough to warn him, to be some kind of barrier between him and . . .

He stood and made for the wine once more. He drank directly from the flask this time, swallowing until he thought he'd choke. Then he called for his horse and guard.

He couldn't stand around here waiting for his court to leave. He had to get on the road now, had to get to Nash before he lost all his courage.

He needed to know he had some left.

A thick swathe of cloud blotted out the highest peaks of the Goleth range, but in his mind's eye, Robert could see them clearly. Memory alone brought forth pictures of the sharp ridges, tall and dipping peaks, covered, at this time of year, in layer after layer of snow and frozen ice. In some places, ice had been caught up in the flow of a rock-slide, turning it grey and black, crumbling the rock before its time, etching the paths and passes of this range with treacherous footing.

The stand of trees sheltered his position as he gazed beyond the foothills. It had been perhaps three days since the last snow here. There was almost no green to be seen, just the unbroken white, bordered by fences, trees and the welcoming warmth of St Germanus Abbey, perched on the hillside like a forgotten trinket.

He remembered days spent in that abbey, trying to forget. Meeting a man who learned to see right through him.

His wounded side throbbed insistently. He would have to stop on the way home to buy some more of the pain-numbing potion. Though it barely worked, it would be enough to ensure he got some rest, to allow it to heal again.

'I wish you'd come with us. Even just for a few days.'

Robert glanced once at Finnlay. 'You know I can't.'

'Mother wants to see you.'

'And I want to see her.'

'Then come. Please.'

'I can't.'

A silence grew between them then, uncomfortable and hungry.

'Tell me,' he blurted out a moment later, 'have you learned anything more about how to find the Calyx?'

'The Calyx?' Finn repeated, puzzled. 'No – though I wish we had. It might have avoided this whole thing.'

'True.'

'Why?'

Why? Wasn't it obvious? Hadn't Finnlay always been the one driving the search for it, however unsuccessfully. 'What about Patric? Any recent word from him?'

'You get the same letters we do. I've heard no more recently.'

'I see.' So still no hope from either avenue. 'Do you have any idea yet what the Calyx actually is?'

Finnlay frowned and faced him. 'No, not really – though the Key said it was a receptacle or cup.'

'Really? Kenrick called the bowl holding Helen's blood a calyx. I'll bet he got the word from Nash when he learned the whole disgusting process.'

For a moment, Finnlay just blinked at him. 'So a calyx is . . .'

'A thing that holds something else.'

'But what?'

Robert shrugged. 'Information?'

'Like a book?'

'Possibly. Or a library of some kind.'

'Oh, hell, Robert, if we've been looking for a library, don't you think we'd have found it by now?'

'I'm just guessing here, Finn. We know from our own

sources that the Calyx is supposed to hold some information, don't we?'

'True.'

'And we also know that Nash isn't interested in finding the Calyx at all.'

'Unless he already has it.'

That made Robert pause. 'Yes, he could have it. Or – he might not know about it.'

'Why wouldn't he?'

'Because he's only interested in the Prophecy and the Key? In the power of the Key and the Word of Destruction.'

'You're talking hope there, Robert. We don't know what's really in that man's mind.' Finnlay looked up at the mountains in front of them. 'You honestly think that if he had the Key, if he had Jenn and the Word, he wouldn't also go right ahead and kill every Salti alive just because he could?'

Finnlay was right, of course. But if Nash already had the Calyx, then Robert couldn't use it, nor find answers within it, leaving him with Patric as his only link to hope.

'What are you planning?'

Robert blinked, scrambling back from the shadows. He picked up his cloak and swung it over his shoulders. Deliberately, he forced a light tone, made his words glib. 'I was wondering when you would ask.'

'Don't!' Finnlay held up a hand. He dropped his voice so Helen wouldn't hear him. 'Just don't do that, Robert. Not any more. I can't keep interpreting what you say when things like this happen. It's just too much. Can you understand that? I want . . . I need to know why you didn't kill Kenrick. Surely, with all he's done now you . . .'

Robert turned and faced Finnlay. There was passion in his eyes, but all of it was blood-thirsty. Ironic, really. 'You would have me murder him?'

'Why not? He nearly murdered my daughter! Your niece! And his men *did* murder Liam!' Finnlay shook his head, bemused and frustrated. 'What difference does it make *how* he dies, only that his miserable existence is done with.'

'So I kill him in cold blood, and let the country run the

rapids without a King? Is that what you want?' Exactly what he had been so tempted to do?

'Do we need another war to get it? Or another King? Serin's blood, Robert! What are you waiting for? A sign from the gods? Isn't this enough? And if not, what *will* be enough?' Finnlay took a step back, as though afraid of what he would do if he got too close. 'I believe in you, Robert. I've always believed in you. What I can't believe is that you won't move because you're afraid.'

Robert suddenly found it hard to breathe. Weight pushed down on his chest from some invisible place. He couldn't look away from Finnlay, from the dark eyes bright with unshed tears.

'You don't understand,' he murmured eventually, the words breaking him from his freeze.

'Those are just words, Robert. How can I understand when you won't . . . you won't trust me?'

'No!' Robert snapped. 'I'm not going to discuss this with you. I never said I didn't trust you.' But he didn't, did he? Couldn't afford to, because betrayal could come from anywhere and Finnlay was living with the daily influence of Jenn.

'You'll have your answers in the spring. I can't tell you more until then.' He turned for his horse, taking up the reins.

'I'm not asking for all your secrets. I understand the need for silence.'

'Do you?' Robert turned back swiftly, searching for something he couldn't name in his brother's eyes. There was a flash there, and he spoke to it. 'What makes you think I'm not afraid of what's to come, eh? Why shouldn't I be afraid?'

As though he'd said something magical, Finnlay's tension faded away and was replaced by warmth and the beginnings of a smile. 'No reason, Robert. As long as it doesn't keep you from—'

'My destiny?'

'From doing what you know is right.'

'And murder is not right.'

Finnlay grinned. 'Spring it is, then. Anything I can do?'

Robert almost laughed at the sudden casual manner, at the

abrupt return to normality between them. The gift touched him where nothing had for eight years. He breathed deeply to ease the tightness in his throat. 'Aye, spring. And you'll know what to do when the time comes.'

'Of course,' Finnlay half-laughed. 'It just wouldn't be you without at least one cryptic instruction.'

And that gave Robert permission to smile a little. 'Well, we wouldn't want things to change too much.'

'Heaven forbid.'

There seemed nothing more either could say then. But this silence stretched easily now, their gazes meeting where their principles would not. 'You have to go.'

Without another word, Finnlay came forward and swept Robert up in a hug that almost squeezed the life out of him. There were more words than he could count in that gesture. When it was over, Robert turned to find Helen.

She stood waiting for them, holding the reins of her horse, eyes wide and knowing, and yet still fringed with an echo of fear. She was still weak, pale and far beyond normal robust health, but she would regain it quickly with rest and proper food. She'd been lucky. They'd *all* been lucky. Except poor, dead Liam.

Helen looked up at him, a smile in her eyes. 'Bronwyn and Anna are going to be so jealous that they didn't get to meet you.'

'I'll trust you to tell them as many stories as possible to make up for the omission.'

'Can I say anything I like?'

Robert had to smile. She was such a delight to be around, his niece. 'Feel free.'

She nodded, taking the double meaning without blinking. 'When you come back, will you visit us?'

For a moment, he couldn't say anything. He could feel Finnlay's eyes on him, willing him to say something. He bought time instead, by taking the girl into an embrace, hoping that his touch, and the touch of those who loved her, would be enough to one day erase the memory of what Kenrick had done to her. 'I will do what I can.'

She kissed his cheek and hugged him back hard. Then she let go quickly and he helped her up onto her horse. He stepped back to let them go. Finnlay said nothing, but Helen raised a hand and a smile. 'Goodbye, Uncle Robert.'

And then they were riding away, towards the invisible mountains curtained by layers of grey and white.

How was a man to know what he loved most in the world?

18

A howling wind tore across the road, whipping up powdered snow in blinding swirls, almost obliterating the lights of Ransem Castle. The ice-laden air made DeMassey huddle down further onto his horse, draw the cloak closely about his face and keep his eyes on what little of the ground he could see. In front of him, the last of Kenrick's guard trudged towards the gate, equally huddled, each man longing for the shelter of stone walls, for the comfort of a fire and perhaps a hot meal after a very long week on the road.

Small comforts. Little things designed to keep the body functioning and usable. Not enough to give answers from which to create solutions.

From the white darkness, colourless stone walls drew near and, with an ironic shiver of relief, the wind dropped and then faded almost the moment he passed through the gate. Chaos reigned then as servants sought to bring the soldiers inside, to take care of the horses within a courtyard not designed for such a large group. Kenrick had sent the bulk of his train on to Marsay, choosing to bring only a hundred men with him to report to Nash.

Perhaps he hoped so many would protect him from the man's wrath?

DeMassey spent little time worrying about the fate of the King, who, by the look of it, was already indoors, away from the vagaries of the weather, but perhaps infinitely less safe. Kenrick was an idiot, still bound up with the superficial pleasures of instant gratification, rarely thinking in terms of where he would be in a year, or ten years.

In reality, of course, DeMassey should have been concerned with Kenrick's fate. After all, the young King was almost the last thing that stood between him and Nash, but weariness and his own, concealed fear brought an element of quiet disdain and as he slipped down from his horse he barely glanced up at the lighted windows above. Instead, he turned and headed towards the south tower, where, on the rare occasions when he had no other choice, he spent the night in a room on the second floor.

The sudden silence inside was almost frightening after the icy gale. He climbed the stairs slowly, stripping sodden leather gloves from his hands, pushing his hood back to brush crusted snow from his hair. When he arrived at the landing he almost smiled. His door was open, the room lit with candles and the deep yellow glow of a blazing fire.

He stepped inside, closed the door and waved a warning over it from habit. Trust was something he'd long ago sacrificed in favour of survival. Barely suppressing a groan, he pulled his cloak from his shoulders and dropped it over a chair, then made for the fireplace and the man who stood waiting for him, a cup of steaming wine held out.

DeMassey said nothing as he took it in both hands. He sipped, swallowed, not caring that the liquid was hot enough to burn his mouth and sear his throat. Spices assailed his senses and he breathed them in, welcoming the fragment of comfort. Only when he'd drained half the cup did he turn to face Gilbert.

'Better?'

'A little,' DeMassey answered. 'What are you doing here? I thought you were headed back to Karakham for the winter.'

'Oh,' Gilbert placed his hands behind his back and turned it to the fire. 'Nash decided that I would be more useful here, though he's given me precious little to do.'

'Which bothers you not at all.'

'I manage to keep busy.'

'I'm sure you do.' DeMassey did smile a little then, putting the cup down long enough to draw off his damp jacket and pull out another from a chest under the window. He'd known Gilbert Dusan all his life. They'd grown up together at Karakham and though the man undoubtedly kept his own secrets, he had been a friend these long years and had certainly never betrayed DeMassey. Nevertheless, he did work for Nash, in his own way. As grandson to Aamin, leader of the Malachi, Gilbert held a unique place amongst his people, though he appeared happy to report to Nash on the workings of the Chabanar without a single squirm of conscience.

Like most men in this farce, Gilbert played his own game and shared it with no other.

Just as DeMassey did.

'What happened?'

The question speared into his drifting concentration. He pulled on the jacket and returned to the fire, his face almost hurting with the heat. 'Kenrick's men picked up two Salti children. They managed to kill the boy before we discovered what they were. Then Kenrick tried to bleed the girl, but he claims she was rescued by the Douglas brothers.'

'Claims?'

DeMassey shrugged.

'By the blood! If those two are around again, trouble can't be far off. He said *both* brothers?'

'Yes. Why?'

Gilbert frowned. 'Kenrick didn't tell you anything of what was said?'

'And why would he tell me something like that?' When Gilbert rolled his eyes, DeMassey added, 'I was thinking that perhaps it was a trap, but they left Kenrick alive.'

'Or perhaps it was a trap to see if these law changes were in earnest.'

'Possibly.'

Gilbert said nothing for a moment, then leaned into the fireplace to pick up the long-handled pot sitting on a grate above the flames. He poured more wine for DeMassey, then filled his own cup. 'I think you need to be very careful, my friend.'

Turning, DeMassey surveyed his friend. Gilbert had been an ungainly child. Never handsome, he'd grown positively ugly as an adult, with thick black eyebrows hovering over eyes of deep amber. With skin marked from a childhood disease and a nose that dominated almost every expression, Gilbert was as oblivious to his looks as DeMassey was proud of his. The long rust-red hair had always been kept in a plaited braid, though now there were swathes of white in it, enhancing the confusion of colours about the man's face.

There were too many things he didn't know about Gilbert any more, too many distances between them, too many things he had to hide for safety's sake.

'Careful?' DeMassey radiated innocence in every aspect of his stance. He'd had eight years to perfect it, after all. 'In what way and with whom? Is there trouble with the Chabanar?'

'No,' Gilbert said, 'it's not Aamin. I'm talking about Nash. You need to tread very carefully with him.'

'Why? What have I done now?'

'That's a good question.' Gilbert tilted his head to one side, smiling enough to reveal hopelessly crooked teeth. 'A question he wants answered.'

'You're talking in riddles.'

'Which is the only way to deal with this, I fear.'

Showing more than a little irritation, DeMassey turned away. He pulled up a chair and sat, kicking his boots off towards the fireplace. His feet instantly ached. 'Just say whatever it is, will you? I'm too tired for games tonight.'

Gilbert was silent a moment, then said, 'He suspects you of something. He doesn't say what, but he is sure you are up to . . . something he wants to know about. Are you?'

DeMassey laughed a little. 'Nash sees enemies in every shadow. I've never worked against him.'

'Haven't you?'

He looked up at that and a wave of discomfort brushed over him. Was it possible that Gilbert knew? Had followed him? Found out something?

Friendship or no, if that were the case, Gilbert would have to die, no question about it. DeMassey couldn't afford another person to know, not even one he trusted this much.

'What are you talking about?'

'You remember my niece? Sairead?'

'Of course.'

'She told me,' Gilbert paused, 'when you were injured and about to flee from Shan Moss . . .'

'That was years ago,' DeMassey tried to dismiss this with a wave of his hand, but Gilbert persisted.

'She was there, with you and Valena and you said things.' Gilbert lifted his chin. 'You and Valena were planning to kill Nash then, were you not?'

DeMassey didn't answer. He just sat back, stretched his feet out and laced his fingers across his stomach. 'What's that got to do with warning me now?'

Gilbert didn't answer immediately. Instead, he watched DeMassey, appraising and evaluating without blinking. Then abruptly he drained his cup and placed it down on the table. He collected his cloak and swung it about his shoulders. Only then did he reply. 'I don't expect you to trust me. I understand why you can't. I just thought I'd ask, in case you thought you might. Even so, my warning is valid. Nash is having you watched. He has questions about your activities that seem to have no answers. If you *do* have something to hide, I suggest you curtail your behaviour enough to allay his suspicions. Either that, or do something about them. I don't think he's going to wait much longer.'

Gilbert didn't wait for a reply. Instead, he made for the door. With his hand on it, he paused, turning slightly. 'My guess is you have perhaps until spring before he demands answers. And then he's going to ask you where Valena is. You'd better have an answer prepared.'

'You did what?'

Kenrick clenched his jaw, determined not to flinch as Nash stormed up to him, fire-spitting fury surging through him, filling the room.

'You idiot!' Nash bellowed. 'You had a Salti child in your

hands and you let the Douglas take her away from you? And why? Because you couldn't wait to get the little girl's blood, was that it? Or did you plan to use her for some other purpose? By the blood of Broleoch, she was a Douglas! If not his daughter, then certainly his niece. Her blood would have been enough for me! I could have regenerated fully – but no, you had to get your childish revenge, didn't you! Had to get your filthy paws all over her and destroy the only chance we are ever likely to have! You fool!'

With that, Nash raised his hand so fast, Kenrick didn't see the blow until he staggered back against the desk, eyes wide at the force, the power behind it.

Nash wasn't as weak as he made out, that much was certain. A wave of horror surged through him, intermingling with his fear.

The old man pursued him, grabbing his collar, hissing into his face with a visage torn and mangled by his fight with Robert Douglas. 'I trusted you with that orb – and now *he's* got it! Do you have any idea the damage he could do with it? Damn it, I knew it was a mistake to give it to you! And now it's too late!' With a disgusted grunt, Nash threw him off. He straightened up and turned away, pacing hard and fast without the aid of a stick.

Shaking, Kenrick steadied himself on the desk and straightened up. Be afraid of Nash, Douglas had told him. He'll use you and throw you away.

But only if I let him.

He held himself in, containing the desire to strike down Nash where he stood. A simple blade would be enough and if he wasn't warned, the old monster wouldn't be able to stop him.

How had he managed to give this man so much power over him?

'So he's moving about now,' Nash threw words about the room like seeds in a fallow field. 'He's well recovered from *his* injuries and moving about, doing things, paying attention to what *you're* doing. But he didn't kill you. He could have, but he didn't. Why?'

Kenrick blinked as Nash turned to him, demanding an answer. Quickly, Kenrick dredged up the words, deliberately ignoring what Douglas *had* said. 'DeMassey and the rest of his Malachi were almost at the ruin. He didn't have time . . .'

'Time? He could have killed you in a second, no more. About the same amount of time it would take *me* to do it.' Nash turned and resumed his pacing. 'No, he didn't kill you because of something else – but what? Oh, but of course, he wouldn't do it, would he? He's a man of strong principles and beliefs. A man who wouldn't stand against your father because he'd made a foolish oath of allegiance when only a boy of seventeen. But still, surely he would have made some attempt to . . .'

Nash came to a halt and Kenrick could see part of that ravaged face in profile, firelight dancing across the scars, enhancing the ugliness.

'Did he say anything to you?'

The question was asked lightly, as though it bore no particular weight, and yet, for all the temper he'd displayed since Kenrick had entered the gallery, these words struck him most deeply.

Feigning nothing, for that would give him away, Kenrick answered with his own question. 'No. What could he have said to me?'

Nash listened, said nothing for a moment, then turned his back, facing the fire squarely. 'Get out of here before I forget why I need you alive. And if by some bizarre miracle, you ever get your hands on another Salti, you bring him here, to me, immediately. Do you understand? Do you?'

Rage and fear seething within him, Kenrick deliberately didn't reply. He just turned and walked out, slamming the door behind him.

Washed, changed, fed and exhausted, DeMassey climbed into bed leaving only the remaining glow from the fireplace to light the room. As he settled back, his gaze returned again to the door, to the memory of Gilbert standing there, his words echoing in the soft darkness, soaking into the floorboards, gathering in the cracks.

Panic sat in the background of his mind. It shadowed his every thought, every attempt he made to avoid going near the subject Gilbert had mentioned.

His time was almost up. He had perhaps a few short months, no more. And with the weather, there was little opportunity to do much in the meantime.

He should have moved before, years ago, when it would have been possible to do it and get away with it. But back then, they'd had no idea just how imperative it would be.

They'd both been blind. Equally stricken, equally to blame. Even so, the solution still fell on his shoulders. He was, after all, the only one who could do anything about it.

He settled further into his bed, pulling the covers up against a cold that would steal into the room like a murderer. He had no options. He had little time. The panic could wait until morning before it overtook him.

Deep snow damped everything, even the sounds of the morning, of Kenrick's soldiers trooping out of his gate, of their calls to one another, of their relief to be leaving. Cushioned by that all-encompassing white, they escaped in flat grey light, turning east, making for safety in Marsay.

Nash watched from his bedroom window as row after row of liveried men, their horses and the others that had accompanied the King – others such as DeMassey – moved off.

As always, his behaviour had been immaculate. Nash's spies had reported nothing in recent weeks to engender more suspicion. There was nothing in his actions that Nash could pinpoint, and yet, there was still that underlying feeling that DeMassey was up to something, absences he could not account for, questions filled with evasive answers. Unfortunately, there was a limit to what Taymar could discover. He had no powers of his own and had to rely entirely on stealth – skills too fragile to succeed with a man of DeMassey's abilities. Not only that, but the Baron had a host of highly trained D'Azzir at his beck and call: men and women who had volunteered to work for Nash's cause, but who would follow only DeMassey's orders.

A problem that seemed to have no solution: getting to

DeMassey required he risk the wrath of the entire D'Azzir, if not the whole Malachi nation. It was a risk he wouldn't be willing to take normally, if he didn't already have an idea of what the man was hiding. Proving it was one thing – doing something about it another matter entirely.

The last of the soldiers below filed through Ransem's gate and the enormous barbican was lowered behind them, a faint tremor beneath his feet indicating that it was closed. Immediately the silence became almost palpable. Cloud drifted down lower and everything, it seemed, came to a slow, steady and numbing halt.

Robert Douglas had come back.

The shadow had stepped back into the light where Nash could almost see him, almost touch him. Close, but not close enough. And healed, too; certainly enough for him to move around as Nash could only dream of.

And if he was moving like this, content to show himself to Kenrick in such a manner, then he was much more advanced in his plans than Nash was!

He gazed into the snowy morning, his eyes burning with the glare.

He'd run out of time.

It was entirely possible that he had overstepped the mark with Kenrick. That boy lived on an edge of fear that normally thrilled him and previously, Nash's temper had served only to keep them wary and alert to each other. He had two choices, find a way to woo the boy back to him, to keep him happy, to keep him willing to remain allies – or he could wash his hands of the entire mess and begin looking for a replacement.

Of course, there was no reason he couldn't do both, was there?

Andrew Eachern, Duke of Ayr, Earl of Elita. Only fourteen years old, the same age Kenrick had been when Nash had bargained for their alliance. While Kenrick had been brought up with his ruthless father and learned many wily skills along that road, Andrew was being brought up by his aunt and uncle. Bella and Lawrence had taken the boy in and treated him as their own. All the reports he'd gathered of Andrew told him of the boy's gentle nature, his pleasant demeanour, his earnestness in keeping the comfort of those around him.

A *good* boy, just as his mother, the Ally would produce. But he'd been damned difficult to spy on. Nash had sent people down to Maitland to work, to report back to him – and every single one of them had, within a week, lost their positions for one reason or another. There had never been any unpleasantness, no strong words or threats. No accusations. Often there were even attempts made to find these people places elsewhere. But whatever the cause, Nash, despite all that, had no spies inside of Maitland Manor. Instead, he'd had to make do with watching the boy when he came to court.

Nash pulled up a chair and sat, shifting his useless arm so that it rested on the table before him, reminding him.

A dozen and more times over the years, Nash had tested Andrew. If the boy had any powers, they were so well buried, they'd never see the light of day. But he was sure there was nothing there, despite the odd way Andrew had behaved the day he'd first met Kenrick, as though he'd known Kenrick had abilities.

How hard would it be to take that good boy and turn him into the tool that Nash needed? How quickly could he do it? And what would happen if he did? Would his mother emerge from the void into which she'd disappeared?

Oh, yes. She would do that and more. But if he was ready for her . . .

The risks were incalculable. As were the rewards.

Nash stood abruptly, kicking his chair back out of the way. 'Taymar!'

The young man arrived within seconds, breathless and ready. 'Yes, Master?'

'DeMassey and Dusan left with the King, didn't they?'

'Yes, Master.'

'How many unBonded Malachi have we here now?'

'A working pair, Master.'

That had been DeMassey's doing, his blatant display of distrust. Though Nash had vowed not to use Malachi to regenerate, DeMassey had ordered his people only to work in pairs, believing that in his current state, Nash would be unable to overcome two Malachi in one go, in order to get what he wanted.

An illusion, like so many other things. One he was about to shatter.

He'd run out of time.

'I have reports here that there has been some anti-Guilde protests in a town north of here. Send the pair to investigate.'

'Yes, Master.'

'Then send my four best Bonded Malachi after them. I want it to look like the pair were killed in a fight with the townspeople. I want them brought back here, unconscious and bound – but not drugged. Understand?'

He looked up to find Taymar with a faint frown on his face – a rare occurrence. 'I understand, Master. But . . .'

'But what?' Nash turned and faced him.

'If the Baron DeMassey discovered you have regenerated using Malachi blood . . .'

'These two are not powerful enough to help me fully regenerate, only enough to heal these wounds, to allow me to move around. DeMassey may suspect, but he will never know, and without being certain, he will say and do nothing about it. But regardless of what he thinks, I can no longer afford to sit around here watching things from afar. I will heal these stinking wounds and then I will move my base back to court, where I can keep a closer eye on the young King. Once you have given DeMassey's men their orders, you can begin making preparations for moving me back to court.'

Wide-eyed, Taymar asked, 'When will you leave?'

Nash sank into his chair, almost enjoying the pain and weariness this ancient and battered body forced him to endure. But in a few hours, he would push risk aside and take what he needed from men who trusted far more than they should.

'As soon as I have absorbed the blood of the Malachi.' Nash smiled. 'Prepare to leave in four days.'

19

The wan morning light filtered through rain-speckled windows to splash over the piles of paper and vellum, books and journals stacked on Godfrey's desk, giving them a dirty grey colour that only served to feed his distaste for what he was doing. Doing his best to ignore it, as he had been doing for the last few weeks, he dipped his pen in the ink once more and finished transcribing the next line.

A quiet knock on his door interrupted further work. He got up and opened it. Archdeacon Francis stood there, a questioning look on his face, a tray of cups and fresh, steaming brew.

'I thought you could use this.'

'Thank you.' Godfrey stepped back to let the priest in, then closed the door. Francis placed the tray on the table before the fire, poured a cup then handed it to Godfrey.

'I noticed you missed morning mass again.'

Godfrey took a sip and headed straight back to his desk. 'I'm behind schedule. I don't have time for—'

'You are a priest first, Godfrey,' Francis reminded him, not ungently.

'And a murderer second?' Godfrey looked up, the weight of too many nights without sleep sitting badly on him, not to mention a conscience that would not let him alone. 'You know what will happen to Brome if I don't get this finished by tomorrow night. Kenrick wanted this by Caslemas. I did not want this task, nor this responsibility – but both the King and Bishop have forced me into this. I can hope the gods will forgive me for missing mass as I'm not sure they will forgive me the work I do instead. Please, Francis, you were one who *told* me I should do this!'

Francis stood there with his hands clasped together, the hood around his head softening his otherwise hard features. 'You haven't spoken to Brome yet, have you?'

'No, I haven't!' Godfrey snapped, then held his hands up in apology. He closed his eyes a moment to ease the sting of tiredness, then faced Francis once more. 'Forgive me. This is not your fault. No, I haven't told the Bishop what I'm doing yet.'

Francis nodded, accepting the apology. He poured himself a cup of brew. 'When do you plan to tell him?'

'I'm not sure I can.'

Francis turned with surprise on his face. 'Then how will you get him to sign?'

'I . . .' Godfrey looked down at the papers on his desk, at the work he'd put into rewriting the Church's laws on sorcery and the crimes therein. 'I intend to forge his signature.'

'What?' The cup in Francis's hand fell to the floor, shattering. The priest leaped back and stared down at the mess before looking once more to Godfrey. 'Are you . . .'

'Mad? Yes, probably. Just stand there and I'll get a cloth.' Now that he'd admitted to his intended crime, Godfrey felt much more calm about it – though really, it wasn't fair to force Francis to share his sin.

He picked up a towel from the wash-basin in the corner and mopped up the worst, collecting the broken shards and placing them on his desk. Francis stepped closer, dropping his voice in case somebody should be listening.

'I understand why you want to do it that way – but it won't be legal. We'll be passing out laws that have no foundation in . . .'

'Brome asked me to do it in exactly this manner – he was just expecting me to do it *after* he died. And this way, if I do end up . . .' Godfrey swallowed down the horror even as he said the words, 'if I end up taking his place, then I can ratify the new laws with my own signature. I promise you, Brother, there is no other way to do this. He fears for his immortal soul and believes signing his name to this will consign him to the flames of hell. How can I argue with that?'

Francis folded his hands beneath his surplice. 'I see.' He wandered towards the door, but without intent, his head angled as if in thought. 'In that case, when you are ready to send the papers out, let me know. I will make sure his doctors and those who attend him say nothing of what is happening. As his senior secretary, I can ensure that no document mentioning it goes before him and can intercept anyone who would wish to discuss it. You will, however, need to field all such enquiries until other members of the Bishop's staff are as familiar with the laws as yourself. Until then, may I ask, as a fellow monk, that you try to get as much rest as you can. I myself will say prayers on your behalf should you need to miss mass again.'

Godfrey was touched by this unbidden support; a tide of relief flooded through him. He'd been in this struggle alone for too many years. He'd forgotten that while he had secrets to keep, in principle, he had many people who were on the same side as he was.

'Thank you, Brother,' Godfrey managed, though his voice came out thickly. 'I appreciate your help.'

Francis just smiled, a rare gesture for him, then he let himself out, closing the door gently behind him.

The muted light of a dozen different colours washed across the floor of the Basilica, streaming from stained-glass high in the walls. Each window depicted some event in the lives of the gods, some lesson to be learned, some grain the faithful could take away with them. These windows were famed across Lusara for their unique beauty and the depth of their wisdom, but sitting in his seat, gazing up at them, Osbert couldn't remember ever having really looked at them before.

He found the colours calming. Though the Basilica could never truly compare with his own Guildhall, this building did have true beauty: the smooth stone walls and the high dome above the altar, tall sweeping spaces captured within arches and shadows, breathing air into the soul. Support pillars, gilded and carved, stood like massive giants' legs, holding up the buttressed roof. Red and white tiled flagstones covered the floor, cool and hard, soft and measured: an atmosphere of contemplation amidst a soaring display of material faith. There were things in the Basilica the Guildhall could not claim as its own.

Today the Basilica was filled to capacity, a quietly seething mass of living faith, compressed together, silent, watching each step of the sacraments of Caslemas with an awe Osbert could not quite match.

What was it about faith that caught so many people up in it? Or were the hundreds of common folk crowded in the back of the building there for the same reasons as those like himself – for the preservation of some kind of hope. Kenrick was trying to do his best not to look bored. Most of his court looked equally disenchanted. They were obviously here for appearances only.

Osbert believed in the gods, in the divine beings of Serinleth and Mineah, whose day this was. That he believed in the evil Broleoch he had no doubt at all. But could these celestial creatures be swayed by the worship and prayers of these people? Or did some people have more influence than others; people such as priests or Kings?

Or sorcerers?

The gods knew how Osbert had been praying for years, all to no effect. And in a very short time, when he had his next audience with the King, his most recent prayers would prove a failure.

Or perhaps he was just praying for the wrong thing.

Andrew did his best to sit still through mass, but the Basilica and its shadows, even the smell of incense, made him uncomfortable. There were memories in this place, going back to some time when he was much younger. To when his father had died and his mother had vanished from his daily life.

He didn't recall very much of that day, but he could still see himself sitting almost in the same place as today, Aunt Bella on one side of him, holding his hand tightly, Uncle Lawrence on the other side, both pretending that Jenn was in one of the caskets before the altar, and that they mourned the man in the other.

Everyone had hated his father. Even those most loyal to Tiege Eachern had sighed with relief to know he was dead.

Restless again, he shifted for the tenth time and was rewarded with a look from Kenrick at his side.

'A few minutes more, Cousin, that's all. If I can manage that, surely you can too.'

'Sorry,' Andrew whispered out the side of his mouth. Kenrick shook his head in resignation.

Incense rose thickly from the thuribles swung by two attending priests and with a final bow towards the altar, the seven Archdeacons turned and began their procession back along the nave, heading for the huge west doors that were even now being opened for them.

Along with the rest of the congregation, Andrew rose to his feet, following a step behind Kenrick, eager to escape this place for the open air.

Outside it was cold, but the sun was shining in the square where hawkers had set up stalls preparatory to the evening's entertainments. Andrew knew he shouldn't look forward to all this, because it was, after all, a religious day, but even so, there was a tangible atmosphere he couldn't entirely ignore. He almost bounced from one foot to the other, eager now to be rid of his official duties to the King and be about the best part of the day.

'Oh, be away with you!' Kenrick sighed. 'You make me feel old just looking at you.'

Andrew grinned. 'How old?'

Kenrick loomed close, his voice heavy with mock warning. 'Let me count the years out with my whip.'

'I'm going, I'm going.' Andrew sketched a quick bow and darted into the crowd. Now that he was away from the royal party, the press of people made it hard to move, but he wanted to see Godfrey and headed towards the east door of the Basilica where the Archdeacons traditionally gave Caslemas greeting and blessing to those who wished it.

Godfrey saw him coming, his long face creasing into a smile both ironic and pleased at the same time. 'Well, it's about time you came to see me. I thought you'd decided to shrug off all your old friends in favour of the new.'

'What new friends?' Andrew paused, puzzled.

'You mean you haven't made any?'

'Oh, er, no.' The admission was softly spoken. Andrew did his best, but a lot of the time, such things were beyond his abilities. He quickly changed the subject. 'You know Father John has . . . gone away for a while?'

'Oh?' Godfrey's interest shone bright in his gaze, though his tone was light, casual, giving nothing away to those who could hear them. 'I wish him luck. I will pray for him.'

Andrew did his best to show something in his expression that would let Godfrey know that John was heading for Flan'har, hoping to find Bishop McCauly. After a moment, Godfrey nodded slowly, his smile deepening, and Andrew knew he'd succeeded.

'How are your Aunt and Uncle?'

'Very well, thank you.'

'Will we see them at court this spring?'

'I believe they intend to visit, yes.' Andrew's voice dropped a little. 'How is Brome? I've heard so many conflicting reports.'

Godfrey said, 'I'm not a doctor, I can't really tell you much, except that he's not getting better.'

'Oh, I'm sorry.'

'I know, my son. Still, you should—' Godfrey broke off, his gaze shifting to somewhere behind Andrew. 'Good morning, my lord Proctor.'

Andrew turned, his smile fixed in place. 'My lord.'

Osbert gazed down at him and bowed properly. 'Your Grace. Caslemas greetings to you and your family.'

'Thank you.' Andrew knew he should stay and ask questions, learn about the laws and about other things the Guilde were doing, but there was something far too forbidding in the Proctor's gaze. 'If you will excuse me, my lord, Archdeacon. The King is expecting me.'

He knew Godfrey saw the lie, but didn't care. There were better things he could do with his time today, and he wanted to be about them. He gave both men a smile, then headed for the first row of hawkers' stands, his nose already twitching with the enticing scents.

*

'He doesn't like me, does he?'

Godfrey stared at Osbert, surprised at the admission, and that Andrew's likes and dislikes should matter to Osbert at all. 'I don't know whether he likes you or not. He's never said.'

'He made a quick exit. And see, he's nowhere near Kenrick. Maybe that's the problem, he's in too close with the King. Still,' Osbert paused, still frowning in the direction the boy had vanished, 'he just doesn't seem to be the type to fit well with Kenrick.'

'You mean he's neither stupid nor apathetic?'

Osbert grunted a laugh, the first Godfrey had seen from him in a long time. The Proctor let out a long sigh. 'I need to speak with you. Alone.'

'Now?'

'Yes, now.'

Vague noises echoed against the walls of the vestry, seeping through the stone from the crowds outside. Despite the weather, Caslemas had always been Godfrey's favourite time of the year, and being able to celebrate mass without Brome along to spoil it only made it more enjoyable. He felt warmed and refreshed, ready to face whatever the new year might have waiting for him. Almost.

He locked the door before making his way to the robing table. Osbert watched him, his recent smile far from his current expression.

'What's wrong?' Godfrey carefully removed the silver stole from around his neck, giving it a ritual kiss before placing it on the table.

'When you gave Kenrick a copy of the new Church laws, what did he say?'

'Very little. Why?'

'I don't know. He's been different since he got back. Haven't you noticed?'

'I haven't seen that much of him.' Godfrey lifted the embroidered surplice from his shoulders and laid it beside the stole.

Osbert remained silent as he did so, then he spoke again, his voice both harsh and hesitant. 'I need you to listen to this as a confession.'

Godfrey stopped, eyes wide. 'Confession? Why, you haven't made confession since . . .' And the last time he'd had such a request, it had come from DeMassey.

'No – I don't have a confession to make – well, I probably do, but this isn't about that. I just need to have your most solemn vow that you will never repeat this to anyone. If you do . . . by the gods, if you do, I am a dead man for certain.'

Godfrey looked up into hollow eyes reflecting a ghostly light. 'Of course. Whatever you wish.'

Osbert seemed unable to release the tension lying in his chest. His fingers touched the edge of the table, tapping lightly. 'In a few minutes, I . . . Kenrick is expecting me. Expecting me to give him something. A . . . a translation. I have no idea where he got the original scraps of text but they're ancient and I . . .'

Moving carefully, Godfrey reached out and placed his hand on the Proctor's arm. Rarely had he seen the man this agitated.

Osbert took the gesture of reassurance and continued, 'I think he stole it from Nash. I don't think Kenrick – or indeed, any of us – are supposed to know anything about it.'

'How do you know?'

'Because the translation is . . . is a prophecy of some kind. It's filled with terms I can't begin to understand, but it warns of the most terrible consequences if somebody called the . . .' Osbert swallowed and continued, 'the Angel of Darkness is allowed to triumph.'

Godfrey's hand dropped as shock flashed through his body. Too many things began to make too much sense. All his previous contentment dried up as the awful truth soaked into him. 'Angel of Darkness? A . . . Dark Angel? Sweet Mineah!'

He turned away, his thoughts reeling, but Osbert hadn't finished.

'I did the best translation I could, but there are still things I can't make out. However, I have prepared a lesser version to give to Kenrick. I have no idea what he intends to do with it, but I can't imagine his knowing the truth would be a good thing, do you? Or do you think I should give him everything I have?'

For twenty, perhaps thirty years the Hermit of Shan Moss, and a dozen other lesser prophets, had been foretelling of a dark angel who would come to Lusara and tear the Church in two, along with warnings that Mineah would once again take on human form and help fight the war against sorcery. But how much of that was real and how much interpretation had always been impossible to tell.

But Nash knew. He'd always known.

'Godfrey?'

His hands clenched against the fear he could no longer deny, he said, 'Give Kenrick as little as you can get away with. If he's sworn you to such secrecy, the chances are he won't risk giving it to someone else to get a better translation. Besides, there are few men outside the Guilde who would have either the knowledge or the resources to do it. I doubt Kenrick can do anything terrible with such a prophecy anyway – but let's not take that chance. After that . . .'

'What?'

Godfrey lifted his chin, taking a chance of his own. 'You have to pass the information on to . . . Robert Douglas.'

There was little change in Osbert's expression. He just looked away, pale light from the misty windows bleaching colour from his face. 'That's your solution, is it?'

'Solution? I don't have one, Osbert! Why do you keep thinking I have?' Godfrey strode forward, grabbing the man's arm again. 'This is something beyond you and I. We neither have the power nor the forces to battle this – but *he* does. You have to give him every ounce of ammunition you can or you hinder his ability to win.'

'And if he does?' Osbert hissed. 'Will we be any better off than we are now?'

'Could we be worse off?'

'Oh, yes, I assure you we could.' Osbert pulled away, pacing up and down. 'You don't know Nash like I do. The things he's said, the things he's done – you have no real idea what you're talking about. No, I can't . . .' He stopped, his chest working hard, his back to Godfrey as though he were afraid of what he would see. 'You could be right – but if you're not, if Vaughn was right and Robert and Nash are in league together, then . . .'

'They're not in league, I promise you!'

Osbert did turn then, his eyes full of sadness. He made no attempt to question how Godfrey knew so much about Robert. Instead, he said, 'They're both sorcerers, Godfrey. It goes against everything I've been taught. I just can't . . . trust, the way you do. I don't have that kind of faith. I'm sorry.'

With that, he unlocked the door. Seconds later, there was nothing left of him but the sounds of his footsteps on the stone floor beyond.

Another clash of steel had the crowd cheering. Another grunt had the crowd silenced in anticipation. Another scuffle of sawdust against stone had them hissing with mass empathy. The audience moved in a single action, one goal, one emotion along a single line.

Kenrick stood on his balcony, bare hands pressed against the stone balustrade, and looked down. Brilliant torches circled the courtyard, flashing yellow against the dark walls, making faces detached and iridescent in the night. The fight continued below, two master swordsmen from Sadlan in the north, their curved blades and bright clothing sufficiently exotic to cause more than a ripple of interest. They circled one another, each carrying his own minor wounds. Kenrick had wanted a fight to the death, but the Church had frowned upon such a means to celebrate the goddess Mineah.

Another cry from the crowd set his head aching again. His friends, or rather, those young men who attended him out of either fear or greed, lounged at tables and in chairs along the width of the balcony, either watching the fight or drinking or playing some game or other.

Why did he bother with them?

His skin itched. It burned over the place under his shirt

where he'd put Osbert's translation. He'd had only enough time to read it once before having to put it away, out of sight of these listless fellows.

A prophecy. Secrets Nash had been keeping from him. Something called the Key. Others called the Enemy and the Ally. A history going back perhaps a thousand years or more, Osbert had said. But there were things missing, words Osbert had been unable to trace, meanings he would only be guessing at. No amount of pressing had made him commit further, so Kenrick could only assume he was telling the truth – Osbert was a notorious coward.

He needed to *do* something. Merely knowing Nash had a plan and goals that did not include him was one thing. But did he want to be involved? Did he want to stop Nash getting what he wanted? Was it worth trying to take the prize from him at the end, whatever it was?

And if he didn't, if he did nothing at all, if he let Nash have his head, go on and achieve whatever it was he believed was his destiny, then where would that leave Kenrick?

Alive or dead?

'Sire?'

The quiet voice came from his left, away from the others. He looked up to find a cup of something held out to him, offered by his cousin. 'What's that?'

'Honey mead. Your head aches, doesn't it?'

'Yes.'

'Well,' Andrew shrugged, 'my aunt tells me this works wonders for an aching head. She made me try it last year when I fell from my horse and hit that tree, you remember?'

'The way I remember it,' Kenrick added, taking the cup, 'you hit the tree and then landed in a bog.'

Andrew's eyes drifted innocently away. 'Er, yes, that might have been the same occasion. I can promise you that the mead did me no harm. Aunt Bella says it's easier on the body than ale or wine.'

When another shout from below hit Kenrick hard, he took two swift mouthfuls of the stuff, surprised to find it nowhere near as sweet as he'd been expecting, and tasting faintly of lemons. Frowning in puzzlement, he drained the cup and looked back at Andrew. 'What's in it?'

'You like it?'

'I've tasted medicines much worse.' Kenrick handed the cup back. 'Tell your aunt to be careful. She should remember that it's against Guilde law to go about practising the healing arts.'

'Oh,' Andrew rushed to clarify, 'this is no healing remedy. It works the way warm milk does, when you can't sleep.'

'Warm milk?' Kenrick could only laugh. Though his cousin had spent half his childhood here, at court, the other half was filled with the pleasantries of country life and a gentleness that Kenrick could barely imagine. He wandered around behind a veil of naïve innocence, emerging with this friendly smile and solicitude for those in need. An odd combination for anyone in this dangerous world. Occasionally, Kenrick was tempted to wipe that genial smile from the boy's face, awaken him to the harsh reality of life, but those thoughts never lingered long. 'Warm milk is for old men and babies.'

Andrew wasn't offended. He was never offended by anything. He just shrugged, his gaze drifting down to the crowd below. Musicians played on the other side of the courtyard while outside the castle gates were tumblers and jugglers and many other festivities.

Kenrick wished they would all just go away.

'How is your head now, Sire?'

With a frown, Kenrick turned back to him. The pain, to his surprise, had almost gone completely. 'Are you sure there is no medicine in that?'

'None at all, Sire.' Andrew was grinning, looking a little smug, and despite his mood, Kenrick couldn't quite bring himself to say anything to dispel it. At least somebody was enjoying themselves tonight.

With another roar, the crowd announced the end of one fight and the beginning of another.

'Is it something you can talk about?'

'No,' Kenrick shook his head. 'Not this time. I told you not to ask, didn't I? That I would talk if I needed to?'

'Of course, Sire. I'm sorry.'

'Damn it, Andrew!' Kenrick straightened up, but Andrew had already backed away, just one step, but it was enough to make Kenrick pause.

His whole court, in fact, the entire country was afraid of him. All except this boy, his cousin. His father's cousin's son, to be precise, but the nearest thing to family Kenrick had left within Lusara. Until he could win Tirone over and get the Princess as his wife, Andrew would remain the only person he could place any trust in at all – however fragile. He had no faithful, Bonded Taymar at his beck and call, no powerful Malachi allied to him. Instead, he had a country which feared and despised him, courtiers who dared not disagree with him, a dying Bishop and a cowardly Proctor – and this fourteen-year-old cousin who had never done anything to hurt him and seemed to genuinely desire to help him.

He often thought he hated the loneliness more than anything else.

On any other night, he would have called for DeMassey to bring him some private entertainment, but he doubted he would enjoy it this time. He was too tired, too sick of the whole silly game – and his flesh burned with the need to make some sort of decision about the prophecy.

With a sigh, he reached out and swung his arm around Andrew's shoulders, as close to an apology as any King could allow himself. Then he let the boy go, asked for another cup of mead, then retired for the night, heading for the darkness of his bedroom and the quiet he would find there.

For a while after Kenrick left, Andrew didn't move from the balcony. He didn't dare. He knew the others were all looking at him, could almost feel their stares raking up and down his exposed back.

They hated him, each and every one. Hated his kinship to the King, his youth, and perhaps most of all, his almost-casual relationship with a man who terrified them with his unpredictable moods.

His stomach tumbled and squirmed at his own temerity, at the need inside him to offer the hand of friendship to one who was in league with Nash. He could never explain it to his mother, or Micah or anyone – but he'd never been able to help himself. Kenrick was like a sponge, Andrew the few drops of life-giving water. The need was there and he had no choice but to provide as much as he could. Even if it made him ill, even if the mere proximity to Kenrick brought black images surging forth in the distant recesses of his mind. He would have nightmares tonight, as he always did, but what was a little lost sleep, if he succeeded in soothing another of the King's moods.

His own head began to ache, but he didn't reach for the mead for himself. It didn't work for him, only for those he gave it to. Instead, he bade goodnight to those who could not hide their observation of him, then retired quickly and silently.

Thick, swirling clouds drifted around him, warm and welcoming the way clouds weren't when he was awake. But was he awake now? Or was he sleeping, drawn down to the depths of non-being where he could make his body do anything, where his powers were all sharp and alive and enough to overcome any threat, either from friend or foe, where he was not alone but instead walking some parallel path that gave him the strength his father had had, and not the weakness that had killed him.

It was too dark in this place he'd made for himself. Too dark and too damned cold. But this was the dungeon he'd created with his own hands, carved out of rock too old to bring back to life, too wasted to do more than shed blood upon it and feast the black-eyed demons inside him who were always so hungry.

He'd been a baby when they'd come for him. A child no older than the one who was his only friend now, though what kind of friend would he be if he saw these demons, the ones who never really left him alone, so did that mean he wasn't lonely with them, or that they made him lonely? They'd come out of his skin when he was just a child, come out and ate away at whatever feeling he'd had for his mother so that when she was killed before his eyes, he felt so little that it might have been a dream, like this one, except that he was not asleep now but mercifully—

Awake.

Kenrick pulled in panicked air, then held it, listening too hard, so hard that his heart pounded and deafened him. His eyes were wide open, painfully darting from one black corner to another.

He was *not* alone. Somebody, some *thing* was in his bedroom and he didn't dare move a muscle in case . . .

'Ah, my King, I see I have awakened you.'

Kenrick's entire body twisted up in shock and horror and half-asleep terror. He scrambled up the bed, pulling blankets with him as though they would be protection against this real, live demon.

'Nash!' his voice came out sour and hoarse. 'What the hell are you doing? How did you get in here? What . . . how did you get all the way from Ransem? I thought you couldn't travel . . .'

A light flared across the room, not too brightly, but enough to make him squint for a moment. The candle moved, approaching to the accompaniment of steady footsteps. Nash halted by the side of the bed and raised the candle.

Kenrick's heart stopped.

'Forgive me,' Nash smiled with a face entirely devoid of scars. 'I had intended to surprise you, but it seems I have mistimed my attempt. Perhaps I should have waited until morning.'

The pain in Kenrick's chest beat him into breathing again, though it was harsh and uneven. He knew his mouth was open, but his eyes could not stop roving over the man before him, picking out things he'd thought were lost forever: the useless injured arm now holding the candle aloft, the eye, once burned from that face, now gazing steadily at him alongside its mate.

Nash had healed his wounds. Had he regenerated fully?

Kenrick wanted to throw up. He swallowed bitter bile and blindly reached out for the cup of mead he'd left on the bed table. He drained the liquid in one mouthful and sat up properly. 'What did you do?'

'Don't concentrate on what I *have* done, but on what I haven't.' Nash placed the candle on the table and sat down, pulling a bag onto his lap. 'This is but an interim measure, enough to allow me to move around, to complete some pressing tasks that can wait no longer. I still need to regenerate fully, to regain the bulk of my powers – but this will serve me in the meantime. If nothing else, it will allow me to spend more time at court, to help *you*.'

Blinking hard, Kenrick frowned. 'Help me? To do what?'

'Why, whatever you need. Tirone's girl, for one thing.'

The prophecy. The question tripped across Kenrick's tongue like a threat and vanished down his throat. No, not yet. Not until . . .

'And to celebrate my return to Marsay, I have brought you a small gift.' Nash reached into the bag and brought forth an orb, larger than the last one and almost pulsing with an energy Kenrick could feel from the other side of the bed.

Despite his fears, despite his nightmares, the orb drew him closer, his nausea replaced by anticipation. 'Is that . . . what I think it is?'

Nash nodded, a small smile on his face. 'I was a little unfair to you over the Salti business. It was my fault for not preparing you better. If you can forgive me, I would share this blood with you, to heal those wounds of yours that are most visible. Unless you no longer wish to . . .'

'Yes!' Kenrick almost reached out for it, but stopped, his eyes on Nash. 'Yes, I want it.'

'Very well. Lie back down and turn your palms open over your chest.' Nash put the orb between his hands and instantly Kenrick felt the sudden drain on his energy, almost pressing his eyes closed. 'You need do nothing else. Just allow yourself to go to sleep. In the morning, your face will be healed and you will be a little tired, no more. After another day, you will feel better than ever before. That's it, let your eyes close. There, my King, just trust me. I will take care of you.'

Though the morning was the warmest so far this winter, Osbert could not stop the icy chill which rattled down his spine to pool in his belly. No numbers of decades' practice could give him control of his expression as he stared at the young man seated so casually at his breakfast table, sipping something that smelled of honey and pulling the meat off a piece of chicken with good appetite.

'It's a miracle, isn't it, Osbert?' Kenrick took a bite of crusty bread, munched on it, then turned to another plate before him. The bedchamber was empty now, servants and pages having been shooed away for this audience. 'I have already sent word to the Archdeacons to say a mass of thanksgiving. As they left, I heard murmurings that it was the work of Mineah, since it happened on her day. I do feel blessed that she has seen fit to touch me in this manner. Help yourself to wine, Osbert, before you fall down.'

Osbert poured from the first flask, tearing his eyes from the scarless face. He swallowed hard and fast, almost choking on the liquid. Kenrick didn't seem to notice.

'About that matter we discussed yesterday.'

'Yes?' Osbert looked up, then immediately wished he hadn't. Kenrick had not only lost the ugly scar on the side of his face, but appeared healthier and stronger than ever before.

His thoughts rebelled at what might really be the cause.

'Yes,' Kenrick continued, popping a slice of peach into his mouth before gazing up at Osbert with a smile of pure serenity on his face. 'Some time over the next day or so, I wonder if you could have the matter whispered in a few taverns here and there.'

Osbert frowned in confusion. 'Sire?'

Kenrick swallowed again, laced his fingers together and began carefully, 'That prophecy you gave me – I read it a few times and it seems to me, this Enemy is supposed to fight the Dark Angel in some way. I want you to have it whispered that *I* am this Enemy. The people must see that I'm the only thing standing between them and whatever evil they fear. But it must be done subtly, understand? There is to be no suggestion that either you or I had any hand in starting the rumours. Can you do that for me?'

Suppressing the desire to roll his eyes, Osbert said, 'Yes, Sire, I can do that.'

'Very good. That's all.'

Osbert put his cup down, bowed and headed for the door, but Kenrick's words brought his feet to a halt.

'Just remember, it must be done secretly and subtly. With Nash back at court, I can't afford to take any chances.'

Osbert fled. He made it to the nearest privy in time to lose his breakfast, but no amount of determined mental arguments could stay the trembling that ran the length of his body.

Nash was back.

20

From the window of his bedroom, Andrew could see only the edge of the clouds blacking out the morning sky, but from his sitting room, the entire southern vista crowded in, like hounds baying for blood. He had to ride into that, had to turn his horse, say his prayers and hope the gods would be kind to him. Just how far south he would get today was a guess he didn't fancy making at this point. But he had no time to play with; he was expected to meet Micah tomorrow, then his mother expected him home after that, and the weather couldn't stop him.

'Your Grace? Your horse is ready and your guard awaits you.'

Andrew turned from the window and took his cloak from the page's hands. His feet itched to get out of the city, and it was all he could do not to make a run for the gates. But in all his years visiting Marsay, and those that he had lived there, he'd never once given in to that temptation, and he wasn't going to today.

'I'm coming now.'

The boy bowed and ran in front of him, leading the way through the castle, down massive staircases, along stone-flagged passages, through rooms dimly lit and secretive.

It was impossible to ignore the rumours. Even if he hadn't heard them himself over the last two weeks, he could see them in people's eyes as they passed him. Some looked upon him with disdain, neatly couched in a smile. Others glanced at him as though he might be a spy, or some saviour come to say that none of it was true.

But it was. He'd seen the evidence with his own eyes. So had the rest of the court. A face once scarred and ruined was now whole and new.

He couldn't avoid those looks thrown at him, though he said little to the greetings murmured in his direction. As Kenrick's cousin, they expected him to provide some answers, shed some light on the rumours, and say whether they were true or not. He could almost feel their disappointment that he knew no more than they did.

And then there was light, though it was too bright, too cheery, as though denying the snowstorm to come. His guard waited for him on the other side of the main courtyard, a little apart from the other traffic. They too seemed anxious to get away. Maitland was a calm promise in the midst of such chaos.

He'd done his best upon hearing the first whisper. He'd followed it through, tracing it back as far as he could. As casually as possible, he'd sent a number of his guard out into the city, into the taverns and markets, to listen and learn. But all they'd come back with were words that struck a different kind of fear into him.

A prophecy.

Kenrick had ordered a mass of thanksgiving to be said, which the entire court had been forced to attend. He had been blessed with a miracle cure, his face purified of scars he'd gained in battle – though Andrew honestly had no idea how the scars had come to be on Kenrick's face. But mass had been said, prayers offered up – and then the whispers had begun.

A prophecy speaking of a dark evil come to Lusara, and of a man born to fight it. With a fresh miracle under his belt, Kenrick looked ready to step into the shoes of both saint and saviour. The people, wracked and torn with oppression and fear, were willing to latch their hopes onto anything.

Just being within the walls of Marsay was more than Andrew could cope with now. After two weeks of these rumours simmering over a flame of discontent, it was only a matter of time before the discord erupted, and he wanted to be nowhere near it when it did. Besides, he needed to tell his mother and Finnlay about this.

They would want to know where these words of prophecy had come from. And perhaps where Osbert had disappeared to, since nobody had seen him since Kenrick's miracle.

Andrew strode across the courtyard, pulling his cloak over his shoulders, shoving his hands into his riding gloves. With a spring of urgency, he swung up into the saddle and headed for the castle gates.

The black sky loomed ahead, growing darker, more menacing by the moment.

The blizzard struck minutes after dusk. Robert barely had time to jump from his horse before the first blast smacked into him, knocking him sideways. He stumbled in already-deep snow, twisting his ankle. The reins slid through his icy gloves and the horse stomped back, eyes wild in the tempest. As a milky swirl of snow blinded him, he lunged forward and grabbed the dangling leather, using the animal's weight to get back onto the road where he could regain his bearings.

He'd thought he'd have another hour at least before the snow hit. The last village was more than a league back, the next another day's ride away.

'Damn it!' He had no choice but to cut across the ridge and down the eastern side. There was an empty barn there he knew well. Shelter was now paramount.

He wrapped the reins about his hand and used the other to hold the hood over his head, keeping his eyes on the darkness ahead, hoping his enhanced sight would keep him safe.

He didn't have time for this – if he missed his chance this time, it could be months before another came along, and he had neither the energy nor the patience to wait again. He'd already had more than his fill of waiting.

Cold leached into him, numbing his feet, his hands, his face. The old wound at his side ached sharply. It would probably bleed again. He could numb it later with the potion, but again it would take longer to heal.

On and on he stumbled until his outstretched hand smacked

against something hard: a wooden wall. Gasping with relief, he moved along it until he found the door. He lifted the latch and dragged the horse inside.

He had no strength left with which to make a light, but his eyes adjusted quickly, once he'd scraped the ice away from his lashes. Old rotting hay was strewn in places over the hard-packed dirt floor. Up the other end, there were some chicken coops, and in the roof was a dovecote – all very empty, just as he remembered. But it *was* relatively dry, and out of the wind, for all that the walls rattled like a warning of Hell. Robert took his horse into the nearest stall, dragged the saddle from its back and picked up a fistful of hay. He rubbed the horse down as best he could, using the exercise to warm himself. He found an empty bucket, scooped some snow into it and put his hands around it. It took minutes for his powers to wake up enough to melt the snow. He drank, let the horse drink, then he curled up in a corner, wrapped in his one blanket and cloak.

He'd had many more comfortable beds in his life, but few so welcome.

He knew the dream moments after the agony struck. The pain, deep in his side, snatched his breath away as he struggled to chase after Nash. Every step was a battle of its own, every second of his existence another touch of war. When would it end? When would he finally stop running, stop struggling and just sink into oblivion?

He fell to his knees, hands sinking into the sodden ground of the battlefield. Behind him, a wind swept through Shan Moss, tempting him with promises impossible to keep.

'Robert?' A hand on his shoulder made his flesh tremble. He looked up to find Jenn kneeling beside him, her blue eyes almost violet in the odd light which washed across the empty battlefield. 'Robert? All this pain, it's just the demon. It's not real. You have to believe that. You have to believe me.'

But she'd betrayed him. How could he believe her?

'Please, Robert,' her voice distant now, as she turned towards Nash, as the Prophecy said she would. 'Please understand.'

Robert lurched forward, reaching out to grab something of her, but his hand touched nothing but icy stone, his knuckles grazed. He opened his eyes and sat up. Immediately the old wound yelled its complaints loud enough to make him groan.

It was still dark, but the wind had died a little. His horse seemed content, shifting slightly from one foot to the other, eyes almost closed.

Robert couldn't go back to sleep. Instead, he reached over for his saddle-bags and pulled out the sack buried at the bottom. He weighed it between his hands, feeling its round-ness, its faint warmth.

He'd resisted this moment. But that was silly. After all, if he'd not wanted to learn about the orb, why had he taken it from Kenrick – just so Kenrick wouldn't have it?

There were side benefits to this, but there was also another driving purpose in his actions. This orb was identical to the Key, only much smaller. In what other ways was it the same?

Without thinking, he slipped the orb from the sack and placed it carefully on the floor in front of him. He crossed his legs, planted his elbows on his knees and studied it.

Only Finnlay had ever even seen one of these before, in his too-close encounter with Nash. Back in the days of the Cabal, they'd been common, but the knowledge of their purpose and uses had been lost, along with a lot of other sorcerer heritage.

Robert reached out and picked it up. The surface was hard, with a texture that felt both smooth and rough at the same time. His fingers skimmed over it, feeling for indentations and scars, any indication that it could be opened. It appeared to be made of stone, but it also glistened a little, as though moistened by dew.

Was that how the Cabal had made the Key, five hundred years ago? They'd simply put together an orb, ten times the size of this one, and placed within it all the things they'd needed kept safe? Or was the Key, like this orb, capable of much, much more than that?

Nash used these orbs to collect blood he later used to heal his wounds and regenerate himself. Somehow a sorcerer's blood could be absorbed into the stone and the power used to heal in a way that nothing else could. So was it Nash's own powers that made it happen, or something about the orb itself?

Kenrick had been about to use it, probably to heal those scars on his face. Old scars, so he'd only just got the orb. So Nash had given it to him. And Nash hadn't been around.

So the power was *in* the orb.

Taking a deep breath, Robert closed his eyes and gingerly sent his Senses out over the intriguing surface. He had no idea what he was looking for, but it was worth a try.

For seconds, he felt nothing, and then, as though gradually awakening to his aura, the orb's surface changed, became more open, like a sponge. Wary, Robert probed further, allowing his Senses to be absorbed into the orb.

Darkness gathered at the edges of his awareness. He might have been looking into an unlit room from a window high above, but there were subtle differences. This room had the power to suck him in. Already he could feel the pressure on his muscles, as though he would be bodily consumed. He pushed back and suddenly the thing began to heat up beneath his hands. Warmer and warmer it grew until, with a hiss, he dropped it back onto the floor, his eyes open, his body scrambling back out of the way.

'Serin's blood! It's . . . alive!'

He reached out for it again, ready to fight, but the orb was cool once more. Carefully, he put it back into the sack, but as he twisted to replace it in his saddlebag, he noticed something odd. His wound no longer hurt. The constant dull ache that kept him company most days had vanished. Curious, he prodded his side with gentle fingers. Yes, it still hurt when pushed, but the ordinary pain was gone.

Shaking his head in wonder, he curled up inside his blankets again. Perhaps he would get some more sleep now.

Or perhaps he would lie awake for the rest of the night pondering this new horrifying question – why had the orb dulled his pain, when nothing but a drug could normally have that effect?

'But Micah, that doesn't make any sense!' Andrew almost

twisted around in his saddle to pursue his point. 'Why would he do such a thing knowing it would fail?'

'It makes perfect sense,' Micah kept his eyes on the road, on picking out where the snow wasn't so deep and where the horses wouldn't founder. 'And failure wasn't the issue. Simply causing doubt was enough.'

'So Duke Robert had men hang things in Shan Moss, linen and bells and other stuff, all to make it look like the forest was haunted? Surely somebody noticed it was all faked?'

Micah couldn't help smiling. It had certainly been an interesting idea. 'I'm sure there were many men in Selar's army who looked and saw nothing but the props. But there were also men who saw and believed the forest was full of sorcerers, or ghosts, or some other monster. Father Godfrey reported hundreds of men ran away that first night. Those were men who did not face the Duke's army the next day.'

Andrew kept his silence for a while. Micah waited for the next question, the inevitable quiz every time the subject came around to Robert. But this time, there was something else beneath the surface, something prompting the interrogation which had begun almost the moment Micah had met up with him, the moment the guard had been sent back to Maitland and left them alone to travel south.

'What is it, my lord?' Micah asked softly. 'Did something happen at court?'

Andrew looked up guiltily, then recovered quickly. 'No, not really. I mean, nothing more than usual.'

'Since you rarely speak about what is usual, I find it difficult to imagine.'

When Andrew said nothing else, Micah pressed on, needing to know for his own sake as much as the boy's. 'Are you having difficulty with your friends?'

A shrug was quickly followed by a dry laugh. 'I don't exactly have a lot of friends at court, Micah. I'm Kenrick's cousin. My father was a man everybody in the country hated. Why would anybody want me as a friend?'

'But you can't help your family. Any reasonable man would know that. If they got to know you . . .'

He broke off. The look on Andrew's face spoke more than any words might. It was enough to make Micah remember exactly how it had been at court with Robert and Selar, the machinations, the scheming and manoeuvring by some who would stop at nothing to gain power and influence. Proctor Vaughn had been such a one, and Robert had fallen from grace as a result.

'Tell me something, Micah.'

He looked up, composing his expression. 'If I can.'

'Do you think my father was an evil man?'

For a moment, the thought almost made Micah laugh out loud, but he quelled that impulse and instead, focused on the memory of Tiege Eachern, the man who had married Jenn.

'Well?'

Andrew was looking at him with a little fear in his eyes, and also, perhaps, a need for confirmation of something. Micah had to tread very carefully here, or he could cause some irreparable damage.

But he could also not forget that Eachern had beaten Jenn, had almost killed her with his own hands.

'I don't know that he was evil. I only knew the man for the months after your mother's marriage, until you were born. I did my best to stay out of his way.'

'He didn't like you, did he?'

'No.'

'And you didn't like him?'

Micah shook his head slowly. 'No.'

Andrew looked away, his gaze drifting out towards the distance where the flat plains rose eventually into hills that would lead them further south.

'I barely remember him,' Andrew whispered eventually.

'And that worries you?'

'If people are going to hate me because of him, I think I should know why.'

There was something horribly sharp in Andrew's tone, though he had spoken softly. Micah frowned, but couldn't stop himself asking, 'Do you remember the night your father died?'

Colour flushed his face. Andrew kept his eyes averted and said, emphatically, 'No, Micah, I don't.'

And there was a finality to those words that rang a deep warning in Micah, a warning he could do nothing about.

The first thing Robert noticed was the wind dropping. He got up from his uncomfortable bed and crossed to the barn door. Peering out, he saw the snow had stopped and a weak sun had appeared.

Quickly, he packed up his things, saddling the horse with hands still cold from the bleak night. He'd slept badly, again. He should have felt rested, but the orb – or worrying about the orb – had whispered throughout his slumber, leaving him with an urgency to be away, to hurry to make up for lost time.

Pulling the horse behind him, he pushed the door open enough to get them out into the cold air. He turned to shut it, but he was no longer alone.

'Step away from the horse. Keep your hands where I can see them.'

A flash of movement from the corner of his eye, and the animal was taken from him. Something hard and sharp was pressed to the small of his back, encouraging him to face the wall. Brisk hands relieved him of his sword and the dagger in his boot and then he was abruptly released.

Silence followed, then, 'You may turn.' This voice was different to the other. Vastly different. This had the tone of absolute command to it.

Robert moved. The barn stood on the side of the ridge, sheltered from the worst weather by scraggly trees above. The slope here was gentle, covered in white, disappearing into a view below invisible in the grey mist.

To his left stood a dozen men, one of whom held his horse, another held his weapons. They watched him like he had the plague, keeping their distance. But it was the man who stood before him who commanded his full attention. The man watched him with an odd mixture of caution and interest. His robes were of the highest quality, but sombre and dull in colour. He was not especially tall, but thin, almost gaunt. Silver hair was cropped closed to the skull above a face that might have been sixty or so years old. Scars of some childhood disease marked one side of his face, while one eye drooped a little beneath brows fine and expressive.

He looked oddly familiar.

'I was told you might pass this way,' the man began and the soldiers behind him shifted with unease. 'I was also told I was a fool to expect to find you and yet, here you are. I should add,' the man paused, turning his head slightly to indicate his men, 'that I was also warned I would pay for this risk with my life, that even taking your sword from you would mean nothing. So tell me, will you kill me as you killed my brother?'

'Your brother?' Robert murmured, frowning. He hadn't killed anyone's brother since . . . 'By the gods! Tirone!' With that, Robert bowed deeply before the King of Mayenne, shock washing cold through his body. When he straightened up, he found the soldiers gone and Tirone studying him with genuine curiosity.

'Forgive me, Sire,' Robert continued, 'I did not recognise you.'

'Had Selar and I grown so different then?' Tirone waved a wrinkled hand to dismiss the subject. 'Not that it matters. As children, he was fair where I was dark, tall where I was not. I made no attempt to emulate his other attributes. I cannot say I am disappointed you failed to know me immediately.'

There was definitely a resemblance, Robert now realised, but surprise still addled his mind a little. What was Tirone doing here, in secret? Or had he come with an army at his back? Surely things hadn't grown so bad so quickly?

'You're surprised to see me.'

Robert nodded, pulling his gloves from his belt. 'Of course, Sire. Your letters never mentioned you might visit in person. And I agree with your men, you have taken a great risk coming here.' He shoved his hands into his gloves. 'Why did you?'

Tirone met his gaze without tremor. 'I thought it was time we met. Time I finally saw you in person, when I have already placed so much trust in you.' He shrugged. 'And I wanted to see what a sorcerer looked like with my own eyes.'

Robert listened to the list, believing not one word. 'Now you've seen me, Sire. We have met. Was your trip worth it?'

Tirone's gaze darkened. 'What are you waiting for? Did you want me to come here, asking these questions of you myself? Is that what you need before you finally move? By Serin's blood, Dunlorn! What must I yet do, what must any of us do, to have you make a stand against my nephew?'

Robert frowned again. 'Has something changed?'

'Tell me when you plan to move.'

'No.' Raising his hands to soften the response, Robert took a step forward. 'Forgive me, Sire, but you know I cannot say.'

'Why not? How could I possibly be a danger to your plans, eh?' Tirone shook his head and looked away, barely containing his anger. 'You try my patience with your evasions, your questions and your neverending request for trust.'

'Have I failed you yet?' Robert held his breath. So much depended on keeping this man content. If Lusara was to have any chance at survival, its relationship with Mayenne needed to remain peaceful. So far, Tirone had been willing to work with him, to keep his armies over the border and not react too quickly. 'Sire, if something has changed, you must tell me if I am to—'

'Tell me,' Tirone began evenly, his gaze directed towards the valley below, 'what do you know of my nephew?'

'In what respect?' Robert shook clear images of his most recent brush with Kenrick and the fate Helen had almost suffered because of him.

'In respect of him marrying my daughter.'

'What?' The word was breathed with such horror that Tirone glanced back at him, a flash of fear in his eyes which was quickly hidden. 'You can't be serious! You would give your consent for Olivia to marry Kenrick? But—'

'You prevaricate and dally,' Tirone snapped. 'I have lost two sons already and I have no desire to lose my last! If I let Kenrick have Olivia, I at least retain a chance my remaining son will live to his majority.'

'You will condemn him to death, Tirone, you know that as

well as I do. Kenrick wants Mayenne, just as your brother did – only the boy at least has the sense to see he can get it with the loss of only three lives, rather than chance it on thousands. You can't honestly be thinking of backing down now.'

'Do you plan to move soon?'

'Yes!'

'When?'

Robert shut his mouth. He could say no more.

Tirone watched him without moving, then slowly nodded. 'Very well. You have three months. If you have made no obvious move by then, I will make my own. Whether I give your King my daughter or take his country from him will depend entirely on you.'

'How?' Robert whispered in horror.

'Either *you* neutralise the threat to my family and my country, or I will. The choice is yours. But I need to see some evidence that you *can*. I warn you,' Tirone paused, his voice dropping, 'the day my son is murdered is the day I declare war on Lusara and no amount of pleading on your part will stop it this time. Do I make myself clear?'

'Yes, Sire.' There was nothing more Robert could say. Assurances would not bring the man's two dead sons back to life. 'But I beg you, do not invade.'

'You? Beg?'

Robert lifted his chin. 'My country may appear weak and feeble, but my people will remember who gave Selar the army he used to conquer us. You may well create a greater hazard than the one you seek to allay.'

Tirone's gaze narrowed. 'That's a pretty threat.'

'No threat, Sire.' Robert pulled his cloak around his shoulders and prepared to leave. 'I know my people. All they want is a tangible enemy to fight and there will be bloodshed far greater than any your brother caused. If you value peace, don't make the same mistake he did.'

When Tirone gave no response, Robert bowed once more. 'I hope your journey home will be safe. Farewell, Sire.' With that, Robert turned and walked around the barn, where he knew the soldiers waited with his horse.

Three months, or disaster would strike. From one evil to another.

At last the choice had been taken from him.

21

'By the gods, Finn, it looks so forlorn!'

'I was just thinking it looked better than I remembered – but I suppose there is a lot of snow on the ground. It's bound to hide a lot.'

When Jenn said nothing more, Finnlay looked aside at her. She stood on the ridge overlooking her old home, absently stroking her horse's nose, the pale afternoon light making her eyes dark and sad.

She travelled carefully in this part of the country. Too many stories already abounded about her supposed fate. She was unwilling to add to them. So she wore boy's clothes, bound her hair up in a braid and either put a cap on her head or kept her cloak hood pulled up, as she did now. From a distance, her slight figure aided the illusion.

Over the years, he'd grown to see that this was perhaps her greatest skill, that of creating illusions. Before Finnlay had met her, she had travelled as a story teller, creating myths and legends for any who would listen. Now there were so many layers to her illusions, he wasn't sure she knew where the truth ended and the lie began any more.

He turned back to the ruin which drew long faint shadows up to the forest beyond. The lake was iced over and clogged with weeds near the castle foundations, along the lines where tall proud walls had once stood. Odd piles of snow were scattered all over the place, covering the stones which remained. The keep, like a sentinel, stood alone in that pristine wasteland, dark and empty.

Hard to believe that this place had once been teeming with life, that on one day, fourteen years ago, it had been surrounded by Malachi in Guilde clothing under the orders of Nash. That Robert had succumbed to the will of the Prophecy and used the Word of Destruction to flatten everything within half a league.

Hard to believe that so much time had passed since.

Unable to stop himself, his thoughts turned once more to Robert, as they had done every day since they'd parted in the shadows of the Goleth mountains a month before. The same questions still rattled through him, shaking him, leaving him more than restless.

What was he planning? When would it happen?

What would happen?

He'd said nothing to Jenn. Of course, he'd told her of the rescue and assured her that Robert looked well and fit – but he couldn't say more. He doubted she'd want to listen.

'Are you sure this is such a good idea?' he started. 'Bringing Andrew here? Don't you think it might . . .'

'What?' She breathed, turning towards him. 'Might make him question the blind faith he has in Robert?'

'Showing Andrew the power of the Word won't do that. Why, *is* that what you want to achieve? Shouldn't a boy be allowed to look upon his father with *some* faith?'

'Please,' she said wearily, 'I can't keep going over this. Can't we just leave it alone for once?'

Finnlay didn't bother to disguise his heart-felt frustration. 'If you wish. Come on, we'd better move or we'll miss them. I don't want you standing around in this area any longer than necessary.'

This was not something Micah could play a part in, and yet still he watched, fascinated, as Andrew took his first look at Elita, the place where he'd been born, in all its dubious glory.

He asked little in the way of questions, just requesting a few details about which building had stood where.

Micah thought Finnlay was a little distracted – or perhaps he too was replaying those events that had brought them all to this place.

Here, Andrew had been born, and here, moments later, Robert had used the Word of Destruction. What was it

McCauly had said? If ever a birth had been marked by signs and portents?

Finnlay's eyes rose, met Micah's for a moment, then moved away. There was something there that made Micah frown, though he said nothing. But when Jenn began to lead Andrew down the path to the lake, Micah held back with a hand on Finnlay's arm.

'Is there something I should know?'

'We need to talk, yes. Let's go make camp while Jenn and Andrew relive old times, eh?'

Though there was a smile in Finnlay's eyes, it did nothing to quell Micah's unease. Still, he kept his silence as they journeyed down. As Jenn and Andrew mounted again and headed towards the keep, Finnlay led Micah around the other side of the lake to where the forest edged up against the crag. There was a layer of pine here, before the older trees of oak and ash. Finnlay took him deep into cover, finding a clearing not far from the narrow river just as the last of the light vanished.

Without a word, Finnlay tied up his horse and began scraping together firewood. Micah helped until they had enough for a warming blaze. He stood back as Finnlay used his powers to set it alight, then held his breath as the other man turned to him.

Finnlay reached into his jacket and drew out a piece of paper, folded several times. He half-held it out before saying, 'I'm sorry, Micah. We . . . I didn't want to just send this on to you. I thought it might be better coming from . . .'

Micah took the letter but didn't open it. He couldn't. His fingers simply refused to move. 'Is it . . .'

'It's from your brother, Durrill. Your father . . .'

'Hell,' Micah whispered, turning away. In the flickering firelight, he opened the letter until it glowed orange from behind, enough to let him read. The words were clear, giving details and times and meanings, but none of it really sank in.

He'd tried. For most of his life he'd tried to make his father understand *why* he was here, working alongside first Robert and now Andrew. But David Maclean had been a man of strict principles and Robert had failed every one of them. So, in turn, had Micah.

And it burned hard and deep inside him to know that his father had died disappointed in his youngest son.

'I'm sorry, Micah,' Finnlay's soft voice drifted to him in the early dusk.

'So am I,' he replied, suddenly glad of that dark shelter.

Within it, he could hide from everything.

'Are you sure it's safe to go inside?'

Andrew paused on the threshold of the keep, peering in to the darkness beyond. His voice echoed against walls that felt leagues away. There wasn't even so much as a single thread of moonlight to tell him where he was.

He felt a hand against his lower back. 'Go on, just be careful where you put your feet. There's a staircase to your right, leading up to the next floor, but it's not so close you can trip on it. To the left, at the other end of the hall, is a doorway and short corridor beyond. My father's study was that way, though it's all gone now.'

Gingerly, Andrew put his foot into the great hall, listening intently for other sounds, ones that shouldn't be there. It wasn't the darkness that scared him exactly, but more the . . . history of the place.

He shivered.

'Are you cold?'

Carefully, he reached out to his right, found his mother's hand and held it. He could see very little, but he turned to her anyway. 'Have you come back here since it was all destroyed?'

'Yes, once. Four years ago, on my way to Maitland to visit you.'

'How does it feel?'

He heard her breath catch. 'How does what feel?'

Andrew took another few tentative steps forward, without letting her hand go. 'You had such a . . . strange life as a child.'

'No stranger than my life as an adult.'

He smiled at the laughter in her voice. 'You were three when you were abducted by Nash and taken to live in Shan Moss at an inn which has long since burned down. And then, fourteen years later, you met up with Finnlay and Micah and Duke Robert and became a sorcerer and they brought you back here, and your father welcomed you?'

'Yes.' He could *hear* the smile in her voice, and that made him glad. 'He was amazed and disbelieving – but he was also wonderful. Though I'd been happy with my life at the inn, Jacob made me feel loved and wanted – and that meant everything to me.'

'Tell me about him.'

'Let's see if we can find the stairs.' Jenn led him forward, stumbled briefly, then gently urged him to sit on the bottom step.

'Are you sure it's safe for us to be here?'

'I know I'm not much of a Seeker, but I can tell at least that there's nobody in the vicinity but Micah and Finnlay.'

Andrew settled then, feeling his mother sitting close by. 'Tell me about Jacob.'

'Well, he was strong, opinionated, well-read and proud of his family's history. He insisted I resume my education, making me study every day to catch up all I'd missed out on. He valued books and history, and how both needed to be appreciated. His people loved him, admired and respected him. They were devastated when he was murdered.'

All suggestion of laughter had gone now and Andrew sat quite still, letting his mind fill in the blanks. 'I was born just after that, wasn't I? After the gate was brought down?'

'That's right.'

'I wish I'd known him.'

'I wish he'd known you.'

'Would I have liked him?'

'You would have adored him – and he would have been so proud of you. He wanted so very much to have a grandchild to carry on our House. He was often so frustrated being confined to that chair, dealing with the limitations of riding only short distances – and yet, he still managed to do so much with his life.'

Andrew turned to her, seeing something of her now his eyes were adjusted to the dark. 'You still miss him, don't you?'

She was silent for a long time and he couldn't guess what she was thinking. Then she said slowly, 'Yes, I still miss him. There's been many a time when I could have used his advice. And sometimes, I'd just like for him to . . . be around.'

Andrew leaned forward and pressed a kiss to her cheek. That brought a smile to her face.

'What did he look like?'

'Oh,' Jenn remembered, 'gruff, white-haired, strong. He had a way of looking at people that seemed to go right through them.' She paused then, facing the hall neither of them could see clearly. Then she raised her hand a little, frowned in concentration and abruptly, the air before them shimmered, as though an invisible wall had appeared out of nowhere, glistening with icicles.

Andrew held his breath. He'd seen her do this a number of times before, but never quite like this. Slowly the crystals collected together and formed a shape, suspended in the darkness. The shape shifted again and again until it became a face.

He stared up at eyes he knew so well, though they were so different. A grin split his face, but before he could say a word, the illusion cracked and shattered, disappearing into nothing.

Andrew wrapped his arms around his mother and gave her a big squeeze. 'Thank you! That was . . . Can we look upstairs?'

Laughing a little now, Jenn agreed. 'Just be careful. I can't afford to make any light. We're too close to the village and you know how suspicious people are nowadays. If they think they're seeing ghosts, there'll be big trouble.'

Andrew sprang to his feet, holding his hand out for hers, no longer afraid of the dark. 'Let's go to the top and see what the view is like.'

Finnlay brought out the smoked ham he'd purchased that morning and busied himself with beans and vegetables until he had a pot of something delicious simmering over the fire. Just sitting close to it made his stomach rumble. Occasional plumes of steam would rise from the pot, drift and dissipate into the night air, urging him to have just one more cook's taste.

It was good to give himself something constructive to do. He wanted to keep an eye on Micah, but the man had busied himself gathering more firewood until there was a pile at the edge of the clearing big enough to last them a week. When the pile drew almost to Micah's eye level, he'd come to a halt and turned back for Finnlay's fire, drawing a couple of moss-covered rocks close by to use as seats. He'd even gone to the trouble of cleaning them off so they could dry before Jenn and Andrew got back. When he appeared ready to find some other constructive thing to do, Finnlay handed him a cup of ale, sat him before the pot and ordered him to stir.

And then, quite deliberately, Finnlay had told him all about the runaway children – and Robert's timely intervention.

Micah had kept his head bowed a little, the flash of firelight dancing in his pale eyes, but there was no mistaking the gleam in them, nor the studied stillness in his body. Though he pretended disinterest, underneath, he was just as hungry for news as Finnlay.

By the gods, it was so hard to sit back and watch this. Robert and Micah had once been so close, the very best that friends could be to each other. They would disagree and voice opposing positions, they would even occasionally have their silences, but Finnlay had believed that their loyalty to one another was utterly unshakable. Finnlay had even been jealous of it on occasion.

Yet, for the last eight years, they had both done their best to ignore the very existence of the other, neither admitting to the split, nor the pain it so obviously had caused.

And what would happen when they once more faced each other?

Finnlay got up and began scraping snow, leaves and twigs aside to make space for sleeping. Jenn and Andrew would return soon, and Micah still hadn't said a word.

'Where is he now?'

The low voice almost made Finnlay jump, and he forced himself to keep working, rather than turn. 'I don't know. He

318

said he was going home – but the gods only know where that might be. Possibly over the border again, maybe Bleakstone?'

'How did Murdoch know where Robert would be?'

'I didn't ask him.'

'Why not?'

Finnlay did turn then, to find Micah's gaze on him, flat and impermeable. 'There are rules, unwritten, perhaps, but they're there nonetheless. Murdoch tells me what he can without breaking Robert's trust.'

Micah looked away. 'Of course.'

'Being bitter won't help.'

'I'm not bitter.' The voice was easy, but the words were forced. 'I'm . . . disappointed.'

Finnlay could say no more to that, for it was written all over Micah's face. He returned to his ground-clearing, but stopped when he heard a soft noise to the east. Micah was on his feet in a second, but Finnlay held up his hand.

Then a face appeared in the shadows, followed by another, and Micah relaxed. By the time Jenn and Andrew reached the clearing, Micah had returned to the pot, picking up the wooden spoon as though it was all that separated him from madness.

And as he watched, Andrew walked over to him, placing a hand on his guardian's shoulder. 'Mother told me about . . . about your father. I'm so sorry.'

Micah froze, then got to his feet, gave Andrew a wan smile, and murmured something about going for a walk. All they could do was stand there and watch as he walked away down the hill towards the river.

For all that he often complained about it, Finnlay wasn't a bad cook if he had enough time to prepare and a good fire to work with. Andrew was almost too hungry for words and went back, not only for seconds, but thirds. He did, however, make sure there was enough for Micah when he came back.

Andrew peered again into the darkness, but he could see little except for the faintest trace of shallow moonlight glittering off running water.

He couldn't imagine how Micah was feeling right now. He got to his feet, his eyes once more searching the darkness.

'He'll come back when he's ready,' Jenn said quietly. 'You know his feelings for his father were complicated.'

'Yes,' Andrew said, 'but he might have gone home when instead he stayed . . .' He pulled up short then. Micah had not chosen to go home simply because of Andrew – but also because of Sairead.

Micah had kept her a secret from him – and now he had to keep her a secret from his own mother.

He turned around with what he hoped was a smile on his face. 'This is near where you were abducted, isn't it? Down by this river? You were playing by the old mill, weren't you?'

A flicker of something flashed in her eyes. Then the mysterious expression was gone. 'Yes. If you follow the river along about fifty paces, you can't miss it.'

'May I go and take a look? I promise I won't go further.'

Jenn gazed steadily at him for a moment, then started, 'Just . . .'

'Be careful, yes, I will.' With that, he headed down the hill, stepping carefully around thick tree roots hidden by crusty layers of ice and snow. It wasn't as cold tonight as it had been since he'd left court, but even so, his fingers felt it, along with the tip of his nose and the tops of his ears. He'd stay warm if he kept moving, which he did, finding the river and the trace of a path along it, overhung with bracken and brush, naked of snow.

Micah had come this way.

He knew he couldn't say anything to make it better. He knew he couldn't do anything to fix it. He knew Micah wanted to be alone. So why was he out here, looking for the ruined mill, but keeping an eye out for his friend?

He saw nothing but more shadows, the silvery thread of bare branches above and the trail of moonlight on the river beside him.

It had been so interesting walking into Elita for the first time, though. So . . . very real. Hearing about his grandfather in the place that had been his home, walking into the empty room where he'd been born, treading the keep looking down at what had once been a mighty castle had all struck up odd and exciting images in his mind that filled him so that he knew he would never get to sleep.

And if he kept on this path, if he watched where he was going, he would find the mill where his mother, at the age of three, had been abducted by Nash, setting the whole chain of events in motion.

Although, of course, if the Prophecy were to be believed, that chain had been begun a thousand and more years ago.

Some shape took on form in the darkness ahead, something square and solid with what might have been the remains of an arch. His step quickened, dodging boulders and fallen branches and ice puddles until he came to a halt before the remains of a wall, encrusted with moss cold to his touch.

A smile warmed his face and without a qualm, he stepped inside—

Something didn't feel quite right. Something about this place. There was no roof and the walls closest to the river were almost gone completely. And the shadows were thicker here, as though . . .

He shivered. This was silly! How could this place be different inside than out? He was being childish!

And yet, there was an urge, deep in his gut, that called to him to leave, to just move out beyond the door.

He deliberately took a step forward, then another – but the fear rose in him, strangling the breath from him. As carefully as he could then, he turned and stepped back through the archway and only then did his breathing slow.

The odd feeling vanished.

Obviously he'd been imagining it. There was no other explanation – especially since he didn't have any powers of any kind. But still, it had been worth it just to see the mill, though so little of it still stood. Best he get back now, before he got too—

A faint brush of air behind his ear and suddenly the ice cold of steel pressed against his throat. Another arm, terrifyingly powerful, pulled his hand behind his back, almost lifting him off the ground. Between the two, he could hardly breathe, though his pounding heart insisted he should.

'Finnlay?' It had to be him. He was trying to teach Andrew something, surely . . .

'No,' a harsh whisper, little more than a suggestion of breath. 'And if you say another word, you'll die.'

22

Icy cold air burned Andrew's breath, making it steam into clouds as it left him, hard and harsh. He wanted to move. He wanted to see. He wanted to know.

He could hardly think, he was shaking so hard.

But the blade at his throat kept him as still as the threat whispered by the man holding him and then his breath came harder, the air not going in properly or out properly and dizziness threatened . . .

'Don't panic,' the half-voice came again. The grip on him shifted, fractionally, keeping the dagger edge against his skin, but no longer pressing. 'Do as I tell you and you'll live.'

A big hand clapped over his mouth, cutting off his air completely. For a second, Andrew thought he would suffocate, but then his vision cleared, his heartbeat slowed a little and the hand dropped.

'This way.'

Andrew had no choice as the man turned him, steered him around the ruin through thick black shadows to where two horses stood in a thread of moonlight.

If he could just call out. Jenn and Finnlay weren't far away . . . and Micah. He would be close by, wouldn't he? They could overpower this . . .

A rustle in the bushes and the man holding him froze. Andrew nearly cried out with relief as Micah came striding towards them, his sword already drawn. But then he came to a halt, his face easily visible and very pale, his eyes wide almost in disbelief.

The fear twisting inside Andrew clenched hard at that, at the sight of Micah's sword lowering, of the threat vanishing from his stance as he stared at the man holding Andrew prisoner.

For a terrifying moment, silence filled the winter night, then Micah shook himself, lifted his chin and asked, 'How long?'

'As long as it takes.'

Micah nodded at that, then his gaze met Andrew's with an expression he could not fathom. Why wasn't Micah doing something? Why was he putting his sword away? Why wasn't he fighting . . . wasn't that the task he'd set himself? To guard Andrew from all danger?

'Move now,' Micah said, stepping back. 'Before it's too late.'

The stranger shifted, pulling Andrew further towards the horses. Then he stopped. 'Thank you.'

'Don't.' Micah's voice was nowhere near as hard as it might have been. 'You've given me no choice.'

'The choice . . . was always yours.'

Before Andrew could take another breath, a gloved hand brushed over his eyes and he could see no more.

He woke up to movement, rhythmic, pounding, unceasing. His head ached and he could see nothing, but he could hear: the forest around him, the horse beneath him, another to his right, the jangle of bit and leather, a rustle of wind through leafless trees above.

He opened his mouth and found he could speak. 'Who are you?' His voice was a croak and he coughed, needing to wet his throat. 'Where are you taking me?'

There was no answer.

He tried to move his hands. They were bound to the saddle, along with the reins; though Andrew's body retained enough control to stay on the animal's back, he still had no power to move his own limbs, nor turn his head, nor see anything but blackness and that could only mean . . .

Serin's blood – this man was a Malachi!

And Micah had just *let* him be taken!

After all those words about trust and betrayal . . .

'Not far now.'

The words jerked him back to the present and he blinked

hard, clearing the odd mist that suddenly appeared before his eyes. Slowly his sight returned to him and he found he was in a different forest, with more snow, trees further apart, the ground sloping and rocky.

And then the stranger slowed the horses, walking them for a while until at last he came to a halt in the shelter of a tall rock the size of a cottage. Beyond it was a blank shadow against the sky, perhaps a cliff. He heard the man dismount, move around behind the horses and then approach from Andrew's left.

'I'm going to free you now, but I'll keep your hands tied for the moment, I think.' And then the man came to his side, unleashed the rope tied to the saddle and Andrew got his first look of the man's face.

Sweet Mineah!

Strong, square jaw, level eyebrows, black wavy hair falling past his shoulders . . .

He'd not changed, not one bit, he was just as Andrew remembered him . . .

He looked up, and Andrew was mesmerised by eyes that looked right into him.

'You remember me. Good. You can dismount now – but be careful, your legs have probably lost some feeling.'

Andrew wanted to move, but couldn't. It wasn't until a hand was placed on his arm that his body woke up. Gingerly he swung his leg over the horse and slid to the ground. His hands, however, remained tied. He looked down at them, then up back into that gaze.

'No. I don't trust you not to run off back to your mother, so for the moment at least, you are my prisoner. Here, drink some of this.'

Andrew shied away from the flask held to his lips.

'You honestly think I'd poison you, all the way out here?' An absent chuckle was lost in the snowy silence. 'I could have killed you a thousand times since we last met – but that doesn't mean you should trust me. However, we have a long walk ahead of us. It's up to you, but you might want a drink first.' With that, the flask was placed in Andrew's hands and he was left alone to make his choice.

He *was* terribly thirsty, so he took a sniff of the contents. It smelled like water. He swallowed a mouthful, then drank greedily. The flask was taken from him and the rope attached to his hands picked up. Then Andrew was forced to walk along behind, with the horses, as his captor found some invisible path and began climbing the ominous black cliff.

Andrew tried to keep up, but he could hardly see a thing before him, just the ropes binding his hands, which affected his balance. He stumbled every few minutes, but he was warm and the ropes weren't painful, at least, as long as he didn't pull on them.

The path wound back and forth, zigzagging up the almost sheer cliff-face, and not for one moment was the pace slowed for him, no matter how many times he fell. His boots were sodden within minutes, the snow melting on them, turning his toes to ice. His head pounded with each step, almost deafening him to everything else. When he could, he'd look up, hoping to see that the top was close by, but it seemed forever impossibly far away, as though it would always keep moving, no matter how many hours or days he trudged like this.

And then, abruptly, when he'd given up hope, they did reach the top and he was allowed a moment to rest, to catch his breath and take another few drops of water. Then they were moving again, down at first, then up again, onto open moorland now, swept by wind and rain. There was little snow here, but the ground was soggy, his boots sinking into mud that sucked all the energy from him. There was enough light now for him to see this moor stretched far in every direction, to the end of the world, perhaps.

He passed the night in a terrible daze, his body aching in every joint, until his thoughts shut down, his curiosity died and nothing mattered any more except for maintaining his balance. He barely noticed when the path began to drop again, when wind petered out and high gully walls surrounded him. When the pressure on the rope ceased suddenly, he dropped where he was, his body not caring that he was half on rock, half on sodden grass.

He closed his eyes and let sleep overtake him.

*

Finnlay couldn't tell what it was in the air that made him look up, made him stand up. He'd been keeping the usual watch, as he always did when out with Jenn, because there was no way of trusting that some danger might not appear if he wasn't paying attention; usually he could work out what had alerted his instincts, but this time, he couldn't.

And his instincts alerted Jenn's. Though she had poor Seeking abilities, her Senses were well-trained enough and after the first moment, she too was certain there was something odd in the night, something that hadn't been there before.

After standing and listening for a moment, they turned to each other.

'Anything?'

'Nothing . . . specific. But you know me – I'm not sure I'd notice anything specific unless it . . .' The grin faded from her face as she turned slightly, almost sniffing the air.

Micah had been gone an hour, perhaps; Andrew only ten minutes. Finnlay suddenly didn't think it a good idea to try shouting for them. Quickly, he pulled out his *ayarn* and sent his Senses forth – but Jenn was already standing.

'Come on.'

The moment he reached the river path, he began looking closely for signs of passage, for clues that might indicate some other danger. Perhaps they were overreacting, but Andrew was too valuable to take such chances – and, damn it, he shouldn't have let the boy go on his own in the first place.

There was nothing to see on the path, nothing to indicate . . .

'Listen!' Jenn's hand on his arm, her swift whisper sent a shiver down his spine.

Two horses, galloping hard on the snow-laden ground, getting further and further away.

He took off running, leaping over obstacles in his way until he reached the ruin, his hand ready on his sword, but he could be too late already . . .

The ruin was empty, but on the other side was—

'Micah?' Jenn rushed forward, but Micah barely noticed her. Instead, he stood gazing into the forest, left hand on the hilt of his sword, and the oddest expression Finnlay had ever seen on his face.

He didn't appear to be injured, so Finnlay kept going, finding two sets of footprints in the snow, and then two horses, both coming and going back in the direction in which Micah was staring.

Finnlay turned, strode up to Micah and said, 'Where's Andrew?'

Micah blinked twice, then roused himself from his daydream. His eyes looked bleak as he said, 'He's gone.'

'Gone?' Jenn struggled to contain her fear and her anger. 'What do you mean, gone? Gone where? With whom?'

'I don't know where. He didn't say.'

Finnlay grabbed Micah's arms, shaking him a little, icy threads of panic beginning to rise in him. 'What the hell's wrong with you? Was it . . . Nash? Did he take Andrew? Did he do something to you?'

'Nash?' Micah half-smiled, then said, 'By the gods, no. You don't understand. I didn't. But now . . .'

'Micah,' Jenn threatened, 'if you don't tell me where my son is—'

'He's safe,' Micah rushed to assure her, before adding. 'Robert took him.'

For a moment, Finnlay was sure he'd misheard, or at least, misunderstood, because it simply didn't make any sense that Robert, of all people would simply abduct . . .

Soon . . . spring . . . you'll know what to do . . .

He dropped his hands and took a step back, horror and excitement thrashing together inside him so violently, he couldn't form thought, let alone words.

Robert was going to use Andrew.

By the gods!

A flash of movement caught his eye. Jenn had grabbed Micah's arm and was trying to urge him back to the camp for their horses. Finnlay, struck into motion, held up his hands. 'Wait! Jenn, what are you doing?'

'What am I doing?' she snapped, her eyes ablaze. 'I'm going to get my son . . .'

'*Robert's* son!'

'*My* son, Finn! And Robert can't have him. I'm going to get him back. I'm going to stop him . . .'

'Stop him what? Doing what you're afraid to do yourself? Is that it?' Finnlay took a step closer to her, but was wise enough to make no move to hold her still, to calm the fear and anger that radiated from her. Deliberately he dropped his voice, keeping his tone reasonable. 'I tried to warn you, the day Andrew was born.'

'Fine! Don't help me. I'll go alone!'

'Jenn!' This time Finnlay did catch her arm, pulling her around to face him. 'You know there is no way you will ever be able to find them. If Robert doesn't want to be found, you don't have a chance. Serin's blood, will you just listen?'

She stood still before him, shaking, stiff panting breaths catching the air, her eyes speaking volumes she couldn't trust to words. Then, finally, her eyes filled. 'Damn you. Damn you for believing him.' And she turned to Micah. 'And damn you for letting him take my son. And I suppose you told him as well, didn't you? You always wanted to.'

'No.' Micah's voice betrayed the shame he obviously felt. 'Robert can't know now.'

Finnlay frowned. 'Can't know? Why not?'

Micah stared at the ground a moment longer, then squared his shoulders. 'There is no way that Robert would ever sanction putting his own son on the throne of Lusara. You've finally got one thing you always wanted, Jenn. I now promise I will never tell them.'

'You knew?' Jenn's horrified whisper slit the night. 'You *knew* this was what Robert was planning? That's why . . . oh, sweet Mineah, please, don't tell me that's why you . . . all these years, that's why you stayed with Andrew, looking after him, guarding him . . . because you knew Robert would do this.'

Micah bravely held her gaze for a moment though he gave no verbal answer. Slowly he headed back towards camp. He took three steps, then paused, not facing them. 'My father died believing I was a traitor to my people. If nothing else, Robert taught me where the path of honour lies, and no matter what you might believe, I have never strayed from it, even if you can't see my footprints.'

And then he was gone, merging into the shadows as though he would become one with them.

Bright morning light forced Andrew's eyes open, though reluctantly. He blinked up at a pale blue sky streaked with horse's tail clouds. For a moment, he kept still, but then the fear returned, awakening him fully to the new day.

He turned his head left and saw nothing but a gently smouldering campfire in a clearing in the stones. To his left, tied beneath a young, spindly pine, were the two horses, stripped of their saddles, lazily munching on fistfuls of winter-brown grass – but other than that, he was alone.

What was he doing here? And why had he been taken without a word to his mother . . . or Finnlay, even?

And why had Micah just . . .

He groaned loudly as he sat up. His hands were still bound, but the rope was loose enough for him to flex his fingers. The rest of his body, however, complained at his movements. He looked down to find two thick blankets had been laid over him. Frowning, he picked them off, rolled to his knees and got up.

His head spun and he stumbled back against a narrow tree trunk until things righted themselves. When he opened his eyes again, he looked down, searching for footprints in the brown slush. They went off in every direction.

'Hungry?'

He flinched as the word reached him. He looked up to find the man emerging from the woods, a branch of something tucked under his arm.

'Could you . . .' Andrew's voice faded as the enormity of the situation pressed in on him, waking him completely.

He was in the presence of a legend.

'I suppose you want those ropes removed, eh?'

Green eyes gazed down on him steadily, as though expecting some kind of trick reply.

'Yes,' Andrew managed, then flinched again when a knife

was sliced through his bonds. Immediately he pulled the ropes away and began to rub his wrists. The moment he was finished, a hot cup was pressed into his hands.

'Drink. Eat. We've a long journey ahead of us.'

'A journey?' Andrew swallowed, and his stomach replied with a growl. 'Where to?'

'Wait and see.' Another sea-green gaze swept over him and then the man turned his back and returned to the woods, as though what remained behind was of no interest to him.

Robert sat on a rock and watched the clearing below. Andrew was stomping around the space, like a rat in a trap, eating bread, looking for a way out.

Of course, Andrew assumed, like all rats, that there *was* a way out in the first place, that it was just a matter of finding the right words, the right actions, arranging the timing and the resources, and the problem was solved.

Now the boy was checking the horses, running his hands over twitching animal-flesh. Was this real interest? Or was it purely boredom?

How much work would he have to do? So far the boy had not reacted as he'd expected, though that was not necessarily a bad thing. What other surprises awaited him?

With a sigh, he stood up and stretched. There was only one way to find out.

'Jenn, you've got to stop,' Finnlay urged gently, placing a hand on her shoulder. He crouched down beside the rock she was sitting on and studied her pale face, the closed eyes which slowly opened to stare without focus at the ground before her.

'I can't stop. I have to know where they are. What they're doing. What . . . Robert's doing.' She swallowed hard and Finnlay put a cup of brew into her hands.

He looked at the camp they had made for the night, to where the fire was ready to die out, to where the horses were saddled, ready to move, to the empty place that Micah should have occupied. Finnlay had no idea where Micah was, but he wouldn't go far – just far enough away from Jenn and what she might say to him.

She felt betrayed – and the worst of it was, Finnlay couldn't blame her. Micah was her oldest, most steadfast friend – even though she'd always known his first loyalty was to Robert. But for the last eight years, that had been replaced by loyalty to Jenn, and Andrew.

Finnlay sighed and turned back to find Jenn readying herself to try Seeking again, as she had all night, stretching her meagre abilities as far as she could in the hope that she could find something shielded more strongly than her own soul. Now, in the light of morning, she was just as determined, even if it exhausted her.

He reached out and placed a hand over hers. 'Please, Jenn. No more. Micah said he believed Robert would bring Andrew back—'

'But Robert didn't say that, did he?' She looked up at him, eyes wide, hoping for something, but expecting nothing. 'I don't want this. I never did. You, Robert . . . even Micah . . . You're all so . . . ready for this, for what it means. But I . . .'

Her voice trailed off and she took another sip of her brew. She was pale, blue eyes peering out at a world she had struggled to find a place in. There was hardly a moment in her life where she'd been wholly free to make any choice, and yet, that struggle still continued, with the same determination as ever.

'Micah was right about one thing,' she murmured after a moment.

'What's that?'

'I can't ever tell Robert. Not now he's done this.'

This mood of hers was frightening Finnlay a little, as though she'd made some decisions she knew he wouldn't like. Braving it, however, he said, 'But you never planned to, did you?'

'Yes,' she replied, 'one day, when all this was over. I . . . you'll think me stupid but . . . I'd hoped to keep Andrew safe for him, the way I know Robert never will.'

A shiver of fear ran down Finnlay's back. 'What do you mean?'

Her eyes flickered to him and then away, as though she was

now afraid of admitting the truth – but she had begun, and she would not now stop. 'I can't afford him knowing, can't afford him growing attached to Andrew, don't dare allow him to . . . love his own son. I wish I could, but . . .'

'Why not?' Finnlay held his breath.

'The Key told me how the Prophecy ends, Finn. It's Robert's ultimate destiny to destroy what he most loves.'

Finnlay sank to his knees to the ground and let out a long, low whistle, shock radiating through every muscle in his body. It all made sense now, didn't it? Everything Robert had done, his fierce determination to keep Jenn safe, to keep her out of the Prophecy as much as possible. Why he could never allow himself simply to love her, as any other man would.

And now that he . . . Did he no longer love Jenn? Is that what she believed? And that if he didn't – and if he did learn about Andrew, and learned to love him, then it would be Andrew who . . .

'I'm sorry,' were the first words that slipped from him, to his surprise. A smile tilted the corner of Jenn's mouth, but it did not reach her steady gaze.

'The irony of it is, Robert will still end up loving Andrew, if he gives himself the chance.'

'Yes,' Finnlay agreed, 'not even Kenrick has the heart to hate your boy. Robert hasn't got a hope. Is that why . . .'

'I don't know what I was expecting. All this apparent evidence that Andrew is connected with the Prophecy – and yet, there's no direct mention of him, and the Key has never once acknowledged his existence. But there's just no way around his ancestry and the fact that he's the last living male of the old royal line. It shouldn't matter, but I know it does, especially to a people who have suffered as much as these. But Andrew . . .' She paused. 'I'm not sure he has it in him to be King. He's not hard enough, inside. Not . . .'

'Ruthless?'

'No. He is . . . his father's son.'

Finnlay got to his feet and held out a hand to her. She took it and stood, tipping the remains of her brew onto the ground. 'And?'

She almost laughed then, would have, if there hadn't been so much sadness in her. 'Robert will see what Andrew is — and what he isn't — and he'll set about changing Andrew to suit his needs.'

'To suit *Lusara*'s needs,' Finnlay felt obliged to point out.

'Come on, Finn,' she admonished, 'you know as well as I do those two things have always been the same.'

He could only agree. 'Well, we can't sit about here waiting for them to come back. I suggest we head to Elita, find some shelter inside.'

Jenn was moving back to the horses by then, kicking dirt over the fire to put it out. 'And what if we're seen?'

'From what I hear, the locals stay clear of the ruins. They fear ghosts.'

'As they should. As we all should.' She took her reins and swung up into the saddle. She tilted her head a little, then pointed towards the stream. 'Micah's down there, somewhere. You'd better go fetch him. I'll see you at the keep.'

23

'Does he still breathe?'

The doctor leaned over Brome, listening to his heart with an instrument of some kind. Godfrey looked at Francis standing beside him and tried to steel himself against the answer if it should be no.

'He still lives,' the doctor pronounced, straightening up. He turned to his apprentice who held a tray of strange concoctions, bottles and other potions, which had been given to Brome in one form or another over the years, and none of which had helped the Bishop at all.

Godfrey took a step back from the bed, his spine twitching at what he had thought would befall him this day. But then, it would still happen, wouldn't it? Brome, though mostly incapacitated over the winter, *had* made sure instructions were left, with his signature on them, clear notification that Godfrey and no other was to succeed him to the Primacy.

The doctor grimaced in displeasure and Godfrey's stomach did an uncomfortable lurch, as it had done every few minutes since Brome had sunk into his current state. The Bishop was now almost beyond speech, movement, and Godfrey doubted Brome could even hear.

And soon Brome would stop breathing, and then it would be all over. For both of them.

Something of his thoughts must have told on his face; Francis firmly took his elbow and steered him to a far corner of the sumptuous room, away from the other priests, the doctors, the servants hovering with fresh sheets, bowls of steaming water, rose petals and rose water to alleviate the stench of the doctor's prescriptions and the sickness, to rid the thick carpets of it, the heavy drapes and tapestries which covered every inch of stone, and even some of the carved oak panelling that graced the wall behind the massive bed.

'Please, Francis,' Godfrey couldn't take his eyes off the room, 'if you are around to see it, when I'm like this, please do not let me use people like this, use my position to . . .'

Francis kept hold of his arm. 'This is not *Brome*, Brother – this is because he is Bishop. This is entitled to him because of the importance of his position, no more. You will be entitled to no less.'

'There has to be something we can do, Francis, something we haven't tried, some doctor from another country, another region that might know something. Perhaps if we—'

'No.' With a firm grip, Francis whispered harder and louder, to stop Godfrey. 'Brother, calm yourself, I beg you.'

The plea silenced Godfrey. He took a long breath and let go all the tension building in his stomach. Francis watched him carefully, then gave him a little room.

'Forgive me,' Godfrey murmured, deliberately turning his eyes back to the room, watching the doctor move about, continuing his work, consulting with his bearded colleagues.

Putting it off would not change it. Brome had seen to it that Godfrey would become Bishop in his place and it didn't matter that he didn't want the mitre, didn't feel worthy of it – or that, in his mind, Lusara *already* had a Bishop, even if living in exile

– none of that mattered. Brome would not last the next month, the doctors said. Probably less.

'I have taken the precaution,' Francis murmured, 'of sending letters to our most outflung Archdeacons and Abbots, to give them sufficient time to arrive for both Brome's funeral and your—'

Godfrey held up his hand. 'Don't say it, please. I'm not doing anything until Brome's instructions are ratified by the Synod.'

'Of course,' Francis said. 'But I'm curious to know how the King will take your new position. Will he even care? Should he?'

Godfrey met Francis's gaze and the open question sitting there, so far unanswered. Godfrey gave a grunt of ironic laughter, but didn't take his eyes away. 'Kenrick will form his opinions regardless of what I do or do not do as Bishop. He will have other sources than my actions to base such opinions on.'

'As you say,' Francis agreed.

Godfrey knew what the real question was – and knew that Francis had been sent by others to ask it. The problem was, Godfrey didn't have an answer. He simply didn't have it in him to stand there and promise he would be the King's man, as Brome had, nor could he say equally that he had rebel's blood flowing through him and that at the first opportunity, he would open the city gates and let them in. He couldn't – he knew too much about the Malachi and Nash to be so foolish.

So where did that leave his answer to Francis? What did he and the others need – or want – to hear?

Godfrey closed his eyes, lacing his fingers together as if in prayer, and thought back to the last time he'd seen Aiden McCauly, the exiled Bishop who still commanded his loyalty. 'I can only pray,' Godfrey replied eventually, allowing words that might have belonged to McCauly to emerge from him, 'that the King will forgive whatever shortcomings I may have, in the sure knowledge that I will always act according to Church Law and within the bounds of my faith and my conscience.'

Francis's gaze flickered over him, perhaps looking for something else, what, Godfrey could only guess. Then, with no noticeable change in demeanour, the Archdeacon turned back to the rest of the room and said, 'I think I shall order some lunch brought up to the anteroom. The doctors will want refreshment when they're finished, and you can't afford to let your strength wane. I'll be back in a moment.'

With practised hands, Francis pulled the cowl up over his head, moved to the door and slipped out, where, Godfrey was certain, the air would be clearer, the room cooler, and there would be men who would listen very carefully to what he had to report.

The one question remaining in Godfrey's mind was: had he just signed his own death warrant?

A blast of noise and heat greeted DeMassey as he pushed open the tavern door and stepped inside. Oil lamps hung from the low ceiling, but these gave out poor light in comparison to the firepit sitting in the middle of the room. A pig was roasting over it, turned on the spit by a small boy perched on the edge of a stool. The child turned his handle absently, his eyes fixed on the men and women around him, and probably – like DeMassey – half deafened by the noise they were making.

This place, the Two Feathers, was as far from the castle as it could be and still remain within the walls of the city. It had become, for reasons DeMassey had never fully understood, a kind of sanctuary for Malachi working within the capital, a place where they were not looked down upon by those in the court whose titles, wealth and position allowed them to be superior and act accordingly, no matter how new their nobility. And of course, the locals didn't know that the men and women they drank with were, in fact, sorcerers. That small fact alone was enough to draw his people here.

But it was also that fact that made him wary of the place. If his D'Azzir, along with other Malachi, were comfortable in this environment, what guards would they let down, what small comments would slip through?

Though the laws against sorcery had been lifted . . .

His face twisted, as if to smile, but he suppressed it.

Some noticed his arrival, but DeMassey paid no heed. He worked his way across the room, stepping between crowded tables, allowing the noise, the smoke and the smells to drift over him until he reached a booth at the back where Gilbert sat alone, waiting for him.

'I was getting worried,' Gilbert said by way of greeting. 'I did say sundown.'

'I had things to attend to.' Important things that could no longer wait: arrangements to make that would soon see him clear of this place, for he could not send Valena out without his protection and he could not trust anyone else to look after her, not even Gilbert. 'Is this really a suitable place for us to talk?'

'As suitable as any other. If Nash wants to spy on us, there's really no way we can stop him.' Gilbert raised his hands and smiled, showing crooked teeth. 'We don't have much time. He was looking for us earlier.'

'Then what did you want to talk about?'

Gilbert stared at him a moment, as though he'd expected more – but what more could DeMassey give? He'd already betrayed everything he believed in, including his own people.

'Aamin's thinking of making a trip to Marsay, now that Nash is back.' Gilbert sat back in his seat, fingering the jug of ale in front of him and surveying the room almost with affection. 'He sees Nash's sudden reappearance as a sign.'

'Of what?'

Gilbert's voice dropped meaningfully. '*We* have no idea how he managed to regenerate, Luc. He vowed he wouldn't . . .'

'Wouldn't use Malachi?' DeMassey let out a bitter laugh. 'He made that promise, but you know as well as I do, Nash can be trusted only as far as you can throw him. I have no doubts at all that he used our people to heal his wounds. I'd kill him for it if I could. But we can't *prove* it was our people – and he knows it. That's why he's been so bold as to come back and show us what he's done.'

'Luc, if you hate him so much, why do you . . .'

'Why do any of us work for him?' DeMassey needed to get out of there. 'We were all fooled into believing he could wrest the Key from the Salti and give it to us. That ancient promise, and we all fell for it.'

'Are you saying he can't get the Key?'

The bitterness filled DeMassey's throat then, almost choking him. 'I think he can. I think he *will*. It's what happens after that which bothers me. Nash has always been far too secretive about his real purposes – and I'm sure you've heard the whispers about a prophecy?'

'I have.' Gilbert leaned forward, lacing long fingers together on the table. 'But I think you despair too quickly. I also think you underestimate both the power and the will of our people. Once Nash has the Key, it will be a relatively easy thing to take it from him. We have the weight of numbers on our side.'

'True – but he has the weight of evil on his.'

Gilbert's mouth dropped open. 'Meaning?'

'Meaning, there is *nothing* he will not do to win.' Even as he said the words, DeMassey's stomach lurched at what he himself was trying to do. It had always been a contest between him and Nash, except that now, the stakes were much higher, the risks infinitely greater.

'Come on,' Gilbert rose sinuously to his feet. 'We have to go. You know what he's like if we're late.'

Nash finished off his wine and put the cup back on the table so that Taymar could hold up the jacket for him to put on. He slipped his arms into the rich fabric, allowing his fingers to smooth over it; it was such a reawakened pleasure to wear fine clothing again. He hadn't bothered for years, with a body that was twisted and scarred. Now that – on the surface at least – he was whole, the experience was entirely satisfying and one he intended to continue.

Taymar began clearing up his supper things and Nash moved over to the tower window. His rooms in the castle had been left untouched and had required only cleaning and airing before he could move back in. It was almost as if the last eight years had never been – except that, inside, he could feel the seconds slipping away from him; there was still so much to do.

He was whole, but he was not regenerated fully. Powers he would once barely have thought about he now struggled to use, or they failed him completely. Seeking in particular, a skill he had excelled at, often left him numb and blind, unable to see beyond the room he was in.

Frustration boiled inside him. Kenrick had come back to him, once more eager to be of service, anxious to achieve all they had planned together, but there were other things Nash still needed to achieve, and one of those was his immediate and total regeneration.

His eyes strayed over the view below him. From this window, he could see the city and its lights as it sloped down the hill towards the waters of the Vitala River. To his left beyond the castle gates, the enormous white dome of the Basilica sitting beside the famous beauty of the Guildehall.

Osbert.

Evasive, truculent, terrified and yet still evasive. Nash had not seen so much as a whisker of the man in the four weeks he'd been back at court. Perhaps he was trying to pretend Nash didn't exist – or maybe he was afraid of being asked to do something.

Nash smiled, admiring his smooth reflection in the glass before him.

'Master?' Taymar stood at the door. 'They're here.'

'Good.' Nash turned in time to see DeMassey and Gilbert come into the room. They had both entered into a bargain with Nash without ever looking deeper into what was expected of them. Gilbert appeared to fulfil his responsibilities without hesitation. DeMassey, who followed every order to the letter, managed, however, to maintain an air of silent rebellion. Well, perhaps it was time to push a little and see what would happen now that Nash was close enough to watch him personally.

'Any further word on young Andrew's whereabouts?' he began without preamble.

It was Gilbert who answered; his men who had ostensibly followed Andrew from the city. 'I had scouts all along the route he usually takes from Marsay to Maitland. I don't know where he is now, but I can tell you for certain he never made it home.'

'Surely he wasn't the victim of highway vagabonds?' Nash asked this without inflection, surreptitiously watching for some reaction from DeMassey. There was none. Whatever his schemes, it was fairly certain Andrew Eachern was not a part of them.

'His guards returned to Maitland unscathed and, as far as we can tell, without any alarm being raised. I can only assume that Andrew never intended to return straight home. Beyond that, I can't tell you. I send people into Maitland and they last perhaps three days before they end up leaving again.'

'Yes, I know,' Nash said absently. DeMassey was paying attention, but saying nothing, which was unlike him. Nash continued, 'So it wouldn't be a stretch of the imagination to suggest that the boy has gone to visit his mother?'

DeMassey did look up at that, frowning slightly. 'I thought you weren't going to touch him because of her. I thought you didn't dare risk . . .'

'That was before.' Nash moved to the table and poured himself a fresh cup of wine. He enjoyed it so much more now that he was healed. He enjoyed *everything* so much more. 'DeMassey, I want you to put twenty of your best people together. Go down to Maitland, surround the place from a safe distance and wait for the boy to return home. When he does, I want you to take him *alive*. I don't mind who you kill in the process, but you make sure it looks like he's perished in some tragic accident. If either the Ally or Kenrick are suspicious at all, I shall hold you personally and wholly responsible. Do I make myself perfectly clear?'

DeMassey's expression was utterly unreadable, but he nodded, almost too quickly. 'What do you plan to do with him?'

'Andrew? Why?'

'Can you use him to regenerate fully?'

There was something in DeMassey's eyes that Nash couldn't fathom, and it bothered him. 'I doubt it – as far as any of us have been able to tell, he has not a whit of power in him. Unfortunate really, as he would have been perfect otherwise. No, I have entirely another purpose in mind.'

DeMassey blinked once, slowly. He was obviously calculating, but Nash could glean nothing more from the man. 'Very well. I'll leave in the morning.'

'Tonight,' he pressed.

Final acquiescence was long in coming, then DeMassey turned and walked out, Gilbert following closely behind.

Smiling, Nash turned back to his window and let his eyes drift once more to the Guildehall.

Osbert picked up another piece of paper from the pile beside him, scanned its contents and placed it on the fire with the others. He didn't pause long enough to watch it crisp and burn, but continued working, eradicating, cleaning and removing anything and everything that Nash might somehow be able to use.

He'd done little else over the last few weeks. He'd barely left the building. Though tired from too many nights without sleep, too many days without fresh air or exercise, he couldn't stop until he was done, shoring up whatever holes were left for Nash to sink his claws into.

Osbert had always been so sure, so confident that he was smarter, quicker, better prepared than anyone else around him – perhaps not a brilliant philosophical thinker, but certainly well versed in the realities of life and political understanding. He'd built a career in the Guilde, working his way from a lowly recruit to the very top of the tree by making the right friends, having the right contacts, paying enough spies to tell him what he needed to know and being able to provide the right service at exactly the moment it was needed. He was everything a Guildesman could and should be.

And that's what he'd done when allying himself to Nash so many years ago. The young man had displayed certain talents, abilities, had developed a unique relationship with King Selar, had proved infinitely useful in so many ways – how in Serin's name was Osbert to know the viper he was so unwittingly aiding?

Nash was going to kill him. It did nothing to aid his appetite, nothing to ease his sleep, nothing to stop the pacing his body demanded when even hours of careful and useless planning failed to calm him. He was lost – but he would not allow the Guilde to fall with him.

He might have days, perhaps hours left, but he would not waste them, no matter the looks his staff gave him, nor the rumours which were flying – he'd started half of them himself, at Kenrick's urging, following orders like a good Proctor . . .

The door opened behind him and he froze, his fingers involuntarily clenching on the paper he held. Nobody was to be admitted to his presence after dark.

Nobody.

'Good evening, my lord Proctor.'

Bile rose in Osbert's throat and he swallowed hard. He came to his feet and turned to find Nash standing before him, the door still open, his face whole and complete and entirely without conscience. 'Nash.'

The man took another few steps into the room, looking about him at the furnishings, the changes that had occurred in his absence. 'I take it Vaughn's old study brought back too many bad memories. Still, this is a good choice. A better view, by far – and more room to move around in. Of course, it doesn't have that little secret chamber hidden in the wall – or does it?'

His voice flat and devoid even of fear, Osbert could honestly reply, 'No. Nothing like that.'

'A pity. Still, it would have been a little too obvious, wouldn't it?'

Osbert didn't answer the question. He simply stood there, waiting for whatever came next.

Nash stopped before him, an absent glance taking in the papers and files, the layers of black ash that fell about the stone fireplace, the bits that had made it onto the brick hearth. 'You don't seem surprised to see me.'

'Why should I be? You are, after all, a Guildesman, are you not?'

A faint laugh greeted that comment. Then Nash clasped his hands together before him. 'I wanted to talk to you about the rumours I've heard.'

'Which rumours? There are a number.'

'So I've noticed. Some are, however, intriguing. Those concerning a prophecy in particular.'

Again Osbert refrained from replying. He had nothing of worth to contribute that would not result in his immediate death.

Nash continued, 'Would you happen to know where they started from?'

'I have no idea,' Osbert lied fluently. He had spent hours practising when he should have been sleeping.

'It's just interesting, really,' Nash went on, as though only mildly involved. 'Do you recall those books I asked you to look for? The ones Vaughn had in his secret library in that hidden chamber? The books you assured me had been destroyed by your illustrious predecessor? Well, I believe we would have found information about such a prophecy inside them.'

Osbert caught a drift of courage, from somewhere. 'I thought you said those books were merely history texts.'

Nash smiled as though he'd been found out for taking an extra slice of bread at supper. 'Well, of course they are. History from the earliest days of the Guilde, running up until the eradication of the Cabal and the battle between the old Empire and the last sorcerers. So, yes, history texts without doubt.'

Though this was only what Osbert had suspected all along, it was another thing entirely for Nash to be so open in his admission. 'But as you say, Vaughn destroyed them.'

'No, as *you* say,' Nash looked up, his face expressionless. 'However, I am beginning to suspect that somebody here, within the Guilde, may have found a way of rescuing one or more of those books before Vaughn could burn them. I believe that's where these rumours have begun. As a dutiful Guildesman, I feel I should warn you that such texts would be dangerous in the wrong hands. I suggest you—'

Osbert almost closed his eyes, knowing in his bones what was coming next.

'—question your men, set up an enquiry. I don't know about you, but I would be very interested in getting my hands on such books – and of course, placing them into safekeeping. We wouldn't want somebody like, say, the King, to find them, would we?'

'No, of course not. I agree completely. We have many trades and professional skills documented within the Guilde libraries. It is our sacred duty to keep such knowledge from those who would abuse it. Thank you for bringing this to my attention. I will start such an enquiry immediately.'

If Nash was surprised by Osbert's acquiescence, he didn't show it. Instead, he nodded, performed what could only be a mock bow and left, leaving the door open behind him.

As the seconds drifted by, Osbert's body began to react, trembling until he could not hold himself still any longer. Turning swiftly, he strode to the window, tweaked the curtain enough to see the empty square below and the imposing castle gates.

Nash was walking through them, alone and unchallenged by the guards, walking without looking back. Osbert watched until Nash disappeared from sight, then went to his door, calling for a servant to bring Godfrey to him at once.

He had one ally left and it was time to put him to good use.

And with that one ally, came one single plan. No matter how desperate, he no longer had any choice.

Though the summons was abrupt and odd, Godfrey was nevertheless somewhat relieved to have an excuse to leave Brome's sickroom after an entire day standing around watching the man ail further. Prayers were being said constantly, and four masses this day alone had been performed in the hope that a miracle would give them all a little more time. Godfrey himself could do nothing more than wait, and waiting alone was killing him.

He was escorted from the Bishop's palace by four armed guards who stuck close to him, as though expecting an attack at any moment. This did nothing to still Godfrey's sudden fears. He was brought into the Guildhall, then hustled up staircases, along passages and into areas that no non-Guildesman had ever seen. He had no time to stop and admire the fine workmanship that emerged in every arched doorway, every cornice and panel. Instead, he was marched through an ante-chamber and into a long, wide study where Osbert waited for him, pacing impatiently, awaiting Godfrey's arrival.

'Leave us,' Osbert waved at the guards. 'Stand outside and let nobody else in.'

The guards bowed, silent in their obedience and then, with the solid click of the door behind, they were alone.

'I'm sorry about this, Godfrey,' Osbert began, almost hovering in the middle of the room, as though he wasn't sure whether to offer Godfrey some wine to go with his apology, or a seat. 'How is Brome?'

'Dying, but hanging on. What is it? What's happened?'

'You once said that . . . that I should trust . . . trust in a man I don't know.'

Godfrey's eyes opened wide in surprise, though he didn't say the name out loud. He'd never thought this would happen. He waited for Osbert to continue.

'I assumed, rightly or wrongly, that you meant to hint that you had some means by which you could contact this . . . man. Was I wrong?'

'I . . .' This could be a trap and the risk wasn't his to take. 'What would you have me do if I could?'

Osbert's eyes darted to him and then away. 'I apologise. I don't want to compromise whatever you've . . . *If* it were possible to send him a message, I would wish that you would . . . ask him to come here, to meet with me. I have something I . . . need to . . . discuss with him. Yes. I need to discuss something with him. If it were possible to get a message to him, urgently, that would be very beneficial to . . . to all of us.'

Though he had worked for ten and more years towards this very end, Godfrey had some trouble taking this sudden turn at face value. Nevertheless, Osbert's agitation was genuine and deep. Godfrey had never seen him like this before and could only assume it had something to do with Nash – no other person had ever had this effect on Osbert.

Which didn't mean it wasn't a trap.

'If he did come here,' Godfrey had no choice but to ask, 'would he be free to leave afterwards?'

'What?' Osbert looked up, disbelief plain on his pale face. 'You think *I* would have the power to keep a man like that . . . Oh.'

As Osbert considered the deeper implications of his request, Godfrey moved closer. 'If I could be sure this summons was not to deliver him into hands that would destroy him . . .'

Godfrey left the rest unsaid, not flinching when Osbert met his gaze steadily and without artifice.

'I can only give you my word, my friend,' Osbert whispered. 'We are . . . on the same side, you and I. The rest you will have to take on faith.'

Godfrey smiled at that. It was all he needed to know they were finally speaking the same language. 'Very well. I will do my best to explore the possibilities.'

24

'How do you feel?'

Andrew looked up at the man saddling horses. 'I feel fine.'

'No aches and pains?'

'Not really.'

'Good.'

For most of his life, Andrew had heard stories about this man. Within the Enclave, Robert was nothing less than a legend, loved by some, feared by a few, even hated now and then. At Maitland, he was viewed with constant suspicion, and yet, no open hostility. At court, this man was a rebel, an outlaw with a very high price on his head – and yet there appeared no intent to capture him. His deeds, no matter how innocent, were retold in the light of treason, as though to ensure his reputation would be destroyed no matter what. And Andrew had heard stories of the rebel on the road when he travelled, in taverns and inns where, after a few ales late in the evening, some man would recount his part in the Battle of Shan Moss, or some such other skirmish Robert had fought in, and out would come the story of the hero, of the brilliant general or the commander who knew the names of most of the men serving under him. And there would be tales told of his laugh, his sense of humour, the calm confidence and easy charm with which he dealt with others, no matter their station, without ever leaving out the darker side of the man, his powers, his skills as a swordsman: he was the kind of man one would be most unwise to make into an enemy.

Robert Douglas was a man of too many faces – and yet none of those Andrew had heard of matched this one. Not even Finnlay had told him anything he could use here, no hint as to what might be in store or how he should speak to a living legend.

Perhaps he shouldn't try – maybe he should just wait for Robert to tell him. Suppressing a sigh, he got to his feet and put away the last pieces of cold rabbit he'd been picking at for breakfast. Since they were moving on, he began throwing handfuls of snow onto the fire, watching it melt and sizzle until only a dull wisp of dying smoke rose into the morning sky. Then he turned back to the man by the horses, watching as he carefully set and tested each girth strap, tied each saddlebag so it would not shake loose, felt for the lee in each bridle.

'My mother will be worried about me,' Andrew ventured after a moment. He didn't want to upset anything, but he was concerned.

'She knows you're with me.' This was followed by a short laugh. 'Of course, that might only make her worry more.'

'You said you'd kill me,' Andrew blurted – then wished he hadn't. His mouth was not listening to his mind's caution.

'Would you have taken me seriously otherwise?'

'Did she know? My mother? That you were going to take me?'

'No.'

'Then won't she be looking for me?'

'I don't know. I hope not.'

The smooth, connected answers and the unconcerned tone in Robert's voice set Andrew's teeth on edge. Robert didn't

347

seem to give a damn who he hurt. 'She'd try. I know she would.'

'Perhaps. But I think Finnlay would stop her. Why? Do you want to be rescued?'

'What would be the point? Micah would only turn me over to you again, wouldn't he?'

Robert stopped at that, his hands still, his head turning until Andrew was caught in that deep green gaze, as though it ran straight through him. It only lasted a moment. Free again, Andrew opened his mouth to apologise, but . . . 'He hates you, you know.'

Robert finished with the horses, then picked up his cloak, swinging it over his shoulders. 'Come, mount up. I want to show you something.'

His face burning with shame again, Andrew tried to keep his voice level, make it look like he was trying to do anything but provoke this man. So he moved to his horse, picked up the reins and said, 'Does it have anything to do with why I'm here?'

'It has *everything* to do with why you're here.'

Robert didn't look back as he led the way onto the path. He kept his Senses alert, looking out for danger, or any other disturbance. These hills were largely uninhabited, but that didn't mean they wouldn't come across somebody, and Robert had no desire for *anyone* to see them now, especially together.

It felt strange being around the boy and, by the gods, it was hard to look into those blue eyes and not see Jenn. But after so many years of planning, the anticipation rippled through him, setting everything on edge.

He took a path up to the plateau. There was wind as usual, but only enough to ripple the heather. He came to a halt at the top of a gentle rise, where a rocky tor was almost buried beneath lichen orange and old, and where the sweep of the plain rolled away before them. Directly west was the huge shadow of Nanmoor, the mountain he had come to know as Omaysis.

Now he would have to be very careful.

He jumped down from his horse, watched the view for a moment, then said, 'This is a dangerous place.' He didn't turn, said nothing else, but listened as Andrew fiddled with his reins a moment, then slid down to the ground. Slowly he walked forward until Robert could just see him from the corner of his eye.

'Why is it dangerous?'

'The land is not what it seems. It looks solid enough from here, but as you work your way east, there are sharp gullies invisible until you're on top of them, and bogs you can't see until you're knee-deep in them. There's mud here in spring, enough to bury a horse, and the weather can change so fast, you'll think you skipped a season or two in a single hour.'

Robert looked once at Andrew, to find him staring warily out at the view. 'Do you know where we are?'

'No.'

'This is Seluth Common,' Robert looked down at the boy. 'The battlefield where Lusara lost her freedom, where Selar crowned himself King and where my father died.'

Andrew's eyes widened in genuine surprise. He turned back to the view, frowning, trying to imagine it, trying to see and hear things that had happened almost thirty years ago now.

Robert continued briskly, 'Ten thousand men were killed on this battlefield alone. Another five thousand were wounded. This heather grows on the bounty of those men's blood. You have read about it?'

'Yes, but only the books Father John was allowed to give me,' Andrew replied, apparently forgetting his previous quiet. 'Mother said her father gave her another book, a secret history written by one of the surviving Lusaran lords, and it had lots in it about the Troubles and how Selar invaded, but it was lost at Elita when you . . .'

'When I used the Word of Destruction and destroyed your mother's home?'

Andrew's cheeks turned a faint pink and he nodded, his gaze dropping to his feet. Robert let him find his own way then. He had to be patient.

'How old were you?'

The question both surprised Robert, and pleased him. 'When I used the Word?'

'No, I mean . . . when your father died.'

'Fifteen.'

Andrew's eyes shot up, searching, curious and yet, not intruding – an odd combination at the best of times, now especially puzzling. Surely Finnlay would have told the boy all this?

'What are you afraid of?' Robert asked, leaving his horse and sitting on a cold rock.

'Nothing,' Andrew replied quickly. 'Why?'

Robert allowed himself a small smile. 'Are you afraid of me?'

'No.' Andrew's gaze darted to him and away.

'Not even when I said I would kill you?'

Again Andrew's face reddened, but he didn't hang his head, and Robert learned in that action a great deal about this boy he would make into a King.

'He bled to death,' Robert whispered, hoping Andrew would hear him over the wind. 'My father. Just over there, where that patch of heather looks cut away. I never saw who dealt the fatal blow, but he'd taken wounds throughout the day. His men, Sir Owen Blanchard and Sir Alexander Deverin, did their best to shield him as he went down, but both received their share of cuts in the process. I was fighting close by and saw my father fall. I couldn't get to him quickly enough. By the time I did, he was dead.'

Robert looked up to find Andrew watching him. 'How do you do it?'

'Do what?'

'Did you hate him?'

'No! I loved him. He was a great man.'

'Then how do you do it? Talk about him like that? Without . . . feeling?'

'By putting thirty years between myself and his slaughter, that's how. Have you . . .' He paused, not sure he wanted the answer to this question just yet, but Andrew seemed receptive.

'What?'

'Have you ever killed a man?'

'No.' Andrew blinked at him a moment, then looked around as though he needed something else to focus on. 'Are you going to tell me why I'm here?'

'That depends. Do you know what you are?'

'What? What am I?'

'The next King of Lusara.'

'I . . .' Andrew froze, eyes wide, mouth open. Abruptly, he sat down on the heather with a thud, his eyes still glued to Robert's face.

Robert got up and pulled a flask of sweet wine from his saddlebag, pouring out a cup for each of them before returning to his rock.

'Is that . . . I mean . . .' Andrew paused, looked at his cup, then back up at Robert. Taking a brave breath, he said, 'Did I do something wrong? Is this a . . . I don't know . . . a punishment for something? Because, I really don't know what you're . . .'

'You know your ancestry, don't you? Four or five generations back? The House of Ross was founded by the younger brother to the King. Thanks to wars and plague and various other troubles over the decades, you are the last living male member of the Ross family. If it weren't for the fact that your father was so close to Selar, I doubt you would have survived infancy.'

'But that doesn't mean,' Andrew laughed a little, almost forcing it, 'that I'm going to be King or anything. I mean, I don't know anything about how to be a King and even if I did, what about Kenrick? He's already got the throne and he's going to be married soon, if he can get Tirone's permission, and then I'm sure he'll get an heir. Having royal blood that goes so far back . . . and well, making something out of that will only cause trouble and I don't want . . .'

'To cause trouble?' Robert interrupted with a sigh. 'Son, you're going to do that sooner or later, whether you want to or not.'

'Why?' Andrew scrambled to his feet, offended. 'I've never hurt anybody! I don't *want* to. Why would I want to be King? I know Kenrick's not the best King in the world but—'

'He's the *worst* kind of King.'

'He's my cousin!'

Robert took in the flushed face, bright eyes and stubborn stance of the boy almost more than the words he uttered. How much further dare he push this?

And how deep was his loyalty to Kenrick?

There was only one way to find out. Keeping his expression flat, Robert raised his hand, exerted just enough power to immobilise the boy, but leaving him speech. Then he moved closer, reading that surface betrayal so easily, but using it now, rather than ignoring it.

'Move,' he said softly, pacing a close circle around him. 'Go ahead, move.'

'I can't. You've done that . . . that thing to me again.' Andrew clenched his teeth and tried to keep his eyes on Robert as he circled.

'It's not that strong. If you try really hard, you can break free. Go ahead, I want to see just how determined you are.'

Andrew closed his eyes, effort flushing his face. Then he grunted, frustrated and irritated, watching Robert walk slowly around him. 'I can't move! You know I can't! This is not fair when you've got powers and I haven't!'

'This isn't a competition.' Robert kept pacing, keeping his voice low, watching carefully for a crack, just one. 'I promise you, if you keep trying, you will get free.'

'But how can I when you've done this to me?'

'So you're just going to give up then, are you?'

'You won't leave me here for the rest of my life, so what's the point in trying?'

'So, you would rather wait for me to set you free than free yourself and be proud of the achievement?'

'You said this wasn't a competition.'

'It isn't. How can it be when you won't fight me?'

'I told you I don't want to fight anyone!'

'In that case, you should do what I tell you and get yourself free.'

Andrew let out a cry of frustration then, straining his entire body to free himself of a power Robert kept just high enough to restrain him. 'This is a test, isn't it? There's some sort of trick to this and I just have to work it out? Is that it?'

'No, no trick involved. It just requires effort.'

'No it doesn't! I try and try and I can't get free! You're lying!'

'Of course. But what is the lie and what's the truth?'

'How should I know? Why, everything you've said so far could be a lie!'

'True. But equally, everything I've said might be the truth. How are you to know unless you test it yourself.'

'Oh, so now this is a test for you? Is that it?'

'Move!' Robert snapped, raising his voice deliberately, shocking the boy into silence. 'Arguing with me won't set you free. Being clever won't set you free. Being feeble won't set you free, and nor will giving in.'

'But . . .' Andrew panted with the effort, his face red and straining, 'it still doesn't work! I still can't move!'

'No,' Robert swooped down, whispering harshly in the boy's ear, 'you can't. Because I won't let you. And how does that make you feel, eh? You're right, I was lying. I can keep you suspended here for as long as I want to and nothing, absolutely nothing you can do or say can change that. You won't get free until I say so, so you're my prisoner, and you are utterly, utterly powerless. So, tell me, Andrew, *how do you feel*?'

Andrew fell silent, his struggles ceasing instantly. With dark eyes, he watched Robert step back, paid no attention to Robert's gesture of release and, instead, remained exactly where he was.

The wind rose a little, blustering over the tor and whipping streaky white clouds across the sky, leaving darker, heavier clouds behind, promising more bad weather for the night. The horses, startled by a flock of birds squawking overhead, took a few steps away, then resumed their casual nuzzling for odd strands of grass amongst the heather.

'What do you want from me?' Andrew said finally.

'The same thing you want from me.' Robert replied. 'I want you to set me free.'

'But how?'

Robert caught the boy's gaze with his own, holding it steady. Making sure. 'Kill Kenrick and take his crown.'

The wind flew flat against his face, tossing his hair around this way and that, sweeping the breath from his mouth and the moisture from his eyes, making them sting and burn and close against the day's sun and every single word he had just heard.

Andrew turned, crouched low, huddled, wrapped his arms around his legs and sheltered his whole body behind a brace of heather until all he could hear was the dry rustle and the eerie echo of some past he couldn't imagine.

Why hadn't he understood that it was the accident of his birth that kept Micah by his side, watching over him, ensuring his continued safety? Why Finnlay and so many others struggled to teach him things, to give him powers, to make him *more*. Why his mother had insisted he live his life at Maitland, when he would have rather been with her.

And now they would turn him into one of them. They would put him in a cage, feed him raw meat and know that when they finally let him out, he would roar like the wild beast they would have him become.

He didn't want to kill. And he certainly didn't want to kill his own cousin.

He felt the wind comb through his hair, cooling the heat that boiled inside him. He opened his eyes and looked out across the dense, empty Common.

Robert stood some distance away with the horses, waiting by the edge of a sharp slope down, some drop Andrew couldn't see from here. Another path he would have to follow blindly. But at least this time, he understood why.

He unfolded himself and stood up, straightened his clothes, pulling his cloak around him and over one arm to avoid getting tangled in the wind and the heather. Then he began to walk, taking one long stride after another until the wind began to propel him and he started to run. He went faster until it was almost too late to stop, but then he did, startling the horses and making no impression on Robert at all.

'What if I say no?'

'I wasn't asking.'

'Then I have no choice?'

'No prisoner has a choice.'

'So you will make me do it, no matter what I say?'

'I will not need to make you.'

'Then I won't do it.'

'Yes. You will.' Robert tossed him his reins, took hold of his own and swung up into his saddle. Before Andrew could say another word, he was riding away, down the path they'd originally come up two days ago.

It took so little for Robert to become the thing he most hated. It took so much to endure it, to set his features against giving anything away, to harden his heart against saving that innocence when so much else in this country had to suffer.

The darkness crawled in around him, cooling more than his body, less than his raging thoughts.

In the act of salvation . . .

This would save Lusara from Kenrick, from Nash, from the bubbling evil they would pour over the entire world. But what would his country be left with? A boy who now trusted nobody? A young King who valued himself now only by dint of his breeding?

It would be this boy, this vengeful, hurt, angry, confused, bitter, innocent boy who would ultimately prove whether Robert would fight the Prophecy, or succumb to it.

He'd known it would require patience, skill and diligence to shape the boy's mind and attitude, to break apart what others had spent fourteen years building with pride. He just hadn't counted on it being so hard.

Andrew didn't pay attention to the night. He didn't look up at the stars, or listen for foxes and owls and mice scurrying beneath the scrub. He just rode behind Robert, his gaze attentive enough to steer his horse down the path, but not enough to take in details.

'Kenrick's got powers,' he said into the silence of hooves on crumbling rock. 'How can I kill him?'

'That's entirely up to you.'

'He'll kill me first.'

'Then you must be quicker and better.'

'Well, why can't you do it?'

'I have no wish to be King. That throne belongs to you.'

'It belongs to Kenrick. His father won it by right of conquest. That's as legal as any other means.'

'Only as long as he's alive. Once he's dead, *you* have it by right of conquest.'

'But I don't want to kill him.'

'I know.'

Andrew kicked his horse enough to pull up alongside Robert. He had to see that face in whatever light there was, needed to see what expression was there, in the eyes which seemed to say so much more than anything else. 'You . . . you know?'

'Of course. If you *did* want to kill him, I wouldn't let you close enough to try.'

'Why not?'

'Well, largely because you might not want to stop at one if it meant that much to you.'

'Oh,' Andrew replied, not sure whether that made him feel better or not. 'So, I get to do this because I don't want to?'

'No, you get to do it because of what you are.'

'But the more I protest, the more sure you are that I'm the right person for the job?'

'I'm afraid so.'

'I suppose it's too late to change my mind? To . . . jump up and down with glee at the prospect?'

Robert's mouth pulled hard in an attempt to stifle laughter, but it emerged anyway, warming the night. It did make him feel better. Not very much, mind, but a little at least.

'So, where are we going to now? Another battlefield?'

'Of a different nature. You need to begin paying attention to where you are. Look around for landmarks you can make out—'

'In the dark?'

'Especially in the dark. You don't know when you might need to find your way here.'

'Here?'

'Almost here.'

'Can I ask you a question?'

'Certainly.'

'Where's almost here?'

A smile was flashed towards him, pale in the night. 'Here, is my home.'

They dismounted then, turning into another gully that rose steeply, with walls so high on either side Andrew lost sight of the sky. But he did as he was told, looking around him, picking out useful shapes in the shadows, of rocks and bent trees, certain turns in the nonexistent path, until he almost crashed into Robert's back.

'Watch.'

Robert laid a hand on a wall of rock that stood before him, almost seamless with the mountain. Then, with a grating complaint, the rock slid sideways, revealing a tunnel beyond and air drier and colder than that outside.

'Give me your hand.'

Andrew's palm was pressed against the rock, hard, like he would leave an imprint. Then it was let go.

'If you ever need to hide somewhere, if you need shelter, or rescue or some resource I have here, come. I am not always here, but come and take what you need. Place your hand on the rock and it will open for you. Once inside, do the same and the rock will seal up the cave. Go ahead.'

Andrew led the way inside, his horse trailing behind. Robert followed, then stayed back to allow Andrew the honour of closing the sorcerer's door. With a face trying hard not to grin, he pressed his palm to the cold rock. Almost instantly, it began to shudder and slide. With a loud grating crunch, it shut off the outside world and Andrew turned in the total blackness, his face hurting from smiling so hard.

'I've never done any sorcery before! That was amazing.'

'I'm glad you enjoyed it.' A torch flared into life and Robert took it down from its sconce in the wall.

'Why are you doing this?' Andrew asked.

'Why not?'

'No,' Andrew reached out and grabbed Robert's arm, holding him still. 'Really. Why are you doing this?'

That gaze, reflecting flickering yellow inside the deep green, gave out glints of too many things too quickly. Then abruptly, they all vanished, leaving behind the now-familiar easy confidence.

'Because I have to.'

25

Andrew wasn't sure what he'd been expecting, but finding Robert lived in a cave buried beneath the mountains of Nanmoor was not it. And the main cave was so comfortable and full of colour. He stared, taking in the bookshelves, the rug, the corner kitchen and earthenware jars of dried foods, the ingenious ventilation system.

'You live here?'

Robert deposited their bags on the table and turned to set wood for a fire. 'Here as much as anywhere else.'

'But I thought . . .'

'What?'

'Well, I think everyone thinks you live in Flan'har.'

'Everyone? The Enclave everyone or the Kenrick everyone?'

Andrew felt his face redden for the hundredth time in two days. It was getting annoying. Still, he swallowed and did his best to meet the gaze levelled at him. 'Both.'

Robert said nothing for a moment, then, with a casual wave of his hand, the fire leaped into life. 'I think that's enough for one day. You can sleep over there. There are blankets in that chest. Get some rest.'

Andrew hesitated. If he said nothing else, surely Robert would assume his silence to mean he agreed. 'But what about—'

Robert's voice was gentle. 'We'll talk tomorrow. Go on.'

With no choice, Andrew turned for the other wall, opened

the chest and pulled out the blankets to make up a bed. He kicked off his boots, laid down and huddled into the thick, warm-smelling wool.

Within minutes, he was asleep.

It was a grey, misty morning when Robert took Andrew outside. The top of the gully was invisible, as was the distant forest. They could have been walking through a cloud.

He'd been planning this for years. He must have listed in his mind a hundred times the things he needed to teach the boy. In the wake of Tirone's threat, he knew exactly what he needed to achieve.

Andrew was not what he'd been expecting. More to the point, he was not what Robert had been hoping for, nor what Lusara needed. He was soft, unguarded, easily provoked. Certainly bright, yes, and very likable, but perhaps most disappointingly, he appeared wholly ignorant of the effect his cousin had had on the country. It was impossible to believe that he didn't care.

Was that the boy himself, or was that his mother's influence? Would she have deliberately blinded herself to his potential in order to protect him? If so, then Robert would have to work counter to all that she had taught her son, and he would have to do it quickly. Some time in the next three months, he would have to turn this boy into a King.

A King who was prepared to kill.

'Come,' he said to the boy following behind him in silence. 'Let's go and set up some rabbit traps.'

'You said we'd talk today.'

'Then talk.'

Andrew was silent a moment, then ventured, 'Why do you want me to kill Kenrick?'

'You can't take his throne if you don't.'

'But I don't want his throne, and if I don't want it, I won't have to kill him.'

'But you will.'

'Why do you keep saying that! Why can't you just . . .'

Robert stopped chopping wood, rested the axe on the log he was splitting and deliberately let his eyes settle on Andrew, knowing such close attention would only provoke him. 'Why can't I just – what? Leave you alone? Do it myself? Come, Andrew. If you have questions, ask them. Don't stand there waving your arms about expecting me to read your mind. Ask and I'll answer. Be ready to learn, and I'll teach. Be prepared to listen, and I'll tell. Show any mark that proves to me your maturity and I'll treat you like an adult.' Andrew stood before him, his mouth open, his face suffused with red. Robert picked up his axe again and swung, ready to chop. 'But I notice you have yet to ask me why I would want Kenrick dead.'

The boy flinched as the axe split the wood, but a moment later he darted forward and picked up the two pieces, placing them on the stack. Robert continued to study him subtly. There was a deep frown of concentration on Andrew's face and he seemed oblivious to the cold and the splinters in his hands. He picked up two more shards, standing another in place for Robert to split. As Robert swung once more, Andrew said, 'Why can't you do it?'

Robert aborted the swing, then stuck the point of the axe into the log. With a dry glance at Andrew, he turned for the flask of water and drank deeply. He wiped his sleeve across his brow and turned back. Andrew required not only information, but to learn how to arrive at such conclusions himself.

'Why should I?'

'If you want him dead, then you should kill him.'

Robert almost smiled at that. 'Since he's your cousin, I assume that means you would stop me?'

Wide eyes stared at him a moment, then dropped, though not sullenly. This boy didn't appear to have a mean bone in him, but this innocence would have to go.

'Do you honestly think that if I had any choice in the matter, I wouldn't do it myself? Eh?' Robert dropped the flask to the forest floor, looked up at where he thought the sun might be, then picked up the axe once more. They had to move to the more important questions, the more difficult plans. 'Andrew, you have a mind. You've been well educated. You tell me. Why must I have you kill Kenrick?'

He split two more logs, but Andrew didn't move. When Robert finally stopped, Andrew met his gaze, hesitant and sombre, a little of that innocence vanished into the grey morning. 'You have to fight Nash.'

Robert clamped down hard on that first leap for hope. He kept his voice hard, 'And?'

'And . . . Nash is in deep with the Malachi. They've been working with him for years. There are always some at court. I can . . . feel them. If you tried to fight Nash with them around, they'd . . . they'd fight you as well and you'd be . . .'

'Finish it,' Robert prompted.

Andrew shook his head, taking a step back, distress flooding across his face. 'It would be just like Shan Moss, when you were injured and then had to fight Nash. And if Mother . . .' He stopped then, and looked up at Robert with horror, as though he'd just said something he shouldn't.

The boy needed reassurance. He needed to know that his mother would not be involved, that there would be a good and happy outcome, that he would not be required to bloody his own hands. From somewhere deep inside, the urge to give him that reassurance rose in Robert, sweeping through him like a gale.

But to do so would condemn Lusara to an eternity of evil.

Robert took a step forward, deliberately intimidating. 'I need you to kill Kenrick. I need you to survive the fight with him and take the throne afterwards. I can see you're not ready to do that, but when the moment comes, you will be, believe me. This incessant whining doesn't become any King, much less one *I* would put onto the throne.'

And then he saw it: a flare of anger in the boy's eyes. He rejoiced silently.

'Whining?' Andrew began, his voice rising. 'You kidnap me, steal me away without warning to my mother or your own brother – and then you tell me I have to kill a member of my own family, just to take a throne I don't want! And why?

Because you don't have time? Because you don't want the throne yourself?'

'No,' Robert snapped back, 'because Kenrick lives in Nash's pocket. I need to separate them and the chances are I will not survive the fight with Nash, and if my efforts are to free Lusara from her chains then you, my boy, must be the one to do it!'

Andrew stood blinking at him, a thousand thoughts flying across his face. 'Tie a bundle of those sticks together and bring them inside. I'll leave the door open for you.'

With that, Robert pulled his sack of logs over his shoulder, grabbed the axe and headed back to the gully, leaving Andrew behind, stunned and silent.

Shame filled him. It followed him, shadowing him, sneaking up on him whenever he thought he might finally be rid of it. He didn't dare look at Robert for fear he might see it leaking out of his eyes. But still the shame wouldn't leave him. He asked no more questions. Instead, he helped with what work was required, answering with a nod or a shake when he was asked something.

So Robert showed him more of the caves created by a once-mighty river and he couldn't help comparing this place to the Enclave. Apart from Robert's living cave, there were perhaps two others that would be fit for people to live in, a couple of others that would serve as stables, but apart from that, the remainder were passages leading from one place to another, all in darkness.

This wasn't a home, it was a refuge. And the more he thought about it, the more he remembered exactly where they were – right in the centre of Lusara, where Robert could reach almost any place in the shortest possible time.

Andrew couldn't help watching him. He studied how Robert moved, how he spoke, how he raised his eyebrows in a manner faintly self-mocking. He smiled easily and often, and yet there were shadows around his eyes, moments when he gazed inwards, haunted.

I want you to free me.

'You're very quiet,' Robert observed as they made their way back to the main cave. 'I thought you wanted to talk.'

'I changed my mind,' Andrew replied, then bit his lip as he heard how sulky that sounded.

'So you don't want to know? But I thought you had an insatiable curiosity.'

Through the shame, Andrew felt the prodding. He stared at the back of the man walking in front of him, lit by a light in front. 'All right. I do want to know. You're the rebel. You're the one who can raise an army to defend Lusara against Selar or Mayenne or the Sadlan. How is it you've not finished off Nash by now? Why have you waited so long?'

Robert came to a sudden stop and Andrew nearly crashed into him. When Robert turned around to face him, there was nothing nice in his gaze at all. 'There are moments when you are astonishingly like your mother, did you know that? She too is fond of asking questions for which she already has the answer.'

'But—'

'And if I'd fought Nash before now, and assuming I survived, assuming I could maintain some degree of support – do you think it would have been particularly wise of me to put a young child on the throne?'

'Why use me at all? You could have taken the crown yourself—'

A hand shot out to his throat and he was shoved back against the wall so hard he lost his breath. Robert's face came close, his eyes black in the shadows. Andrew gasped and the pressure abated a little, but not enough to free him.

'Never again will you say that to me. I was not born to wear that crown. You were, whether you can see it or not. Whether you want to believe it or no, you will be King, and you will be a good King, the kind of King I could never be. So you will never mention this, either to me, or to anyone else, again. Do I make myself clear?'

His heart racing, Andrew could only nod. The moment he did, Robert released him, a flash of distaste in his eyes. He moved as if to speak again, and to his surprise, Andrew could

363

almost read an apology written on that enigmatic face. Then it was gone and Robert had turned once more, heading off down the corridor, taking his light with him. 'Come, it's suppertime and I'm hungry.'

Andrew ran after him, stumbling a little on the uneven cave floor. He arrived back at the main cave in time to help serve up the rabbit stew they'd made earlier and Andrew did his best not to flinch every time Robert came near him.

He was being silly, of course. Robert wouldn't hurt him. He knew that with complete certainty. It was just that . . .

How did he know that?

He ate in silence, concentrating on his food, keeping his eyes on his plate. He didn't know where to look any more. Didn't know what to think or feel. All he did know was that he *didn't* want to kill Kenrick. He didn't want to kill *anyone*!

'Tell me something,' Robert began easily, as though there hadn't been that moment of violence in the other cave. 'How is it that you have managed to survive in Kenrick's court, when so many others around you have lost their heads? Literally.'

Andrew swallowed hard and nearly choked. 'They . . . committed treason. I wouldn't—'

'No matter what? Do you think Kenrick protects you? Because you're his cousin?' Robert picked the last meat off a bone. 'You could be right. I hadn't thought he could have such feelings for anyone.'

'You don't know him,' Andrew offered, looking up, wondering if there was any chance he might grasp here. 'Kenrick is not like Nash.'

'Oh?' Robert turned to look at him, his eyebrows raised. He moved from the kitchen area and settled on the floor by the fire, where two large cushions added a modicum of comfort. He picked up a book, left it open beside him, then pointed at the empty chair. 'Not everything needs to be a confrontation between us, you know. There is no requirement that you and I be enemies. Please, sit down.'

'Please?' Andrew asked, surprised.

Robert shrugged, smiling slightly. 'You forget; when you've done as I've asked, you will be *my* King as well.'

King? This man's King? Would he still be a rebel then? Would he bow and obey orders and pledge allegiance? And if Andrew told him to do something, would he do it?

It was too silly even to play with such an idea. Robert would never take orders from anybody. Oh, he'd say Andrew was King, but in reality, he would never bow to anyone . . .

And yet he was there, waiting patiently for Andrew to sit down, and there was no proud expression on his face, no arrogance in anything he said or did. In fact, Robert had always displayed the most alarming honesty, an honesty far greater than Andrew had ever experienced from an adult before.

He got the feeling he could ask Robert *anything* and get an answer.

His mind reeled at the thought and, still a little stunned, he came over to the fire and carefully sat down.

The moment he was settled, Robert poured himself some wine and began talking again, but this time, the subject had Andrew's attention snagged totally.

'You know of the Prophecy and some of the trouble it has caused so far. Well, the truth is, there's a great deal of ambiguity involved. Even so, there appears to be a deep and lasting connection between the Angel of Darkness and the Ally.'

Angel . . . that was Nash – and his mother was the Ally. 'What kind of connection?'

Robert wasn't looking at him. 'Nash told me he loved your mother and that they were destined to be together.'

You lie. The words sat there on the tip of Andrew's tongue, like poison, needing to be spat out – but how could he? There was so much his mother had never told him, things she said he wouldn't understand. Was this one of them?

He looked down to find those green eyes on him again, watching openly now. Robert continued, 'I could never trust the Key and I told Jenn, when she became Jaibir, that I wouldn't be able to trust her because she was joined to it. And after that, she . . . joined Nash and me on the battlefield.' Robert paused and Andrew held his breath, waiting. 'She stopped me from using the Word to destroy Nash.'

Andrew's throat grew tight and he swallowed the lump forming there, desperate to take a full breath because his chest wouldn't fill properly and it was starting to hurt. 'Are you saying that she . . . deliberately . . . took Nash's side? Are you telling me my mother is . . .'

'I don't know what I'm telling you. I haven't spoken to her since, so I can't say what she is thinking.'

'She said she was trying to save your life.'

Robert's eyes took on a haunted aspect as he gazed into the fire. 'My life didn't matter; destroying Nash did.'

'You . . . you're trying to poison me against her, aren't you? Because you know she won't support what you want me to do. She's never said anything about me becoming King or anything!' Andrew pushed himself out of his chair, blinking to rid his eyes of bitter tears that might spill onto his cheeks; he couldn't stand that kind of shame and be angry at this man at the same time. 'She's never said *anything* against you! She just said that you're . . . you're not always what people think you are, but she never suggested, not once that you might be a . . . a traitor to your own people! But you, you want me to kill my own cousin and now you want me to believe that my own mother would sell Salti and all of Lusara to the man she most despises in the whole world? How can you say that? I thought you and she were at least on the same side!' Robert was on his feet now, but Andrew backed away, holding his hands up in warning. 'No, I'm not going to listen to any more of this! I want you to take me back now because I'm *never* going to help you, do you understand? Never!'

And then he turned and ran out, because if he didn't he was going to cry and he hadn't done that even when his father had died and his mother had left him at Maitland.

Robert stoked up the fire, laid out the blankets for Andrew's bed, put away the last of the dishes and heated up some water to have a wash. He whistled as he completed each task, careful to keep all outward signs cool, containing the true depth of his concern hidden.

Now was not the time to falter. He had so little time.

Andrew was soft, gentle, kind, sensitive to any small change in Robert's mood and it felt so strange having him around, reminding him painfully, as each minute went by, just what it had felt like with Jenn in those few, brief, heady hours when he'd allowed himself to believe that they were in love. That belief had sustained him through so much: knowing she knew him, knowing how she understood him, had meant more to him than he'd ever been able to say. Cutting himself off from her had left some part of him bereft, as though a limb was frozen in paralysis.

And this damned boy came in, looking at him with Jenn's eyes, asking questions Jenn would ask and laughing at what she would laugh at, challenging everything he said in exactly the same way. It hurt.

While he waited for the water to boil, he pulled out his saddlebags, packed what things he would need for the next trip and left them by the door. On impulse, he pulled out the orb, still wrapped in its coarse sack. He put that in his bags, unwilling to leave it, even here, where it was completely safe. Then he made himself a cup of brew and went out into the connecting passage, sat on the ground with his back to a wall, raised his voice enough to carry to wherever Andrew might be, and said, 'If I'd thought your mother was a traitor to her own people, I would have killed her long ago.'

There was no response. Andrew was still here, somewhere; he could feel it without trying to Seek him.

Or was the boy able to sense the lie in that last statement?

'She never told you, did she? About Nash? About how they became friends? Did she ever tell you about how Nash would come to visit her at Clonnet? About how she would look forward to his visits? You must remember seeing him there a few times? Tall man, about Finnlay's height. Black hair, black eyes, a short beard. Neither handsome nor ugly. The kind of man you wouldn't notice unless he spoke to you. Of course, your mother had no idea who he was. She just thought he was a Guildesman who liked to talk to her. It never occurred to her that he might have another motive.' Robert was about to continue, to tell the boy how his mother had allowed Nash to kiss her at Shan Moss, but he could never replace his own confusion with cruelty to this boy.

'Despite all this, I'm not trying to destroy your mother. I'm just trying to make you see that none of this makes a lot of sense. Not to me, not to her. So don't go looking to understand it all. She did what she had to do, for reasons I don't understand – just as she couldn't understand that I was willing to end my own life if it meant Nash would go with me at the same time.'

There was still no response, but when he paused, he caught a faint scrape of leather against stone, just a hint of movement, though he could see nothing in the dark tunnels that led away from him.

'Andrew, you need to understand that I can't do this again. I don't have an infinite number of times that I can face Nash and expect to live to fight him again. But even if I could, this country won't survive another ten or twenty years like this – especially if Nash expands his influence, as he seems to be doing. I don't want to make your life impossible, but I will if that's what it will take to make you understand. I can't afford to fail again.'

'And you can't afford to trust me, can you? Like you couldn't afford to trust my mother?'

Robert didn't turn as the question was asked. Instead, he let Andrew emerge from the shadows on his own. 'No, I can't.'

'So you're going to make me kill Kenrick. One way or the other.'

Slowly Robert got to his feet, faced the boy and placed a hand on his shoulder. Andrew looked up at him with eyes older than a few days ago, wary, still a little angry and yet, prepared to learn. 'I'm not going to lie to you and say it's your destiny, Andrew, because you're right; it's just a trick of fate that gave you the ancestors you have and if it *were* my freedom I was talking about, chances are you and I would never have met again. But, for reasons I cannot fathom, my fate is tied in with that of Lusara. Every day that I am imprisoned thus, so is she and I will never be allowed to rest until the last chain has gone. I could raise another army. I could start another war.

And at every turn I made, Nash would be waiting, prepared to destroy everything in my path to hinder and stop me. Those are sacrifices I'm no longer willing to make.'

'So you sacrifice me instead?'

'*You* will survive, and so will Lusara.'

'But I have to kill Kenrick to make sure.'

'I can't handle both him and Nash at the same time. You're the only person I know who can get close enough to kill him without an army at your back.'

'So I must betray him? Because you tell me to?' Andrew asked. 'I need a better reason than that.'

'You should already have all the reason you need. If you'd had your eyes open these last years, you would see what I see. Kenrick is not fit to be King.'

Andrew lifted his chin. 'I live half of every year at court. I see more of him than you do—'

'My point exactly.'

'And you're expecting me to just take your word for it?'

'You would trust him before me?'

'I don't know you. I do know him.'

Robert folded his arms. 'Have I ever done anything to harm you?'

Andrew raised his eyebrows. 'Has he?'

'Have I ever hurt those around you?'

Andrew blinked owlishly, considering this. 'With the obvious exception of my abduction, no. Has Kenrick?'

Robert paused a moment, needing to choose his words with great care. 'My brother tells me you are fond of his daughter, Helen, and friendly with a boy called Liam?'

Andrew froze. Then he took a step forward, his eyes abruptly dark, and Robert knew then that he could do it, he could make this boy into a King. There were things in this world that had deep and powerful meaning for Andrew. All Robert had to do now was to use those to mould that agile but stubborn mind.

'Helen? What's happened to her?'

With a gentle hand, Robert took him back to the fire, sat him down and told the story, carefully. Andrew listened in silence. When he finished, Andrew sighed.

'I can't . . . he isn't . . . he never . . . Poor Liam. Is Helen all right?'

'I'm sure she is. She had already recovered a little when I left her with Finnlay.'

'He never said . . .' Andrew got to his feet, his eyes down, his movements distracted. 'I'm . . . going to bed.'

'We have an early start in the morning.'

'We do?'

'I have a number of places where messages can be left for me by various people. I have to go and check on one of them. It's not too far from here. After that, I'll take you back to your mother.'

'My mother?' Andrew stopped and looked up at him. 'But—'

'I will give you two days to make what arrangements you need. After that . . .'

Andrew closed his eyes, pressing his fists against his temples as though a great pain throbbed there. He said nothing more, merely turning to his bed, throwing off his outer clothing and burying himself in his blankets.

Robert had no trouble reading that message. He'd often had the desire to shut the world out and never go back.

And this was definitely one of those times.

The early start felt like the middle of the night to Andrew's sore eyes and weary body. Too little sleep and too much to think about. He needed to see what was lying beneath the surface now, or somewhere along this crooked line, he was going to start screaming.

He hardly knew himself any more, but he was getting to know the man who rode beside him, hood pulled down against the driving, icy rain so that his face was almost invisible and that stark gaze was safely hidden. Thankfully the rain gave him an excuse not to talk, and Robert an excuse not to reply. They could both hide within the silence.

The sun never made a showing. The constant downpour dragged their progress through sodden ground and mud the horses struggled to endure. This was spring at its worst, the time of the year the poets forgot about, before the blossom and lilies bloomed, before leaves appeared on the trees all new and bright and pristine. This was the ugly part of the season, where the hard work was done, where the earth was prepared for planting, rivers and lakes filled and those who were foolish enough to be out in it paid for the privilege.

At least it gave him something else to think about. Something that wasn't Kenrick, or even Helen and Liam. Just brushing against that subject made him want to be ill and he had to swallow hard to dissuade his body from reacting.

They didn't stop for a meal, so by the time the thin church tower appeared through the gloom, Andrew's stomach was growling loud enough to unsettle his horse. Robert paid no attention, but led him down the slope, through a tiny rotting gate and up to the lee wall of the church, where they were sheltered a little from the weather.

Robert swung down from his horse, his feet landing with a splash. He barely looked up at Andrew, but his voice came clear. 'Wait here. I won't be long. There's some shelter not far where we can light a fire and dry off a little.' Then he was gone inside and Andrew sat there, looking out over the grey landscape filled with grey fields and the grey trees in the fuzzy distance. Of course, spring was welcomed because it brought colour back into the countryside. After months and months of winter blankness, even Guilde yellow would be a welcome . . .

'Robert!' Andrew kicked his horse around to the door of the church and leaned down, bellowing at the top of his voice, 'Robert! We have to go! Now!'

A second later, Robert burst through the door, a leather pouch in his hand, already pulling the hood over his head. He grabbed his reins from Andrew's hands and leaped into the saddle, his gaze following the line Andrew was pointing.

'Damn it! Come on, this way.' He pulled hard on the reins, turning around the other side of the church, then kicked off at a gallop, heading for the nearest trees. Andrew stayed close, but looked again and again at the half-dozen Guilde soldiers who advanced on them from their ambush positions.

But after a minute he had no more time to look back and

instead had to concentrate on watching where he was going as his horse stumbled and skittered down a rocky hillside littered with half-stripped pine trees and rotting stumps. At the bottom was a river which Robert rode straight into, coaching his horse to work with the flow, rather than against it. Andrew held on, too scared to look back now, too afraid to look forward. He had to trust. Robert hadn't stayed alive and free all these years by being a fool.

Shivering, the horses brought them up the other side in one piece and immediately Robert got them moving again. The forest was thicker on this side, but the moment the horses began to regain confidence, Robert urged them back into a canter. Trees flew past as the rain flew down until, without warning, Robert brought them to a halt beside a long-deserted lake. Breathing heavily in time with his horse, Robert held up a hand for silence, half-closed his eyes and turned his head slightly.

He was Seeking, looking for the faint aura of humans in those following them. Andrew glanced back the way they'd come, searching for any flash of yellow in the unending grey expanse.

'They've lost us,' Robert announced after a moment. 'Did they see your face?'

Andrew frowned. 'No. At least, I don't think so. They weren't very close when I first saw them and I had my hood down.'

'Good. Now, let's see what all the fuss was about.' With that, he pulled out the leather pouch, tore the glove off his right hand and held his cloak up for shelter with his left. Andrew could just see an edge of paper, but no more.

'Who is it from?' When Robert looked at him, Andrew said, 'If you want me to be King, you can't keep secrets from me.'

The corner's of Robert's eyes crinkled then, the briefest of smiles. 'It's from Archdeacon Godfrey.'

'Godfrey? He writes to you?' Andrew was happily amazed, and not really very surprised. Godfrey was a good man. It was nice to know he was actively working on the right side.

The right side. *His* side?

'What does it say?'

Robert finished reading, then folded the paper up absently.

It wasn't too hard to read the gestures. 'So you think it was a trick? The message? Who else knew to send you letters there?'

Robert's frown deepened. He gathered his reins and began moving again along the bank of the lake. 'Godfrey's been Sealed, so he couldn't tell anybody about the church. But the message was about Osbert wanting to meet with me urgently. I can only suspect that Osbert had men follow Godfrey's courier.'

'So it was a ploy to ambush you?'

'Oh, I doubt it.'

'Why?'

Robert pushed his hood back and looked up at the sky, reading the clouds. 'Osbert is no fool. He wouldn't bother sending only six men to capture me.'

'Then why send them at all?'

'Why do you think?'

Andrew hated questions like this. 'To make you notice? To . . . make sure you go to see him? So you know it really is important?'

Robert grinned widely at him. 'Ah, so you're not so dumb after all, are you?'

'Who said I was dumb?'

His answer was a chuckle.

And then he knew it, knew what it was that had been bugging him all this time, that thing, that unexpected question or that niggling answer that had been hiding in the corner of his eye.

'It was you, wasn't it?'

'Me?' Robert raised his eyebrows, not understanding. 'Me what?'

'You who . . . You've been putting books in that alcove in my window, books for me to read. It was you all along, wasn't it? Writing those notes, answering my questions . . . just like you've been doing these last few days . . .'

Robert let his horse wander to the edge of the lake, allowing it to drink. 'It will take the rest of the day to circle around and head south again to meet your mother. I'll try mindspeaking her tonight and tell her to meet us at Maitland.'

'No.'

'No?'

'No.' Andrew drew himself up. 'I'm going with you. To Marsay.'

Robert's gaze narrowed. 'To what end?'

'I . . .' Andrew struggled, but nothing came to him. 'I don't know. I just think I should . . . go with you.'

'Because I gave you books to read? Because I answered your questions? Made you think?'

Unable to help himself, Andrew's cheeks burned again, but he didn't look down this time. He just nodded. 'That's as good a reason as any.'

'It's a bit thin, as reasons go.' This came out just as serious, but Andrew got the impression Robert was laughing, just a little. 'And we won't be going in as though we belong there, you know? If you travel with me, you become what I am: a rebel.'

'That's what you want to turn me into, isn't it?'

'I suppose so.' The faintly whimsical air vanished then as Robert lifted his chin. 'Can you obey orders? To the letter? Can you trust me to know what I'm doing? To keep you safe? Are you prepared to put your life in my hands?'

This answer came without any thought. This was the question Andrew had been waiting for all this time. 'Yes, I can.'

Robert considered it a moment longer, then said. 'Very well. Let's go find a change of horses. We've three days' hard ride ahead of us.'

26

As the first bell rang, Andrew squeezed himself back into the too-small crevice and held his breath. He could see almost nothing, but he could hear and smell a side of Marsay he'd never really experienced before.

And judging from the stench, he wasn't sure he wanted to.

'As soon as the market is closed up, we'll move. See that alley over there? A few strides down it you'll find some steps leading down to a door. If we get separated, meet me there.'

'If we get separated?' Andrew twisted his head as much as he could, but from his awkward position, he could barely see Robert. Dozens of people shuffled past their hideaway, going about their business at the end of the day, ignorant of their presence. 'Why would we—'

'You think I can foretell the future as well?'

Andrew shut his mouth, not sure whether he could hear laughter in that soft whisper.

'Just remember that if anything happens to me, you make your way to Godfrey as quietly as you can. He'll hide you or get you out of the city, whatever he feels is necessary.'

'Yes, yes, I remember everything you said.'

'Now you do, yes. But what about if I get caught? Are you going to recall every word while you're shivering with fear?'

Andrew chewed his lip, not wanting to make some dumb statement about being afraid, and yet not wanting to let Robert think he was a coward.

The decision was taken from his hands. 'Come now. Follow me and stay close!'

And he was away, scurrying across the cobbled alley, moving as Robert did, letting his body merge with the growing darkness.

He didn't need to wait for Robert to get captured. He was scared enough right now.

There was something a little unsettling about the Guilde guards who waited for him outside the Basilica. Godfrey could still hear the echo of the choir, smell the warmth of incense, and yet neither of those comforts gave him reason to refuse another abrupt summons from Osbert. Chill from more than the weather, he accepted the cloak laid about his shoulders and stepped out into the cold spring evening.

Soon the nights would be shorter. Soon the dark mornings would be brighter and sunshine would last more than the time between two thick clouds. And then there would be that change in the air, some indefinable essence that existed at no other time of the year. A warmth, perhaps, or even the subtle scent of blossom arriving on the breeze – whatever it was, it only ever lasted a week or so and then was gone, but it always heralded the very last days of the long, long winter.

His solemn-faced guard steered him around the people lingering in the square, almost stifling the noises of the busy city. And then he was once again at the doors to the Guildhall. For the second time in his life, he was taken to Osbert's study, almost in secrecy, the door closed solidly behind him.

Osbert wasn't pacing this time. Instead, he was standing before the fireplace, hands behind his back and an expression of bleak fatalism on his face. 'I'm sorry, Godfrey,' he began in a voice grey with apology. 'I know you don't deserve this. In fact, you deserve so much better for the friendship you've offered me over the years – but this matter has gone beyond my needs. I just want you to know now, before it's too late, that I'm genuinely sorry.'

The fine hairs on the back of Godfrey's neck rose all at once. He steadfastly kept his gaze on the man before him and didn't look over his shoulder the way he wanted to. He was not sure if he really wanted an answer.

'Sorry for what?'

'Are you sure about this?' Andrew whispered in the creaky darkness of the roof space he was huddled in. Of course, if he was huddled, Robert must be bent double, but the rebel held his finger to his lips and pointed downwards.

He'd always imagined the life of an outlaw to be rather pleasant, with no master but yourself, a degree of freedom he'd often envied and a certain measure of excitement bound up in unnamed and clandestine activities. The truth was so far removed as to be laughable.

Robert had hesitated at every turn, pausing long enough to Seek for danger, to listen, sniff the air, extending his Senses to ensure Andrew's safety. Of course, he probably shouldn't have insisted on coming along, but then again, Robert hadn't put up too many objections, so perhaps he'd done the right thing for a change.

Not that his legs agreed with him at the moment.

The dust in the air tickled his nose and he rubbed at it, holding his breath. For a second, the irritation went away, but then a huge sneeze came upon him suddenly and before he could stop it, a large gloved hand clapped over his face, stifling everything.

Andrew kept completely still, not daring to move a single muscle. When the hand finally dropped, he took a brief shallow breath, to find the sneeze had vanished before it could kill them and Robert was looking at him in query. Andrew took a deeper breath and then nodded, relaxing a little. Robert beckoned him to follow, then took off further into the shadows, squeezing between two stone walls before emerging into a more open area lit from a glow in the plaster floor below.

This roof space was almost oval-shaped. Huge oak beams stretched from one stone wall to the other, with more beams rising up to support the slate roof. Beneath him, curving downwards, were the plaster domed ceilings of some important church or hall. He took each step very carefully, walking only on narrow wooden workmen's platforms positioned here and there in the roof space.

He'd had no idea that buildings were structured like this, on the inside, where nobody could see. He burned to ask Robert a hundred questions.

A wide hand-waving tore his gaze from the domes below and he hurried after Robert once more, treading softly. Robert took him to a wall on the far side of the roof, leading him between another gap in the wall where a horribly narrow staircase squeezed into the depth of the wall itself, so small Robert could only walk sideways. This ended before a midget door through which Robert had to crawl, and all silently. When Andrew finally joined him, breathing hard, he found they were no longer in the roof cavity, but a level lower, crouched on a hidden balcony or clerestory, obviously used by workmen doing maintenance on what looked to be a very grand building.

But where were they?

He wasn't stupid enough to try looking over the balcony, but he didn't need to; simply looking up at the domes now above him was more than enough. The stone walls, the ceiling, every surface he could see, was painted. A midnight blue background, incredible gold stars and highlight, brighter red and light blue, yellow and green, pictures he could hardly focus on this closely, the shapes odd and out of proportion – of course, these paintings had been designed to be seen from the ground below, not here, but even so, this place was extraordinary! How had he lived so many years at court and yet never known that Kenrick was . . . What? As evil as Nash? Was it possible he'd been that mistaken about his own cousin?

A voice nearby strangled his wonder with a close reminder of the danger they were in. Robert put a hand to his shoulder, squeezed to indicate that he stay where he was, then moved further along the balcony and rose up enough to look over.

Andrew concentrated on the words he could hear, piecing together what he could.

That voice . . . that was Osbert – by the gods, they were in the famed Guildehall!

Any other day, Andrew would have whistled in amazement.

'. . . no, I can't risk it,' Osbert was saying. 'If we need to make up an excuse to explain his absence, then we will, but I won't do anything unless I have to. They know where to find him if something happens.'

'Yes, my lord,' another, younger voice replied, obedient, but not servile.

'I want you to stay with him and if I give the order, you are to obey without question. Do you understand me, Lyle?'

'Yes, my lord Proctor.' There was a faint layer of regret in that voice, almost perfectly matching that in Osbert's. Andrew couldn't begin to guess what they were talking about, though it didn't sound very promising.

'Are you sure of your timing?'

'Positive, my lord.'

'And what about—'

'I have questioned my men at length. There were two of them at the church, but more than that, they could not say.'

'Very well. Go. Now.'

'Good luck, my lord.'

There were footsteps then, quiet leather on worn stone, the clank of an ancient handle and the low creak of a heavy door opening and closing. Then silence. Of a kind.

Andrew listened as hard as he could, but it was almost impossible to hear anything over the pounding of his own heart and those noises he didn't want to hear, like the bells of the Basilica so close by, calling for a service he could not track. He had no idea how late it was, or how dark it was outside. There was enough glow from lamps below to illuminate the incredible ceiling above, and that encompassed his entire world.

Moving slowly, he turned his head, his eyes opening wide as he watched Robert unfold himself from his crouch. He put one, then both legs over the balcony railing, turned on his stomach, then silently disappeared over the side.

Osbert waited. Without patience, without self-respect, without too much hope and with too much desperation. But some desperate and stubborn train of thought kept insisting that this would never really happen, he would never need to put aside all his own better judgement and place what little trust he had left in the hands of a man who, by his very nature, *couldn't* be trusted.

Insane acts were often committed by those in perfect command of their faculties.

As the door closed behind Lyle, he closed his eyes and offered up more probably useless prayers, and willed yet more patience. If the man didn't come tonight, then perhaps he would come tomorrow night. But too many more nights and Osbert would run out of time.

He waited in silence.

And in the silence he heard it, turned in time to see a figure in black land on the floor at the opposite end of the Hall. The man then straightened up – and something deep and mournful inside Osbert sighed in relief.

Robert hadn't changed, hadn't aged so much as a day. His hair was just as windblown, perhaps a little longer, but the face, the eyes which drifted over Osbert casually, then roamed the rest of the Hall, the mouth, set but not grim, the jaw, determined but not threatening – no, nothing had changed at all.

Except the circumstances. Last time, they'd been on opposite sides of badly drawn battle lines. Today they were . . . allies?

Robert moved forward, his pace relaxed, as though he were here to take in the sights and nothing more. 'I can see why this place has such a reputation. The workmanship is exquisite.'

'You've not seen it before? I'm surprised.' The temptation to shift into casual conversation was enormous. An almost overwhelming curiosity blossomed in him then, a desire to know what this rebel was doing, what he was planning, and when, *when* it would happen.

And, by the gods, that it *would* happen!

'I don't know why you're surprised – or have you forgotten how much Vaughn hated me?' Robert half-smiled at him, as though it was of no concern. 'And I'm not one for walking all over something held sacred by others.'

'And yet you're here now.'

Robert turned slightly, to look up at the ceiling again. 'You changed your laws. I was . . . invited and you seemed ready to talk. Are you?'

'Yes.' His rebellious stomach twisted in anticipation, then settled. He'd had plenty of time to think this over; there would be no last-minute changing of his mind. 'When Nash first joined the Guilde, I noticed his abilities and his obvious talent in certain areas where I needed such expertise. So I sponsored him, ensured certain opportunities were put his way and generally supported his rise through the ranks until his obvious close relationship with Selar overwhelmed any need he had of me.'

Osbert looked up to find Robert's gaze on him, flat, steady and very, very interested.

'Of course, I had no idea at the time just what he was – none of us did. By the time I began to suspect, it was far too late for me to do anything about it – assuming I ever could. But what you need to know is . . .' Osbert paused just long enough to swallow, 'soon after his rise with Selar, Nash began to ask me about a supposed secret library he believed was housed somewhere here, within the Guildhall. I didn't like the sound of his questions, so I put him off as long as I could. When I could avoid the issue no longer, I . . . drugged Vaughn one night and he told me about a secret room adjacent to his study where traditionally the books had been housed. But Vaughn, believing you and Nash to be working together, had the books moved, leaving the room empty.'

Robert had moved much closer now, but his silence was complete, the patience in his eyes unnerving. Osbert hurried on, 'I dragged together some old tomes from our library, books nobody would miss, and set them alight, while Vaughn was still drugged. Then, at the first opportunity, I showed the room to Nash and convinced him that Vaughn had burned all the books he'd been looking for.'

'And he believed you?'

Osbert twisted his hands together, his heart pounding, just wanting to get this awful tale over and done with, so the solution could be put into motion. 'But almost a week ago, Nash came to me . . .'

'What?' For a moment, Osbert was trapped utterly within a sea-green gaze, snared like a rabbit and powerless to escape. The questions came softly, intense like burning coals. 'He came to you? He's back at court?'

'Yes,' Osbert whispered. 'He's back.'

A shiver ran over Robert, but he contained it. He couldn't afford to scare Osbert now. 'He's back.'

'I thought you knew.'

How could he have known?

But more importantly, had Andrew known and said nothing?

It hardly bore thinking about, but he would have to, later. 'Go on.'

Osbert continued, his hands still twisting, his fear still sweating itself out on his forehead as though this was high summer rather than bitter spring, 'Well, he'd heard some rumours about a prophecy—'

'Prophecy?' For the second time in as many minutes, Robert's heart stopped. 'What prophecy?'

Osbert flinched, like a deer startled in the hunt. He blinked twice, then continued stringing words together. 'There have been rumours floating around the city, some mention of a dark presence, and one who has come to save us from him.'

Robert wanted to laugh; instead, he shoved that to one side as well, and gestured again for Osbert to continue. So far this visit was proving to be more than profitable.

And that boy would have some very tough questions to answer before he saw his mother again.

'Nash insisted that such rumours could only be made by a man who had read the books I'd claimed were destroyed. He admitted what Vaughn had known, and I'd suspected – that those books contained information about sorcery. He then charged me with finding them and I know that if I don't, he will tear this place apart until he has them.'

Robert's gaze narrowed. 'And you want me to find them?'

'That's right.'

'How do you know I can?'

'I don't know that you can't. I do know that Vaughn would have hidden them somewhere within the Guildehall, because to him there was nothing more sacred and more safe.'

'So why did he move them from the secret room?'

'The books had been there for centuries. He was never certain he was the only one who knew about it. By moving the books with his own hands, he could die with the secret.'

'I assume Nash also looked for them?'

'Yes, but I have no idea how. While Vaughn was alive, Nash was busy with Selar and did very little, and since then, he's only been back at court a short time.'

Robert had to ask, for his own peace of mind, if nothing else. 'How short?'

'This last month.'

So. He'd been right not to trust the boy without question. Very well. At least he knew now where they stood.

'What is Nash planning?'

'How would I know? I told you, it's been a long time since I had his confidence. He'd never tell me anything that important.'

'But you've not heard rumours? Whispers? Anything that might warn me when he plans to move?'

'Nothing.'

He turned back to Osbert and raised his hand to indicate the Hall. 'So you want me to find these books, but you don't know where they are?'

Osbert swallowed hard. 'No, but when I had Vaughn drugged, he said that he'd hidden them, "where none shall seek and none shall find".'

What was that?

Robert frowned, stepping closer to Osbert, unable to still the flutter of excitement which rippled through him. 'Those were his exact words? "Where none shall seek and none shall find"?'

'Yes. I've gone over them a thousand times since that night. I'm sure. Why? Do you know where . . .'

Robert was already moving, striding towards the door so fast, his thoughts almost had to hurry to catch up. Quickly he waved a warning over the door, so he'd know if anyone approached, then he placed his hand against the flat painted stone of the nearest wall.

Oh, this would be too much, wouldn't it, if he could find the very books he'd been searching for for so long, here, in the Guildehall? After years of risking his and his men's lives, to find them here, in the one place he'd not dared to try looking . . .

He closed his eyes, pulled in a breath and held it. As his fingers felt the surface of the painted wall, he let his Senses flow out from his fingertips, not at all sure what he was looking for.

Seeking worked only with people, sorcerers. The only time he'd ever done this with an inanimate object was when he'd focused on the properties of the Key and found the silver rod he believed might be part of the Calyx. But that process would never work here.

'What are you doing?'

'Seeking.'

'What's that?'

'It's something sorcerers can do, to find . . . something.'

'Will that help you find the books?'

'I don't know – but that's what Vaughn meant, and I believe he got it out of one of the books in the collection.'

Osbert's confusion was obvious. 'But how can you know that if you've never seen . . .'

'Because it's a line out of a book called *Flail an Feer*, a book sorcerers have been reading for centuries. There's little chance Vaughn would have come across – or read – that book if it didn't belong to such a library. And it's exactly the kind of book Vaughn would be afraid of and want to hide.'

Robert held up his other hand for silence as his senses slipped beyond the walls and out into the rest of the Guildehall. Room after room he passed faint auras, and other things he would have liked to examine more closely; he pushed it hard, unwilling to concede that it couldn't work. But—

'No.' Robert came to an abrupt halt and opened his eyes. There was no sign at all, and yet, he couldn't fault Osbert's logic: Vaughn *would* have hidden the books here, and he wouldn't have destroyed them – he was clever enough to know how valuable they could be to him.

And, of course, that was how he'd learned to make that Bresail.

He sighed. 'Where none shall Seek and none shall find. What's the complete quote?' He half-closed his eyes and summoned up the words, '*Allaying hope and placing it where none shall Seek and none shall find, until again it comes, against all but those who would destroy, and those who would confuse, to feed where hunger will deny*. That's . . .' his words tailed off almost to a whisper, voicing the thoughts as they came to him, 'that's a section about the Calyx . . . written in . . . No. So, if none will Seek it, then none will find it, but if I Seek it . . .

Why would none Seek it? Because they wouldn't know what to look for—'

By the blood, he was such a fool – too busy making it more complicated than it needed to be.

Why *wouldn't* these books have some connection to the Key? They were about the same age, from the same origins.

Once more he moved to stillness and held his breath. As he had done when he'd found the silver rod, he framed all he knew of the Key in his mind, then let his Senses free, to roam where they might, giving them no direction.

For long, blissful seconds, he lost himself in the images that washed through him. Then, abruptly, a corner of his awareness was snagged sharply, turning him, focusing him on the central pillar of the Hall.

'Sweet Mineah,' he breathed, long and slow. Then his face, without asking, shifted and creased up into a smile he could not control.

He'd found them at last: the answers he needed. They would all be here, in the books Vaughn had tried to hide from him.

'Well?'

Osbert's voice cut into his thoughts, barely jilting his elation. 'It's here. I don't know how he did it, but it's here.'

Wide eyes darted from him to the pillar, the face snapping from relief to horror and back to relief so fast Robert couldn't keep up. 'Are you sure?'

'Positive.'

'I'll get some tools . . .'

'No need.' Robert replied quietly. 'Anything a Guilde stone-mason can put together, a sorcerer can take apart.'

'But you'll bring the roof down!'

'I'll be careful. Just move back a little.'

Osbert straightened and shifted out of the way.

Robert knelt down in front of the pillar base where each block was carved with a different animal shape, all of them in some kind of motion. He felt along the edges of one stone, to discover it was a facing, not a support stone. He pressed his hands against it, let the power shift from his belly, out through his palm and into the stone. He felt it slip and alter its weight. He moved back a little and the stone came away.

In front of him was a space in the pillar, a gaping hole that led somewhere deeper into the floor. He reached into the darkness until his hand came to something. Something dusty and bound in leather. With another grin he pulled it forth and held it up for Osbert to see. He blew once, sending a cloud into the air, then opened it up to the first page.

Osbert grabbed his shoulder. 'Bring the others out.'

'Of course.' Robert reached in again, and again, passing the books to Osbert to stack on the floor. And still the books came. He lost count after fifty. Then finally there were no more and Robert was surrounded by more freedom than he'd *ever* hoped for.

He reached out, his fingers itching to touch and discover, his eyes soaking in the sight of so much of the future clearly written in the past. These books would contain the Cabal lore that had been lost when the Enclave library had been destroyed in a fire. There would be records here, of the work Cabal and Guilde had done together, of how they had both served the Empire. The Guilde had always seen it as their sacred duty to gather knowledge and write it down, for safety's sake, to be a part of handing that knowledge on. This had always been the central core of all that the Guilde was.

And with them working so closely together with the Cabal, for so many centuries, there *had* to be mention of the Prophecy in there somewhere, its origins, its purpose, and perhaps even a copy of the text. Nash himself believed it to be so – and he knew far more than Robert did. He might finally have a weapon he could use. And the Enclave could regain so much lore that had been lost.

He picked up the first book to hand, reverently brushed the dust from its surface and opened to the first page. The language was obscure, the text open and curvaceous – but he was sure he'd seen it from somewhere. Certainly enough to let him get—

'Destroy it.'

'What?' Robert looked up to find Osbert standing before

him, beyond the line of books, holding his robes away as though he would be poisoned.

'I said, destroy it. Destroy them all.'

Robert frowned and scrambled to his feet. 'This is a joke, isn't it?'

'No joke. I'm sorry,' Osbert said apologetically, 'but I never intended for you to keep them.'

'You never intended . . .' Robert gestured down at the books and scrolls, some bound in tooled leather, some in plain. All shapes and sizes, along with a few unbound manuscripts: possibly the most valuable collection he'd ever seen in his entire life. He looked back up at Osbert. 'But don't you see, if you give them to me, then they can only help ensure Nash's defeat. Serin's teeth, Osbert! You had the sense all these years to know they were dangerous! Don't make me destroy them now, when they could be such a powerful weapon against Nash and his kind.'

Squaring his shoulders, Osbert turned and faced him. 'But I don't know that you and Nash *aren't* the same kind.'

'But . . .'

'No!' Osbert snapped. 'You seem to forget what you are – and *where* you are! Have you forgotten that it's the Guilde's sacred duty to eradicate sorcery from the face of the land? That's been our goal for more than five hundred years . . .'

'And those are Vaughn's words, not yours. Can't you see that suspicion, prejudice and bigotry are all that stands between you and me? We are the *same*, Osbert – we just have different skills! Damn it, man, don't destroy these books just because you don't understand!'

'I'm not going to destroy them. You are.'

Robert straightened up. This was utter insanity, and he had to stop the man at all costs. 'And if I say no?'

'Your friend Godfrey dies. If you try to save him, I'll burn the books while you're gone and raise the alarm that you are here.' Slowly Osbert raised his hand and pulled Godfrey's wooden trium from his robe pocket. He drew it up to hang before Robert, leaving it there long enough for him to recognise it.

His breath caught in his throat and he swallowed hard, fixing his gaze once more on Osbert. Even now, he could still smell fear on the man – a fear of so many things. His voice emerged soft and very sad. 'You have done such a brave thing, and now you will destroy what good you would do. And what will you tell Nash when next he asks?'

'That's my concern, not yours.'

'You'll lie to him? And make him believe? Then why not let me take the books and lie to him still. Or . . .' Robert scrambled for a compromise, something that would leave him with a little hope, 'or let me look through the books and choose those most useful, and then I'll . . . destroy the rest. Just don't . . .' He knew he was begging, but he didn't give a damn. What was dignity compared with stopping a catastrophe? If he didn't beg, if he didn't back away from this, the demon would let loose. 'Please, Osbert. You've trusted me enough to get me here, to let me see them. We never knew each other well before, but you must be able to see I'm not the same as Nash. I beg you, don't make me do this.'

Osbert stared at him, as though he couldn't believe that he actually had Robert in this position. But still he shook his head slowly, his face pale, his words short. 'Do it. Now.'

Could he? Could he somehow protect the books from Osbert, and still get through the Guildhall and find Godfrey before Osbert could call the alarm? But there were soldiers beyond the door, more than Robert could handle on his own, and at his first appearance, the alarm would be raised and Godfrey would be a dead man. If they did get away, they would have to escape the city, at night, after the gates had been locked, with all Kenrick's army looking for them.

And the future King of Lusara sat waiting above, relying on his protection, looking down and watching. Learning.

But he couldn't destroy these books.

He turned back to Osbert, but the man's gaze was stony and convinced, terrified and reaching for hope, just as Robert was.

And Osbert *was* right about one thing: if Robert did destroy these books, Nash would never be able to use them against Lusara or the Enclave.

Still his throat grew tight as he stepped clear of the books. His eyes stung as he raised his hands. He needed only to relax his control a little, but even that was enough to scare him so he almost strangled it. But the power filled him all the same, coursed through him as though delighted that he would be the one to shatter his own hopes. The demon loved moments like these.

He let the power loose, flying from his fingertips, landing on the floor in a bright flash of fire more intense than any seen before in this Hall. Then it was done. No smoke, no over-whelming stench: just a mountain of black ash stirring slightly in the air currents.

'You have no idea the damage you've just caused,' Robert murmured, his voice as black as the ashes. He waded into the pit, causing a wave to rise about his ankles. 'Set Godfrey free. I did as you asked.'

'No, you haven't. What's that there?' Osbert moved forward, but stopped short of the ashes.

Robert bent down and lifted one surviving book free of the black dust. 'That's odd. I don't know how that survived.' With almost loving hands, he placed it on the stone he'd removed from the pillar, and raised his hand again. Another, smaller flash split the air, but the book remained untouched. How could that happen? He picked it up and turned to Osbert, who was staring at him, eyes wide.

Then Osbert's gaze changed completely and regret edged into his tone. 'Very well, you may take that one. I don't care. Now, please go. Whichever way you choose, but just go. Nash could come any time and I don't want . . .'

'*You* don't want?' Robert would have laughed if he hadn't felt so numb. He tucked the book inside his jacket, doing up the buttons. The weight of it was small and puzzling – and of little comfort. He stepped clear of the ash, almost following Osbert to the door. 'I have your word about Godfrey? Your promise?'

Nodding, Osbert hurried to his freedom, only to find his feet frozen in place.

'Your promise, Osbert,' Robert gave in to the impulse to scare the man. 'Or you'll have my revenge.'

Osbert's response was fast and honest. 'My promise. I go to release him now.'

Robert freed him, staying long enough to watch Osbert reach the door, but there the Proctor stayed for reasons of his own. He reached into his pocket once more, drawing forth a piece of paper. He folded it over in his hands a moment, then looked up.

'Those rumours of prophecy? You didn't ask how I knew they were fake.'

'Fake?' Robert blinked, but went along with the odd question. 'How did you?'

'Because I started them myself.' Osbert looked at the paper again. 'Kenrick asked me to. After he had me translate this. I think he stole it from Nash. You might be able to read it better than me. Do with it what you will. I . . . Thank you for your help.'

Robert took the paper, but kept his gaze on Osbert as he turned and unlocked the door, closing it firmly behind him.

27

For a moment, Robert just stared at the paper in his hands. Thick parchment, solid ink. Words he couldn't read, a language he would have to research.

He turned swiftly, pushing the paper into his jacket next to the oddly surviving book and ran across the Hall to the wall opposite. Taking a leap off the ground, aided only slightly by his powers, he caught hold of the balcony edge and hauled himself up and over – to find a pair of huge blue eyes staring at him in wonder.

'I . . .'

'Shh,' Robert urged. 'We can still be heard. Come, let's get out of here before I decide to pull that pillar down after all.'

With Andrew behind him, he retraced their steps back into the wall, up the impossible stairs and out again into the roof space. There he had to stop to shift the book around beneath his jacket, because it wasn't sitting right and he didn't want it to slip out at the wrong moment. He picked up their cloaks and tucked them under his arm. Then he led the boy across the roof. Not once did he trust himself to look back and see if Andrew was still following.

He lost track of the route back to the street. His nose knew the path, even if his eyes weren't paying attention.

It was dark outside, and too cold, but it was enough to hide them from prying eyes. Nobody would ever believe that he would come back to Marsay – even in secret. Not even Nash.

He stepped into the street, pulled up his hood and dodged around a pair carrying a shrouded stretcher between them. He was on his way again when he realised there were no footsteps behind him.

Andrew stood by the wall, his cloak pulled around him, his eyes following the deceased as it was carried down the dark street, towards the city walls where it would be slid through Dead Man's Gate and into the river, aided by a few rocks sewn into the shroud. A beggar's burial.

'What's wrong?' Robert asked, in no mood to be gentle.

Andrew started, then replied, 'Nothing.'

'Good. Try to keep up.' Robert didn't wait for him to follow. He just took off, keeping his pace steady but purposeful, unhurried, but quick as he could. Dark or no, there were some places in this city he dared not go without heavy disguise, even after so many years.

But there were also some places he did dare, and he made for one of them, keeping to the shadows, and climbing to the hayloft above a stables that shut down at night. He pulled his cloak around him, stood at the tiny window and checked the street to make sure they hadn't been followed.

He chose his words without any care at all. 'So I was right to doubt your loyalty.'

'What?' Andrew's voice was hushed, confused and slightly breathless. Hay rustled beneath his feet as he approached from behind, but he stopped before he reached the window. 'How have I—'

'Nash has been a month back to court. You left here, what, three weeks ago? Are you going to tell me you didn't know?'

'I didn't!' Outrage split the air. 'How could I possibly know? I've never even seen him—'

'Are you sure?' Robert spun around and grabbed the boy's shoulder, exerting more than a little pressure, enough to make Andrew wince. 'He and Kenrick are close, very close. How can you have lived so many years at court and not seen Nash once in that time?'

Andrew's mouth opened to cry forth another denial, but no sound came out. There was enough streetlight bleeding through the window, enough strength in Robert's sight to see the deep blue eyes wide and afraid – and devastated.

For a second – a very brief second – Robert softened a little, convinced that Andrew had to be innocent.

But he'd been fooled before – and by this boy's mother, at that.

'And were you ever going to tell me,' he began again, his voice softer this time, but just as harsh, 'about the rumours of prophecy?'

Horrified eyes widened again, giving Robert a glimpse of something. Then they squeezed shut. Andrew dropped his head and Robert let him go. Stunned, surprised, and . . .

The boy *had* been telling the truth about Nash. Robert had seen it in his eyes. He *knew* this with a certainty he'd never felt before, and instead of scaring him, it—

'Tell me,' he said quietly. 'Tell me what you know of the rumours.'

Before Andrew could say a word, Robert turned, sat on a bale of hay, pressed back against a wall and pulled the rest of his cloak around him. He'd make supper soon. He needed answers first, however, before he could stomach eating.

'I'm . . . sorry,' Andrew whispered, his voice full of wretchedness. 'I didn't mean to . . . I just forgot about it with everything else . . . you and everything . . .'

In the face of such dejection Robert said, more kindly, 'Sit, boy, before you fall down. Just tell me.'

Andrew sat, more from the desire to obey an order than from need. 'I never saw or heard of Nash being anywhere near Marsay. Ever. Not ever in my whole life. And I would have said

392

something to Mother if I had, because if nothing else, even if I don't understand the Prophecy or anything, or where my mother fits into it, I *do* know that he wants to kill Finnlay and I couldn't be on his side for that reason alone.' Andrew still didn't dare to look up. Instead, his fingers played with each other. 'About two weeks before I left to go home, Kenrick appeared without the scars he'd had on his face.'

Robert sat forward. 'Two weeks? But that . . .'

Slowly, Andrew looked up. 'What?'

Robert studied the timidity in Andrew's hunched shape, in the timbre of his voice, in the tentative question. How much of it was an act, and how much could he afford to let the boy keep?

His tone level, he asked, 'Nothing. Did Kenrick say anything about what had happened to his scars?'

'Just that it was a miracle. He had a thanksgiving mass said in honour of the occasion. The . . . rumours started after that.'

'And?'

'I tried to find out as much as possible, without drawing attention to myself. People kept asking me questions because, well, Kenrick's my cousin. But he told me no more about his scars and all I could find out about the rumours were just what Osbert told you, that some great evil had come to Lusara and that a man had been born to fight it. But—' Andrew paused for a moment, then continued, 'I think perhaps Kenrick is trying to make it look like *he's* that man.'

'So,' Robert asked when Andrew met his gaze, 'Can I trust you or not?'

'You can! I promise you!' Andrew's reply was instant and passionate.

'I take it,' he replied with a smile, 'that means you *want* me to trust you?'

Andrew paused, frowned in thought a moment, then said, 'Yes – but that doesn't mean I've committed to anything.'

Robert just stared at the boy for a moment, this boy he would make into a King. This confused, ill-prepared, immature, sensitive yet still powerfully promising boy would soon sit on the throne of Lusara. For the first time, Robert could actually *see* it.

Lusara *would* be free.

As relief threatened to overwhelm him, he deliberately looked away, keeping his voice dry, his heady thoughts to himself. 'No, heaven forbid you should trust me in return. Stay here. I'm going to get us some supper.'

He was almost at the ladder and ready to climb down to the stable when Andrew called after him, 'What about the book?'

The book: the one that hadn't burned. It was impossible for it to have survived the fire, especially as the second blast had been smaller, but twice as powerful. Which meant that—

Robert spun around so fast, Andrew almost crashed into him. He strode back to the window and prayed as he never had before in his life.

For it to survive his power like that, the book had to be shielded.

He'd tried Seeking for things with properties similar to the Key. He'd let the Key fill his mind, opening up every memory, every experience he'd ever had with it, every word they'd exchanged, every dark, twisted game the orb had played . . . and he'd found the books.

In a library gathered together from the time when sorcerers were openly a part of the Guilde, where their knowledge and learning were welcomed, where they had felt comfortable and safe. A library that had, by Osbert's admission, contained many, many powerful works on sorcery.

A library that had remained virtually untouched and undiscovered for hundreds and hundreds of years.

A library in *Marsay*.

He could hardly draw breath. With trembling hands, he reached inside his jacket and gently withdrew the book, two inches thick, big enough for him to hold comfortably with one hand.

It certainly felt like a book. He opened it up, found words written there – in Saelic, which could be a positive sign, or might mean nothing at all. And yet.

With a gentle hand on Andrew's arm, he pushed the boy back enough to give him some space. Then he put the book on the hay-strewn floorboards. He smoothed down the thick, worn leather covering of the book in a childish gesture of good luck, then he straightened up.

Last time he'd tried something like this, he'd had an *ayarn*.

He concentrated, struggling to still his excitement, pulling his thoughts down to a single point, place and second, then reached out and touched the book—

And saw it flash gold, brilliant, jewelled, carved, bowl-shaped, intricate designs just like the silver rod made by . . .

And the swirl of inscription along one side, set into the metal.

And he heard something powerful, pounding in the background, like the Basilica bells, only louder, overwhelming, deafening, like the Key when it awoke, painful, shuddering—

Nothing.

Stunned, Robert breathed in, feeding lungs suddenly starved. The book looked unchanged and he glanced up quickly to see if Andrew had witnessed the same. One look at the boy's face told him this had been no dream.

This was real.

Reverently, he picked up the book, holding it like the treasure it was.

He brought it to his lips, like a saint's relic, breathing in the essence of more than a thousand years of secrets.

This was victory.

And he held it cradled in his hands.

This was the Calyx!

28

'There they are again.'

Jenn immediately put out her small light, shut the book she'd been reading and joined Finnlay at the tiny window which looked down at the lakeside and the old road leading into the village of Fenlock. 'What are they doing?'

'I have no idea. But look, it's not all the same people who were here last night, or the night before. The one carrying the torch looks familiar, but the others . . .' He paused, looking around the large room they had used for the last week. 'Where's Micah?'

Jenn kept her gaze on the dozen or so folk below as they walked in solemn procession towards Elita. 'He went to check on the horses, I think. Finn, do you suppose it's something to do with my father? That these people worked for him and now . . . I don't know, come back and pay their respects?'

'In the dark? Every night?'

'Well, there is a small Guilde presence in Fenlock now, since they took over the healing work from the monastery. Perhaps they're afraid of being seen coming out here. They certainly don't look like they mean any harm and nothing inside the keep has been damaged in any way – which I suppose in itself is a little strange.'

'You know there are stories about this place.'

'Of course, but that's my point. Surely those stories would keep people away, rather than draw them here.'

'Do you recognise any of them?'

'How can I? It's dark and they're too far away.' Jenn sighed. This was too strange. Of course, if they hadn't been hiding out here for the last week, they would never have noticed these odd nocturnal visits to the ruins of her home. People would walk up from the village, gather together before the rubble of the old gate and listen while one or the other spoke. An hour later, they would turn about and walk home in darkness. None of them ever came near the keep, let alone tried to enter. Such regular visits made hiding out here more than difficult when there was still so much snow on the ground and too little cover between here and the forest.

'Did you say Micah's gone to check on the horses?'

'Yes. Why?'

Finnlay pointed out of the tiny slit window. 'Then I suppose that man down there must be his twin.'

Jenn almost pushed him out of the way – but he was right. Micah had emerged from the darkness, joining the village folk and walking with them, talking to them as though he had every right, as though he wasn't a fugitive, as though . . .

Jenn?

She reached out for support against the cold stone wall.

Jenn? Can you hear me?

Robert?

Yes. Why? Were you expecting someone else?

She ignored the barb. *Where's Andrew?*

Safe, with me. I won't tell you where we are as you'll just get all upset.

As though it would be irrational of me to get upset over the way you abducted him?

This is not the time for that discussion.

How did I know you were going to say that? With you, Robert, there's never a right time to discuss anything you don't want to discuss. Very well, what do you want?

I just wanted to tell you that I'm bringing Andrew back to you.

That made her pause. *When?*

We're on our way to Maitland now. I guess you're still at Elita. We'll meet you at the clearing near Dormund Spay, on the other side of the rock pools, in three days.

Three days. And he was gone before she could ask him anything. Three days meant they had to get moving tonight.

But why was he bringing Andrew back at all?

'Jenn?'

She opened her eyes to find Finnlay watching her. She gave him something of a smile. 'Robert says he'll meet us at Maitland in three days. He's bringing Andrew back.'

The war which played itself out over his face was breathtaking: from surprise to disappointment, to concern, to consternation, to nothing, all in the space of a few seconds. Jenn turned to begin packing.

'Did he say . . .'

'No, Finn, he didn't say anything else to me. Why would he? I'm the enemy, aren't I? I'm the one he can't trust, who's joined to the Key and who may or may not ultimately side with the Angel of Darkness. Why in Serin's name do you suppose he might tell *me* what his plans are?' She picked up a saddlebag and rolled up her blankets to place them inside.

'You don't know that's how he feels,' Finnlay didn't disagree with her, but his voice sounded more sad than angry.

'I do know that's exactly how he feels. That's how he's supposed to feel. That's how any man would feel in his position.' That was how she'd wanted him to feel, so he'd be free. Amazing how much success she'd had, really, no matter how much it still hurt.

Jenn shoved blankets and her few other possessions into the bag, then stopped herself before she could do real damage. She sat back on her heels as Finnlay moved around the room packing his own things. He was so transparent, especially after all these years. 'You know, if he tells you his plans, he won't let you tell me?'

Finnlay looked at her, surprised.

'And if he does,' Jenn continued, still watching him, 'I can't allow you to keep your seat on the Council.'

His gaze hardened then and he opened his mouth, but stopped himself, angrily collecting things with more fervour than they deserved. 'You know, you have this amazing ability to make things so much harder than they need to be. We're not adversaries, and yet, you keep pushing me, treating me like I'm your enemy.'

'No, Finn, I don't.' Jenn did up the last buckle of her saddlebag and got to her feet. She stared down at him for a moment, until he looked up and met her gaze. Then, with a sigh, she added, 'You and Micah . . . you've always been Robert's men. Neither of you will ever trust me the way you trust him. And where do you think that leaves me?'

She didn't wait for a reply. She simply gathered up her cloak and opened the door. She almost walked straight into Micah, who looked surprised, and full of news.

'Are we leaving?'

'Yes.' Jenn squeezed past him and headed out to the horses.

Micah took one last look around the room to make sure they'd left behind no sign of their visit, then picked up his bags and hurried out after Finnlay. He hadn't missed the undercurrent of tension between him and Jenn, something which seemed to happen with increasing regularity. It had to be because of Robert.

Wasn't everything?

'Finn!' He ran across the empty hall, his boots making huge noises as he caught up. 'Wait. I need to tell you something.'

Finnlay barely looked at him as he pushed the heavy wooden door open and squeezed through, holding it for Micah to follow. The night air was sharp and bitter, promising rain or sleet later. There was no sign of Jenn; by now she would be in the wood, saddling the horses.

Micah matched his stride to Finnlay's, picking his way between the snow-covered rubble towards the open field and the shelter of the forest. Even though Jenn couldn't hear them from this distance, he still kept his voice low. 'I spoke to those villagers.'

'Oh?' Finnlay didn't seem very interested. 'What did they say?'

'In words, not too much.' But it hadn't just been the words, or the prayers, or anything else tangible. It had been in the way they walked, held themselves, in the looks they shared and how they'd viewed him as either an enemy, or a potential convert.

'Anything we need to worry about?' Finnlay swung his saddlebags over his shoulder.

'That depends,' Micah replied, not at all sure this was such a good idea. Actually, he *was* sure it wasn't a very good idea at all.

'On what?'

'On how many rumours you've heard over the last year or so.'

'Which rumours?' Finnlay's voice betrayed his underlying irritation, but Micah ploughed on regardless.

'The ones about the incarnation of Mineah coming back to battle against the evils of sorcery ravaging the land at the moment.'

Finnlay sighed. 'What about them?'

'These people believe that . . .' he swallowed, then continued, 'that she's been here a while and that . . . well that she's . . . Jenn.'

Finnlay came to a halt. 'Are they serious?' he whispered. 'And that's why they come up here?'

'To pray, yes,' Micah agreed. 'Look, I've heard a hundred different things about Jenn over the years – mostly because of her appearance at Shan Moss after she was supposed to have been killed in the fire at Clonnet. Enough people saw her to recognise her, and too many people saw her use some kind of power *against* two sorcerers.'

'But that doesn't mean they could . . .'

'Finn,' Micah put a hand on the man's arm. 'I've been to Alusia, remember? Robert and I went to the site of the last battle with the Empire, when Mineah was supposed to have fought against the Cabal. I saw the marks in the earth, caused, according to legend, by *her* power.'

'And Robert said that only meant she might have been a sorcerer.'

'Isn't Jenn? Isn't she a different kind of sorcerer?'

Finnlay raised his eyebrows at that. 'How bad are these rumours?'

'I've had them whispered to me in the odd tavern here and there. It's not a flood – but if she's seen again, and people hear about it, it could gather momentum. These people are very serious. They've already got men walking the country delivering the message. I get the impression that these nightly visits are a prelude to building some kind of shrine. As this is her birthplace, they see Elita as a holy place.'

'This is not my area of expertise, you know. I wonder if McCauly has heard about this.' With a deep sigh, Finnlay said, 'And we can't tell her.'

'Why not?'

'Would you want to be told there are people out there who think you're a god? She's already got too much to worry about at the moment. Let's see what happens with Andrew and Robert. Then, if I get a chance, I'll tell her when we get back to the Enclave.'

It made sense. Besides, Jenn probably wouldn't believe him anyway, given their current problems. 'And if she asks?' Micah said.

'Tell her they're here saying prayers for her father's soul. She already half-believes it. And I might suggest Murdoch comes back here in the summer, see if he can find out more.'

'Good idea.'

'Come on. If we keep her waiting, she won't speak to either of us for the rest of the journey.'

'One can only hope.'

Finnlay let out an involuntary laugh, then elbowed him sharply. 'That's not nice.'

'Sorry.'

But they were both grinning as they entered the forest.

Andrew tried not to fidget. He tried to focus his attention on the forest around him, on the cottage he could just see through the trees, tried to practise the things Finnlay had taught him about listening and sensing changes in his natural surroundings – but he failed miserably. It had nothing to do with where he was, who he was with or the fact that he'd just spent the last five days in the saddle. He just didn't feel like settling, sitting down in one place and not *doing* anything.

For the tenth time since they'd arrived, he looked over to where Robert sat with his back to a tree trunk, not ten feet away, that book open in his hands, reading as though he had no other concerns in his life, as though *things* weren't happening all around him. The light was fading, and Jenn and Finnlay and Micah would be here soon, but Robert kept on reading.

Andrew had tried asking about the book, about the odd way it had changed shape for a moment, but Robert wouldn't be drawn.

Didn't they have things to discuss?

Robert hadn't mentioned Kenrick again, nor what he claimed had happened to Helen and Liam. If it was true, why hadn't Jenn said anything to him? Or Finnlay? Surely they knew he'd find out about it the moment he returned to the Enclave. Or would they . . . find some way to fold the truth and leave some parts of it out? After all, they hadn't told him the truth about Robert, had they? And there were still dozens of questions Jenn had said he was too young to know the answer for.

Answers that Robert had given him quickly and openly. Answers that made him feel very . . .

He leaped to his feet, ready to start pacing.

'Where are you going?' Robert murmured without looking up from his damned book.

'Nowhere. I just want to stretch my legs.'

'Can't it wait?'

'For what?'

'Until your mother gets here?'

'Why?'

'Because I'm holding a mask over us at the moment, and if you move around, somebody could see you.'

'But I live here!'

'And you spend hours sitting here, in this part of Lawrence's forest, don't you? In the company of a known sorcerer and rebel.'

Andrew sniffed and sat back down, wrapping his arms around his knees. He watched Robert for a few minutes longer, then sighed. 'I thought that wasn't really a book.'

'Of course it's a book.' Robert seemed quite capable of carrying on a conversation while reading at the same time, a feat Andrew had never quite mastered. 'How could I read it if it wasn't?'

'Is it interesting?'

'Quite.'

'What's it about?'

'Well . . . it says here that young Dukes who don't let their betters read in peace receive punishment of the most dire proportions.'

Andrew struggled, but his grin won out. He kept his silence for a few minutes longer, but the truth was, there *were* things that needed discussing, *before* his mother returned. 'So, do you know why it did that strange shape-shifting thing, back at the loft?'

Robert's answer took a second to emerge. 'I think so. Why?'

'Well, it's just that . . . well, it didn't keep its shape after it changed, like the Key, you know? Of course, my mother has to be present for it to shift from that bell to the orb, but once it does, it stays like that until she's finished with it.'

He stopped talking to find Robert's gaze had lifted from the book and was fixed on some place in the middle distance. Then his eyes narrowed a little and the faintest suggestion of a smile danced across his face. He nodded once and returned to his book.

But there was no more. No explanation, no discussion. All those years, the books in the alcove, the notes they'd exchanged, the discussion they'd had – even this abduction – all to one purpose. So he would kill when ordered to.

It seemed Robert didn't trust him after all.

'So what happens now?' He'd hoped to keep the bitterness from his voice, but failed there as well. Well, Robert could just interpret that however he wanted.

'Now you go home, explain to Bella and Lawrence and your mother that you will be going away for a while. Concoct some story between you to cover your absence. When I made my first visit to the Enclave at the age of nine, I arranged with my parents to go on a retreat to a monastery for a month. Then you can collect what small belongings you feel you must have and meet me here again in two days. When you do, I'll tell you the rest of the plan.'

'The plan where I kill Kenrick.'

Robert turned his head slowly and pinned Andrew with his gaze. 'Are you really so shallow, so selfish, as to think that's all this is about?'

Again Andrew's face flushed and he looked down. 'No. I just don't . . . I mean, I want to . . . I don't know what I'm doing here. Nobody ever said that I would . . .'

Robert got to his feet, his voice soft. 'Tell me something: why don't you have any powers?'

'What?' Andrew frowned up at him.

'I can Sense them in you. You have a sorcerer's aura and yet you walk about blind and deaf. Why?'

Andrew pushed himself slowly to his feet. 'You can Sense them?'

'Of course,' Robert said. 'Can't everybody?'

The silliness of that question forced a smile on Andrew's face, answered by one of Robert's. 'Well, no. Mother can, and Martha and I think, Arlie – but Finnlay's never been convinced and he's tried to teach me things, but I can never do what he says. If I *do* have powers, they don't work very well.'

Robert stared at him for a moment, then said, 'Close your eyes.'

'Why?'

'Just close your eyes.'

Wary for no good reason, Andrew shut his eyes against the darkening forest. Abruptly he was set adrift, unable to feel the ground beneath his feet or the cold air against his face. He opened his mouth to speak, but a wave of dizziness almost knocked him over and he stumbled, opening his eyes again to find Robert reaching out to take his arm, steady him.

'What was that?'

'Let me ask you another question first. What would you do if you did have powers?'

'Do?'

'Yes, do. Would you do as I ask and take care of Kenrick?'

'I . . . I don't know.'

'I see. So what would you do with them?'

'What do *you* do with them?'

'Fight a very small rebellion and contain the bloodshed as best I can.'

'Oh. Well . . . I suppose . . .' Andrew had never really thought of this, and now that he had, it was irritating not to have an answer. 'I'd think of something.'

Robert's smile was almost overpowering. 'Yes, I'm sure you would. Come on, let's go. Your mother is arriving.'

'But . . . is that it?'

With a sigh, Robert turned back to him, his gaze hooded and deep. 'You'll tell your mother all about our little jaunt, won't you?'

'I . . . am I not supposed to?'

'You'll fill in all the details, making sure you tell her much of what I said to you word for word. Am I wrong?'

'You . . .' Andrew swallowed hard, understanding dawning on him too slowly. 'You don't trust her. You don't trust that she won't tell Nash. But . . . if Nash is looking for the Key and if she was on his side, why wouldn't she just give it to him?'

One side of Robert's mouth lifted in a sardonic smile. 'Is that all Nash wants?'

Andrew frowned. 'I don't know. But does that mean you don't want me to tell Mother?'

'No, that means I want you to decide for yourself.' With that, Robert turned away and headed into the dark forest, away from where the others were just arriving. 'And in case you're wondering, this time it *is* a test.'

Andrew, turning back to the Spay, saw the approaching horses step carefully amongst the rock pools. He hurried forward, bursting into the clearing in time to sweep his mother up into a hug. It felt like he hadn't seen her for a year.

Robert watched the boy run towards his mother. Though it was almost completely dark inside the forest now, and she didn't have his enhanced eyesight, he knew she would know he was here. But he didn't move forward.

This was so stupid. So . . . predictable. So unknown. What he felt for her shouldn't matter any more: he'd once loved her, and believed she'd loved him. But she'd lied and betrayed him in the same breath and that put an end to it.

She'd never told him about her meeting with Nash in Shan Moss. Never told him that the Angel of Darkness had kissed her. Instead, she'd told him she'd never loved him and had stopped him from destroying Nash.

Had she *really* never loved him?

He could feel the warmth of the Calyx close to his skin, the book a hard shape, and comforting. But did he dare try to change it again – what if he unleashed something he couldn't contain?

He didn't dare, not without the right setting, and perhaps

some help if something went wrong. But what was the right setting? Jenn? The Enclave – and would it be safe to trust them with such knowledge?

Jenn would not want to turn her son into a killer, or a King.

Robert turned for his horse, tightening the girth strap and making ready to leave.

'Robert?'

He froze, hands still on the saddle, Senses vanishing in the wake of her too-familiar aura. Like a statue he waited.

This was simply not fair.

'I'm sorry,' she said evenly, betraying nothing. 'I realise you don't really want to talk to me but there are things we need to discuss.'

'Isn't that what mindspeech is for?' Suddenly unfrozen, his hands finished their work and he moved around the horse, ashamed that he felt the need for such protection against her.

'Only if it *is* used – and more than twice in eight years.' She took a step closer and he had no choice, as he had never had a choice, but to look at her.

Like himself, she had been touched by the Key that day, and now she stood before him unaged, unchanged and yet so terribly different in ways that made him quake inside. He saw the long dark hair, bound up in a thick braid which fell over her shoulder. He saw her oval face, so like her son's, the eyes, nose and mouth, familiar and yet not the same at all. Andrew was everything Jenn would have been if she'd been a man – but did he have her courage? Her determination? Her ability to manipulate those around her to achieve goals she never spoke about?

Had she been like this since joining with the Key, or had he been blind to it for years before that?

'What do you plan to do with Andrew?' Her voice held memories. 'Or can't you tell me?'

'You know the answer to that. You always did have the habit of asking questions you already knew the answers to. I'm sure you, Micah and my brother have discussed it at length.'

406

'So it's true?' Her eyes went wide at this. 'And what if I want to stop you?'

'Don't.'

'Could I?'

And suddenly, he knew how to keep the fear at bay and yet hold the demon in check. He moved back around his horse, dropping the reins, walking up to her, noting how she became wary, but not afraid, as though fear between them still didn't exist, as it never had, and then he was there, before her, his arm slipping around her waist, his hand catching under her chin, lifting her face towards him.

He kissed her.

Fear, like desire, rose in him, flooding through his body, awakening him like nothing had over the years since he'd last seen her. Something in her fought him, but without strength, and that was enough to encourage him, to take whatever it was he needed without giving anything back.

They broke apart, breathless. For a moment, he retained his hold on her, then he dropped his hands and stepped back. Her gaze was locked on his, open and yet wholly closed to him. She was shaking slightly, but she said nothing.

'Don't try to stop me.'

He caught up his reins, led his horse past her and on towards the clearing. He stopped then, unable to avoid facing Micah. Pale blue eyes watched him without blinking, without expression, and Robert knew it was up to him to speak first this time.

'I'm sorry about your father.' There was a faint flicker in those eyes, and Robert continued, 'I spoke to Durrill. He said your mother and the rest of your family are well.' His voice trailed off. He couldn't say any more to his once-closest friend. The time for that had long since passed. But no matter what else, Micah *had* spent the last eight years protecting a future King, and for that, Robert added, 'I am very sorry about David. He was a good man.'

For a moment, Micah just continued to stare at him. Then he nodded slowly. 'Thank you, my lord.'

In the ensuing silence, Robert looked at Finnlay, then at

Andrew. 'I'll see you in two days.' With that, he swung up into his saddle and rode away, kicking his horse into a gallop, invisible ghosts snapping at his heels.

Andrew stared at the patch of darkness Robert had disappeared into. Why did he feel like he'd just failed somehow?

He turned back to the others, in time to see the last of a look pass between Micah and Finnlay, something far beyond anything he was privy to. And then his mother emerged from the forest, deliberately looking at neither of the men, but keeping her attention on Andrew instead.

The clearing drew forth the last of the afternoon light, helping the odd silence. It was just enough to see something glisten in Jenn's eyes, then she gave him the kind of smile he had never seen before on her. It touched him deeply, but left him unsettled – like so much else that had happened in the last hour.

'You and Micah should go on to Maitland. You're a day late already and Bella will be worried.'

The words, tone, gestures, all seemed so normal, but he couldn't escape the conviction that something very important had just happened and he was the only one who didn't understand it. 'What about you?'

'I'll follow on my own. Finnlay will have to wait for us at Micah's cottage, as usual.'

Micah could get away with going through the gate after dark, but anybody who saw his mother would immediately recognise her, since she looked so much like her sister.

He watched her for a moment, remembering the strange look shared by Finnlay and Micah, and blurted, 'Mother, will you walk back to my horse with me?'

Surprised, she said, 'Yes, of course.'

He caught her hand and she walked alongside him into the darkness of the pine trees, to where his horse was tethered. 'What happened?' he murmured. 'Between you and Duke Robert?'

He felt her stiffen beside him. 'I tried to ask him about his plans for you.'

'And?'

'And he wouldn't tell me.' She came closer, brushing his hair down with a gentle hand. She had always touched him, always made sure he knew how much she loved him, how important he was to her, even though she'd chosen to live in the Enclave, rather than live with him.

'Andrew, are you all right?'

'I'm just . . . I don't know, confused, I suppose.'

'I don't know what to say to you, my love,' she whispered. 'I know you have questions and I know you need answers. I wish that he . . .'

Andrew held his breath, waiting for the rest of the wish, but it never came.

In the silence, he found he could only leap head first into the test. But at least it didn't have to be entirely on Robert's terms. 'Just tell me one thing, Mother.'

'I'll try.'

'Can I trust him?'

She muttered under her breath, 'When I get my hands on him, I'll . . . what he's done to you . . .' She stopped abruptly, faced him again and put her hands against his cool cheeks. 'Yes, you can trust him. You *have* to trust him.'

Shock washed through him. 'Does that mean you agree? That I should do as he says?'

She pulled him close then, as she had when he was a child. 'It means, my love, that I can't help you in this. I would fight to the death for you, but in this, I . . . I cannot stand against him.'

He pushed away from her. This couldn't be his mother speaking! She would never condone something like this! And yet, it *was* her. He grabbed his reins and headed back to the clearing. 'We'll talk about this tomorrow.'

'Andrew, wait!'

'Why?' Stubborn and defiant, he turned to face her.

'There are things you don't understand.'

'And that's *my* fault? If you'd wanted me to understand, you should have told me a long time ago.'

'I was trying to protect you.'

'And that makes a difference? That makes it right? Mother, do you have *any* idea what he wants me to do? Do you? What in Serin's name were you trying to protect me from? The truth of who I am? Was that ever going to change it? Make it go away? No! So now I have to listen to . . . him and what he says and you tell me you can't stop him.' Andrew came to a crashing halt, his throat tight, his eyes stinging. 'I . . . worshipped him, Mother. And he thinks I'm a coward and a traitor. I . . .'

Jenn moved forward, her hands reaching for him. 'I'm sorry, love. I never wanted this to happen—'

But the moment she touched him, he flinched, unable to believe such comfort now. Nor could he look at her. 'Don't, Mother. Just . . . I'll see you tomorrow.' He didn't wait for more. The moment he reached Micah, he swung up into his saddle and kicked the horse into movement. Micah joined him as they headed north, to join up with the road they were supposed to be travelling.

They rode in silence, after a while passing through a crossroads with a busy tavern, when they made it look as if they'd come directly from Marsay. All necessary lies. All sacrifices to the gods of survival.

He felt ill.

So this was the life of a rebel, then. Doing things under cover of darkness, hiding, pretending, keeping secrets and living with half-truths. No wonder Robert had such a problem with trust.

'Micah?'

'Yes, my lord?'

'Could you have stopped him?'

'Taking you?'

'Yes.'

'I don't know.'

'That means you could have if you'd wanted to, doesn't it?'

'You've spent a week with him, my lord. Can you honestly tell me any man alive has the ability to stop him doing anything he wants to?'

Andrew could see the lights of Maitland Manor appear in the distance, but even as they gave him that familiar welcome, something about them had changed. Or perhaps it was he who had changed. 'My mother stopped him from killing Nash.'

'No, she didn't.' Micah replied so softly Andrew almost didn't hear it. 'She stopped him from killing himself.'

'How do you know that?' Andrew wanted it to be a question, but it came out more like a demand. He turned to look at Micah, to read the expression in the pale shaded moonlight, but there was something wrong. Micah didn't appear to be thinking the question over. He seemed to be concentrating on something—

He heard it then: the pounding of hooves from the forest all around them, calls in the darkness and the unmistakable rasp of steel against steel.

'By the gods, my lord, turn and run!' Micah pulled his horse around and drew his sword all in the same motion, nothing more in that moment than pure warrior. 'We are attacked by Malachi!'

29

DeMassey shouted out another order, sent two men around to flank the pair dodging every attempt to surround them. Then he barked at a man to ride and gather the rest who were guarding the other approach. He kicked his horse, galloping towards the front of the group, ducking under low-hanging branches, rolling each time the animal stumbled beneath him.

It should have been easy. With the experience of his men, their skills, their abilities, the ambush should have been over within seconds. But long minutes after they'd made their first strike, they were still chasing the boy and his guard, running parallel to the road. Two of his men were already wounded, the guard fighting like a demon, continually keeping himself between the D'Azzir and his charge.

They needed to get this done. If they got too much closer to Maitland, the alarm would be raised and any hope of keeping the abduction from the Ally's eyes would be lost.

But he couldn't use too much force, didn't dare give the

order for his men to use combat abilities. One stray shot – and in the darkness, under these conditions, it was too possible – and the boy would be dead. And so would they all.

The road dipped down before them and with his men flanking, his prey stumbled into a shallow gully, hedged with trees. The guard perched ready to fight, turning his horse this way and that, picking out what he could see in the dark. The boy did the same, but with terror in his eyes, his sword pointing warily but effectively.

Without warning, a single bolt of power flew from De-Massey's left and hit the ground beneath the two as his men surrounded them. Panicking, both horses reared up. With a yell, the boy slid to the ground and DeMassey's men closed in.

Turned out this was much easier than it had looked.

The night crammed close and hostile, forcing Jenn to her feet again and again, to pace before the fire Finnlay had made. They could have gone to Micah's cottage, but she'd only have to come back this way to go to Maitland. So Finnlay sat by the fire, wrapped in his cloak, a bundle of stark silence, and Jenn paced back and forth, memories of Andrew's comments deafening her.

'Will you *please* sit down!'

Jenn came to a halt, staring into the clearing beyond the line of trees in the direction of Maitland. 'Is it time for me to leave yet?'

'I'd say they would be going through the crossroads by now. So, no, not just yet. Not unless you want to get to Maitland before Andrew?'

'No.' Her fingers itched. She pulled her gloves off and rubbed her hands together, but it made no difference. 'Are you sure about the timing?'

'Am I ever wrong?'

'Not that you've told me.'

'Well, I'm telling you now, sit down and calm down.'

Again she began to pace, rubbing her hands and shaking her head. She shouldn't be feeling this just because of her argument with Andrew. Or was it that Robert had kissed her? A tremor ran through her. Wanting and needing had too often taken second place to larger concerns. Just seeing him, standing there whole and alive, had touched something inside her. But Robert hadn't kissed her out of affection, or love. There had been the taste of revenge on his lips.

What had he tasted on hers?

Something dark swept before her eyes, like a bat flying in the forest, but larger. She stopped, searching for the shadow in the black night. Abruptly all the dissonance coalesced inside her and, terrified, she ran for her horse.

'Malachi! They're going for Andrew!'

Andrew landed hard on the ground, the wind knocked out of him, the sword bumping from his fingers. Another flash of fire split the night around him, blinding him for a moment. A shout followed it, an order to cease or else, and Andrew blinked, trying to find Micah in the chaos.

'Andrew? Are you hurt?'

A hand beneath his elbow dragged him to his feet. As his sight returned, his sword was thrust into his hand.

'Stay close.'

'What do they want?' Andrew hissed, seeing more now: perhaps a dozen men, mounted, heavily armed. Malachi all. And he recognised the leader – Baron DeMassey.

'Make it easy on yourselves,' DeMassey called out. 'Stand apart, drop your weapons and nobody will get hurt.'

'What do you want?' Micah spoke up boldly, neither moving away nor dropping his sword.

'Just the boy. You can go free. Get back on your horse and ride away.'

'He's lying.' Andrew was shaking so hard his teeth were chattering, but he still knew a lie when he saw one. 'Don't believe him.'

'If you want him, you'll have to take him,' Micah called back, defiant, so much strength in his voice that Andrew felt instantly ashamed. How did he get to be so brave when he was the one facing death?

No order was given that he could hear, but before he could

move, the Malachi jumped down from their horses and advanced. The first blow sent him reeling backwards, unable to counter the greater weight of his opponent. Micah stayed with him, but he had his own opponents. Two men crowded in on him and he swung around to put his back to Andrew's so they could cover each other.

Frantically Andrew tried to remember everything Micah and Finnlay and all his other teachers had tried to pound into him, but every time a sword crashed down on his own, the impact drummed all thought out of him. Hard, jarring, loud and shocking, the noise alone crowded in on him, shattering every ounce of confidence he'd ever mustered.

They were going to die.

Where were his powers?

Sweet Mineah, help us!

Robert was swept away by a terror that flooded through his bones in a tidal wave, blinding him, tapping into the demon directly and stealing his soul.

He pulled his horse to a halt, gasping for air, staring into the night.

Jenn?

No answer.

Jenn!

The silence darkened. He tugged on the reins hard, wheeling his horse. With a savage kick, he sent it into a flat gallop

He would be too late.

He moved as one with the horse, breathing as it did, letting it make all the decisions, leaving him ready, power surging through him, held back only by his will and nothing else.

The demon sat around him, his cloak of darkness, champing to be set free, to blanket everything . . .

Blinded, Andrew couldn't see anything, only feeling the blows he tried to fend off, tried to duck. His hands ached holding the sword; they were sweaty and losing their grip. But he had to stay close to Micah or the Malachi would cut him down in a heartbeat.

He couldn't think over the fear. Everything was bigger, sharper, harder, more vicious than anything before. Everything was darker; the violence consumed him.

Could he hear his name being called over the shouts of the Malachi? He ducked another blow and behind the Malachi were Jenn and Finnlay and they were fighting too, fighting to get close to him.

But the forest was on fire, and they were so far away.

And then he did hear something, something thundering beneath everything else: pounding hooves on the hard winter ground. Coming closer, bright and vengeful.

Robert. His sword alight with fire, raised ready to strike, heading straight towards them.

He could see everything. As he raced towards the mêlée, he counted off twenty-four men, eight of them dead and three with bad wounds. And DeMassey was there; this was Nash's doing.

It should have been darker. It was night, but the forest was lit by trees burning, branches dripping flames to the snow-covered ground. And there were Jenn and Finnlay, beset by Malachi, their blasts filling the air, neither giving ground. But Jenn was far from Andrew and Micah.

Too slowly he moved. To his right, the Malachi aimed a combined burst of fire at a tree above Jenn and over the noise, he could hear its mighty trunk crack under the blast . . .

To his left, Andrew cried out as his sword was finally knocked from his hands and, defenceless, he faced . . .

Robert's horse stumbled. With a cry of blind rage in his heart, he pulled it up, kicked it hard again and headed left.

Towards Andrew.

His fingers numb and slippery with blood, Andrew tried to duck down and grab his sword, but the men facing him got too close, pointing to his throat, making him freeze. From the corner of his eye, he could see Robert galloping closer, and then he was upon them, his sword swinging, cutting down two men at the first pass, another two on the second.

Terror tore through the Malachi like wildfire, but still Andrew was trapped. Then, just as Robert was upon them, Micah seized his arm and, with a shove, pushed him right into Robert's path. With a violent wrench, Robert grabbed him and swung him up onto the saddle behind him, his sword cutting more fire into the night.

And then they were free of the Malachi, galloping into the forest until, with a hard turn, Robert headed back, his sword still flaming. Andrew clung on to him, heart pounding, hands shaking, desperate to find Micah in the mess, to find Jenn and Finnlay, but all he could see were Malachi racing to their horses, leaving their dead behind, their cries of panic illuminating the night.

Then his eyes did see. The flaming tree, the warning cried out by Finnlay, his mother looking up too late to move, to get out of the way. With a deafening crash, the tree fell.

'Mother!'

Robert barely registered the fires, or the marks in the snow, the horses milling around, the scars of blood and the bodies on the ground. Something inside him said he should go after DeMassey and his men, make them pay for this. His horse stumbled to a halt on scorched grass sodden with wet ash. He slid from its back, landing lightly. Action, his body demanded, action, but there was no enemy left he could fight.

He dropped his sword and ran forward until the heat of the blaze forced him back. Smoke filled the air and he choked, coughing, squinting into the unholy glare.

He was too late. And in the end, the Prophecy . . . *in the act of salvation . . . destroy that which he loved . . .*

'Robert!' Finnlay staggered towards him, Micah following. They were both bleeding, but neither badly. 'I can't find her, Robert!' Finnlay grabbed his sleeve. 'Seeking her. I can't find her. She was wounded. I—'

Robert shook him off, closing his eyes, though he could still see the fallen tree engulfed in flame. He heard Andrew run forward, and Finn and Micah hold him back. After that, he shut the world out.

Jenn?

Jenny? Please? Answer me!

Please?

He closed his eyes, summoned the power, all the raw power that had been building in him since that first moment of blind panic, all the way here, all the way to this moment in his life. He let it go, surging through his whole body. Seeking, burning through the burning forest, looking, knowing he would find what he needed because he had to, because she couldn't be dead. The Prophecy couldn't be real. It couldn't win. Not like this!

He gasped and staggered forward, but Finnlay kept him upright, kept him breathing, and he could feel Micah close by, steady in his silence, See their auras in the black, inky night, see the faint humming glow of the fire and the bloody wastefulness of it and he kept pushing, sliding and slipping until the demon burst inside him, clawing at the power, vicious and cruel and sending it further and harder than he could on his own.

He could no longer control it, but the demon had only ever struck her once, and then with no power. As his terror blossomed, he let the demon free.

His eyes snapped open, feeling for, finding, grabbing hold of the most frail, the most tentative . . .

Sweet Mineah, yes! Yes!

He twisted out of Finnlay's hold, moving forward, both of them following.

'Robert, wait! You can't go in there! The fire's still too hot!'

'She's alive, Finn. She's shielding. She won't last long.' He didn't bother with further explanations.

He threw up his own shield, but it thinned before such forceful natural power and the heat almost blinded him. Then he grabbed hold of the demon inside him, closing his eyes, letting his Senses work as they were born to, making the world out in the darkness, giving him what he needed.

With the vengeance of the betrayed, the demon lashed out, rolling pressure before it like a wave crashing onto a rocky shore. He heard it before he saw it, his eyes opening late to find the tree moving, falling and tumbling back, taking the worst of the fire with it, sweeping each last piece from where he would be.

He was there without thought, pushing at glowing timbers, kicking things out of the way until, at last, there she was: Jenn, huddled beneath a blackened branch, alive.

He pulled her free, cradled her in his arms as Finnlay dashed forward and helped him. Together they stumbled away to where Micah waited, their gathered horses ready.

Robert laid Jenn down then stood back, to give his brother a chance to check her injuries with hands more steady than his.

'She's bleeding, Robert. I need water and bandages and—'

'We can't stay here,' Micah interrupted. 'If they decide to come back—'

'Yes.' Robert turned in the direction the Malachi had gone. He should go after them. He should make sure—

'Finn, get on your horse. Micah, help me get her up to him. We'll go to your cottage, tend her wounds there. Andrew, let's go.'

'No! We can't!' DeMassey repeated, his temper running raw as his wounds were jostled. His men gathered around him, those who had survived, who had left their dead friends behind as they'd fled before a wave of unbridled panic. It had hit them all, without exception, a force that could only have come from the Douglas.

'We have no choice, Luc,' one man on his left insisted. 'When Nash finds out we killed the Ally, we're all dead. And we'll never get the boy now!'

'The best we can do,' another joined in, 'is to make it look like it wasn't our fault! That what happened had nothing to do with us. You must see that!'

'And what do we say about the boy?' DeMassey tried to insert reason into this rage. His men were angry that they had been so afraid, and were now determined to get their courage back, no matter the cost.

'Say he died in the fire.'

'How is Nash going to know the difference? How important can the boy be if it's taken Nash this long to get him?'

'Come on, Luc! We don't have much time!'

No, it wasn't their fault – it was *his* fault, for not considering that the boy's mother might still be in the area, or the Rebel; for risking their lives on something that had nothing to do with them or their ambitions – for dragging his people into Nash's web of lies in the first place. And because it was his fault, he tried for reason now. 'You honestly think that burning Maitland is going to achieve that?'

His men clamoured to answer.

'It would serve them right!'

'We can make Nash believe. If we all tell the same story, how can he doubt us?'

'Don't even say the Ally was there!'

'We gave them a chance to surrender. It's not our fault they died – and I'm damned if I'm going to die because of that bitch and her whelp!'

With cries of agreement, his men turned almost as one and galloped towards the manor house, leaving him inside the shadows of a mighty oak.

After that, he could only sit by and watch.

30

Finnlay dropped the bags on the rug before the fireplace as Micah quickly piled logs for Finnlay to light. The cottage was freezing cold after Micah's long absence, and smelled faintly of damp. Then Robert brought Jenn in, carrying her as though she were made of glass. With gentle hands, he laid her on the bed.

He was afraid. Finnlay could see it in his brother's eyes, in his short breaths, in the pale cast to his skin. Robert was afraid.

Finnlay quickly pulled things he needed from his bags. Hopefully, Micah would have more. He turned to Jenn to find Robert smoothing the hair back from her forehead, frowning down at her, unsure whether he should stay or go.

What was it about these two? Was it Fate that drew them together, then tore them apart again? Or was it something within themselves that refused to see what was so painfully obvious to everyone else around them?

Micah brought bowls of clean water, cloths and bandages. Without saying a word, he moved Robert out of the way and began to clear away the area surrounding Jenn's wounds. Robert stood back, Andrew at his side, wincing as each new cut was revealed, not seeing the same expressions on Andrew's face.

Finnlay bent his head to work. 'Robert, you might want to try Seeking for DeMassey.'

'I don't know his aura well enough to Seek him.'

'Or perhaps just check to make sure they're not on their way back – or that anybody else is approaching. I need some time to get Jenn ready to travel. If we can get her to Maitland, we'll be a lot safer.'

'Of course.' Robert took two steps towards the door, then turned back to Finnlay, his face hopelessly vulnerable. He went to say something else, but then shut his mouth. He closed the door quietly.

'Andrew?'

'Yes?' The boy was immediately at his side, his face as pale as his father's.

'Go and dig out the driest wood from Micah's pile outside. Just small stuff that will catch and burn quickly. We won't be here long enough for a big blaze. Can you do that?'

'Yes.' Andrew paused a moment longer, then turned and ran outside as though speed alone could help his mother.

'This is not good,' Micah murmured, pasting some sweet-smelling salve into the fold of a bandage before pressing it over a wound in Jenn's side. 'How did she get these . . . Damn it, I knew she should have had more combat training – and with a sword at that. By the gods, I was supposed to be protecting her!'

'No, your job was to protect Andrew, mine was to protect Jenn. Let's make sure the blame is apportioned correctly.'

'Oh, right, fine. Whatever you say.'

'Trust me, Micah. If he thinks it's your fault, he'll kill you if she dies.'

'And he won't kill you?'

'I'm his brother.'

'Yes,' Micah whispered, the black humour gone from his voice. 'You are.'

In the few minutes it had taken to get Jenn and Andrew settled inside, Robert had completely forgotten that it was still winter outside. His cloak was muddied and covered in ash, smoke and blood, but he pulled it around himself, as he paced away from the cottage, digging his heels into the slimy snow being drilled down into icy water and further, into mud.

He'd let the demon go. He'd allowed it free rein and it had done no damage.

This once. For the first time, in fact.

But he'd still let it go.

He closed his eyes, pushed out with his Senses, looking for anything – *anything* – out of place.

His feet wouldn't let him stand still; his restlessness was broken up by bouts of freezing terror when he could only turn his Seeking backwards into the cottage, to make sure he could still See her, wounded badly, her aura so pale, broken in places, but still surviving.

He came to a halt, doubling over, stomach lurching with swallowing the fear for so long. He'd come so damned close.

He pulled himself upright, closing his eyes once more and Seeking tightly and firmly, regaining more and more control as each heartbeat flew by.

No. Nothing close by – and beyond that, his abilities refused to go so far from the cottage. If he wanted to be sure they were safe, he would have to do it in person and ride the perimeter. He should go to Maitland, get Bella to send over a cart to carry Jenn. If they had a Healer or a doctor or something, that would help.

Slowly his stomach steadied, balanced by the cold and the presence he could still Sense inside the cottage.

He paused only long enough to stick his head inside to tell the others where he was going. Then he took the first horse and headed northwards. From there, he would sweep southeast and stop for supplies at Maitland.

He'd already taken enough risks tonight to last him a lifetime.

Andrew brought in wood, armloads of it, dry and split, stacking it onto the fire and watching it flare up until the heat was almost unbearable. Then he brought more inside, stacking it against the stone fireplace, just in case it was needed. Without being asked, he went out again, to the well, filling a bucket with water to warm on the fire. Then he got another. After that, he rummaged through their saddlebags, looking for food. Micah's cupboards were next as he sought and found flasks of ale and wine. He was about to find something else to do when Finnlay caught him, steering him to a seat by the window.

Andrew swallowed hard and looked up; Finnlay avoided his gaze. Instead, he checked the cut Andrew had on his forearm, and the other he had on his shoulder. Neither were deep, and he'd long since forgotten about the pain. Finnlay exposed both, cleaning them and applying a bandage to each.

Andrew's gaze drifted to the bed where Micah was still tending Jenn. 'How is she?'

Micah heard this and turned around, plunging his hands into a bowl of bloody water. He dried them off and straightened up, but it was Finnlay who answered him. 'She's not so good, I'm afraid. She had three wounds, two deep. A number of cuts and bruises. She's lost a lot of blood, but she's already stretched herself beyond safety levels, trying to shelter from the fire.'

'But . . . she's going to be all right, isn't she?'

'Yes,' Micah answered before Finnlay could. Andrew saw a look shared between them, then Micah turned back to his work and Andrew faced Finnlay squarely.

'Is she going to . . . die?'

'Andrew, she . . .'

Finnlay's voice also trailed off as he turned to find Rober standing in the open doorway, his expression grave.

'Get Jenn ready to travel,' he said, 'we're heading straight t the Enclave.'

'The Enclave?' Finnlay asked, frowning. 'Why?'

But Robert almost ignored him. Instead, he came into the cottage, closed the door behind him and stood before Andrew. 'I'm sorry. It looks as though DeMassey took his . . . frustrations out on Maitland.'

'His frustrations?' Andrew could barely squeak out the question before dread folded into him, making him quake inside. 'Aunt Bella? Uncle Lawrence?'

Robert met his eyes for long moments, then slowly shook his head. 'I'm sorry, son.'

'They're dead?' Andrew murmured. 'Both of them?'

The silence was louder than the fresh wind battering against the shutters.

'Micah, you can't be serious! Surely it's not that bad. And waiting a few days isn't going to make any difference.'

Micah stepped around the horse so that Finnlay couldn't see him again. It was dark and cold and very close inside this tiny stable. There was just enough room for five horses and a bag of oats. Two extra people made moving around almost impossible.

But the animals needed saddling, and despite his shoulder wound, Micah was determined to do it all himself, leaving no space for Finnlay to help. That wasn't the only thing Micah was being stubborn about.

Finnlay pressed himself up against the wall, easing the nearest horse's head out of his way to see where Micah was up to. 'You can't do anything for Bella and Lawrence now. Staying back isn't going to make any difference – and if those Malachi decide to come back . . .'

'They won't come back, and you know it. They wanted Andrew.'

'So why stay? Is it really because you don't want to travel with Robert?'

Micah's expression hardened in the yellow lamplight, making him look suddenly old beyond his years. 'The three of you will be fine getting Jenn back on your own. I'll follow two days behind you.'

'But—'

'Why bother arguing with me, Finnlay?' Micah looked up with a smile that didn't reach his eyes. 'You're not going to change my mind. Now why don't you take these two horses out and tie them up beside the woodshed. That will give me enough room to finish the others.'

'Mother? Mother? Can you hear me? Micah says you should be able to wake up, but Finnlay says you exhausted yourself too much. I think you should rest anyway. We're going to take you back to the Enclave. Duke Robert says the closer you get, the more the Key will be able to help you. He told me how it healed over all his old scars that day when you became Jaibir, and that the Key did the same thing with you – but can it heal new wounds like this? You said I should trust him.

'Mother, I'm sorry. I . . . should have been able to help you. Even Duke Robert says I've got powers in me. I tried, really I did. I tried so hard but . . . but . . . I'm sorry. I don't even know why they wanted me.

'Aunt Bella and Uncle Lawrence . . . they . . . I'm so sorry, Mother. Just rest and get better, please.'

Robert knew he wasn't supposed to hear the whispered plea and for a moment he considered pretending he hadn't. But Andrew's throat constricted, his voice broke and his entire body tensed to ward off tears he should have been able to shed.

Saying nothing, Robert came inside, closed the door behind him silently and moved up behind the boy, intending to do no more than be there. But his hand came up and rested on Andrew's shoulder and his gaze drifted down to where she lay.

She *was* pale, and blue-grey shadows welled under her eyes. She rested on her left side, the right bearing the wounds now stitched and bound and ready for travelling. Her aura was still fragile, worrying him, but the bleeding had stopped for the moment.

At least she wasn't in any pain.

'You'd better take your things out to your horse,' Robert

ventured quietly, nudging Andrew. 'We'll be leaving in a minute. I'll stay with her.'

Slowly, Andrew got to his feet and turned. His face was grey, but there was no sign of tears. He was finding strength he hadn't known he had. With his back straight, he picked up his bag and headed out of the cottage.

Left alone with Jenn, Robert sat on the bed beside her, not touching her, not looking at her, but Seeing her purely with his Senses. He could do nothing more to make amends.

They took what supplies they could carry, leaving Micah with just enough to last him three days. After that, he'd be on the road and heading towards the Goleth. Finnlay still didn't like the idea – but strangely, Andrew didn't argue with the decision. He'd just studied Micah long and hard and then turned away, as though there was some secret neither dared speak about.

The night stood about them, black and icy, an evil wind blowing from the north as they mounted up. Finnlay led the spare horses which carried the bulk of their things, and Robert had Jenn on the saddle in front of him.

She had not yet woken up.

And then they were riding into the grey light and Finnlay spared a glance over his shoulder at the man who had fought and lost, like so many others. After that, he kept his attention on the road before them, and on a nephew who seemed so unnaturally quiet, matching the unholy quiet of his brother.

Micah slept after they left, awaking, hours later, his body aching, his shoulder burning. He got up long enough to relieve himself, then fell back into bed and slept again, empty, unable to even mourn.

By the time he woke again, it was almost dark. He couldn't do much about his shoulder, but he made some food and forced it down, drinking as much water as he could, staying clear of the small keg of ale he kept in the pantry. Fortified then, he set about cleaning the cottage, burning bloodied rags and bandages, sweeping the mud from the floor, washing and putting away the cups and plates they'd used through the night. Finally he sank into his favourite chair by the fireplace, a cup of brew heating the palm of one hand.

Poor Bella. She'd never understood her sister, she'd never really given Jenn a chance, even from the first – and yet, she'd never turned her back, never once let Jenn or Andrew down, as though understanding was not a prerequisite for loyalty.

Well, it wasn't, was it?

Had *he* felt the need to understand Robert before he'd give his loyalty?

He sighed. It was so long ago now, how could he remember? He'd been a boy of six, Robert thirteen. Back then, going to live at Dunlorn had been a dream come true, with more wonderful things surrounding them than he'd ever seen in his life. Questions like loyalty and understanding hadn't existed for a long time – and then, by the time they did, there was no question at all.

And look how it had all changed. Trust and loyalty, understanding and forgiveness had become no more than shallow tokens and Bella and Lawrence lay dead in the blackened ruins of their home.

Micah put his cup down, blew out the lamp and went back to bed. He closed his eyes and saw not the look Andrew had given him as he'd left, nor the look Robert hadn't given him, but instead, how Finnlay had looked back with worry, and how Jenn always smiled when she saw him.

To some people, loyalty was not a prerequisite to understanding.

For a moment, he couldn't work out what had woken him – but that alone was enough of a clue. He held still, listening to the night above the pounding of his heart. Then the door latch lifted and Micah opened his eyes, knowing the shape of her as she slipped inside, obviously hoping to catch him asleep.

She never did. Robert had trained him far too well for that.

She crept up to the bed, kneeling down beside it before leaning forward to brush her lips over his. His arm whipped out, going around the back of her neck and pulling her closer, down onto the bed. She squealed with laughter and kissed him hard this time, then abruptly pulled back. With a snap of her fingers, the lamp burst into life again and she looked down at him, her hand moving out to his shoulder and the dressing.

'Is it bad?'

'No.'

His tone must have alerted her. Her stark gaze switched from his shoulder to his face in a single heartbeat and then she was abruptly off the bed, standing before him ready for battle.

Sighing, Micah sat up and swung his legs over the side of the bed. He ran his fingers through his hair and looked up. 'How did they know?'

'Know what? Are you suggesting I was with them?'

'Sairead, don't leap to the defensive, please.'

'How can I not, when you ask questions like that.'

'You're assuming I don't trust you, or that I blame you.'

'Are you going to say you never thought to blame me? Not once, not for one brief second?'

'Wouldn't you, in the same position?'

'We're *not* enemies!'

She said this with so much heat, there were tears in her eyes and Micah got up quickly, not holding her, but instead, taking her hand in his, just keeping a touch between them. 'No, *we* are not – but your people and mine have always been enemies, and always will be.'

'We've never asked questions like that of each other. How can I tell you how they knew? I wasn't with them. I have no idea who did this, and if I ask . . . Micah, please!'

He reached out, brushing a thumb over her lips, feeling her tremble beneath his touch. He could feel nothing. No guilt, no fear, and it didn't seem to matter any more that somehow he had been betrayed, even if it wasn't by her.

He kissed her, gently, felt her move in close to him, put her arms around his waist and bury her face into his shoulder. 'I'm sorry,' she whispered. 'You lost people you loved.'

Micah couldn't bring himself to ask if she thought that Andrew and Jenn had died in the fire. He didn't trust his own reaction if she showed no surprise.

'Micah?'

'Yes, love?'

'I . . . I wanted to tell you something.'

'Something good?'

She lifted her head at that, watching him with those crystal blue eyes again, now faintly green in the firelight. 'Yes, I think so. Something very good.'

Micah began to smile – then froze. Second after second drifted by as the numb feeling inside him dried up, to be replaced by a burning curiosity and an answer to a question he'd almost given up asking.

Sairead was grinning at him now, almost laughing. 'Oh, you should see your face! What, did you not think we would manage it somehow, despite the fact that we see each other for perhaps a month out of every year?'

'But . . . how . . . I mean . . . when?'

'Last time I was here. So tell me, is it a good thing?'

Micah smiled hugely. 'Yes, the best.' He pulled her to him then, kissing her deeply, just feeling her there, in the room with him, holding the memory for the months they would be apart.

How in the name of the gods were they going to manage this? They'd kept their marriage secret all these years because it was necessary – and they'd never had any children to complicate matters. Now . . .

'Shh,' Sairead pressed a finger to his lips. 'Let's not concern ourselves with the problems just yet? Please, let's just rejoice together.'

'Very well. Then let's be comfortable.' He turned to pull her back on the bed—

The door crashed open and the cottage was filled with men Micah vaguely recognised. Instantly he reached for the sword he always left beneath the bed, but a single gesture from the lead man made him stop.

These were Malachi, and a sword would do him no good.

Sairead took a step until she was in front of him, her shoulders back, chin raised, ready for defiance. He had never loved her so much.

'What are you doing, Uncle? Did you follow me here?'

428

The man she addressed looked around the room, three of his men ready behind him. The others, Serin only knew how many, had gone back outside. Micah could hear them moving around, probably looking for tracks.

'You're my niece; I don't need to follow you.' The man turned back to her, looked Micah up and down once, then turned away, moving to stand before the fireplace where the flames abruptly flared brighter. 'This is really very cosy, isn't it?'

'Uncle Gilbert, please let me explain—'

'Trust me, Sairead, there's nothing you could say that would make any difference. After what I've witnessed tonight . . .'

Micah held his breath, tightening his grip on Sairead's hand. 'What do you want?'

Gilbert turned slowly and faced them. Once more his attention sat firmly on his niece, his expression appraising. Then he met Micah's gaze. 'I want no more than what you want.'

'Am I to trust that? After what's happened here?'

He got a smile for that, a wry, displeased smile. 'I gave you my word, Micah. Now is not the time to doubt me.'

'If you were in the area, why didn't you stop them?'

'I had only four men with me, and I can't afford to make an enemy out of either Nash or DeMassey. You know that.'

'I knew this was a bad idea.'

'But it's too late to back out now.'

'Micah?' Sairead was frowning at him. 'You two know each other?'

'Yes, my dear, we do.' Before Micah could stop him, Gilbert added, 'Micah and I have become allies. Didn't he tell you?'

Her gaze didn't move from his face, her eyes pale and deep and full of half-imagined wrath. He would pay for this secret, as he'd paid for all the others – but he hoped that this time, the price would not be another life.

'Micah?' Her pale whisper sliced into the room. 'Please tell me this isn't true.'

He took her hand, pressed the back of it to his lips. 'Very well. Just remember that I love you.'

31

'I didn't know! I promise you, I didn't know anything about this until a week ago and it's taken me all this time to get the answers you needed. Do you really think I would lie to you after all these years?'

The hand around Osbert's throat tightened fractionally, cutting off the air supply. His face felt overlarge and swollen, his eyes ready to pop out of his head – and then just as suddenly, Nash released him and stepped back, his expression as dark as Osbert had ever seen it.

Free, Osbert brought his own hands to his throat in tardy protection and kept his silence as Nash turned away, pacing back down Osbert's study like a predator prowling for prey.

And just as it had been with Robert, Osbert could almost feel the power in the room with them, felt again the physical evidence that this man was a sorcerer, and more evil than he'd ever imagined.

Had he felt that same thing with Robert? He could hardly remember now. It had all become tangled up in a week and a half where he'd worked harder than ever before in his life, had struggled to give Godfrey some kind of weak explanation for his hours of incarceration, and then pushed himself to practise, rehearse and repeat the denials, go over any and all questions Nash might ask him, to memorise and engrave into his own mind the lies he would need in order to guarantee his survival, and indeed, that of the Guildehall.

He had waited until Nash came to him, waited until the information was forced from him with reluctance. Nash would believe nothing else.

He stood now, at the end of Osbert's table, hand on the polished timber, gaze fixed on the garnet ring he always wore, the stone of which seemed almost to glow in the wan afternoon light. He no longer bothered to wear the robes of a Guildesman, nor even the gold badge of a Governor. Instead, his clothes were as rich as any King's, the dark green fabric and black velvet trim displaying workmanship as fine as any Bishop's. The cloak sitting about his shoulders was lined with silky black fur, a diamond and gold brooch holding it at his throat.

But it was the face which gave so much away: those unremarkable features that had fooled Osbert and so many others into believing that Nash was what he seemed to be: innocent, unambitious, self-effacing, willing to serve for the honour of it. Osbert could take no comfort in knowing that he'd not been the only one caught in this trap. Now he watched those black eyes narrow, watched a hand run through short black hair – and he noted that the scars of his fight with Robert had disappeared completely.

Osbert almost flinched when Nash looked up at him again, the edge of a vicious smile playing about his mouth. 'And you looked?'

'Everywhere. I had men go through every book in the library in case they'd been hidden there under different covers. I've had all the mortars checked, the roof spaces searched, every room, every dormitory. I even had men probing the courtyard garden in case a chest of something had been buried there.' Osbert said no more. Too much elaboration would ruin the lie. Not that there was too much of a lie involved. After all, he *had* ordered a thorough search. He'd just already known beforehand that nothing would turn up.

A thread of fury was barely contained in his tight voice as Nash said, 'Then how do you explain the rumours?'

Osbert spread his hands. 'I cannot. Perhaps it's just the old fear of sorcery coming in after all those Hermit visions. I can tell you that they have nothing to do with the Guilde, or any books here. Or perhaps . . .'

Nash grunted, 'Perhaps?'

'Has it occurred to you that perhaps the rumours were begun by your enemy, Robert Douglas?'

At the look of surprise in Nash's eyes, Osbert almost wept with delight.

There was a moment of total silence, where even the noises of the city faded completely. For a time he stared at Osbert, dark eyes glinting with some neatly hidden anger. Then he nodded once, turned and stalked out.

Osbert almost wept with relief.

By the time they got DeMassey onto the bed, the bandages were ready to come off. Releasing his held breath, he eased himself back, rested his head against the wall and hoped the dizziness would wear off quickly. He heard one of his men shut the door on the tavern noises, another rummage in a saddlebag for more medicines and dressings.

He would be safe in here, they'd told him. The Two Feathers stood under the protection of the Malachi contingency at court, and all of them would swear allegiance to the Master of the D'Azzir long before they would to Nash or Kenrick.

So he was safe for the moment. But he was also in pain. He bore the usual minor cuts and burns, not unlike the men who had brought him here, but he also suffered a deep cut in his chest, which made breathing difficult, and which gave him a raging fever most nights. They'd begged him to wait, to rest a little before he returned to Marsay. Others, more quietly, had begged him to avoid Marsay altogether and head directly back to Karakham.

He could do neither, for he had sworn allegiance to Valena on the day he had given her his heart. He could no more abandon her than he could his own soul.

He hissed when they removed the old bandages and closed his eyes when fresh salves were applied. Then he watched them, these men, his trained D'Azzir – those who had survived to bring him back. They brought him a Healer who looked over his wounds, gave his advice and left a tonic and a poultice, but the glint in his eye said more than words.

The door opened again and Rayve, his youngest warrior, brought a tray of food in for him as the rest of his men quietly moved out. They would wait downstairs and do their best to protect him from whatever trouble might come in his direction.

As Rayve set his tray down, DeMassey shifted in his bed, finding a hand ready for him, eager to help.

He'd brought his people into this nightmare alliance with Nash – and yet they still showed him such blind loyalty it made his throat hurt.

Rayve held a cup for him to drink ale, broke off some bread and placed the bowl on his lap so he could soak it in juices from a wine-flavoured stew. He ate what he could, but swallowing was difficult and his stomach rebelled at every turn.

'That's all I can manage,' he said after a while, waiting until Rayve took the bowl away before sipping the ale once more.

He had choices. He could go to Nash now, giving up all hope in the process – but that would mean breaking every promise he'd ever made. He could run, get Valena away and hope that Nash might never find them – but that might mean he would lead Nash straight to her. Or he could try braving it out, and hope that Nash would not kill him for his failure.

Nash had never liked him, had always resented having to ask for help in the first place so many years ago. And there had always been the issue of Valena, something that had stood between them for more than twenty years.

Rayve moved to leave and DeMassey stopped him, making a decision in the space between one heartbeat and another. 'I want you to do something for me.'

'Of course, Master.'

'Sit.'

The boy returned to his stool and watched DeMassey with cool brown eyes. He'd done well on this mission, followed orders, hadn't panicked, had done his best to fight and protect his brother D'Azzir. He was the right man to trust with this task – the task upon which might rest the fate of both the Malachi nation and this entire country.

'I don't know how long I can hide out here,' DeMassey began carefully. 'If I'm lucky, I might get two days' rest before word will reach Nash of the fire at Maitland. After that, if I don't go to him, he will hunt me down.'

'We will protect you, Master. This failure was not yours.'

DeMassey couldn't help smiling a little at his passion. 'Nash will not see it like that. However, no matter what happens in the coming days, I want you to make me the most solemn oath, that you will carry out my instructions as though your very life depended on it. You must share this with nobody.'

Rayve's eyes widened at this. He sat up straighter, squared his shoulders and asked, 'What do you wish me to do?'

'If I'm dead, I want you to find Archdeacon Godfrey.'

'The priest?' Rayve asked faintly, as though DeMassey had just requested the moon in a handbasket.

'Yes, the priest. Find him and ask him to say prayers for my soul.'

'Prayers, Master?' The boy was schooled enough to show no more than a little surprise at this request. DeMassey offered no more information. Even trusting Godfrey was hard enough as it was. But he had to. This was not something he could force any of his own people to do, no matter how loyal they were.

And much as he hated to admit it, he couldn't be *absolutely* sure that all of his men were loyal. It would take only one traitor for him to lose more than just his life.

'Do I have your promise?'

Rayve nodded slowly. 'Of course, Master.'

'Thank you.' DeMassey rested back then, closing his eyes. He barely heard the door close behind the boy.

He would decide in the morning. He would not give in, but if he was rested enough, he would consider the possibility of running.

One peal of the bell followed another, long and deep, in time with Godfrey's heartbeat. He could feel it deep in his chest, rattling through his entire body, infecting him with the same air as the hum of prayers echoing about the bedroom.

It was almost crowded in here now. Though the doctors had been officially dismissed, they remained in the background, perhaps wishing to be present at the passing of a Bishop, a historic occasion at the best of times.

But this had never been the best of times. This moment would, he knew, remain for him as the worst of times.

The Archdeacons, Deacons and Abbots had come from

434

across the country, warned of what was to happen. The most senior knelt at the foot of the great bed, hands clasped together, chanting prayers. Beyond the open doors stood the others, holding candles in vigil.

Godfrey had long before found himself alone beside the bed, only Francis attending him from one hour to the next as they all waited, his solitude testament to their agreement that he would take up the mantle as Brome had demanded.

Like a terrified child, he watched each rise of that chest, each fall, hoping for the next rise, but knowing each one could be the last.

And then it was the last. Brome was dead.

The cloying scent of incense hung heavily in the room. Godfrey watched as one doctor came forward, placed a hand against Brome's throat, left it there for another long time. Then he stood back.

Godfrey bowed his head and tried to ignore the change in the prayers. He closed his eyes, but felt the movements around him as one priest after another came close to the bed, blessed Brome with the sign of the trium before filing out into the antechamber. Even so, he knew precisely the moment when he was alone.

He got to his feet, feeling his knees complain and wishing for the humour to argue with them. Without a qualm, he turned to Brome's still body, his memory extracting for him the promise he'd made to this man. His hand reached out, traced a final trium, saying farewell. Then he turned and faced the open doors and the solemn priests who awaited him.

Though no words had been said to him, he knew they would have made preparations for this moment. He knew how important this was, how urgent that he step into those shoes with the utmost expediency. And, strangely, now that Brome was dead, though he'd prayed this day would never come, he wanted this done as quickly as possible.

They made room for him as he came out, every man meeting his eyes with some variation of pride or acceptance. Either way, no matter Brome's decision, Godfrey knew they had agreed. They began to file out of the room, two abreast, walking slowly. He was caught up in the middle of them, another priest, walking to mass.

They'd prepared the chapel for this ceremony, as though they'd known all along that Brome would die in the middle of the night. Tall, thick candles surrounded the altar. Flowers decorated it, rich cloth draped over every surface. The air was cooler in here, allowing him to breathe a little – but only for a moment.

They brought him to a halt before the altar. The four most senior priests attended him then, removing his outer clothing, washing his hands and feet, drying him with the softest linen – all in complete silence. Then they began dressing him again, in new robes, and the priests behind him began to sing, a hymn he'd always been very fond of. The gentle, caressing sound of their voices soaked into him and he allowed himself to relax a little, to remember why he was here in the first place, to open his eyes and gaze up at the trium on the eastern chapel wall.

For love of the gods, he had become a priest. For love of duty and obedience, he had accepted one position after another, rising through the Church in the most turbulent of times. But it was for love of truth that he stood here this night, dressed in what would always be for him borrowed robes. Love of truth, and a desire, heartfelt and wrenching, for freedom.

The hymns changed, lifting him higher, to the place he needed to be. He barely shook as they began the ceremony, as they placed each symbol of his office in his hands, or around his shoulders. He gave the responses like a man born to it, his voice solid and sure. When they brought him the trium to kiss, he did so with all the love welling up in his heart. When they had him say mass, he did so with all the passion he had ever felt for the sacrament. When they laid their hands on his head, giving him their blessing, he felt the power of it filter through his entire body.

And when they turned him to face his brethren, when he saw the hope shining in their eyes, he could do nothing to stop the tears falling down his face at the mockery they had made of the primacy, of the blasphemer he had become, and of the crimes he had already committed against a man he held above all others.

'Forgive me,' he whispered, as they raised their voices once more in joyous celebration. 'Forgive me, Father Aiden.'

They led their new Bishop out of the chapel just as dawn began to break on a new day. As he caught the first flash of sunrise through the gallery windows, he could only pray that this was indeed the path to freedom.

32

Finnlay counted the days, one after another. He kept an eye out for landmarks that would tell him where they were and how much longer it would take to reach the Enclave. He watched each sunset as it fell, longing for sight of mountains and rock and still-frozen ice.

He felt as though they were being followed. No, not followed, chased. He kept asking Robert about it, and his brother would pause long enough to Seek thoroughly – but there was never any sign that they hadn't got away safely.

Some days, Finnlay felt like screaming. Others, he wanted to find the nearest hardwood tree and knock his head against it a good few dozen times – but the problem with that was Andrew at least would ask him why he was doing it, and framing replies for that boy would be more difficult than convincing his brother to lose his temper.

Once again he was merely a spectator, witness to an odd play unfolding before him. Jenn remained ill, unconscious for most the time. When she did wake, she knew none of them and what words she could speak were nonsense. Andrew stuck close by her, holding her hand, trying to get a little water past her lips, running and fetching anything Finnlay might need when attending to her wounds.

And Robert, dark, solid, walking like a thundercloud looking for a fit place to burst, stayed in the background, answering questions, posing few of his own and, when he thought Finnlay wasn't looking, reading from a book he kept tucked inside his jacket.

For three days they rode through into as much of the night as they could bear. Robert would carry Jenn with him, letting Finnlay take her when his horse needed rest. This morning, they had found a hostelry and bought a change of mounts so that even though the sun had set hours ago, they could still keep going. They were past the forests now, skirting the hills surrounding a lake he knew was out there somewhere. He had no choice about the route; instead, he had to trust Robert's Seeking abilities, to ensure they stayed away from villages and farms, once again travelling as though they were invisible, leaving few marks upon the land in their wake.

What had it felt like to be a free man? Fifteen years. So long that he hadn't even noticed.

'We'll stop here.'

Robert's voice cut into Finnlay's quiet horror. He swallowed hard, then slid off his horse, ready to begin the nightly ritual.

She didn't seem to be getting any better, though Finnlay assured him she was. But to Andrew's eyes, Jenn's face was just as pale in the daylight, her gasps of pain just as loud at night. More than once, Robert had knelt beside her, put his hand on hers and released enough power to ease that pain. Then she would quieten down, breathe more easily and rest properly.

It still felt like the journey was killing her.

Andrew attended to his tasks as Finnlay checked her wounds, though how he could see clearly in such bad light, he didn't know. But it was hard not to keep looking over his shoulder instead of gathering firewood, hard to trust that even though Finnlay wasn't trained, he still knew enough about Healing to keep her from getting sicker.

A flutter of panic rippled across his stomach. He turned away from the camp and stumbled downhill to where a few fallen trees gathered around the trunk of a standing one. He pulled at dried branches sticking up, breaking them off with as much force as he could manage, until he had a pile on the ground. But he didn't stop. He just jumped onto the trunk of the next tree and began kicking more branches clear. This was good work. This was physical, better than sitting on a horse all day and half the night, better than having to watch his mother die . . .

A last kick went wild, throwing his balance. With a half-strangled cry, he twisted sideways and fell, landing hard between the two trunks. Winded, he just lay there for a moment, trying to convince his chest to fill again. Then it did, and he heaved in one breath after another, holding onto a trunk with each hand. A little bruised, and feeling more than a little silly, he rolled to his knees and stood up.

A face greeted him in the darkness, eyebrows raised. Robert waited for him, sitting on the trunk he'd just fallen from. For a moment, Andrew didn't move. The moonlight was strong, filtering down through still-bare trees and bathing the hillside with a soft light.

'Running from it won't help. You do know that, don't you?'

'Oh?' Andrew snapped, scrambling onto the trunk and sliding down the other side. 'Is this where you give me the big speech on how to deal with fear?' When Robert didn't say anything, he looked over his shoulder to find himself alone. He clambered over the remaining logs until he reached the down-hill side of the standing oak.

Robert was waiting for him, leaning against the tree, his arms folded, looking out over the hills. Or at least, Andrew assumed that was what he was doing as it was too dark to see that far.

'How much do you remember of your father's death?'

Andrew stopped mid-stride, his mouth open in surprise. 'I . . . not very much. Why?'

'Indulge me.'

'I . . . I remember you on the battlements, fighting him. I thought you were going to kill him.'

'And?'

'And . . .' Andrew struggled. He hated talking about this, hated thinking about it more. But to talk he had to think – and remember. 'He'd been hurting Mother. I . . . I thought she was going to die. And then . . . then he was falling over the battlements and Mother and Father John pulled you up and you got us away.'

Robert turned to look at him sideways. 'But what of the moment when Jenn actually let loose the blast that killed your father. Do you recall that?'

Andrew felt his cheeks flush. He could only hope they were invisible in the dark. 'No. I do know she killed him to save your life.'

'Yes,' Robert murmured. There was enough echo of something to make Andrew frown – but before he could ask, Robert continued, 'Did you hate your father?'

'Hate him?' Andrew took a step back, shaking his head. 'What has that got to do with it? I barely remember him. I was just six when he died. Why are you asking me about him?'

'You asked the same questions of me. I wondered how you would speak of him. Forgive me if I have offended you.'

Andrew came to a halt a second time, forced to reappraise the man before him – the *ambiguous* man before him.

'It was not fear I wanted to talk to you about,' Robert said into the night. 'Instead, I wanted to discuss grief.'

It was suddenly very difficult for Andrew to breathe. He reached out and steadied himself against the tree, closing his eyes and bowing his head.

The voice came close, almost whispering in his ear. 'You cannot change it by not thinking it. You cannot make it go away by wishing it were gone. You cannot pretend they're still alive. Grief is a powerful force, and it will strike you down when and wherever it chooses. Do not deny it. And when it does strike, do not be afraid. Like any other power, it will spend itself and fade soon enough. You *will* survive it. Just don't be afraid of it.'

A hand pressed his shoulder and a tiny amount of power seeped into Andrew as though it were burning him. He twisted away, walking backwards, pointing his finger at the man who would change his life completely – again, for the second time! 'I'm *not* afraid of it! How I feel about my father has nothing to do with you! This is all your fault. If you hadn't . . . I wouldn't have been on that road and my mother . . . if she dies . . . Why can't you just leave me alone!'

He turned and ran then, ran up the hill and past the camp. He kept on running until he could barely see signs of the camp fire. Only then did he stop and catch his breath, falling on his knees because he wanted to pray.

But there was only one thing he wanted from the gods.

'Please, don't let her die too . . .'

She could hear them moving about, hear their voices. Sometimes they spoke to her. She couldn't understand what they were saying. She did know them, the three men in her life. Robert, Andrew and Finnlay. Where was Micah?

She felt so hot inside, like somebody had put a shovel of coals in her chest. And every time she moved, her whole side felt like it was tearing off. Or being clawed off.

Andrew was upset. She could hear that much. She needed to hold him, comfort him. Or perhaps he needed to hold her. But he was fourteen now, fifteen soon. Too old for such things. He was a man, not a child.

Sleep crept up, until the voices all sang together and she knew this was not those who travelled with her, but the one who was always with her. The Key said little, but its voice seemed so strong, stronger each day and it murmured, as though it had something important to tell her when she was well enough. She smiled in her mind, promising to listen.

She longed for the darkness, longed for the peace of sleep. Longed to hear the birds sing and leaves to bud on the trees. Longed to hold her son.

Longed to see Robert smile.

Soft cloud drifted across the moon hours after everyone had bedded down for the night. Robert sat with his back against a tree and watched frail filaments drape over the bright light, diffusing the disk, broadening the glow.

For once he had chosen a campsite on the edge of a sparse stand of trees, rather than within the shelter of a forest. This was the most cover he'd seen since the morning and Jenn had grown restless. He'd had no idea the view would be quite so incredible.

He could see clear across the valley, make out the line of brush at the bottom, the stone walling winding its way up the other side, the change in texture to heather along the eastern ridge, and then the darker, bluer shadows behind, hinting at more hills, taller, disappearing into forever.

He could hear birds, sometimes see their lightning-fast dash from one tree to another, a streak of black in the night that happened too fast for him to really see it. There were rabbits, too, sneaking out of burrows he hadn't noticed earlier. They crept onto the hillside, nibbled, ears and noses twitching, scurrying back underground at the slightest noise.

He tried not to, but he couldn't stop the parallel thought: this was so like the Enclave. It wasn't a fair comparison. Salti weren't frightened rabbits running for cover at the slightest sign of trouble – and they certainly had more weapons at their disposal than sensitive hearing alone. Even so, there was a shared attitude: the Enclave never got involved unless something directly affected it.

And why should it? Why care for a country, a people who would eradicate them if it could?

It was a matter of attitude. And a matter of fear.

He reached inside his jacket and pulled forth the book. He could have made a light to read by, but at the moment, he just wanted to look at it. On the pages was a text in ancient Saelic. Interesting, and certainly worth reading on its own, but there was nothing inside which indicated the purpose behind the book.

And how had it been changed into this shape? How had it remained safe all these centuries? How had it landed in the secret Guilde library at all?

Of course, if Amar Thraxis had really created the Calyx, and he'd done something to it to preserve and hide it from those who would abuse it, then having it stubbornly remain in this inert form was the perfect answer. Everything Robert had ever read about the Calyx supported this idea – but the question was, if it was hidden from those who would abuse it, how was it to be used by those who wouldn't?

And why hadn't he told Finnlay that he had it?

On the other side of the camp Finnlay lay wrapped up in his old travel blanket, the edges a little frayed with use now. His face was peaceful in sleep; Robert could make out fine lines around his eyes, some threads of silver through his hair and beard. They already looked the same age – soon, Finnlay would begin to look older than him.

Finn had been passionate about finding the Calyx all his life. Hadn't he been the one to push Robert into finding it? It had been his ideas that had led to their trip to the caves where Robert now hid his home, that had brought him to discovering the silver rod.

But the rod had been easy to uncover; the Calyx had given him one glimpse of promise, and then hidden from him.

Would it read that *he* was one who would abuse it? Was that why he couldn't tell Finn – because he would then have to admit he was afraid to change it permanently?

With a sigh, he slipped it back inside his jacket, doing up the buttons to keep it safe. As he rested his head back, he idly sent his Senses out once more, roaming the area, checking for pursuit or discovery.

He did this without thinking now. He didn't sleep, hadn't since the fight with the Malachi. He couldn't. Each time he tried, each time he closed his eyes, was worse than any nightmare. It was getting harder and harder to escape that cold, black, empty feeling inside where the demon thrived. The terror stole his breath away, made him struggle back to waking just so he could fill his lungs again, but the fight was so hard, taking forever and when he awoke, shaking, the thought of more sleep made him physically ill.

So he didn't sleep.

Unbidden, his gaze shifted down to where she lay beside him. She was curled up on her side, but as he watched, she turned, pushing the blankets back from her face, settling on her back. Robert waited a moment, then leaned down and pulled the blanket back up around her neck, his hand brushing against her chin as he withdrew.

She startled awake, her eyes wild, looking for safety in the unfamiliar night. Instantly Robert scrambled to kneel by her side, his hand out on hers, the other reaching for the bottle of water.

'It's all right,' he whispered, not wanting to wake the others. 'You're safe. Andrew's safe.'

Jenn blinked hard, frowning a little, before turning to look at him. 'Where are we?'

'Two days short of the Enclave. Can you sit up a little, try to drink something?'

She nodded and he put a hand behind her shoulders, easing her up to sit with her back against his tree trunk. Then he held the bottle for her to drink, letting her take small sips. When she'd had enough, she put her head back and closed her eyes for a moment. Then, in the silence, she said, 'What happened?'

'How much do you remember?'

'Of the attack? All of it. I was . . . protecting Andrew and . . .'

Quietly, Robert filled in the details, leaving his visit to Maitland until last, hoping to soften the blow. 'I'm sorry. There was nothing I could do. Nothing to be done. There were enough survivors to give them a proper burial, to take care of the injured and get them to safety. We couldn't stay longer, not with Malachi still in the area and with vengeance in their hearts.'

'Is that what it was?' Jenn whispered, turning her head to look at him. 'Simple vengeance?'

'They wanted Andrew.'

'Doesn't everybody?'

He'd hoped they could have this conversation some other time, when she was better. 'DeMassey and his Malachi didn't act on their own.'

'How do you know that?'

'What possible interest could they have in Andrew?'

'But why would Nash try to take him knowing that I'd come after him?'

444

Robert grunted laughter at that. The answer was so obvious. 'Because he wants you?'

'So Andrew was just a decoy? If so, then why has Nash waited until now? Why bother doing it on the road to Maitland? Why not just have him snatched at court, where nobody would notice? If he'd done it years ago, Andrew would have been a child, unable to defend himself.' Jenn paused in her attack and shifted slightly. 'Tell me, did the Malachi see you?'

'Yes, but they all fled soon after.'

'Then Nash will know you have come back.'

'Assuming he'd ever believed I'd gone in the first place.' Robert frowned. 'There was no way Nash would have ordered an ambush knowing either you or I were involved. The question is, why would Nash try to take Andrew without you knowing?'

Jenn said nothing then. She closed her eyes again, a deep frown on her forehead. After a moment, he asked, 'Are you in pain?'

'Yes. But nothing your powers can help with.'

He could see moisture glisten around her eyes, hear the sorrow in her voice. 'I'm sorry,' he said into the silence.

'Don't you dare blame yourself for this one,' she hissed, but without much venom.

Robert ducked his head, feeling the rebuke in places he'd thought had long since died. She'd always had an odd but incredible power over him. If it hadn't been for the vagaries of the Prophecy, and the involvement of Nash, Robert would have been just as happy to admit to it and never think of it again. But such luxuries were dangerous in these times, and to accept that power would be tantamount to surrender.

And to love her was to seal her destruction.

He looked up to find her staring out at the view, much as he had done, but there were tears falling down her pale cheeks. Robert said nothing then, leaving her to her thoughts, allowing her the moment he had encouraged in her son.

That boy had as much as lost his parents twice now – and yet, still not a tear from him.

And not a single glimpse of powers, despite the ambush.

'Where is Micah?' Jenn asked softly.

'I believe he told Finnlay he would follow a few days behind.'

'Because of you?'

Robert let his own gaze absorb the blue-black view, fading in and out as one set of clouds after another swept over the shifting moon.

'You need to talk to him, Robert.'

'I cannot if he is not here.'

'Don't be obtuse.'

'Don't be unrealistic.'

'Are you saying you will speak with him when you next see him?'

'You're assuming he wants to speak to me. He's known for the last eight years where to find me. If he'd wanted to talk, he would have before now.'

He looked at her to find her eyes more blue than he'd ever seen before, fixed on him: a midnight gaze, full of night and darkness, with no promise of the morning. She could, if she'd wanted to, bridge the gap between them – and that realisation brought Robert up cold.

For a moment he busied himself pulling the last of the bread from a saddlebag, carefully dipping it in a jar of honey. He handed it to her without meeting her eyes.

It was fortunate that he'd never married her, that he'd never had the opportunity to act on his instincts. As his wife, she would have torn him to shreds. As it was, as an ally, she made a formidable enemy.

'You have a fine son. You have every reason to be proud of him,' he murmured under his breath, listening for, and hearing her small gasp of surprise. Then, and only then, did he turn and face her again.

She was smiling at him. He couldn't help but smile back.

A formidable enemy indeed – but every enemy had a weakness. And Robert was learning to be ruthless.

33

He could feel it, sitting beneath his skin, worming its way into muscle and bone. A presence growing closer, lurking on the line where his awareness dwelt, neither in this world, nor the next.

He was that place where the two conjoined. The figure that walked between shadow and light, visible to neither. He was ready.

Of course he'd known, deep down, the choice would not be his to make. Nash was far too clever for that, would have been looking out for his return, Seeking him to see how close to Marsay he was, perhaps even thinking he might waylay the boy before he entered the city and thus avoid possible questions.

And there was no chance that his men, returning from their day in the city, would be sufficient to put up any real defence against Nash. Besides, Nash would insist he came only to find out how DeMassey was.

He could feel Nash getting closer, without benefit of See-king. It was almost dark now. DeMassey could see the last of the light fade from the window he'd had open all day.

He could hardly move. The potions and dressings, salves and bandages had all failed without the aid of a qualified Healer – and it would take far too long to find one. Much longer than the few precious minutes he had left.

He wished for more time. For better time. That he'd never offered to help Nash. That he'd never let Valena leave Karakham and follow after Nash, that he'd had the strength back then to open her eyes. He wished his own had been open, as they were now.

The door opened. He did not turn his head. The black mess in his room was not of his making. The door closed again.

'Your men are wary, DeMassey. What have you been telling them?'

'Nothing but the truth.'

'About me?'

'Are you afraid of the truth?'

'Aren't we all?'

This made DeMassey laugh and he began to cough. He struggled to sit up in bed a little, finally getting the hacking under control. Then he pointed to a cup sitting on a table by the wall. 'Would you?'

Nash glanced once at the cup, then at DeMassey. With obvious disdain, he passed it across. 'You failed. What happened?'

Settling back, he took in a long, steady breath to avoid another coughing fit. He closed his eyes, no longer willing to look. 'His mother.'

'She was there?' Surprised, he was now. As he would have been then – as he shouldn't have been.

'Yes. We didn't discover that until she tried to stop us taking Andrew. By then it was too late to withdraw.'

'But she saw you?'

'It doesn't matter.'

'Doesn't matter?' DeMassey could almost hear the frown in his voice. 'Why not? What have you done?'

'I did exactly what you told me to do,' DeMassey replied, knowing he was smiling, but unable to help it. He could almost see the fear fading before his eyes. 'Just like always. But your plan was flawed, just like always. You don't look before you push, do you? You think everything is just sitting there, waiting for you to pluck it out whenever you need it. I told you it wasn't a good idea to take him. You're a fool, Nash.'

Nash moved closer, his presence almost searing DeMassey's skin, burning him. 'What have you done!'

'What have *I* done?' DeMassey began to laugh. It was just so simple, so perfect, it was almost a farce. 'I think she died protecting her boy, and he with her. There was another Salti with her. Might have been the Douglas, or his brother. I didn't get a chance to look. But still, you know she died once before. Don't take my word for it this time. Go down there yourself and see.'

He was suddenly crushed by an enormous weight on his chest, forcing the air from him, killing his laughter, making his wound bleed profusely. He opened his eyes, fearless, and looked up to find Nash towering over him.

'You want me to kill you, don't you?' Nash roared and DeMassey knew there would be no help from his men. They would suddenly find it impossible to climb the stairs – and Nash would kill anyone who tried.

Nash clenched his fist in the air and a bolt of white-hot agony split DeMassey from head to toe. His body convulsed on the bed, then fell to twitching, spasms rattling through his muscles for long seconds after.

Nash came close again, his breath harsh-felt along De-Massey's aching flesh. 'You will not die until you give up your secrets. I know you have them. I've had you watched and followed. I've known you too long, Luc, since you were a boy. Known you'd never forgive me for taking Valena from you, for making her my own. Well, I let you have her, to keep you happy – and my reward is your secrets.'

'I have . . . no . . . secrets,' DeMassey managed, each word a trial in itself.

'Every man has his secrets, Luc. And I want to know yours. When you tell me, I will let you die peacefully. You know me to be merciful when it suits me.'

'I know . . . nothing of the kind.'

'Have you been spying on me? Passing word on to the Enemy? Is that what you've done? Betrayed me, betrayed your own people and crossed over?' When DeMassey didn't reply, Nash clenched his fist again.

The pain ripped through him like lightning, blinding him, forcing all the air out of his body, all the blood, all the will to live.

But he wasn't dead. And he wouldn't be. Nash could keep up this level of torture indefinitely. He did no damage to the body, but explored the depths of pain. DeMassey had seen him torture a dozen and more men in just this fashion over the years. He had always suspected that one day he himself would be subject to the same treatment.

449

'What have you done?' Nash hissed again, his anger making his voice ragged. 'Tell me!'

'Tell you . . . nothing . . . monster.' His vision was gone completely now and he could feel nothing in his hands and feet. 'Too late. My secrets . . . safe from you. Promised you . . . would never know . . .'

He did feel hands on his shoulders then, shaking him, questions spat in his face. Then something was picked up, sniffed, then thrown across the room and he knew this last secret, at least, had been discovered.

The blow to his face felt like a caress compared to the agony in the rest of his body. But he was detached from it now, floating an inch above it, still able to feel it, but not experience it.

'You will not die until I say so!' Nash grabbed him again, lifting him from the bed, shaking him. 'You will tell me! What are you hiding? What are you protecting? Is it Douglas? Jenn? Andrew? Kenrick? It's Kenrick, isn't it? You've made an alliance with him . . . no . . . Malachi? Is that it? Damn it DeMassey! You *will* talk!'

And he felt it again, a pushing deep within his gut, an overwhelming urge to speak, to let the truth fly into the evening air, where he could rejoice in it once more before he died.

'Not . . . my secret . . .' he managed. And the breath left him then, wheezing out of his body with no force at all until he was left empty. He felt Nash drop him back to the bed, felt him step back, heard another whispered curse. He could feel the venom tingling in the air that brushed over his skin, feel the evil that had been born with this man soaking into the floorboards at his feet, into the plaster walls and timber furniture. Felt it float on the breeze, and out through the window, venturing into the cold spring night.

And then Baron Luc DeMassey felt no more.

'Forgive me, Your Grace.'

The words, once familiar from his own mouth, now fell sharp about his ears, like icicles in a winter storm. Godfrey

450

looked up from the desk strewn with papers and focused tired eyes on the monk before him. 'Yes, Brother?'

'There is a man to see you. He says the matter is of the gravest importance.'

Godfrey did his best not to sigh. Bishop barely two days and already the demands weighed on him. He'd been besieged with requests to see people since the announcement of Brome's death had been made at mass yesterday morning. He'd tried to keep up with the interviews, but he'd had less than five hours' sleep last night – and he still had no idea what that business with Osbert had all been about.

Then this morning he'd had his first audience as Bishop with Kenrick.

'Did this man give you a name?'

'No, Your Grace. But he insisted that he must see you immediately, tonight.'

'Very well. Is he outside?'

'Yes, Your Grace. Should I bring him in?'

'Please.' Godfrey reached out for his cup of brew, but it had gone cold since he'd last looked at it. The piles of papers on the desk had not budged since he'd sat down to go through them. Even with expert help in the form of Francis and Ohler and a dozen others, the work of the Bishop had been largely neglected for the last few years. Godfrey could only pray that he was up to tackling some of it.

The door opened again and the monk led a young man into his new study. The man came forward, bowed a little awkwardly, then glanced nervously at the monk.

'How can I help you?' Godfrey began, smiling a little, hoping to put the man at ease. He did look vaguely familiar; Godfrey was sure he'd seen him somewhere around at court.

'Yes, Father . . . I'm sorry. I am unfamiliar with your ways. But I come on behalf of my master, on his instructions.'

'Your master?' Godfrey raised his eyebrows.

'The Baron Luc DeMassey, Father.'

Godfrey felt faint. A flush of heat spread across his neck.

'He asked me . . . to come see you. To ask you to say prayers for his soul.'

Without realising it, Godfrey had risen to his feet. 'Then . . . he is dead?'

'Yes, Father,' the young man said, his expression grim, eyes dark with deep sadness. 'He begged that I ask for your . . . intervention.'

'Of course,' Godfrey replied. He'd given it so little thought in the beginning, when there were so many questions that appeared to be without answer. Now the moment had come and he had no idea what he should do, or why.

DeMassey was dead.

'Please, accept my condolences. I know the Baron was held in the highest regard.'

The young man narrowed his gaze then, as though deeply surprised to hear such words from a priest – especially one who would now know him to be a sorcerer – but Godfrey had gone beyond such things in the last few weeks, or months. Or probably years. Yes, that would be closer. Somewhere around the time he became friends with Robert. From that point on, his life had completely failed to be predictable.

Not sure that it would be welcome, Godfrey refrained from signing the trium in the air and blessing the young man. 'I will order prayers said at mass tonight and in the morning. Also for the rest of the week.'

'Thank you.' The young sorcerer bowed again, then turned and left. When the door closed, Godfrey was once more alone.

In a daze, he moved to the fireplace and took down the wooden box he'd put there only that morning. He placed it on the desk and pulled out the key which hung around his neck. Unlocking the box felt wrong. Extracting the pouch felt terrible. Sliding out the letter and breaking the wax seal on it set off a wave of panic rolling in his stomach and he had to pour a healthy measure of wine and swallow half of it before he could bring himself to take the letter to one of the candles standing on the mantel.

He didn't know what the letter contained. He knew only of its importance, that responsibility of another sort entirely had been left with him, courtesy of a now-dead sorcerer who had chosen Godfrey because he was a 'good' man.

Godfrey drained the rest of the wine, put the goblet down, then carefully unfolded the letter. There were two pages.

You will read this knowing I am dead. Take no longer than necessary to read my instructions. I cannot stress more how precious time is in this matter. You must leave immediately, telling no one where you go, nor what you do. Absolute secrecy and speed are the only hopes I have of success.

I have included for you instructions on how to reach this place, and what you must do. I have also explained why it must be done, as I understand that, for you, this task goes against everything you believe in – but still, you must do it. I know you will. This is why I have trusted you. I know you are not merely a man of the cloth, but a good man, who has been willing to fight for a long time. I now give you the best, most unique opportunity to do so. Such an opportunity will not come again. If you fail, however, the consequences will be most dire and I can assure you, your hero will not be able to save your country from what will follow.

In closing, allow me to beg your forgiveness for asking this of you. You are my last, most desperate hope. Though you will commit this mortal sin, your gods, I believe, will bless you for your courage and perhaps even forgive you.

Good luck.

A vicious wind whipped around Nash's legs as he went down the steps into the courtyard and he pulled his cloak out of the way to avoid tripping over it. Half a dozen of his Bonded Malachi were already mounted up and waiting, their horses stamping impatiently on the damp cobbles, feisty and ready for the morning's adventure.

Nash took the reins held out to him by Taymar. 'How long ago did he leave?'

'Less than an hour, Master. He was waiting at the gates when they opened this morning.'

'And you are certain he was alone?'

'Positive. Saylin follows at a discreet distance. If you Seek for him, you will find the Bishop.'

Nash swung up into his saddle.

'Master, what should I tell the King if he asks for you?'

Snorting with disdain, Nash looked up at the castle keep. 'Tell him I'm busy.' With that, he pulled on his reins, turning his horse for the gates. With a hard kick, he launched into a canter. He didn't look to see if his men followed.

'Are you *sure*?' Kenrick leaned forward, his elbow resting on the table, his body strung tight, his meal forgotten. 'That's what this man said? Exactly?'

'Yes, Sire, that's exactly what he said.' Forb'ez stood before Kenrick, his shock of white hair cropped short, his face scarred, his body lean and more bent than he remembered. This man had once been his father's most trusted aide, but his father had died alone on the battlefield, this man nowhere to be found.

Now, without warning, Forb'ez approached him with this story of how he had been drinking in the Two Feathers, had in fact made a habit of doing so, because that was where Malachi were to be found, and Forb'ez blamed those people for Selar's death.

Kenrick could not begin to tell him how true that was.

So Forb'ez had overheard a conversation, repeated many times, voiced in shock. DeMassey was dead and greatly mourned, but also, there'd been a fight in the south and others had died.

A fight at Maitland, and amongst the dead was his own cousin, Andrew.

The words echoed about the room, dull and lifeless. His fingers felt numb and this taste swirled through his mouth of milk and sweet honey, some vague scent of spices on the air.

Andrew dead? How? Had DeMassey orders to protect Andrew? If so, why? From whom?

If not – then why had DeMassey been there in the first place?

'Are these Malachi still in the Two Feathers?'

'No, Sire,' Forb'ez shook his head. 'As far as I could tell, they planned to take the Baron's body back to their home, wherever that is.'

Kenrick sat back. Why had the Malachi been there in the first place?

There was only one possible reason – Nash must have sent them, but why? To kill his cousin? To remove some imagined rival for the throne?

But to kill Andrew to do it? The boy was more harmless than his sickly milk drinks! What would be the point in killing him?

He got up from his chair and paced the length of the table, heading for the windows. He was missing something obvious.

'Where is Nash?' he demanded of his nearest guard.

'Gone from the city, Sire.'

'For how long?'

'He did not say, Sire.'

Did not say? As though he answered to nobody – not even Kenrick?

Still, it was hard to believe that Andrew was dead, that anyone could want him dead, or even wish him harm. And if Nash *had* done something . . .

Kenrick turned from the window and gestured towards Forb'ez. 'You will join my guard. I want twenty men saddled and ready to head south with me in an hour – but keep quiet about it. No fanfare, no warning. Can you manage that?'

The older man bowed deeply, obviously expecting just such a commission as reward for his information. 'Of course, Sire. As you wish.'

Godfrey prayed as he rode, bitter, heartsick, hopeful prayers that did nothing to ease his conscience. He could almost feel the growing displeasure of the gods as he left the city, choosing the quickest route up through the hills and into a valley he'd never seen before, away from the trade roads, away from the river traffic. He could feel the gods in the wind which tore at him from every direction, biting into him with spring cold running deeper than any winter chill. He could hear it in the howl burning across his numb ears, snatching the breath from his mouth, freezing his hands on the reins, terrifying the skittish horse.

He shouldn't be doing this. All the years he'd worked, all the effort gone into keeping his position, into holding onto a place whereby he could work for the greater good without losing his own head, or that of anybody else. All that time, he'd been so sure it was the right path, because he'd felt it in his heart, known, from his first breath, what good was, what evil was, and which side he would always make his home on.

And now he was going to sacrifice one to fight the other. How had this happened? How had he allowed himself to believe that he, unlike anyone else, would come through this battle untainted by sin?

But what should he do? Turn back for the city, pretend he'd never read that letter, pretend that he didn't know what would happen?

DeMassey had known what he was about, choosing Godfrey. Wise and perceptive. He'd known Godfrey would do this, get on his horse, hurry out here after memorising the directions, the story, the instructions, before burning them and crushing the ash left behind.

But even now, an hour into his journey, he still wasn't sure . . .

He had to. If DeMassey was right – and he was, Godfrey was certain about that much – then he had no choice. This had to be done and Godfrey was the only man alive who could do this.

Nausea rumbled in his stomach, the same that had kept him awake all night, counting each shift of the secretive moon which had drifted behind one cloud after another, grey and distant. He'd swallowed one mouthful of water after another, praying his horror would die down and let him perform his task, but, fool that he was, he'd known all along that this horror would never leave him. It would stay until he'd done it, and remain with him to the end of his days.

The valley ended, turning him into a lane between fresh-sown fields which flattened out. Beyond were more low hills, trees on some of them, a house on another. He turned towards it, urging his horse to hurry, because for all that this was secret, there was no guarantee he had more than these minutes before he would be stopped.

His lips continued to move in prayer, but he could no longer focus on the words. He rode straight past the house and down the hill, heading for a stretch of ancient forest of gnarled trees swept by too many easterly winds.

Odd that this place should be so close, that DeMassey had taken the risk . . . But this place could simply be another in a long line of hiding places, designed to outwit Nash, to keep him from his greatest goal. For a moment last night, reading through DeMassey's explanation, he *didn't* believe. But a moment later, some scent in the air, some configuration of candlelight against the ceiling, had made him think of Robert, of how he'd stood amidst the ruins of Elita and admitted that it had been his power that had caused so much destruction in the space of a few moments.

Anything that could be imagined could be true.

And so he turned his horse into the forest, slowing, catching his breath, giving the animal its head to pick a path between knotty roots and mossy rocks covering the ground.

Not too much longer and he should be there. He looked once back the way he'd come, praying that he would still be alone on this journey. It was answered in the empty landscape behind him.

It was darker here, where some trees kept their leaves through winter. Godfrey found the stream. He crossed it, going up a steep slope littered with brown beech leaves scattered like thoughts across the barren ground. Further up the slope again, and then down the other side.

And there it was: the cottage, sitting alone. A thirsty stream of smoke rose from the chimney; a solid storehouse stood to one side, with a vegetable garden ranging out into a clearing in the trees, soaking up what sunlight this place could afford.

It all looked so peaceful.

Godfrey slid down from his horse and walked around the garden, approaching the house with great care, as he'd been warned. He left his mount to wander as he walked up to the door. He didn't knock. Instead, the door opened for him, the shadows within initially hiding the face of the woman who stared at him. Then she came forward, both hesitant and confident at the same time.

He knew her. Her face was one of extraordinary beauty, even now, hair of honey gold and eyes dark to contrast. She wore a gown of simple colours, though the quality of the cloth was high. The grace she had been so well-known for still shone from her eyes, visible in the gentle curve of her lips˜ as she raised her eyebrows in question.

Lady Valena Cerianne. The woman who had, for many years, been Nash's closest companion, his . . . whore. Until she'd gone to share Selar's bed, and helped Nash control him with the secrets of her body.

But he could see none of that history in her eyes now. Instead, he saw her as DeMassey had drawn her: gentle, kind, loving – and in danger.

'Can I help you, sir?'

A voice like sweet wine made him shudder with his purpose. 'I'm sorry, my lady,' he swallowed. 'I'm . . . I'm Godfrey.'

It took a second for his words to register. Then her eyes widened. 'By the blood, no! Luc, no!' Another second flashed by as those eyes filled with tears, as a hand came up to her mouth, as the shock of sudden and terrible loss filtered through her. Then she looked up at Godfrey again, forcing her attention, blinking hard, nodded, moving back. 'Come in. We don't have much time. I . . .'

She stumbled slightly as she led him inside, but he didn't dare reach out to steady her. He had no idea what to expect. DeMassey had said they'd agreed this, between the two of them, both acknowledging there was no other answer . . . But how could two people make that kind of decision? How could they, in the cold light of day . . .

'This way.'

Lady Valena took him past a staircase and into a short corridor. On the left was a door and she paused at this, steadying herself, pushing grief back to a place where it wouldn't interfere with her purpose.

Godfrey's hand was on her arm before he knew it, squeezing

458

gently. She looked up at him, eyes red, face damp from where she'd brushed hopeless tears away. 'He loved you.'

'I know,' she whispered, nodding desperately. 'As I loved him.' Her hand moved to grasp his. 'Please forgive us and what we ask of you. Luc was right, I can't do this myself. Not after . . . not now he's . . . gone. But please, Father, I beg you . . . do it quickly?' She paused again, swallowed hard and whispered, 'Do it now.'

Compassion flowed out of Godfrey, through his heart and his hands. He couldn't deny this love, the love DeMassey had had not only for this woman, but his people as well.

But his hands shook. His heart shook. His soul trembled as he turned to the door. Lady Valena opened it for him, preceded him in as though to soften the blow of his first sight.

The room was furnished simply, a cupboard by one wall, a window on another, a fine bright rug on the floor by the bed. A small bed, built out of honey cedar by hands skilled and artful.

On the bed lay the child. A girl, DeMassey had said. Thea. Eight years old.

'She won't wake for a while yet,' Valena murmured, looking tenderly down on her daughter. 'She's been getting worse over the last few months. She doesn't sleep at night and so must nap during the day. I give her a draught in the mornings some-times, when she's had a bad night. She'll . . .' Valena caught herself, nodded. 'I'll hold her.'

Carefully, the mother slipped an arm behind the child, lifting her shoulders. Valena then settled on the bed behind Thea, drawing the girl into her arms, letting her head rest back against the shoulder. She pressed a kiss to a pale temple.

Godfrey could hardly breathe. His heart pounded frantically in his chest, threatening to kill him. His hands were steady, though – they had to be.

He looked once more at Valena. 'If you would say no, then do so now.'

'No!' Valena shook her head, more tears spilling down her cheeks, unheeded now. 'No, Father, please don't ask that of me. I can only do this because I made a vow to Luc. He has died to protect me, so that you could do this. I care not what happens to me after this – but you must not falter. *You* must not doubt. Or would you rather Nash be allowed to get his hands on her? Would you rather he used his own daughter's blood to regenerate? He *needs* this prophecy to unfold! Thea would be enough for him, don't you see? Would you bring eternal destruction down on your own people?'

Godfrey came closer, kneeling down beside the bed in a gesture much like prayer. His voice emerged thick but steady. 'I will not falter. I gave my word to Luc. But I must know, for my own conscience – are you certain she is Nash's child?'

Valena blinked back more tears. 'You can see it in her face, in her eyes. I'd hoped she'd be Luc's. I thought she was . . . until she was born. Until I saw what she could do and how . . . the power burns through her like a disease. She does things she doesn't even understand, hurts people without thinking about it, and when she does think about it, she does it anyway, so she can see what happens. I can barely control her now, and only with the help of these draughts. Luc was always better at dealing with her. He wanted to get her out of Lusara, but moving her is so difficult. And now that Luc is . . . Luc is . . .' Valena frowned and looked up, her hands smoothing the dark hair back from Thea's forehead, raw courage shining in her eyes. 'Please, Father. Don't wait.'

With tears of his own now filling his eyes, Godfrey reached inside his cloak and drew out the dagger he had brought for this purpose. The blade, long and sharp, glinted in the daylight coming through the window.

He would rather have done almost anything than this – but he would not falter now, would not fail them.

But his hands still shook as he raised the blade, as he pressed the tip against the child's breast, over her heart. And his voice shook as he fumbled for a prayer for the girl's soul, cursed without her say, and for the child's mother, who needed her dead, and for himself, a priest who had agreed to commit murder.

His muscles tensed, gathering the force required. He held his breath, pausing between moments. With a cry of his own, he thrust down, the blade biting into flesh, slicing, bleeding, grinding against bone, cutting through resistance as the child rose up against such violence, but sank back again as the hilt stopped against her chest. And a silent wail from the child's mother as she pulled the girl to her, rocking, letting the blood flow over her, letting it soak into the sheets and blankets rather than have it feed Nash and give him the eternal life he'd always wanted.

And then all sound stopped when the door behind them crashed open.

34

Andrew felt no relief as they finally reached the foothills of the Goleth, and began to climb into the frosty mountain morning, where it didn't so much rain as fill the air with a permanent damp mist that soaked into everything and made even the horses cold.

They didn't go via a route he knew; instead, Robert led them up to a steep pass and then onto something of a plateau. He said it was a much harder journey, but it would cut hours off their trip from this direction.

So Andrew had followed along, staying as close to his mother as he was allowed to get – which sometimes became quite difficult. She made an effort to ride on her own, but lasted little more than two hours before the pain became too much. They would stop then and she would sit in front of Finnlay. He would hold her so she could relax back against him, then Robert would work his powers and again dim the pain that etched lines around her mouth and eyes.

But there were no kind words between his mother and Robert. Instead, they had settled into a kind of punctuated silence, where comments were exchanged for travel purposes only, and yet still seemed to have some other meaning behind them. Of course, nobody had ever told him his mother and his hero were enemies, had they? It made his head ache.

And Finnlay's too, by the look in his eyes.

Andrew longed for the gate to appear on the trail before

them, for the safety of the Enclave, where nothing could get in and nobody could ever find them. Where he could find a space of his own and do some thinking.

Outside of that odd silence, all else appeared as normal as he could expect, considering his aunt and uncle had just been murdered, along with the gods knew how many others. Considering Nash was now after him for reasons he still didn't really understand. Considering he was now almost as much a prisoner of the Enclave as any other Salti.

It was almost dark by the time Robert paused on the trail and turned to look at Finnlay, who still held the sleeping Jenn. Andrew rode beside him, his eyes darting from the gate up ahead, to Finnlay, and then to Robert.

'So,' Finnlay began playing with his reins before looking up, 'are you coming in this time? Or are you going to ride off as usual?'

To Andrew's surprise, Robert smiled. 'After all these leagues, you can still ask me that?'

Finnlay didn't smile back. 'Yes, I can.'

Robert peered up at the mountain above, or what he could see of it. 'Then let's go in before I change my mind.'

Finnlay rolled his eyes, but he was smiling when he turned back to the path and took them through the gate.

There was a huge fuss on the other side. Enclave scouts had been on the lookout, boys came to take the horses, Councillors and Healers came to help Jenn, installing her on a stretcher they insisted on using. Andrew followed along behind her, finally relieved that they were safe now, but more unsettled than he'd been the entire trip.

Everyone moved inside, a mess of voices all talking at once, men taller than him and children smaller, and everybody was trying to get around him, or get to Jenn – but almost everybody wanted to get close to Robert and followed him, calling questions out to him, the air of excitement completely unmistakable and totally out of place.

But when Lady Margaret came around the corner, cried out for Robert, tears of joy in her eyes, and when Robert left everyone else and swept her up in a hug that didn't end,

Andrew couldn't stand watching any more. He ducked into the nearest corridor and ran until he was hopelessly and thankfully lost.

Robert tried not to hear the voices around him, the darkness, the shadows, the memories and the guilt. He just wanted to hold on for a few minutes, that was all, but it wouldn't work. He couldn't keep track of the feeling long enough to identify it – and he needed to, or he would lose ground.

His mother was crying. Her tears were damp against his cheek, her soft skin cool to the touch. And her tears touched him deeply, her relief, her gratitude, her hope, all emerging in those gentle sounds made close to him, within the protection of his embrace.

Panic reared up in him and he let her go as quickly as he dared. It was simply too dangerous to hold on for too long, too dangerous to even be here.

He watched his brother hug and kiss his daughters, all three of them, embrace his wife, and saw the smile in Fiona's eyes at her husband's return. Helen gave him a heartfelt hug, full of so much pride it made his gut ache.

Though he was included in the warmth and the welcome, though he received kisses and hugs from all his nieces, and Fiona, he still couldn't entirely suppress a sharp pang of pure demon-loving envy, that Finnlay had all this, all that Robert had ever wanted. And that envy drove him away more quickly than anything else.

He found his room after asking a few directions. Everything inside the Enclave seemed to have changed around. Now Finnlay and Fiona had larger caves, with enough space for their daughters and for Margaret. His mother had moved her things in with the girls, giving him her room. He escaped into it with a sigh of relief, closing the door softly against the turmoil.

He needed rest. He needed to know he could close his eyes and nothing would happen. He needed to know that those around him were not depending on him Sensing any danger approaching.

He needed to know how to sleep.

He pulled off his cloak, draped it over a chair and slowly undid the laces of his thick winter jacket. He pulled out the Calyx and laid it under his pillow. Only then did he gingerly take the jacket off, favouring his wounded side, trying not to hiss at the pain.

In the morning, he would ask Arlie to stop by. A real Enclave Healer would surely be able to help where other doctors had failed.

In the morning. After he'd slept.

He sat carefully on the bed, leaning back a little so he could rest his head against the wall. He closed his eyes.

He'd failed. He'd completely underestimated both Nash and the Malachi. People had died. Andrew had almost been taken and Jenn had . . .

His eyes snapped open and he gasped in breaths that made his side hurt.

Andrew was right; it was all his fault. The worst part about it was, he'd do the same again.

'How does that feel now?'

'Much better. Thank you.' Jenn closed her eyes and breathed in the familiar smells of her rooms inside the Enclave. She could hear Martha pick up the bowls of washing water and the travel-stained clothes. She did her best not to urge Martha to leave everything.

Leave her in peace. Leave her alone.

Martha returned to sit on the bed beside her. Jenn opened her eyes. Her wounds had been freshly dressed before Martha had helped bathe her. Now, wearing clean clothes, her injuries healing, and close enough to the Key to feel its support, she could no longer ignore the reality that even now walked the corridors of the Enclave, leaving more questions in his wake than answers, as always.

'I take it you want me to call a council meeting for the morning?'

'Please. There is news I need to tell them and then, perhaps, Robert will want to . . . I don't know. You could ask him. I really don't have any idea what his plans are, so . . .'

'So I should ask him?' Martha asked. She leaned forward and took Jenn's hand. 'I'm very sorry about Bella and Lawrence.'

'Thank you,' Jenn squeezed the hand, not wanting to talk about this right now. Nor did she know what she did want to talk about. Or perhaps it was that she was trying to talk to the wrong person.

Martha let the quiet grow, leaving the peace before them, light on the air.

'I don't understand,' Jenn whispered, feeling the words drawn out of her by the silence. 'I don't see how he can just . . . formulate these plans, order people's lives, without a thought to what they want, what they're afraid of, what they're capable of. And nobody . . . *nobody* denies him. Nobody ever says no. They need his . . . confidence, his certainty. They want the kind of leadership that brooks no discussion, so they crowd around him every time he comes here, their eyes shining, laughing with him, anxious and eager for whatever challenge he has for them. That's what they want in a leader. Exactly the talents I *don't* have.' Jenn stared at nothing for a few seconds more, then blinked and looked up at Martha. 'I wish I knew what was going to happen. I wish I knew what to do. I wish I could trust him the way you do.'

'And I wish he could trust you the way we do.'

Surprised at that, Jenn asked, 'What does that mean?'

'It means that you're too hard on yourself. You always have been,' Martha replied. '*You* were the one chosen by the Key to be Jaibir, not Robert. And *you* have been the one here for the last eight years, dealing with the aftermath of the Battle, dealing with the discontent, the restlessness—'

'To the point where five children went wandering off on their own? How is that an achievement?'

Martha shook her head. 'It's an achievement when those children have the confidence and skills to make it as far as they did. It's an achievement when they could find the courage to do it. So they chose a bad time, and a bad place—'

'I failed to make them understand, and Liam died because of it.'

'Their parents failed in that, Jenn. You're not responsible for the thoughts of every Salti here.' Martha paused a moment, then added, 'Robert can't take your place, Jenn.'

Jenn stiffened at that, but didn't pull away. Martha had always been far too good at reading her moods, at knowing what to say and when to say it. In too many ways, Martha had become the sister Bella had refused to be, and that hurt.

'You know, I don't know what's going to happen.'

Martha shrugged. 'Does that matter?'

It was a good question. Unfortunately, she had a good answer to accompany it: she'd seen the demon inside him, and the way he still refused to deal with it. She saw the temptation in his eyes, the reluctance in his words. Too much conflict and too little resolution. For Robert, every direction he turned was an opportunity to make the Prophecy come true. With the demon unchained inside him, he was now running towards it, blind and deaf.

'With Robert, yes. It matters more than anything else.'

Finnlay rapped on the door twice, but didn't wait for a reply. He just pushed it open and stepped inside, almost slamming it shut behind him.

'By the gods, Robert, you have some gall!'

'What? What have I done now?'

'What have you done? All innocence, is it?'

Robert struggled to sit up. Finnlay barely glanced at him. 'I'm trying to get some rest, Finn. I'm tired.'

'Yes, I know. You basically haven't slept since we left Maitland, which in itself is a piece of stupidity! Now, do you want to tell me what's going on, or am I going to have to beat it out of you?'

'Going on?'

Finnlay came around the bed and stood with his hands on his hips, forcing Robert to look at him. 'You're through the gate all of five minutes, long enough to let everyone see you've come back – and then you run off and hide in here.'

'I told you, Finn, I'm tired.'

'So tired that you couldn't have spent another few minutes with everyone? With your nieces? Helen is convinced you don't like her any more, and everybody else thinks that either there's something very wrong with you, or you have terrible news to impart.'

'What?' Robert did push himself up then, frowning at his brother. 'Why would they think that?'

'Why?' Finnlay's eyebrows rose in disbelief. 'Have you honestly got no idea at all why people would think that? Robert, they look up to you! They wait for your visits, often planning their lives around your work. They take your lead in so many things – and it doesn't occur to you that your hasty departure would make them worried? Are you joking?'

Robert stared at him without blinking. Then he let out a long sigh. Carefully, he swung his legs over the side of the bed and sat up. 'You're right. I'm sorry. I'm just not thinking . . .' He reached down for his boots, but the pain made him gasp. Finnlay put a hand on his shoulder, keeping him in his place.

'Robert? Don't you think it's time you talked about it?'

'About what?'

Finnlay wanted to sigh, but didn't dare. His brother looked so fragile; it scared him. As soon as he left Robert, he'd get him a sleeping potion. 'Talk about whatever it is that's scaring you.'

'Serin's blood!' Robert groaned softly.

'You can trust me, Robert, I swear.'

'Don't swear. You have loyalties to other people before me. Your family, for one.'

'Oh, and you think Jenn is the other? This is just great, you know? Now I've got both of you doubting me because of my relationship with the other. And once again I'm stuck in the middle, unable to do or say anything, but having to put up with suspicion being levelled against me all the same. Well, so what if I have other people? Don't you? Doesn't every man? Or is that what you wanted from Micah – and that's why you had to get rid of him, because he fell in love and developed another allegiance?'

'Stop right there, Finn!' Robert shook his head, holding his hands up in warning. 'You have no idea what you're talking about.'

'Micah made a *mistake*, nothing more. A simple mistake. You've made enough of them yourself. You should know.'

Robert levered himself to his feet. He made his way to the other side of the small room, to the table placed against a rough-hewn cave wall. He poured wine from a jug and sipped it.

The brother inside Finnlay didn't want to push, could see that Robert was slipping closer to the edge – and had been since the Malachi attack. But the brother in him also wanted to push, to make something happen, to make Robert take the help he needed.

'What are you afraid of, Robert?'

'You know damned well what I'm afraid of, Finn!' Robert snapped.

'No, I know what you *used* to be afraid of. Now, all I see is a man who just keeps running and running. Are you afraid of facing Nash? Of losing to him?'

'No! Damn it, Finn, leave it alone!' Robert kept his back to Finnlay, his shoulders square and rigid. 'I told you before, Nash doesn't scare me. He probably should, but he doesn't. I'll bet I don't scare him, either. And if he kills me, well . . .'

'Then,' Finnlay moved closer, the truth suddenly and horribly obvious, 'you're afraid of winning.'

Robert said nothing.

'Your hand will change the world. That's got to be just a little frightening. It would be to me, and I don't have the Word of . . .'

Slowly, Robert turned and faced him, his gaze flat and unrevealing. So close now, Finnlay had to finish this.

'You're afraid of what happens if you do beat Nash. Is that why you need Andrew?'

Robert's voice gave away nothing. 'I *have* to beat Nash. There is no other option.'

'And the Prophecy says—'

'This has nothing to do with the Prophecy.'

'No?'

'No.'

'Then what?'

The answer was long in coming. Robert, breathing shallowly, moved around Finnlay and headed back to his bed. 'This isn't about the Prophecy, Finn. It's about power.'

'Serin's blood,' Finnlay swore, shaking his head at his own stupidity.

'Ah,' Robert sighed lightly. 'He understands at last.'

'You're afraid of the demon having so much power. And if you've had to sacrifice Jenn in order to beat Nash, there'll be nobody left to stop you, will there?'

Robert barely listened. Instead, he rolled over onto his good side, pulled the pillow close and shut his eyes.

'So what are you going to do?'

'Me?' Robert replied, his words faint. 'I'm going to try to sleep.'

Andrew hung around outside the workroom, watching people go in and out, listening to the background noise of the Enclave, remembering what it was like to be here before he . . .

But he couldn't go home again.

Unless of course he could somehow get to Kenrick first. With the King's protection, Nash wouldn't dare do anything to him, would he?

'Andrew?'

He looked up and came away from the wall as Arlie emerged from his workroom.

'Is something wrong? You want me to have a look at your cuts?'

That was as good a reason as any. Andrew followed the Healer as he went back inside. He sat where he was directed and looked around at the shelves and benches which lined the cave, lined themselves in bottles and jars, in wooden cases and boxes of potions and dried herbs and lotions and poisons and spices for uses that he couldn't even imagine, let alone understand.

But at least he could see what he didn't understand.

'You want to tell me what's wrong?'

Andrew blinked and looked down to find Arlie testing a

bandage around his arm with a gentle finger. Arlie's other hand was missing, chopped off at the wrist. Healed a long time ago.

When had it happened? How had it felt – and why didn't Arlie want to kill the man who had damaged him so badly?

How had Andrew grown up knowing this man without knowing something so important?

'Arlie,' he began, holding his arm steady as the Healer began to change the dressing, 'what happened to your . . . your hand? When did you lose it?'

Arlie, intent on washing the still-tender wound, said, 'That was the day I met your mother. She and Robert helped save my life. Twice. Micah helped the second time. I was a lucky man that day.'

'Lucky? To need to have your life saved twice in one day?'

'Better that than have the need not met, eh?' Arlie smiled at him, which Andrew returned.

'So how did it happen?'

'Martha and I were coming back to the Enclave and went through a village that had some sick children. I made up a tonic and gave it to them, but the Guilde had just taken over the healing and hospice work from the Church—'

'In 1354?'

'That's right. Anyone outside the Guilde practising healing was breaking the law. I was arrested. They tied me to a trium above the village and chopped off my left hand as punishment. I would have bled to death if Jenn hadn't created a diversion so Robert could get me free.'

'That was . . . sixteen years ago?'

'That's right.' Arlie finished what he was doing and put away the salve and dressings.

'And . . . you don't mind?'

'Mind what?'

Andrew waited for the older man to face him before he opened his mouth. 'Don't you mind that Robert didn't rescue you *before* the Guilde took your hand?'

Arlie's eyebrows rose at that. He leaned back against the table and folded his arms. 'I don't know. I never thought about it like that. I suppose I could.'

'I think *I* would,' Andrew replied, conviction sitting hard in his belly.

'Or perhaps,' Arlie ventured, 'you might blame yourself for letting things get so out of hand in the first place.'

'I . . .' Words failed him. But he'd been wrong about one thing. He did understand more than he'd thought. 'How is my mother?'

Arlie took the abrupt change of subject without blinking. 'She's much better now she's close to the Key. Her wounds are clean and healing nicely. She took a great risk, but I'm sure she'll recover completely soon enough.'

A great risk protecting him. As she'd always done, even at risk to her own life? As Bella and Lawrence had done, knowing he would be a target at some time in his life? How could he have lived fourteen years and been blind to so much around him?

'Thank you for looking at my injuries.' He slowly made his way to the door.

'You're welcome.' Arlie smiled, but Andrew couldn't find one to return.

As he walked back out into the corridor, he found Helen waiting for him, a smile on her face enough to throw his thoughts to the wind.

He just wanted to forget for a while.

'Come on,' Helen whispered. 'I'll tell you about Liam if you like.'

'Yes,' he replied. 'But in a little while. For now, can we just sit somewhere?'

She grinned at him. 'I know just the place.'

It wasn't winter in his dream any more. Now it was sodden summer, the western plains quaking in knee-deep mud, wrestling with carts and oxen and an army he didn't recognise. The push for the forest, for the battlefield, was paramount. But the battlefield wasn't the border; it wasn't a war with Mayenne, but a fight with the Enemy. He had to go and fight the Enemy, had to win this time, and make sure the man would no longer be around to hamper his plans, to get in the way of his achieving his ambitions.

But there was so much rain it had washed away the bridge over the river, the river where Vaughn had been swept away, pushed to his death for certain, but there was another bridge further south, closer to the forest, and they'd have to cross there to get shelter, and rest the animals and the army before they faced the Enemy, or they'd all die, yes, they'd all . . . die . . .

Robert sat up in bed, eyes wide, unable to breathe, grasping in the dark for any shred of light.

By the gods! The dream! How could he . . . that wasn't *his* dream . . .

He got out of bed, poured a large cup of wine and gulped it down so quickly his chest hurt. He didn't light any candles. He couldn't bring himself to admit, even now, that he was afraid of the dark.

And besides, it wasn't *this* dark that scared him.

How could he be dreaming somebody else's memory?

Nash's memory.

But was it memory? Or was it just Robert's mind playing more tricks than usual, putting him into Nash's place, seeing things through Nash's eyes? It certainly wasn't his usual dream.

He pulled the covers over his head, deliberately ensuring total darkness surrounded him.

He closed his eyes and concentrated on a breathing exercise that always helped him sleep, even after a nightmare.

And he was instantly back in the dream. A different dream now, but this was his usual dream. This was where he stood upon the boggy and bloody battlefield, his sword ready to fall from useless fingers, his wounds bleeding and deep, ready to kill him, and Nash stood before him, his face ripped and savaged, but still exuding an air of victory.

Why had Nash been so sure he would succeed and that Robert would fail? Had Robert really been foolish in thinking he could kill Nash by using the Word?

And if not like that, then how? In the name of all that was holy, *how* was he to destroy such evil? How could he eradicate it before it filled and consumed him, until he . . .

He Sensed her behind him, walking silently now, betrayal in

her future, in her present as she stepped between them, raising her hands, as she'd done in the past, as she would do again—

Would she? Would she betray him again?

And the dream Jenn lifted up her powers and struck him down, splitting the ground, making the air bleed with sorrow.

Robert looked up at the sky, at the clouds and the rain. He knew now what he should have done, what true regret felt like.

It felt just like . . .

It felt just like anger.

Like the anger he couldn't afford to feel.

Then he was standing again, facing her, waiting for that moment of betrayal, and then, his breath taken, his fear driving his courage before him, he opened his mouth—

And spoke the Word of Destruction. White-hot light incinerated her right in front of him, turned her to ash in a heartbeat, leaving the ground scorched and smoking, desolate and ruined . . .

'NO!' Robert sat bolt upright in the bed, then scrambled to his feet, heart pounding, blind and deaf, nauseated, doubled over with spasming cramps that ripped through his stomach. No, no, no. Never.

But he had. In his dream. The same dream for eight years now and this was the first time he'd . . .

Stumbling, he made it to the wash bowl and retched up the remainder of his supper. He grabbed his boots, shoving his feet into them, his hands finding a jacket to wrap around him, shoving the Calyx inside for safety. Action, that was what he needed. Still he couldn't breathe properly, couldn't see, or feel, or hear—

A hand on his arm almost made him jump. He turned to find Finnlay beside him, half-asleep, worry filling his eyes, a lit candle in his hand.

'Robert? Are you all right?'

He couldn't find words; he could only do what he'd always done.

He ran.

35

Blood.

Everywhere. Sweet, sweet blood, singing to him. He could smell it in the air, on the walls, on the floor, soaking into the clothing of that bitch and that unholy priest.

'Get him away from there! Get the mother away from the girl. Take her into the other room and bind her so she can hardly breathe. I'll deal with her when I've finished. Put the orb there. That's it. Turn the child so the wound can bleed into it. Now, carefully, pull the blade from her heart. Slowly! Damn it, you'll ruin everything! That's it. Not too much in one go or the orb won't be able to take it. You, go and find a bowl, wooden, large. Take what you can of the bedding and try to squeeze as much blood out as you can. Don't waste a drop!'

He was shaking. Dizzy with the perfume. An elixir, yes. Balm to the aches he could suddenly feel all through him.

She had done this: killed his child so he couldn't have her blood. DeMassey had hidden them all these years, plotting behind his back to deny him the destiny that was written in his own blood.

Blood, blood. So sweet, still warm, red-black now dripping down, soaking into the porous surface of the orb, glistening, sensuous, seductive and addictive.

'Get the priest out of here. And get rid of this furniture. I don't want anything in this room except the bed – and when you're done bleeding her, get rid of that as well. Burn the corpse. I don't want anything left of her when you're done. Heat some water on the stove. I'll bathe and be ready when you've finished.'

So many years. One hundred and thirty-four. This was not the blood that was foretold, but it was blood of his flesh, and it was enough for what he needed. He would regenerate and give himself another century of vivid life. He would have the power

474

of ten D'Azzir masters. And the energy. Now he could take whatever he wanted.

The Ally would be his – and this time the Enemy would not be able to stop him.

Wind pulled at the treetops, tearing the weathered leaves, bending branches towards the ground as though they would weep for the child lost, for the mother in agony, for the priest who had done more than he wanted, and yet still not enough.

Godfrey couldn't bear to open his eyes. He just let them drag him out of the cottage, let them haul him to a nearby tree and bind him to the trunk, hand and foot, wad of cloth in his mouth. To be attended to later, he knew.

Had Nash realised who he was? Had the man even noticed?

Sick certainty filled him. DeMassey had not lied. But he had died in vain and Godfrey . . . Godfrey had failed. He should have cut her throat and wrists, or poisoned her. Why hadn't DeMassey thought of that? He'd been the warrior. But they must have assumed they would have more than a few minutes. And a few minutes more would have been enough. Half an hour would have sealed it.

He had failed by waiting, to question, to be sure, not doubting, in reality, but putting off what had seemed to him so abhorrent. And he could never confess it, never bring to light the depths of his sin, for his was a crime not only of murder, but of wilful prevarication. His first days as Bishop, tainted forever by his failure, both as a man, and as a priest.

So Nash would get the blood he needed. Godfrey would weep for Lusara until this Dark Angel took his life. And then Lusara would weep forever.

With his eyes shut tight against the light he'd once craved, he didn't see the man move behind him, felt only the sharp blade at his wrists. He relaxed into it, willing the end to come, but the blade moved away and his hands were freed, the cloth plucked from his mouth.

'Come on, Godfrey, open your eyes! I guess I have less than a minute to get you away before they notice.'

Stunned, Godfrey saw the frowning, gruff face of a man he'd once dared call friend. 'Osbert? But what . . .'

'No time. Answers later. Quickly, I've got your horse.' With that, the ropes around his feet were cut and he was pulled away from the cottage, between thick trees and down a slope until there was nothing left of the house but the smear of smoke torn from the chimney by an angry wind.

He would have stumbled, but Osbert put an arm around him, steadying him, half-carrying him. Godfrey could find no words until they reached the horses, but when Osbert moved to help him mount, Godfrey stopped him.

'Wait! Lady Valena! I can't leave without her . . .'

'Godfrey, if you go back in there, they'll kill you without blinking! They're sorcerers, damn it! Nash's men. We *must* go now, while they're still busy. If we can get back to court, find a way to cover your absence, Nash might just forget it was you, or perhaps he didn't notice your face or . . .'

Godfrey put a hand on Osbert's chest, feeling the pounding beat beneath it, the terror that was filling his friend. From nowhere, a smile emerged on his face and new tears appeared in his eyes – but not of grief this time.

'You came out here . . . for me?'

Osbert swallowed, lifted his chin and nodded. Just once. 'But if he catches both of us, my brave gesture will have been for nothing, so please, Godfrey can we go now?'

Swinging up into the saddle, Godfrey looked up the hill, but he could see nothing of the house now. Then all he could do was turn and follow his friend, through the trees, deeper into the forest, taking a route around and around, keeping them clear and safe.

The first wave hit him hard, harder than ever before. He thought he groaned, but he couldn't tell. It was too dark, too quiet in the room. Just him, the orb and the bare floor beneath him. Naked, he lay curled on his side, hugging the orb to him, panting a little, not wanting to feel it too much just yet.

Then the second wave hit him and he did cry out. The agony was sharp, like the knife wound that had captured him so much blood. Good blood, this. His own. Valena's. The child conceived while he was still enormously strong – and Valena too had power, unpredictable, yet potent. That's why he'd chosen her in the first place, not just because of her beauty.

And she had been beautiful, still was: the kind of beauty that stayed with a man, long after he'd killed her.

He'd always known she would end up betraying him, but for the last eight years, he'd barely thought about her, believing her to have returned to Karakham to be with DeMassey.

Only DeMassey spent just as much time in Lusara.

It would have been easy for them to keep the child from him, with him so handicapped by his injuries. And although he'd chosen Valena in case he failed to capture and subdue the Ally, he'd not really counted Valena as too great a contribution – but already he could feel how wrong he'd been. A child born of Ally and Angel would have guaranteed him immortality, but this blood was—

He gasped as another wave slammed into him, turning his muscles to jelly, leaving him deaf and blind.

Three days it would take to absorb this.

Three more days, then, and he would be virtually invincible. Such pain was a small price to pay.

He breathed in time to the pulse that shuddered through him from the burning thing held in his arms against his chest. One pulse, drumming in his ears. Then another. And another. Buzzing, vibrating inside his bones.

Tiny, invisible strings stretched out from his body, beyond the places where the walls had been, for they were no longer there, and further, into the night, into the forest where trees stood watch over him, anchored in the moist earth.

He was tied to them, to the trees, the earth, to water and fire. Each pulse, each shuddering, buzzing peal of this empty bell sent vibrations along the strings, into the trees and the earth and the water and fire.

Connected to all things.

Dizzy. Drunk. Heady. He rolled about on the floor, on wooden boards supporting his weight, dreaming of nothing, feeling so much, letting the fire spread through his body, a fever of power and lust and ambition and success.

He glowed with it, in a night that didn't exist. He couldn't control it, couldn't feed it, couldn't deny it. It went on and on and on.

The heavens burned, flames climbing high, streaking across his vision, pouring down the walls of his face and soaking into his flesh with inch-long talons. He was burning now, burning alive. His skin was bubbling, blackening, crisping, drying, flaking away, flames licking into his mouth, tasting him, suffocating him, making him swallow, choking him, flooding up to his eyeballs, bursting them, tearing his ears from his head, incinerating his bones, leaving them white dust to be blown away by the conflagration.

A convulsion hit him. And another. Hands grasped around his throat, cutting off the air. Another convulsion twisted him off the floor, until, with a crack, he fell down again, to gasp, live, survive until the next.

Each step, each moment taking him closer and closer.

Stronger.

Structure formed itself, building walls around him, a roof over him, fending off elements that had no influence over him.

The orb stung his skin, prickled, scratched, bit into him, like the fangs of an adder, filled with poison, leaching the strength from his bones.

She'd done this to him: she'd poisoned her own child so he couldn't use her blood. Yes, just as DeMassey had done so his blood wouldn't be used against . . .

His body melted, the fire leaking into his marrow, easing him out on the floor, filling him with contentment.

So beautiful, this.

He'd seen the look on his father's face, seen the features, familiar and hated, the scars that had never quite vanished because his father had balked at using Malachi to regenerate. Year after year, he'd watched that man, helping, learning, sucking the information out of him. Flattered, amused, entertained, his father never once imagined that the boy he had gone such lengths to sire would, in the end, be the one to cut his throat and take away the blood he had spent so many years enhancing.

Surprise had never looked so pathetic.

Nor had failure. His father had harboured ambition, as had his father before him, and his father – and so too had his great-great-grandfather, Bayazit of Yedicale, the man who had created the Word of Destruction, whose son had helped form the Key and who was then killed by that son.

An honoured tradition, passed from one generation to another, parent murdered by child – until parent murders child first.

A line of men, passing ambition on, one to the other, though so few of them possessed the skills required to achieve that goal. Bayazit had the ideas, but it had come to his great-great-grandson Carlan to fulfil a destiny his line had been born to.

Prophecy had a purpose. It had taught him many things: that fear factored in nothing but the actions of his enemies, that his ability could only ever be matched by his imagination, that history was nothing more than the path already travelled.

Above all, it had taught him to be ruthless.

He twitched, one bit of him after another, flinching against the next. And his skin itched, but his hands were useless for scratching. He had no fingers. The fire had burned them all away. He pulled his arms tight and felt the orb against him, itching and scratching the scorched skin on his chest, crushing him.

And then it stopped.

His feet went numb. His legs, knees, fingers, arms, shoulders, all going numb, dying before him, until the only part of him that could feel anything at all was the place on his chest where the orb still lay, destroying him, remaking him and destroying him again.

And then he could feel. Slowly, all over, then more and more; he soared with it, flying higher than ever before, stretching his muscles, popping joints, springing sinews ready to move, to begin, to succeed.

Nothing could stop him now. Not the Enemy, not the Ally, not even the child they might have conceived between them if they had Bonded. The Prophecy had been wrong. He could take all he wanted.

He lay still and listened to the orb. Lying beneath it, looking up into the faces of his father and grandfather and all those beyond, history was simply the path already travelled; none of them had ever got this far.

And now here he was, whole, renewed. Alive.

Full of power.

Nash opened his eyes.

36

He ran, just like in his nightmare. He ran through the winding, tortured passages of the Enclave, where everyone was asleep but him. The shadow of Nash chased him, no, it wasn't Nash, it was, it was the demon, yes, the demon, but the demon was leaking out of his eyes now, his fingertips, his breath coming out in flames, scorching the air, sucking the life from him and there was nowhere safe from this evil because he'd brought it with him. It had been born here, yes, the Key had done this to him, created the demon, that's what she'd said, he'd created the demon when the Key had given him the Prophecy and he couldn't hold it in any more, couldn't be what it wanted and what he wanted at the same time, it was never going to happen, should never have tried in the first place because he just kept failing and people kept dying, she'd said it was killing him and he'd believed her and trusted her and by the gods, she was right, it was killing him, it was, it was—

He landed hard against the door, gasping, holding on, staying upright. Fingers in one hand curled into a fist, threatening. The other, desperate, turned the latch. He stumbled forward, crashing blindly into furniture. Another door, another latch and he fumbled with this one, fingers numb and old, aging faster than he. A click, and he pushed this door open, stumbling again, not caring, falling to his knees when there was sudden light and the startled, unexpected depth of relief in words quickly spoken.

'Oh, by the gods, Robert! What have you done? What have you done?'

He looked up and saw nothing. Nothing but the blackness inside his own soul.

'Help me,' he whispered, afraid of his own voice. 'Please, Jenny, help me.'

Jenn quickly pulled back the covers, eased her legs over the bed and sank to her knees before him. His eyes roved wildly, as though he were blind, the colour so deep as to be almost black. With another wave of her hand she brought another two candles alight, to see him better, but what she was really looking at could not be lit by flames.

'Robert, what happened?'

He wrapped his arms about himself and rocked backwards and forwards, as though trying to contain something trapped within him.

'Robert, talk to me, please!' She could see it so clearly, black and writhing inside him, burning him up like straw on a fire. Damn it, how could he have let it get so bad! Why hadn't he done something to . . . but what could he do on his own? This had always been beyond his ability to understand, and only just within his ability to control.

Now that control was almost gone.

But what could she do? She had Healer's Sight, but she couldn't heal this – and Robert needed someone skilled.

'I'll wake Arlie; he'll be able to help you.'

Robert's hand flashed out and grabbed her wrist. 'No. You. Only you. You . . . *know*.'

His eyes pulled into focus then, snaring hers in that awesome, overpowering gaze that had once made great men tremble, and did no less to Jenn now.

'Only you,' he repeated softly, his mouth barely moving. 'It . . . hurts.'

Jenn blinked at this admission. She didn't have much time to find something to say, something to keep him safe. She'd used all of her words last time – but then, it had been the demon trying to kill him for vengeance. This time it was . . .

Quickly she put her hands on his face, holding his gaze steady. 'Robert, tell me what's happening inside. Tell me what you're feeling.'

'Help me.'

'I'm going to, Robert, but you have to trust me. Now tell me what's happening. I can only see what the demon is doing, I can't see why. How did this happen?'

'Nightmare. Nash. Fighting. Shan Moss.'

'You remember the fight with Nash?' He nodded, trying to close his eyes as if they stung. She let him, but kept hold of his face. 'What else? Is it the same dream over and over?'

'Yes. No. I'm no good at this . . . I'm . . . the demon is evil and I . . . keep failing. My fault. Bella and Lawrence and . . . you. You. I left you. In the forest. Left you because . . . because . . . I had to save . . . Andrew.'

'And you thought you'd made the Prophecy come true?'

'Yes!' His eyes opened with a flash of relief that she'd understood. But she'd always understood this man. That was the tragedy. She'd been born to understand him, as he'd been born to understand her.

This power in him, this awesome power unrivalled any-where within the Enclave, or outside it, for that matter. This power had always been at the mercy of the demon created by a nine-year-old child given the fate of a destroyer. And knowing that fate, he'd again and again taken on the responsibility for so much, taken on the blame and given the demon more and more strength.

That choice in the forest, that moment, had brought alive a nightmare he'd been living since the age of nine. The demon was going to make him pay for that failure.

Robert was terrified.

So was Jenn, but she knew exactly what she had to do: something she should have done a long time ago, for both their sakes.

She settled carefully in front of him, not touching him now, but close enough to reach out if she needed to. He watched her in silence, rocking still, arms wrapped around himself, holding in the pain.

In his eyes were fear, regret and darkness.

If she was wrong about this, she would end up making the Prophecy come true by default. He would kill her, unable to stop himself.

'Robert, I want you to do exactly as I tell you,' she began softly, keeping hold of his gaze. 'I want you to let it go.'

'No!' he cried, scrambling back in horror. 'No!'

'You must! Please, Robert, let it go. I can contain it.'

'No! Never!' And he wrapped his arms around himself again, shutting his eyes and shutting her out.

He couldn't ever let go, not with her here, in front of him, where she'd get destroyed! Wasn't that what the dream was about? What the Prophecy was about? That his anger *would* rule him, like the demon would rule him – and then he would destroy her. How could she ask that of him? He'd come to her for help and this is what she'd . . .

By the gods, it hurt so much, making him sick to his stomach, the dizziness overwhelming, so he couldn't tell up from down, but he was already down on the floor so he couldn't fall any further.

'Robert! Listen to me. You have to do this! You have to let go!'

'No!'

She crawled closer so he could feel her heat, feel her breath on his face. 'Listen to me, you fool! You have to do this. And you have to accept the Prophecy. You can't fight it any more! It's killing you. Please, don't fight it any more. We need you alive, to fight Nash. Stop fighting yourself and fight Nash instead! Please, Robert. Just accept the Prophecy. Let it go! I can contain it, just like you did! Please, Robert I'm begging you. Let the anger go.'

'No!' He struggled to get away from her, but suddenly she caught hold of his face once more and his eyes snapped open, to see the whole blue depths of hers, taking him down to that place where he'd only ever felt peace.

She kissed him. Hard. Deep. Drawing him down further until he was swimming in a blue haze, angry and sharp, vigilant and destructive.

Let it go, Robert. Accept your destiny, as I do mine.

His world shook and trembled and the demon rose up within him, reaching for freedom. Within her kiss, he no longer had the strength to resist.

And the darkness was split by lightning.

It roared through her, massive and uncontrollable. It shredded her, and left her intact. It bound her up, even as it freed her. And even in the pristine agony of it, she could still marvel at the awesome power of it. Of *him*. Of that which he had spent a lifetime containing: such strength, such indomitable will to deny the one thing he hated the most. He had done all this, and so much more, for the sake of his country's freedom, for the Enclave, for his family. For her.

And though the wave of blackness tore through her, as it had done with him, she remained apart from the pain, because it was not her pain, but his. She could share it, but not be destroyed by it.

She fell back, tears falling down her face. She shook, all over, but she was whole. So was the Enclave.

'Jenn? Jenn? Speak to me? Are you hurt? Jenny, please!'

His hands smoothed down her arms, cradled her face, helped her up so she could sit comfortably against the side of the bed. Half-laughing, she tried to wipe the tears from her cheeks, but her hands were still shaking too much. 'Sorry, I didn't mean to scare you. I just didn't expect—'

She looked up at him, ready to reassure him, but stopped when she saw the colour of his eyes. That glorious forest-green she'd always adored was back, restored completely. And she looked further, to where the demon dwelled.

It was gone. She could see no trace of it.

But she'd seen this once before, after the last time Robert

had lost control of the demon, when he'd used the Word of Destruction at Elita.

The day Andrew had been born.

But that time, Robert had *lost* control. Was this time different, because he'd given it up willingly?

He was still frowning, still worried. 'Are you hurt? Anywhere? Did I . . .'

'No, I'm not hurt at all. Honestly. Just a little shaken.'

'I'll get you some wine. Where . . .'

'There's a cup I didn't finish, there on the nightstand.'

He turned quickly and grabbed it, holding it to her mouth for her to sip. 'Is that better?'

'Thank you.'

'I'll get some more.'

'No, wait,' she caught his hand, made him turn back to face her. 'What about you? How do *you* feel?'

He didn't look at her for a moment, then he looked at the door, then at his hands, then, finally, met her gaze. For a time, he said nothing, not moving more than to breathe. When his hand moved out to dry her face, she began to shake inside. She'd kissed him, hadn't she? She'd just done it, knowing it would complete the connection between them, knowing it would force him to—

'I need to know, Jenny,' he whispered, his eyes glistening, darkening again, 'I'm sorry. I just need to know, so I can . . .'

He gave her no time to reply. Instead, he leaned forward, holding her face up so he could kiss her, so she couldn't escape, so she couldn't pretend any more, so she couldn't lie.

This kiss was so different to the one before, in the forest, where he had forced something upon her, and made her pay for it. This was sweet, heartbroken, deliberate and wanting. And no, she couldn't lie.

Her arms were around him before she knew it, his around her before she could think. And then she was slipping to the floor, taking him with her, tasting him, feeling the warmth and passion only he had ever offered.

Her wounds might have been healed completely for all the difference they made in that moment. She broke off, desperate for air, burying her face in his neck, where he wouldn't see her blush, her need, her overwhelming, undeniable relief to just have him close once more.

'You *do* love me,' he whispered into her hair, joy in his voice, and wonder. 'You do love me.'

He kissed her again, harder this time, as though he needed to be sure, as though he needed to make a point. Then he moved back, looking at her with new eyes. Slowly he shook his head; his voice took on a steely quality that would brook no discussion, not a single word. 'Never again, Jenn. You understand me? Never again. No more lies between us, for any reason. I won't have it. Are you listening to me? No more. I love you, you love me. That's an end to it!'

Jenn couldn't decide if she wanted to laugh or cry. She tried to do both. All these chains she'd buried herself in were falling away, leaving her light, almost floating. But how could she promise without telling him about Andrew? Could they be like this, be at peace, without her promise? Could she make it with Andrew as a single, solitary exception – would her conscience allow her?

One look at Robert gave her the answer she needed. 'No more lies, Robert. But . . . you know this can't make a difference. I'm still . . . joined to the Key.'

'Joined to the Key or no, it makes all the difference in the world to me. We'll worry about the Key when it becomes a problem.' With that, he sat up, helped her up as well.

She had to ask. There was no getting around it. 'And what about the Prophecy?'

His gaze was troubled, but not hiding anything. 'I . . . can't change it, can I? I mean, I've spent so long trying to, trying to fight it, find a way around it, learn more so I can beat it. And nothing's changed – except that people have died while I've—'

'No!' Jenn caught his hand, squeezing hard. 'If we're to have no more lies between us, Robert, then you have to stop that! You do that, and the demon will grow again. No more!'

His face was a treat. He blinked hard, as though ridding himself of an emotion he wasn't ready to deal with, and yet, the rest of him smiled wide, bordering on laughter. 'Very well. Just as you say.'

'So what about the Prophecy?'

His words emerged reluctantly. 'I can't just . . . embrace this destiny, Jenny.' He gazed down to where their hands were joined. 'I have to keep believing that somehow there is a way for me to defy the Prophecy.'

'But if you can't?'

Anguish flooded his face; he looked open and vulnerable. 'I think we already know what will happen. I'm sorry, Jenny, I can't—'

She raised her hand to his lips to silence him. 'Don't let the Prophecy be the question, Robert. Let it be the answer. No blame either way. For both our sakes.'

He smiled again, making her want to melt. Then he reached inside his jacket and pulled out an old book. With oddly reverent hands, he placed it on the mat between them. Then he sat back, clasping his hands together. He took a deep breath and looked up.

'I know you're still joined to the Key, and I know I said I couldn't trust you any more but . . . I don't think I ever really stopped trusting you. So . . .'

'So?'

He laughed a little, as though he couldn't quite believe he was doing this. 'So, this is for you.'

'For me? A book?'

'Yes, for you,' he replied, suddenly solemn. 'I think it was always for you. I just didn't understand before. And it's not a book. It's the Calyx.'

When Andrew heard the door crash open the first time, it woke him hard, his heart pounding with some half-forgotten dream. Then another door had opened and shut and he'd heard the unmistakable tones of Robert's voice, along with his mother's. Not that that made him feel any better, especially with them being enemies and hardly talking all the way back here. But still, he got out of bed, washed his face, put on clothes, even though it was still too early to be up.

487

Then, silently, he crept out of his bedroom, into the living area, though now he could hear nothing at all.

For a moment, he considered knocking on her door, but as swiftly decided against it. They might not be friends, but there was no way Robert would hurt Jenn. Andrew was sure of that – especially after the way he'd fussed over her injuries. So Andrew turned for the fire, stoking up the coals, putting fresh tufts of peat down and blowing on them a little to get them to take. Then he put water on for a brew and took out the fresh bread Martha had brought yesterday, along with a piece of smoked ham and the yellow cheese Jenn liked so much. All the while he kept his face to the door so he'd be ready, just in case.

So he was ready when the door burst open and Robert strode into the living area, followed by Jenn, both dressed, both very awake and very surprised to see him standing there, a jug of brew in his hands.

'I think you woke him, Robert.'

'Did I?'

'Yes, when you crashed into my rooms.'

'Oh.' Robert offered a smile to Andrew. 'Sorry. Won't happen again, I promise.' With that, he turned to Jenn, brisk and sharp, as though he were trying to hide something. 'I'll . . . er . . . finish getting dressed and wake Finnlay. I'll be back in a few minutes. Will you be . . .'

Jenn just laughed at him, as she often laughed at Andrew when he was being silly. 'I'll be fine. We'll have breakfast waiting for you when you get back. Go.'

'Right.' Robert headed for the door, then paused, his hand on the latch. He turned, looked at Jenn, then faced Andrew, a frown forming.

Andrew raised both hands. 'No. I don't want any more puzzles, or any more tests—'

'I only gave you one test . . .'

'I don't care.' Andrew was not really ready to do this, but knew he had to. 'If you . . . if you want me to do anything at all . . .'

'What?' Robert asked quietly, and very seriously.

'You have to promise you won't try to . . . turn me against my mother. I can't do that. I'm sorry.'

'You're *sorry*?' Robert's eyebrows shot up. 'Well, good. Not that you're sorry so much, but that you've decided one way or the other. Good. Excellent. Now I have a question for you.'

'Oh? What?' Andrew felt heady, a little dizzy with relief. He'd never expected such a reaction. But Robert's next words wiped the smile from his face.

'Will you help me to get rid of Nash and Kenrick?'

Shock hit him first, followed rapidly by disbelief. 'You're . . . *asking* me?'

'Yes,' Robert said solemnly. 'I'm asking you.'

Andrew didn't know what to say. 'But I . . .'

'Think about it. We'll talk later.' With that, Robert flashed a brilliant smile at Jenn and left, closing the door quietly behind him.

Stunned, Andrew turned to his mother, who approached him with tears in her eyes.

'What's wrong?'

'Nothing,' she murmured, putting her arms around him. 'And thank you! You don't know how much . . .'

'Oh,' he whispered, and hugged her back. The day had barely started and he was already completely confused. 'How many for breakfast?'

The table was a mess, breadcrumbs, knives, half-empty cups, pieces of apple peel and cheese crusts strewn everywhere. But when Robert swept all these aside, Finnlay rubbed his hands clean on his trousers and sat back as Jenn placed the book on the table before him.

'This is it?' he whispered, hopelessly reverent, his fingers itching to touch. 'It looks so . . .'

'Innocuous?' Robert smiled and returned to his seat at the other end of the table. 'That's what I thought. But remember, when we found the silver rod, it was disguised as well. Thraxis was very determined this would never fall into the wrong hands.'

'You're assuming ours *aren't* the wrong hands, I take it?'

489

Robert grinned. 'I haven't tried to open it. I don't know how. I'm hoping the Key will tell Jenn.'

Finnlay looked at Andrew and the rapt expression on his face as he watched the mystery unfold before him. Finnlay felt that same excitement, and there were more than twenty years separating them.

'I'm still not convinced the Key is going to help with this,' Jenn offered, moving around the table to refill their cups. 'No matter how I've phrased the question, it's always refused to acknowledge that such a thing as the Calyx even exists.'

'But it *did* tell you the Calyx was a cup or receptacle, didn't it?' Finnlay sat up, paying particular attention to the way Jenn moved around behind Robert, and the way Robert watched her without turning his head. 'So it knows what a calyx is. And Kenrick used the same meaning, which he must have got from Nash.'

'So you're saying,' Andrew offered, 'that this book is a cup?'

Jenn filled Robert's mug as he held it up for her. To untrained eyes, the brush of their hands would have seemed entirely innocent.

'Well, Kenrick used the term in relation to a bowl,' Finnlay answered the question, doing his best not to smile. 'But essentially, yes, I suppose they're much the same thing.'

'Then how can we find out anything from it? What if it's just a bowl?'

Jenn returned to her seat beside Robert, without even looking at him, giving Finnlay a clear answer to the question that had been haunting him since Robert had returned to his rooms after running out in such a bizarre manner.

They were together again.

They were trying to hide it, certainly, but they were *definitely* together. And Robert looked so good it was almost laughable. Something very important had happened between them, and with that and the Calyx, it was all Finnlay could do not to jump up and down and dance a little, which, of course, would only make them all think he'd gone a little insane and needed to be tied down somewhere safe where he couldn't harm himself.

'Well?' Robert was talking again, drawing Finnlay's attention back to the task at hand. 'What do you think?'

'Well,' Finnlay replied, his eyes turning inexorably to the book – Calyx, rather. 'I can't say I'm not just a little disappointed that I wasn't the one to find it – but it's just incredible that we finally have it. I just hope we can—'

'Make it work,' Robert finished for him. 'That's exactly what I was thinking. Any ideas on how to get it to change properly?'

With the silver rod, Robert had simply touched his *ayarn* to it, but he didn't have one any more. Perhaps he needed to look beyond the obvious. After all, if it was supposed to be easy to find, easy to open and use, they'd have done it centuries ago. So perhaps there was a clue, instead, in something they had written down, maybe in one of the books that referred to the Calyx and . . .

The excitement of it caught him again, and he had to smile. This thing in front of him would, if legend was correct, give them a way to live outside the Enclave in safety. His days of being a prisoner were numbered! He wouldn't die in this place!

'Finn? Are you all right?' Jenn was watching him. He began to shake his head, then blinked.

'Um, actually, I think I do have an idea.'

'What?'

'Robert, you said the first time it changed was just after you got it, right? But then it almost instantly changed back?'

'Yes.'

'And Jenn can touch it, and it doesn't change?'

'That's right.'

'What if you both touch it at the same time?'

Robert instantly got to his feet. 'Why both of us?'

'Oh, come on, Robert,' Finnlay stood as well, unable to avoid the protectiveness in Robert's stance. 'You're both mentioned in the Prophecy. If Thraxis wanted to keep this thing safe – which he obviously wanted to do – then surely he'd also make sure that only somebody special would be able to open it.'

'But that doesn't mean—'

'Actually, Robert,' Jenn spoke quietly, but firmly, 'I think that's exactly what it means. Much as I hate the idea of being involved in the Prophecy, it makes sense that it needs two people to open it. That way, one alone can't abuse the contents for his or her own purposes. If I wanted to protect something, I'd do it that way.'

Robert's gaze narrowed a moment, then he nodded. 'Well, it's worth a try, I suppose. I can't Sense any power coming from it, so I doubt there's much danger involved. Still, if you and Andrew step back, then we won't have to worry about you.'

Finnlay took Andrew out of the way, standing by the fireplace as Robert and Jenn moved towards the book. Such a little thing that could mean so much.

He held his breath. Their hands came out together and, for a moment, they shared a look filled with more hope than Finnlay had seen before. Then their hands descended and touched the—

He didn't see it happen, it was so fast. One second, the book sat there, where Jenn had left it, the next, something entirely different was in its place: square and gilt, engraved and beautiful.

'You did it!' Andrew sprang forward and gave his mother a hug.

Finnlay approached more slowly, suddenly a little shaky inside at the prospect of this *thing* before him.

Amar Thraxis had made this more than a thousand years ago.

Mostly, it kept the shape of the book, only now it was larger and more solid. Along the top face, there were raised silver edges, which looked like they would move if necessary. Even as he watched, however, Robert and Jenn touched it again and these edges shifted and slid upwards, joining together until they formed the inner face of a shallow bowl.

A Calyx!

'It seems to need some power to shift and change,' Robert murmured, his face creased in concentration. 'The moment we stop touching it, it stops moving.'

'The silver rod!' Finnlay almost leaped towards the table. 'Do you still have it?'

But Robert was already there. He pulled a dagger out of his boot and twisted the handle away from the blade. Without pausing, he turned the handle around and inserted it into a grooved slot in the centre of the bowl, giving it the look of a huge, gold and silver flower.

'Oh . . . my!' Jenn breathed into the air. Instantly, Robert's arm was around her waist, but whether he was trying to protect her, or support her, Finnlay couldn't tell.

'What? What is it?'

'Can't you see?' She pointed at the bowl. 'The surface, it's changing. Like the Key does. Like it's covered in oil or something.'

'Don't touch it,' Robert warned, taking her hand away from it. 'Look. There's something else there.'

Finnlay crowded close, but he couldn't see more than a dull polished surface. It neither moved, nor formed any other shape. One glance at Andrew told him only Robert and Jenn could see this – which, of course, was entirely logical if they were the only ones supposed to use it.

'What can you see?' Finnlay urged, unwilling to be left out.

'There's some sort of . . . writing, I think,' Jenn looked at Robert. 'Do you recognise the language?'

'I . . . it looks vaguely familiar, but it's almost as though there are parts of some figures missing. And it keeps shifting and changing. It's not stable at all.'

'Oh, no!' Jenn moved closer, reaching out again.

'What?'

'The writing's gone completely! The surface . . . it's returned to normal. Did we do something wrong?'

'No,' Robert sighed, crouching down to look at the Calyx from below. 'I think the rod ran out of power. I don't think it had that much to begin with, certainly not enough to run the Calyx for more than a few seconds.'

'So what do we do now?' Finnlay couldn't believe that was the end of the line, not after so long and still with so many questions unanswered.

There was a long, deep silence which Finnlay made no move to fill. Even Andrew sat still, saying not a word, but watching intently.

'The Key,' Jenn said without warning.

'No.' Robert's reply was short, and entirely predictable.

Finnlay kept his silence, staying out for once. They didn't need his help for this.

'What other source of power do we have?'

'We don't even know what kind of power it uses.'

'In which case, nothing will happen, and therefore there's no problem.'

'Or the Key's power will conflict with what the Calyx needs and put them both out of action.'

'You're reaching, Robert, and you know it.'

'Why did the rod run out of power? Wouldn't Thraxis have made it to last this long?'

'How was he to know how long it needed to last? Maybe the rod's power was to be supplemented in some way.'

'How? And by whom?'

Jenn paused at that, tilting her head to one side, fixing Robert in her gaze without mercy. 'By *us*, Robert.'

'Now *you're* reaching.'

'You found Kenrick with an orb and a bowl he called a calyx. Finn, you saw Nash with the same combination. Well, what if that's the way these things worked? The two together, in this instance, the orb providing the power so the Calyx can be read.'

'You can't possibly assume Nash's obscene process is related in some way to this.'

'Why not? You got that orb from Kenrick – you know how it was designed to store power. The Key stores power as well. For all we know, this is exactly what it was created for!'

'You're guessing, Jenn. There's no evidence—'

'Do you want answers?' She put her hands on her hips. 'Well? Do you? Because if you want answers, then you have to risk this.'

'That's not the risk that bothers me.'

'I know.' Then she smiled, and if Finnlay was in any doubt

494

before about these two, that smile and Robert's reaction to it swept it away. 'Look, let's just take the Calyx into the cavern, all right? If we get any adverse reaction, or if the Key starts talking, then we can change our minds.'

'Huh,' Robert turned away shaking his head, but not seriously. 'Change *your* mind, you mean. Very well, since you're so damned determined. Let's get it over with.'

Robert walked across the cavern carrying the Calyx in his hands, feeling it grow warmer, heating him, almost singing to him.

The bell began to ring, as though warning him not to approach. He glanced over his shoulder at Jenn, but she just shook her head. Well, if the Key wasn't saying anything to her, then it wouldn't. But the sound was welcome, too, underscoring his anticipation, allowing him to feel the vibration shudder through the stone beneath his feet.

As he drew near the low platform bearing the ironwork pyramid and the bell which hung from its apex, the shape before him began to tremble, to shimmer and glisten in familiar patterns. He kept still as the Key went to work, anticipating his questions, even as he anticipated the answers.

And then, abruptly, the bell and pyramid were gone and before him, suspended in the air where the bell had been, was the Key in its purest form: a black, gleaming orb, bristling with power.

Everything here was disguised, everything as something other than its true nature. Why had he been surprised to find the Calyx also disguised?

Holding his breath, Robert held up the Calyx, not sure if he should go closer, but nothing happened.

Suddenly, he wasn't alone any more. Jenn joined him before the Key, smiling up at him like sunshine in the darkness. Carefully she reached up and removed the silver rod from the Calyx, then put it gently on the floor by her feet. With her expression grave, she looked at him, then placed her hands on the Calyx as well, their fingers overlapping.

'If we do this, Robert, we do it together. Agreed?'

How was a man to know what he loved most in the world? He couldn't, until he'd lost it, and by then it would be far too late.

'Agreed. Together.'

'What now?'

Suddenly the sides of the Calyx began to move, shifting down as though in welcome for the Key. At the same time, there began a faint keening sound, like mourning on the breeze, distant and sad.

'Robert!' Jenn's alarm brought him back to himself and the realisation that they'd both stepped onto the platform and were holding the Calyx close to the Key, as though offering it up as a sacrifice. He tried to pull away, but nothing happened, the Key was pulling them closer. The bell was ringing again, long, low peals which made the ground vibrate around his feet.

'I think we should stop this,' Robert called out over the noise as it built up around them.

'I don't think we can.'

'The Key won't hurt you, will it?'

'No. I don't know. It doesn't . . . feel wrong. Just . . .'

'Overpowering?'

Jenn's response was truncated as, with a violent crunch, the Calyx jerked forward and smashed against the Key. Instantly the Calyx began to shift and shimmer, turning and moulding itself against the roundness of the Key. It began to get hot – too hot to touch any longer. With a hiss, he pulled his hands away, taking Jenn's with him, pushing her behind him for shelter.

And there, right in front of them, shapes appeared on the outer surface of the Calyx. Letters he recognised, words he could piece together. The first he read, Amar Thraxis . . . created . . . this . . . for those who would follow . . . for his . . . people . . . to learn those secrets they lost when . . .

Jenn, can you read this?

Yes, Robert. By the gods, it's incredible!

And the words kept coming: when two worlds died and the Dawn of Ages flooded across this land. Herein lies the history of the Generet and how they were . . .

The Generet? Robert, are they those people we saw in Budlandi?

Yes . . . The Generet, the people who could Sense the demon in him and who had been able to mindspeak each other, to the point where Jenn had been able to hear them. These were the people of Amar Thraxis?

He opened his eyes – but he was no longer standing by the Calyx. Instead, he was swept above the mountain, as though he were Seeking. From there, he could See how the Key shielded the Enclave from discovery, with threads of glowing power, like the bars of a cage, enclosing the mountaintop, and so much below it.

He shook his head, snapping back to the cave hard enough to make him stagger. Jenn caught his arm, her eyes questioning, her mouth moving, though he heard no words. Then she was shouting, calling out to the Key, demanding something.

The Key was glowing now, illuminating the Calyx below, making it translucent, a gold tablet with many glistening facets awaiting discovery.

This feeling was so familiar. This was just like that orb, the one he'd taken from Kenrick. Looking into that was the same as this, only this was so much stronger. And the more power he'd used on it, the more tangled he'd got. The more power it absorbed, the hotter it got.

The closer he got to understanding it – the more dangerous it became.

Jenn, we have to stop this. The Key's been waiting for the Calyx. All this time, waiting for this so it can—

But he was too late.

And then he saw it: the Key's light fading – and the bars fading with it. He saw the protection of the Enclave vanish before his eyes as all the Key's power was absorbed into the Calyx. He heard Jenn's shout of dismay as he climbed to his feet, his body weighing too much, his limbs barely able to function. But he got there, and reached out, wrapped his arms around the Key or the Calyx, or whatever it was now. He wrapped his arms around it and bullied up his own powers, for

497

too long ill-used and wasted. Now he took them and made them into what they'd been destined for.

He formed the picture in his mind of how to split them apart again, of how he could place a wedge between them now, before they were properly sealed together. With total certainty flowing through him, he sent the first thrust into the Key—

Where he was taken and twisted and stripped bare of his protection, just like the Enclave, just like his hopes. He'd always known the Key couldn't be trusted, but he'd hoped, yes, he'd hoped that the Calyx would bring only good. Now it was too late and he was powerless to stop the destruction.

Drowning in a vat of seething, uncontrollable power, he opened his mouth, opened his mind to shout one last desperate warning to Jenn—

He tried again—

And was instantly deafened by a voice. Not the Key this time; this was strong, but far away. Strong; a voice he knew but had hoped never to hear again. Powerful, more so than ever before, and he could only marvel at the change.

Ah, Enemy! I find you at last! But . . . the Ally is with you? Still alive! I knew it!

Robert's despair did nothing to cut the connection. It was sealed by the Key and Calyx joined together and it stripped through his flesh and bone, his agony the lifeline to Nash.

But wait . . . I can see you now . . . Yes! You are hiding . . . mountains . . . high up and yet below ground . . . Ah! The Goleth Mountain!

You can't escape me now, Enemy! The Key will be mine!

Here ends
REBEL'S CAGE
Fourth Book of Elita

The story concludes in
TRIAL OF FIRE
Fifth Book of Elita